TO THE MANOR BORN

FOURTH BOOK IN THE BRIGANDSHAW CHRONICLES

PETER RIMMER

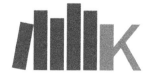

ABOUT PETER RIMMER

Peter Rimmer was born in London, England, and grew up in the south of the city where he went to school. After the Second World War, aged eighteen, he joined the Royal Air Force, reaching the rank of Pilot Officer before he was nineteen. At the end of his National Service, he sailed for Africa to grow tobacco in what was then Rhodesia, now Zimbabwe.

The years went by and Peter found himself in Johannesburg where he established an insurance brokering company. Over 2% of the companies listed on the Johannesburg Stock Exchange were clients of Rimmer Associates. He opened branches in the United States of America, Australia and Hong Kong and travelled extensively between them.

Having lived a reclusive life on his beloved smallholding in Knysna, South Africa, for over 25 years, Peter passed away in July 2018. He has left an enormous legacy of unpublished work for his family to release over the coming years, and not only they but also his readers from around the world will sorely miss him. Peter Rimmer was 81 years old.

AFRICAN TRILOGY

ALSO BY PETER RIMMER

❧

The Brigandshaw Chronicles

The Rise and Fall of the Anglo Saxon Empire

Book 1 - Echoes from the Past

Book 2 - Elephant Walk

Book 3 - Mad Dogs and Englishmen

Book 4 - To the Manor Born

Book 5 - On the Brink of Tears

Book 6 - Treason If You Lose

Book 7 - Horns of Dilemma

Book 8 - Lady Come Home

Book 9 - The Best of Times

Book 10 - Full Circle

Book 11 - Leopards Never Change Their Spots

Book 12 - Look Before You Leap

Book 13 - The Game of Life

Book 14 - Scattered to the Wind

❧

Standalone Novels

All Our Yesterdays

Cry of the Fish Eagle

Just the Memory of Love

Vultures in the Wind

In the Beginning of the Night

❧

The Asian Sagas

Bend with the Wind (Book 1)

Each to His Own (Book 2)

~

The Pioneers

Morgandale (Book 1)

Carregan's Catch (Book 2)

~

Novella

Second Beach

1

JUNE 1923 – OUT OF THE CLEAR BLUE SKY

*T*heir cave looked out three thousand feet above the Zambezi valley with the lip of the escarpment dropping vertically to the valley floor. The sun was rising from the east, promising the warmth of day. In front of the cave mouth, above the great drop, the black man they called Alfred was tending the cooking fire. Inside the cave, a spring welled up with pure, underground water. The spring spilt into a shallow rock pool. Far away, they could see the Zambezi River meandering through the valley. It was beautiful in the morning with the billy boiling for their tea and Alfred crouched at the fire.

One of Ralph Madgwick's small fingers was missing due to the war. A sliver of metal from a German shell had cut it off, clean as a whistle. The same shell that had killed Malcolm Scott. The headmaster had said that Malcolm Scott was going to be someone but now he wouldn't be.

Keppel Howland watched Alfred pour the boiling water into the iron kettle to make the morning tea. They drank tea without milk, as there was no milk three thousand feet up looking out over the Zambezi valley. Livingstone had found the river. He had called the falls further up the river valley after his Queen.

They were looking for gold, diamonds, emeralds. Something of value. They were happy. It was difficult not to be happy down the valley in the dawn before the heat haze took away the sun-glint of the river. They would have liked Malcolm to be with them but he was dead, pieces of him buried deep in the French mud by the German bombardment that had cut off

Ralph's finger. The shell that killed Malcolm Scott had brought them to Rhodesia.

It was Ralph's turn to shoot their breakfast. With a warm blanket over his shoulder, he watched the fire, drinking his tea. In an hour, the sun would be hot enough to drop the blanket. The tea was hot. Ralph no longer missed the milk and sugar. The one bag of sugar had run out months ago. They never ran out of tea.

No one spoke in the morning. The flames burned the dry wood Alfred had collected the previous day. There was always wood for the fire. In June at three thousand feet, the African night was bitterly cold, making them always build a fire, which they slept around. It burned all through the cold night fed by whichever one of them woke. The fire was as much to protect them from the leopards as the cold. Before they moved into the cave, it was home to a family of leopards. There were droppings around the cave. The white calcium of bones showed in the droppings. Yellow fur was tangled in the broken bones where the cats had licked themselves clean. Most nights they could hear the leopards outside their cave. The big cats were frightened of the flames burning in their lair.

In the day when they were away from the camp, the leopards came into the cave to lap at the water in the pool. There would be fresh droppings and the smell of cat. Ralph and Keppel slept with a gun. Ralph said some things in life never changed.

The gun was a Lee-Enfield .303 that had also been in the war. All three of them were good shots. The gun had a bolt action to push the shell into the firing breech.

They mostly ate meat, craving the fatty parts. Sometimes Alfred found them wild spinach. The maize had been finished before the sugar that they had bought in Salisbury just after Christmas. Before the bullets ran out they rode the horses back to Salisbury.

Every year, they had shot elephant, taking the tusks to Salisbury, the capital of the self-governing Crown Colony of Southern Rhodesia. The tusks paid for their provisions. Always an old bull. When they found diamonds, they would not have to shoot the elephant.

During the day, they looked down at the earth. The bush, outcrops of rock, the drop down to the valley. Wild animals. The birds. Predators circling the canopy of the mopane forest down below in the Zambezi valley. Tiny specks of vultures, eagles and buzzards, too small to identify properly. The thread of winding river. Mist from the water until the African sun ate it away and the heat haze shrouded the earth. Then they looked for shade. Looking down at insects on the dry, dusty ground. The song of crickets, the sound of beetles in the trees, butterflies, all colours and sizes, with some as big as a man's hand. The feel of eyes from the dappled bush where the buck stood motionless. The sun relentless. Pressing down. Keeping their heads down and looking at the earth.

At night, it was different. In the cold black air away from the light of the fire. Without a moon. They looked up and wondered. Three layers of stars in the pitch black dome of heaven. All the stars twinkling with light from only God knew where.

For hours, they watched the heavens and the nights without the moon. The splash of the Milky Way. Milky lace splashed from a bucket across the heavens. The Southern Cross writing the poles in the heaven for man to find on earth. Distant signs for the sailors on the seas. For men in the vast wilderness of the African bush.

It made them puny. Ralph. Keppel. Alfred. Insignificant. Less concerned with themselves. Their petty problems of a life so brief. Each, silently, asked himself if there was any point to life. To being who they were if they could only understand. Silently.

They never spoke of the awe they felt looking up at the stars, wondering what they were about.

Ralph wondered if eyes from so far away were seeing Earth as a point of light. He thought, just maybe, Malcolm Scott was up there somewhere. It made him think of God and his lack of faith... Malcolm Scott was as dead as mutton.

The skies at night were too big. Too mocking. Too big to understand in his mind. Man, Ralph thought, was conceited to believe his soul had a place among the stars. He would look one last time with awe and go into the cave to the burning fire. He fell asleep quickly on those nights. At peace with the world. At peace with the stars. He never dreamt on nights like that.

Those same nights Alfred watched Ralph sleeping soundly, the strange man from far away. Alfred told himself he did not understand the men who had left their homes. He would never leave his. On the black nights in heaven, he would feed the fire with wood and lie back to sleep feeling the outside presence of the leopards in the dark of the moonless night.

. . .

THE NIGHT OF THE COMET, the day after Ralph had shot a kudu for their breakfast, it was a black night in heaven. The three men were gathered around the cooking fire on the lip of the great cliff. The fire was low, dancing small sparks at the heavens on the draught of heat. They were tired from a week's worthless searching in the vast bush away from the cave. More dispirited than tired.

"What are we going to do, Ralph?" asked Keppel.

Alfred heard the spoken sounds and barely understood. Only the gesture of despair from the young man with a face as smooth as a child. It would be a long time before they could have a conversation, Alfred thought. The two Englishmen were not interested in learning Shona. Alfred spoke the Kalanga dialect of Shona. The two men were often distracted. They spoke to each other of a great war. That much he understood. There was great noise in this great war. Always this noise. In the war his grandfather had fought against the impi of the Zulu, Lobengula, it had been quiet. Stealth and stabbings in the dark of the night. Only in open battle did they shout their war cries to give them courage before they died.

He tried often to pick out words. Mostly he failed, the sounds of the English flowing along as a single, unintelligible sound. Like the constant chatter of the small birds in the mopane forest searching for the big worms that lived in the trees, hairy big worms, and the most delicious food in the bush when cooked on the fire.

The man called Ralph first pointed up at the long line of fire streaking the heavens, the question of what they were going to do unanswered.

Alfred looked up at the black sky. Fear gripped him. Worse than a lion. Worse than a snake. The heavens were falling apart. He screamed, the sound running out and around in the night without moonlight. He ran into the cave and hid himself as far back as he could... He heard Ralph follow him. Felt Ralph put a hand on his shoulder. He knew it was Ralph.

"It is only a comet, Alfred. A piece of rock from space cutting into our atmosphere. So long as it doesn't land on top of us it will do us no harm."

Calmed by the human hand on his shoulder, Alfred told Ralph in Shona it was a sign in the heavens of eternal death. Earth's destruction. The end of life. The end of man.

Neither man had understood the other's words.

Keppel made some black tea for Alfred, bringing a full mug into the cave.

That night Alfred watched the Englishmen sleep perfectly. Alfred slept not a wink. He was still shivering in the morning when the sun came up. He knew it was eternal death. Not the death of war. Of age. Of pain. His ancestors had spoken to him from the heavens. His ancestors who were close to God. There would be nothing from before. No back or forward. Just a void of nothing.

THE NEXT MORNING, Keppel made the cooking fire, boiling the water for their tea. They could see Alfred was still trembling. Nothing would make it stop. Not even the heat of the morning fire outside in the morning sun.

Tentatively, Alfred looked out at the world. It all seemed the same. By lunchtime, his trembling had stopped. When dusk came, he went into the cave as deep as possible. He was never again going to look up at the heavens. Silently, he prayed to his ancestors to intercede with God and save them from eternal destruction.

Eventually that night, driven to the fireside by the intense cold in the cave, Alfred fell asleep from mental exhaustion.

There were so many contortions in his dreams he remembered none of them when he woke. Only the fear of nothing.

BY MID-MORNING A WEEK LATER, they had eaten three times from the roasting meat of another kudu, each time letting the hot coals cook the outside flesh. The thin, brown and crumbly slices were eaten in their fingers, the fat dripping from their chins. It was a young bull and easily chewed. A lazy morning was spent watching the meat brown, waiting for the exact right moment to slice again the sweet slivers from the carcase. The rich smell of roast venison made them perfectly content.

They had not gone out prospecting on the horses since the comet streaked the night sky. Alfred had mostly recovered from his fear. Secretly, without telling the other, Ralph and Keppel had given up hope of making their fortune in Africa.

The sun had been up for five hours. They ate in the shade of a gnarled tree that grew from a split in the rock outside the cave, perched on the lip of the great escarpment.

The sound came first on the wind and went away again. All three had heard it. Ralph and Keppel looked up. It had come from the sky. Alfred, unable to look up, began to tremble. The wind brought back the sound, only stronger.

"It's one of ours," he said.

"It's a bloody Handley Page bomber," said Keppel. He also got up.

They had seen them fly over the trenches every day towards the end of the war in France.

Alfred looked up, screamed and ran back into the cave. Ralph thought the pilot had seen the smoke from their fire. The aircraft, with its two propellers, was turning, flying straight at them from across the valley. They could see the front of the biplane with the pilot looking out from his open cockpit between the propellers. One of the engines was running rough, backfiring.

"What on earth is he doing here?" asked Keppel, standing closer to the lip of the escarpment. He was waving madly with both hands, the sun in his eyes, the bush hat pulled down over his face with just enough vision to watch the oncoming aircraft. The noise from the engines was echoing back from the face of the cliff, sending the sound back into the valley. Ralph and Keppel began to share in their excitement, yelling at Alfred over their shoulder to come back and look at the aircraft.

"It's civilian," said Keppel. "No roundels on the wings or fuselage. One man flying alone in the middle of Africa."

"He's got to be English," said Ralph as the aircraft flew in low over their heads, making them turn quickly to follow its passage over the mouth of their cave. The pilot was waving a gloved hand, his head trailing a silk red scarf, face hidden by a leather flying helmet and goggles. Another face appeared from the observer's cockpit. It was a small boy with his hands on the leather hide of the cockpit surround. He was gripping it with both hands but they could hear his treble voice yelling at them after the first rush of sound from the engines, the propellers thrashing the air to keep the craft in the sky.

"Well, I'll be buggered," said Ralph. "Did you see that?"

"Poor old Alfred. He'll never be the same again. First the comet in the night sky and now this." Keppel was grinning at the empty entrance to the cave. The sound of the plane was receding.

"Pinch me, Keppel," said Ralph.

"It was real. One of the Rhodesians must have flown in the war and brought a plane back with him."

"One of the fighter aces was a Rhodesian. Harry Brigandshaw. Shot down twenty-three Germans. He was one of the few aces they never gave a Victoria Cross. There was a scandal in the press. Something to do with Brigandshaw's commanding officer. You ever been up in the air?"

"He's coming back again... Go and get Alfred."

"He won't come out of the cave."

They watched the aircraft fly back and circle over their heads, the meat still roasting over the fire. Something was thrown out of the pilot's cockpit, tied in the red silk scarf. The scarf trailed down like an unopened parachute they had once seen in France when a British observer jumped from a basket under an observation balloon that a German fighter was shooting up. The observer had broken both his legs and was sent home to Blighty... The boy was looking straight down at them as a package bounced inside the mouth of the cave. The pilot raised his gloved fist and the aircraft droned away until the sound was gone from the sky.

Keppel easily found the scarf. Tied at the end was a tin of Navy Cut tobacco. The tin was weighted with a small spanner when they opened the lid. Inside was the message, scrawled badly on a calling card similar to the ones Ralph and Keppel had used in the mess during the war. They read the message.

CALL IN AT ELEPHANT WALK ON YOUR WAY BACK TO SALISBURY

ON THE OTHER side of the card was engraved:

COLONEL H BRIGANDSHAW, ROYAL FLYING CORPS

"WELL, I'LL BE BUGGERED," said Ralph again. "The comet was a sign of our luck changing. Not the end of the world. Alfred! Come on out. We're leaving. Load up the packhorses."

"You want to go now?"

"Chances like this never came before. Do you want to wander around the bush for the rest of your life? Let's face it. We're lousy prospectors. Not surprising when we don't know what we are looking for... Oh my God! A hot bath followed by a plateful of fresh vegetables. The smell of a woman. The voice of a woman. Oh my God! It's a double message from heaven. Come on. Get cracking. No time to waste. It's the first bloody invitation we've had since coming to Africa."

"What's Elephant Walk?" asked Keppel.

"The name of his farm. I saw the sign on the road the morning before we crossed the Mazoe River. Twenty miles out of Salisbury thereabouts. Some hundred miles from here. Go and get Alfred before he tries to run off into the bush... I wish he could speak English... Can't believe it. Bloody civilisation beckons again. Maybe Brigandshaw can give us a job... You think knowing his name had something to do with dropping the message? Telepathy. There's a lot more to this life than we understand."

"Doing what? All we are trained to do is kill people. So far as I know there isn't a war going on in Africa."

"There's always a war going on somewhere."

In the end, they packed up everything themselves. Alfred was quite useless, trembling without control... With the three packhorses carrying the paraphernalia of amateur prospectors ready to travel, they pushed Alfred up onto his horse. It was two o'clock in the afternoon when they began the long journey to Elephant Walk. Ralph had looked at his watch to check the time. He was whistling a tune. One of the songs they had sung in the troopship crossing the English Channel when they went home, without Malcolm Scott, at the end of the war in France. When they thought the world would be their oyster before the reality of so many demobbed men looking for civilian jobs became apparent.

The bush was dry in June. There had been no rain since the end of April. The tall elephant grass was brown and brushed the bellies of the horses as they followed the tracks they had made on their journey northwest from Salisbury a month earlier. Nothing had grown without rain. Some of their tracks were scuffed by animals. There was no visible sign of man cutting their trail. The wind had blown dust over the marks in the hard earth cut by the metal horseshoes. Since arriving in Rhodesia at the end of the rainy season, they had learnt to follow their own tracks and to read the stars to stop themselves going round in circles... There were no landmarks. Bush. Trees, not very tall and mostly leafless. Great round granite rocks with bald heads the size of an ocean liner. And grass. Tall grass hiding the teeming herds of animals most of the time, especially the smaller animals. They could see the elephant moving through the bush eating leaves from the tops of the trees with their trunks, pulling off the few succulent ones, bringing them down into their mouths. Tons of fodder every day. The elephant ignoring the yellow and black spotted giraffe, the beautiful camels of the African bush.

They rode on all afternoon, making camp at dusk. They had to help Alfred down from his horse. He was jabbering away to them again in his own language.

"It was a great, red snapping snake. It chased me into the cave. Jumping up into the air and making a terrible noise. Not a snake of this world. Another message from the ancestors... We die now."

The two Englishmen, unable to understand a word of the Shona, ignored him. Alfred was gibbering, his mind unhinged. If they could talk to him it would help, but they couldn't. Luckily for Alfred, Ralph kept the red silk scarf in his pocket. Had he pulled it out like a magician it would have likely stopped the man's heart, killing him on the spot. Alfred was that obsessed with Harry Brigandshaw's silk scarf, and the empty Navy Cut tobacco tin with a spanner inside making all the noise.

They both gave him a pat on the shoulder, sat him on a fallen tree trunk and went about preparing their camp for the night, bringing in firewood and clearing a large enough area of dry grass to make the fire and not set the bush alight.

The light went quickly. The crickets sang in the tall grass and from up in the trees. Their world shrank, becoming smaller with only the pool of light around the flickering fire. As they chewed the cold venison they had brought with them, they could hear animals all round their camp. Alfred ate some of the meat. They hoped he would sleep and feel better in the morning. At least he had stopped gibbering. They were worried about the man they had hired in Salisbury to show them through the African bush.

THERE HAD BEEN a kill not far away from the camp. The hyena were loud and raucous. A wild dog barked and sent shivers down their spines. The scavengers were getting to eat from the kill.

"The lion have eaten," said Keppel. "They won't bother us now. Don't sleep too well. We'll have to keep the fire up ourselves. Poor old Alfred. Aircraft almost frightened him to death."

"It would you if you'd never seen machinery before... What a place to live. Africa. Man living with the animals without all the rubbish of civilisation. Makes you think. Does a man need any more than this to be happy?"

"Just make sure we don't make someone their dinner by letting the fire go out. A hyena can bite right through your leg. Take it right off."

"Shut up, Keppel... You want some more cold meat?"

"The tea is ready."

The sparks from the fire lifted up under the branches of the trees where they had camped. Away from the fire and the soft sparks rising in the heat of the flames, danced fireflies. Small red eyes flitting around in the dark of the bush. Noiseless.

Alfred went to sleep, curled up next to the fire. Ralph covered him with a blanket. The night cold had begun to grip the side of their bodies away from the fire.

"What are we going to do?" asked Keppel.

"I have absolutely no idea... Let the gods decide. We're young."

THEY RODE off after breakfast with Alfred managing to climb onto his own horse. He was still muttering to himself. They hoped someone on Elephant Walk would translate for them the Shona so they knew what he was talking about. There had to be more than an aircraft in the sky. The fear in the black man's eyes was palpable.

By mid-morning, they were in savannah. The grass came up to their knees. They rode through a sea of grass gently blowing in the morning wind. They could hear the tsetse fly following as they rode. When the fly bit them through their khaki shirts it was like a red-hot needle in their flesh. Their wide-brimmed bush hats kept the sun from their eyes, the sweatbands soaked black with sweat. They rode in riding breeches with thick leather puttees that covered from the top of their leather boots to their knees. The blue sky was lightly patterned with soft white clouds as far as the hills to the north that ended at the Zambezi escarpment where they had come from. Alfred was riding again in front, as was his job. Out of the sea of swaying brown grass, a lion's head came up ten yards to the side of them, making the lead horse bolt with Alfred trying to keep in the saddle. The male lion with its long black mane turned to look at the fleeing horseman. The lion did not move. It turned to look at Keppel and Ralph who had pulled up their horses and taken their rifles from the bucket holsters in front of their right knees. The three packhorses had stopped, frozen. The horses were neighing in fear. Alfred was a hundred yards in front of them, at full gallop and still in the saddle.

A lioness stood up in the grass and looked at Ralph with cold, yellow eyes half closed against the direct rays of the morning sun. All around them lions stood up, showing their big heads above the sea of grass. Many of them were only cubs. The packhorses were too frightened to bolt, their sides shivering. All the lions were looking at them. Ralph and Keppel were in the middle of a large pride that had been sleeping in the grass. The black-maned lion yawned and disappeared. As quickly as they had risen to have a look at the interruption, the big cats disappeared back into the grass.

Ralph had the three packhorses on one long line and gently pulled them forward. Guns at the ready, they moved through the grass expecting to trample on a sleeping lion. Searching all around, adrenaline pumping, fear sweating the backs of their shirts.

Slowly they moved away from the hidden danger.

TEN MINUTES LATER, they looked back at where they had been. There was no sign of the pride of lions. In front, there was no sign of Alfred. The horse had bolted out of the savannah. Out of their sight. Into the trees that were mostly msasa. Small with spreading canopies that looked like tabletops from a distance. A large bird was sitting on top of one of the trees using its wings to keep its balance.

"Poor old Alfred," said Ralph. "Just not his week."

"You think he fell off?"

"We'll soon find out. That horse cut a swathe through the grass even my mother could follow... We were lucky. They were sleeping off an earlier dinner... How many did you see?" Ralph wanted to laugh now the danger was over.

"Fifteen, twenty. I didn't count."

"The horse will be blown. We'll have to camp when we find him. How long do you think that invitation will last?" Ralph had taken off his sweat-stained bush hat and was wiping his forehead with the back of his right hand. Then he drank from a water bottle, his old army water bottle that he kept on his hip. The water tasted cool.

It took them three hours to find Alfred's blown horse. Alfred was grinning at them, showing two rows of perfectly white teeth.

"Lion," he said. "Shumba."

They all laughed together from the relief, as much at finding each other again as from being far away from the pride of lions.

The bolting horse had finally stopped on the banks of a small river. It was a perfect spot to camp with tall shade trees on the banks. A troop of vervet monkeys were watching them, their faces peering around the protection of the green leaves. Small round faces with perfect black markings. Every time they pulled back their faces from the canopy of the trees, they thought they were hidden, leaving their long grey tails plain as pikestaffs. All the trees had their roots in the river.

Within five minutes, Keppel had caught a five-pound fish. Freshwater bream. It was the best food they had eaten since making their permanent camp in the cave on top of the escarpment back in February. Keppel had scaled the fish. They cooked it whole over the coals of the fire, and then placed it on their one tin plate. Eating under the tree with the monkeys, the three men sat cross-legged around the dish. They broke into the white flesh of the fish with their fingers. They ate slowly, luxuriously, until they were full. Then they lay back in the shade of the tall tree and went to sleep away from the noonday sun.

When they woke, the monkeys had gone. The tree above them was empty. Buck were drinking from the river on the opposite bank. Waterbuck. The buck saw the waking men and ran back into the safety of the thorn bush.

They stayed the night on the bank of the river and crossed in the morning. The water came up to the bellies of the horses as they crossed. They had fired shots into the water to make a path away from the crocodiles that watched them from a small island in the stream. The crocodiles had big eyes but did not move into the water. All three of them had their guns at the ready to protect themselves with the packhorses in the middle of the small cavalcade.

TWO DAYS LATER, navigating the savannah like sailors far out on the great oceans of the world, they joined the wagon-rutted road that had been cut for fifty miles out of Salisbury by the Southern Rhodesian government to open up the country to the north. Only once had they passed an African village. Rondavels with thinly thatched roofs. Long-legged chickens. Black pigs that ate human faeces and kept the area around the huts clean of disease. Near the village were stalks of old maize stands. The village was on another small river. Near the river were patches of pumpkin with thorn bush fences to keep out the pigs and wild animals. Later, they saw a herd of long-horned cattle that belonged to the village being tended by two small naked and very thin boys. They both ignored the greeting from Alfred. Just stared. Ralph wondered what had happened to the rest of the people, as the village had been empty. Not even an emaciated dog had been seen in another village on their journey north out of Salisbury at the end of the rainy season. It was as though the whole of that part of Africa had been cleansed of people. Ralph wondered about it more than once. Was it war or disease? If the English wanted to farm in that part of Africa, there would be little labour to employ. Even the cattle with the small boys had been skin and bones. Walking skeletons.

The following day they found a sign that read 'Elephant Walk' and turned off the government road that led to nowhere. Later, they found out the new government of Charles Coghlan was to open up the empty land to European settlement. The problem was the tsetse fly that killed people and cattle and fed off the game that was immune to the deadly sickness. To settle the area would mean shooting out the game to eradicate the problem, a task beyond the new government. Africa had a way of protecting its solitude, Ralph was to find out in years to come. Nature always prevailed. Always had a new disease to keep the population of man under control. To stop the bush from being overgrazed by man and beast.

A good, well-worn track led off the road, marked by vehicle wheels along with the ruts of the old wagon wheels. The earth was a strange red. The red dust soon covered them all.

Out of nowhere came an avenue of jacaranda trees. The trees were many years old. At the end of the line of jacaranda were farm buildings and one huge shed next to a well-kept airstrip. They could see the tailpiece of the Handley Page through the open door of the hangar. There were people everywhere going about their business. The buildings were solid and well kept. Between the buildings were lawns. On the lawns, in neat rows, stood farm equipment newly painted. Ploughs. Discers. Ridgers. Some pieces of equipment Ralph had never seen before.

A white man dressed in cotton trousers, open-necked shirt, bush shoes and a large hat, came out of one of the smaller buildings as their horses threaded their way through the brick tobacco barns that rose high on both sides of them, each with a tall chimney rising up to thirty feet above their heads. There were fires at the base of the barns, round, brick-made fires long enough to burn the trunk of a tree. Next to the fires were stacks of trees ready for the next year's tobacco season.

The man was well built, his face turned mahogany by the African sun, and in his mid-thirties. There was not an ounce of fat on his body. His shirt hung like a rag from the back of his trousers. The smiling eyes looking at the travellers were green marbled with grey flecks. Ralph had a way of telling a man from his eyes. He was a little short of six-foot, his hands covered in black grease and old oil. He was trying to clean them with a dirty rag that was spreading the grease up his arms.

"You got my message. Well done. Can't shake hands. Covered in engine oil. Bloody tractor's blown a gasket. You're just in time for lunch. My name's Harry Brigandshaw. Come and meet my wife down at the compound. My man over there is Tembo and he'll look after your man along with the horses."

"This is yours," said Ralph, taking the red silk scarf out of his pocket. "My name's Ralph Madgwick. My friend is Keppel Howland."

"Thanks. Flew with me right through the war… What's wrong with your man? He looked terrified. Oh well, nothing Tembo can't cure. He's a magician. We'll walk. The houses are half a mile from here. The gardens run down to the Mazoe River. What on earth were you chaps doing up there on the escarpment? Saw the smoke from your fire. Couldn't believe my eyes and neither could my nephew."

"We shot a brace of duck at a river on the way here," said Ralph, handing them over.

"Jolly good." Harry gave the birds to Tembo. "He'll pluck and gut or get one of the other chaps to do the work."

"This place is well established."

"The oldest farm in Mashonaland, so my father said. He was the white hunter, Sebastian Brigandshaw. Fact is, we were here before the column hoisted the Union Jack at Fort Salisbury in September 1890. General Oosthuizen was my father's mentor and partner. That was his grandson and my nephew you probably saw. Young Tinus loves my aircraft. Strap him in so he can stand up in the rear cockpit but not climb out. He's seven. I'll teach him to fly when he's older... How about a cold beer?"

The man they had first seen in flying helmet and goggles walked beside them. Another white man was standing in an open-sided tractor shed. A black man's feet stuck out from under the front of the tractor. Another black man was sitting up on the metal bucket seat pulling a lever on the steering column up and down to intermittently rev the engine.

"It's off-season," Harry explained following their gaze. "Maintenance time. Everything on the farm has to be working properly before the new season starts next month. The ploughing and discing. Remaking the contours so the rains don't run off with my topsoil. Farming in Africa is a permanent challenge. Too much rain and then too little. Just as bad. My ambition is to dam the Mazoe River so I can put water on every inch of the farm without staring at the heavens. Cut out half the weather problem. This is a tobacco farm. The maize and cattle take second place when it comes to making money. We sell to the British American Tobacco Company. Jim Bowman over there is the assistant to my grandfather who runs the tobacco. Grandfather has a cousin in Virginia who sent in the first seed and a rundown on growing flue-cured tobacco. I've been away in England on family business for a year. We own Colonial Shipping. Why I have the aircraft to fly me to Beira in Mozambique and Cape Town in South Africa. Talk to the ships' captains. Only way I can spend time in the bush and keep my sanity. I don't like the city life. Jim's from Liverpool. They gave him a commission in the field during the war. Quite a hero our Jim. Lucky to have him. You look too young to have been in the war."

"We lied about our age. Our best friend from school was killed. He was seventeen."

"I'm sorry... Army?"

"Yes."

"We had an easy war in the Flying Corps. My younger brother George was killed in the army. Why I went over. Revenge... Silly, really. They were just the same as us. Young men. Not so young men like me... Why do we always end up wanting to kill each other?... Can you hear that wailing sound? That's my son Anthony. He was born two weeks ago with a first-class pair of lungs. They say children who yell in the cot are going to give the world a lot of trouble. I hope not... Look out! Here come the dogs. They are Rhodesian ridgebacks. A bitch and two dogs."

The dogs had run out from a group of houses that Ralph could see between the trees. The dogs were patted in turn by Harry Brigandshaw and ran back to the houses not even looking at the new arrivals.

Turning back, Keppel could see Alfred and the black man Harry Brigandshaw had called Tembo walking towards what Keppel thought were the farm stables. Next to the stables in a field, he could see a pair of giraffes.

"I say, there are giraffe over there."

"Tame," said Harry. "Fed from a baby's milk bottle. Teat and all. Mother was killed. We all have a soft spot for animals on Elephant Walk."

"Strange name for a farm."

"We're on the migration path of the elephant. Once every decade or so. My father saw them walking through the valley, the baby elephant holding their mothers' tails in their trunks. He called our farm Elephant Walk. Maybe someday soon we'll see the elephant migration again. Just hope they don't migrate through my tobacco lands at the height of the growing season. Typical. But that's Africa. Life really. Just when you think you are winning, something happens to knock you back... Don't worry about your gear. Quite safe. No one has ever stolen anything on the farm. Tembo will unpack the horses in the stables and give them a good rub down. After lunch, we can wander over and you can get what you want. You'll stay a few days, won't you? Plenty of room. Cottage to yourselves. We appreciate a bit of company every now and again. There's my sister, Madge, and her three children. Barend was killed last year so don't ask her about her husband. Poor Madge. My mother has moved in with Madge to help look after the children. They are wild. Their lack of shouting worries me now I come to think of it. The only time you don't hear their treble voices is at night when they are asleep... Their silence is ominous... Grandfather. He's my mother's father. He lives in his own house. Jim and his wife, Jenny, have another house to themselves. My wife and I have the oldest house built by my father. You'll be in the guest cottage. Mostly we all eat together. Seems silly to cook four different meals. My veranda is the meeting place where we are going to get you that cold beer. Ralph Madgwick and Keppel Howland. Have I got the names right? Are you a Manxman from the Isle of Man, Keppel?"

"How did you know that, sir?"

"Please, no sir. Africa is different. Everyone is treated the same among the British and the Boers. The Boers are the Dutch descendants. My nephew and nieces are Boers. Their grandfather Martinus Oosthuizen was a Boer general during the Anglo-Boer War. My sister married his son."

"Wasn't he executed by the British for treason?"

"They hanged him for going out with GJ Scheepers. They were both from the Cape Colony and technically British. One of the reasons the Boers still hate the British. That and the concentration camps where so many of their women and children died of disease all cooped up together. I don't blame the Boers hating the British. Every time you have a war with someone, you sow the seeds of hatred... Your name, Mr Howland. It's Manx. Had a chap with me in France. Same name... There's my wife, Tina. We've only been married six months and you don't have to start counting. Anthony, shall we say, was a little early."

Keppel could not believe his eyes. In the middle of the African bush, as far away from civilisation as man had ever been, walking towards him with a lovely smile was the most beautiful woman he had ever seen in his life. He felt the shock straight down into his loins.

"Meet my wife, Tina," said Harry Brigandshaw. "What's upset His Lordship this time?"

"Life itself," said Tina.

Keppel was gawping at her. Large, brown, bedroom eyes. Brown hair with a hint of red. Mid-twenties. Not even the recent baby could deny the voluptuous body.

She looked from Ralph to Keppel and back again as they were introduced to her by Harry. The thought of new conversation was better than any present. After six months on the farm, she was lonelier than she had ever been in her life. From the fast life of a flapper in London to living on an African farm. Harry, however much she tried to persuade him, was not going back to live in London. He loved the bush, something Tina was beginning to hate. Getting herself pregnant on the SS *Corfe Castle* on its journey from England to Africa was plain stupid. Only half intended. If Barnaby St Clair could see her life as a wife and mother, he would laugh his head off... Trying not to gush too obviously, she began to talk too much as she walked back to the house and her wailing son. There had to be something wrong with him making all the noise. It was a sound she was growing to hate. Demanding. Immediate. Imperious.

"He really has got a good pair of lungs," said Harry proudly. "Where are the others?"

"Tinus Junior poked the baby in his cot under the tree and started him off. They scarpered. Down to the river. With luck, they'll drown."

The men laughed nervously. It was clear the mother of the child was deadly serious but it had to be a joke. Keppel was still gawping at her. Ralph just thought women were curves. Different. The girl was grinning so maybe she was not going to drown the general's grandchildren.

"You see how mothers protect their offspring," said Harry fondly. "I'll have a word with Tinus."

"Won't do any good. Never listens to anyone."

"He needs his father."

"He needs his ears boxed."

To Ralph who was saying nothing, but doing a lot of thinking, all was not well in paradise. Looking at the girl and her husband, there had to be a good ten years or more difference in their ages. Like Keppel, he was following every word out of the girl's mouth. Ralph thought her the most sexually provocative woman he had seen in his life. He felt all the danger signs. When they were alone he would warn Keppel. The last thing Ralph wanted in his life was trouble... And to Ralph Madgwick, Mrs Brigandshaw was trouble. No doubt about it. Trouble with a capital T.

Taking his eyes off the woman, Ralph had a look around the family compound they were walking towards. The grounds between the thatched homes were perfectly kept. The msasa trees had been left standing along with other trees Ralph had yet to find the names of. At the base of each tree trunk, a ring of small rocks held a flower bed. The rest of the spacious garden was well-cut lawns all the way to the river a quarter of a mile down the slope where the trees fed by the river were much bigger. Near the house was one large outside cooking area with a permanent spit, a thick-topped wooden table and heavy wooden benches that had not warped in the sun. The small area around the table was paved with slivers of indigenous rock. Ralph learnt later the paving was made by making a hot fire on top of the big rocks that dotted the Rhodesian landscape, causing the rocks to flake.

Water was being sprayed on the garden. A system of pipes and small metal windmills brought the river water up the slope to a reservoir behind the houses from where gravity fed the sprinklers on the lawns. The engineering was so simple and perfect Ralph smiled as his eyes followed the metal pipe all the way up to the reservoir. Without the water, the gardens would have been a desert, not a riot of green, well-cut grass, flowering shrubs and flowers of every colour.

"My grandfather," said Harry, following Ralph's eyes. "He's something of an inventor. All you need in Africa is water right around the year and everything blooms. Trouble is, it only rains properly for three months of the year and that is never certain. A dam on the river and much bigger windmills to reservoirs on the granite kopjes and water will be plentiful for the whole farm through the year. Can you imagine damming the Zambezi River? The whole of Rhodesia would be the Garden of Eden. Wind, water and man's ingenuity and we'll all live like kings. What the blacks need from us is our engineering. Our knowledge of science. When we got to the farm and before grandfather put his mind to it, we were carrying every drop of water up from the river in buckets. That was before the tractor and fifty-gallon drums on the trailers. Even that was backbreaking hard work... I do believe that son of mine has stopped crying. Come and have a look at him. One day he's going to inherit the farm like I did from my father. I like continuity. Gives a family stability. The sense of belonging. My first wife was shot dead by a lunatic when she was pregnant. Tina has given me back my life. Without children, life has no future. No purpose. What is the point in building something when you know you will die and strangers will inherit your work? That may be selfish but it is the nature of man. I want at least ten children."

"I don't know about that," said Tina nervously giggling. "There's more to life than breeding. Thank goodness for Poppy. Don't know what I would do without her."

Ralph looked across at the large pram in the direction of which he was being marched by the proud father. A large black woman Ralph thought must be Poppy had taken up the child in the fattest arms he had ever seen and was cradling the boy, talking to him in her own language. The loving attention had stopped the son and heir howling his lungs out.

When Ralph reached the child to add his own praise for the ears of the parents the small mouth was gurgling happily, the eyes smiling up at what the child thought was his mother. Keppel was shown the child in his turn and voiced his complete approval. What else could he say? The child stayed in the arms of the nanny.

When Poppy tried to give the child to its mother, the boy abruptly changed from gurgling to howling but once returned to the comfort of his nurse the noise immediately stopped as the danger was over. Ralph shook his head very slightly. There were going to be strange goings-on in Africa by the look of what he saw on the lawn. Then he remembered his own nanny in England, a village girl who could neither read nor write but gave him the first and only love in his life. If he were lucky at bedtime back then his mother would come to the nursery and kiss the children good night. They never saw their father during the week. Their father worked in the City. Catching the six twenty-five back from Waterloo. When father arrived home from a ten-minute walk from Ashtead railway station, the children were meant to be asleep. Ralph still called his father 'sir'. He was supposed to be learning his trade in the Baltic Exchange. To join the family firm. The family were in shipping.

Looking around the farm hoping no one had seen the shake of his head, he thought Harry Brigandshaw was right. Inheriting this beautiful farm was a far bigger prize than a seat on the Baltic Exchange, a three-storey house on five acres in Surrey and the family holiday home on the cliff overlooking the sea at Looe in Cornwall. Well, maybe he would keep the house in Looe. It was the only time for six weeks each year in the summer when the family were all together. For breakfast, lunch and supper. Father out of a pinstriped suit and without his rolled umbrella looking, as Ralph thought smiling back to those summers, ridiculous in shorts, lily-white knees and long socks.

The small entourage left the two-week-old Anthony Brigandshaw with Poppy.

Another servant in white shorts and shirt appeared as they reached the veranda of the largest and oldest house. The thatch was darker and thicker where new layers of grass had been combed on the top each year. It was almost lunchtime. On a long table covered with a white tablecloth was a spread of cold foods on large, oval plates. Next to each plate was a large silver serving spoon. A pile of dinner plates stood at one end of the long table next to three piles of cutlery. Silver dessert spoons. Silver forks. Knives made in Sheffield with ivory bone handles. Another servant brought in a cut-glass bowl the size of a small fish tank full of green salad that caught Ralph's full attention. He was given a poured glass of beer by Harry Brigandshaw.

"Cheers," said Harry. "Welcome to Elephant Walk."

The cook, who had brought the bowl of salad, and Ralph's craving for greens to a climax, rang a gong with a leather-ended stick three feet long. The lunch gong boomed out, calling the rest of the compound.

To Ralph it was quickly obvious a couple more to lunch made no difference to the catering. The others arrived and were introduced to Keppel and Ralph. No one seemed to think the newcomers' arrival abnormal. No one even asked what they were doing in Africa. Everyone drank one cold beer or a glass of cold lemonade from a bowl floating with ice and served with a cut-glass ladle that poured a full glass of lemonade in one go.

Each served himself with food and went out to the long wooden table outside under the trees. Everyone's plates were piled high.

Ralph, taking his own, began to fill it with greens. The salad dressing was oil, vinegar, herbs and garlic, which he poured over his salad.

"You can't eat out after dark," confided a young girl to Ralph. "Mosquitoes. Just before dusk, we slot together the fly screens to close in the veranda before lighting the lamps." The girl had a north country accent. She was visibly pregnant. In the introductions, he had missed her first name. She was Mrs Bowman, the wife of the assistant tobacco manager – that much he knew.

"Strange as it may seem," said Harry Brigandshaw as he filled his dinner plate with food next to Ralph, moving confidently from the laden table, "I think I know one of your family. Madgwick. Not a common English name. Clive Madgwick. Baltic Exchange. We do business together."

"My father."

"Now that is a coincidence. What on earth were you doing stuck up on the Zambezi escarpment the other day?"

"Trying to avoid working for Father."

"You have my sympathy. I hate the City... Come and chat to my maternal grandfather, Sir Henry Manderville. Title's been in the family for donkeys' years. One of the oldest baronetcies in England. Goes back to the Conqueror. Quite a character. My grandfather I mean. He never worked out of the countryside in his entire life."

"Never had a job in my entire life," said Henry Manderville whose grandson had meant him to overhear the conversation.

"Then what's all this tobacco crop?" asked Harry. Ralph thought it sounded like an old family joke.

"Fun, Harry, when work is fun it is no longer work. Any more than connecting up the water system. May I remind you I had the first pull and let go in Rhodesia; Mr Crapper would have been proud of me. I'm sorry, my dear. Rude to talk of lavatories at lunchtime." Mrs Bowman had actually blushed. "You two lads come sit with me and tell me what you're up to. Have to be up to something so far from home."

"Prospecting," said Keppel.

"Any success?"

"None at all," said Ralph.

"Better talk to Harry. Has a degree in geology from Oxford. Never used it, what with this farm and Colonial Shipping. Problem with inheritance, you can never do what you want to do, always what you have to do... Harry has a pile of books in the house. You have to know what you're not looking for, he always says. Then the rare and precious become obvious. You will make him happy talking about geology. How long are you staying with us?"

"A few days."

"You'll need more than that to be a geologist, I think. I've tried reading them. All double Dutch. All you've put on your plate is salad."

"We've lived on meat for months."

"When you have some time, I'll show you how we grow tobacco in Rhodesia. I think I rather started it. Chap who'll inherit my title when I'm dead lives in Virginia. Tobacco country. Used to be a lumberjack in Canada before he went to America. Emily, Harry's mother, is my only child. Now we are plentiful again, with Madge's children and the new heir to Elephant Walk. Don't know what cousin George will do with the title as he can't use it in America. When they kicked us British out of America, they declared a republic. No lords and ladies after that. Rather a pity... Oh, not the lords and ladies. America not being part of the empire. That's a pity. The Anglo-Saxon world against the rest so to speak. When a family divides itself, it falls. In the end. United we stand. Divided we fall... Not in my lifetime of course. But mark my words. Families can't afford to quarrel with each other... This is the way to do it. Communal life. Everyone together... Oh, dear. Here come the children up from the river. Must have been miles away. Why the gong has to make so much noise... Now there'll be a racket. Those children can do nothing in silence. Just look at them! They've been swimming in the river again. A crocodile will get one of them. Harry takes young Tinus up in the aeroplane. Boy says he's going to be a pilot. Just as well the last war was the war to end all wars. Pilots in wartime don't last very long. Harry was lucky. The Germans he killed were not so lucky. But I'm not sure about the end of the war. The retribution forced on Germany at Versailles was far too harsh. You can't blame the whole nation for the mistakes of the leaders. Always be magnanimous in victory. It pays. Only foolish nations bear a grudge... You were lucky being too young for the war."

"We lied about our age," said Keppel.

"Did you now?"

"Our best friend was killed. He was seventeen years old."

"Life isn't all it's cracked up to be."

With both Ralph and Keppel staring at him the old man walked off, his mind seemingly far away, looking at another life. Twenty yards down he turned back to look at them again.

"When you're my age you'll understand. Enjoy the happy times. Always enjoy the happy days... I'm an old man. I'm sorry... Give yourselves another plate of salad... Tomorrow then. We'll do the grand tobacco tour."

"We'll look forward to it, sir," said Ralph.

To Ralph's quiet amusement Harry's mother had sent the owner of the estate off to wash his hands. Despite the earlier cleaning with the rag, Harry's hands were still visibly dirty. The grey-haired woman was coming across to Ralph and Keppel, her stride purposeful.

"That son of mine would eat his lunch off the workshop floor. Has it brought to him to save time. He didn't show you the bathroom before pouring you a glass of beer?"

"No, Mrs Brigandshaw."

"Put your plates down and follow Harry. Civilisation my foot. Without us women, it would all collapse in a week. I've tried making them change for dinner. My father just laughs at me, which encourages Harry... When you come back we'll have a good talk together."

"My mother always...," began Ralph, thinking he was back at school.

"No. No. I believe you come from Ashtead where you grew up. I grew up near Hedley. Hastings Court... How's my salad?"

"Marvellous."

"Made it myself." She was smiling at them mischievously. Hedley was only a few miles from Ashtead. Once Ralph had stood outside the gates of Hastings Court looking up the long driveway. And Harry knew more about the Madgwick family than he was letting on. Dutifully, the two friends went off to wash their hands. Mrs Brigandshaw was holding their plates that she now put down on the table.

"Wow," said Keppel as they hurried after Harry. "That really makes me feel homesick."

The three young children appeared washed and scrubbed.

When Ralph and Keppel came back from their own ablutions, the children were seated on small chairs at a small table eating ravenously. Madge, their mother, was trying to stop them talking with their mouths full.

By the time Ralph and Keppel retrieved their plates, the children's mother had given up and was walking away to the food table. She seemed bewildered. Not quite there. Ralph learnt later the same lunatic who had killed the first Mrs Harry Brigandshaw had shot dead her husband.

Three dogs began chasing each other around the trees that dotted the lawn. Bits from the flower beds flew into the air around them.

·   ·   ·

AFTER LUNCH, Ralph and Keppel were shown the guest cottage where the curtains had been drawn all day against the sun. Within minutes, they were sound asleep on the twin beds, the treble noise of the children's voices background to their dreams. The guest cottage was a rondavel, one round room on the same lines as a native hut. The Brigandshaws had added a small bathroom to the architecture connected to Sir Henry Manderville's system of pipes, windmills, pumps and a Rhodesian boiler that gave the houses hot water.

When Ralph woke an hour later, he could not remember in the first moment where he was. When he pulled back the curtain to the one window in the room, all was quiet outside. The food table had been cleared. The families had gone back to their own houses. Remembering the lunch made him feel quite at home.

They walked back to the stables and retrieved what they needed for the rondavel. The horses had been put out to graze in the fields with the tame giraffes. There was no sign of Alfred or Tembo. With their sponge bags and what went for clean clothes packed in army kit bags, they walked back out into the sun. Passing the tractor shed, Jim Bowman, who had not come into lunch, was still tinkering with the same tractor. They could hear Harry talking to someone in Shona.

A sweet smell permeated the air from the largest of the sheds. They could see the tobacco and trestle tables inside the long shed. Black women with babies strapped to their backs by long towels were standing at the tables piling leaves of what Ralph realised was cured tobacco from the previous growing season. The women were making different stacks of tobacco. When one stack seemed about to fall over, a man collected the pile and took it to another woman who tied the leaves of tobacco into hands. It seemed to Ralph some of the leaves were different and needed sorting into grades. He would remember to ask Sir Henry Manderville what it was all about in the morning. At the entrance to the shed, a square box was being fed with hands of tobacco. Next to the box were square tables of compressed tobacco in hessian sacks. Ralph saw when the wooden box was full of tobacco, a lid was placed on top and screwed down tight to make the square bales. From seeming chaos came neat rows of square bales.

Ralph had had no idea how much went into the cigarettes he had started smoking out of fear during his first enemy bombardment in the trenches. All three were then private soldiers wearing tin hats, and waiting to die. The cigarettes had been their only comfort, glowing in the dark of the wet cold trenches where they stood up to their knees in mud. When the barrage shifted, the fear became more intense, waiting for the German infantry to attack. The glamour of war had gone for them. Ralph had cried in the dark. Much later, when Malcolm Scott was dead and Ralph missing a finger, Keppel admitted he had also cried during the first bombardment. Afterwards, they waited more stoically to die, puffing their cigarettes in the midst of hell. The noise numbed their brains and bodies. By then they had given up on staying alive.

WHEN THEY GOT BACK to the rondavel, someone had put many books on the dressing table. All the books were about geology. They began to read.

2

SEPTEMBER 1923 – LONDON

*C*hristopher Marlowe, Ralph Madgwick's elder brother, was a man of many small talents. He could paint a little. Play the piano by ear. Write poetry that was not embarrassing. He had even once had a small part on the West End stage playing himself: the quintessential bohemian as he liked to think.

After surviving three years on the Western Front without a scratch, he had taken a new look at life and decided he did not like what he saw. The prim, upper-class and well-mannered life he had led was boring. The life of the bohemian was not.

Born Barrington Madgwick, the eldest in the family, he had gone home briefly to Ashtead at the end of the war, four years earlier, to be treated like a schoolboy. There had been a row with his father.

"May I remind you, Father, I'm a major in the British Army and no longer a child. War makes a man change. Sometimes for the better. Your life will not suit me. I outgrew it in the trenches. There has to be more to life than material wealth. Maintaining appearances for the sake of appearances. Keeping strictly to one's class. Fulfilling a parent's ambitions however well-meaning the parent. I want to be an artist but I'm not good enough so all I can do is live the life of an artist. My life, the way I live it, will be my art. I will have friends. I will have enemies. I may well go hungry. But all will be real. Like the trenches and watching all my friends die. I will not live a pose. An appearance. I will not appear to be what society says I should be... I want to live, Father. One life. This life. I want to live it. Really live it every moment every day. So many times, I came within a hair's width of losing my life. A stray piece of shrapnel meant for me. The trench wall not in a timely position. God gave me another chance that I shall not waste. I promised Him that, every time He saved my life."

"You'll get not a penny from me, Barrington. I'll cut you out of my will. You can get out of this house. Don't come back again. Ralph will run the firm."

"You'd better ask him. And, Father, I never wanted your money. Just your love..."

"Get out of my house."

"Sadly, but truly, it will be my pleasure."

WITHIN A WEEK, Major Barrie Madgwick had morphed into Christopher Marlowe and moved into an attic off Shaftesbury Avenue. Soho was the place to be an aspiring bohemian. It was cosmopolitan. Classless. Full of life. Italians. Greeks. Chinese. Indians. A microcosm of the world where a man was judged by what he was and not where he came from: man and woman. Love, and there was much of it, was free. Christopher Marlowe, twenty-six years old, dived in head first, wallowing in the happiness. He wrote to his mother every week, explaining his life. The good son wrote for six months without a reply. To his family in Ashtead, he might just as well have died in France. They were ashamed of him. Wanted nothing further of his life.

Ralph found him in the attic four months after the armistice. The war had made them see the same problem: the terrible shortness of life.

"I can't be like you, Barrie," he told his brother.

"Christopher. Christopher Marlowe. Like the Elizabethan playwright. It has the perfect ring for the long hair to my shoulders don't you think? The black beret on the profusion of my dark hair. The paint spilt down my smock. The attic. The smell of garlic. Music. The new bohemian... Not to mention all the free love... Of course, you can't be like me, Ralph. You can only be like yourself. Anyone who says we are all born equal is a fool. We are all born different. That is what makes us human. Sometimes interesting... Have a glass of wine? My army pay has run out but I still have some wine."

"What are you going to live off?"

"There's a restaurant down the road where I tinkle the ivories. They give me a meal. I may even sell a painting. People don't really know what they are buying. I may beg. I will not steal. We help each other. Most importantly this attic is cheap."

"You will freeze in the winter."

"We froze in France and nobody worried about us."

"I wish I could play the piano."

"How long have you been working for Father?"

"Three months."

"Does he give you a salary?"

"He says I'm of little value until I know the business."

"When will that be? No, let me tell you, Ralph, you will come into your own when our esteemed father passes away to the other world. You will then become rich. You will then be old. Your life behind you. A house in Wimbledon still with a mortgage that your inheritance will instantly liquidate. A shrew of a wife. Six brats all like you and me. Is that what you want?"

"Of course not."

"Why didn't you come and find me earlier? I could have stopped you wasting three good months of your youth."

"They would not let me."

"So you now want to be a bohemian?"

"I don't know. I do know I don't want to catch the ten past eight to Waterloo six days a week for the rest of my life."

"Do you have a friend?"

"Of course. Keppel Howland... There were three of us..."

"I know, Ralph," said his brother gently. "Have you any money?"

"A little. I live at home."

"Go to the docks. Get a ship. You and Keppel. Go and see the rest of the world. The American prairies. The Amazon jungle. The African bush."

"What will you live off, Barrie?"

"Christopher."

"I'm sorry."

"What I live off which is very little, but very nice. Go and live your lives and then come back and tell me so I can write it all down and tell the world. Only then will I make my fortune when I am far too old to enjoy it. When I'm thirty."

"Can't I write it down myself?"

"You can try."

"What shall I tell Father?"

"Probably best to say nothing. I'll bet it will take him a month to find out you are gone... Now. The wine. We shall drink a bottle of wine. Spill a libation to the gods... Did I tell you I met Ivor Novello? Even though he's one of them it does not matter in Soho."

"Have you become one of them?"

"Don't be silly. The Hippodrome is just up the road. All those saucy revues. All those girls with legs that go all the way up to heaven."

"I envy you, Christopher."

"A cliché it is, brother Ralph. But life is what you make of it. Go and make something of your life. Please. I implore you."

SITTING in the attic window with his legs dangling down the slate roof, Christopher Marlowe felt deeply satisfied with his life. The rooftop pigeons were talking to him. The September sun was shining. Down below in the small garden the grass had just been cut by Gert van Heerden who lived in the room next to Christopher's that did not have a window. The smell of newly cut grass drifted up in the late summer evening. Only when the sun went down would he go to the supper club where he played the piano to the after-show diners who flocked to Soho from the West End theatres, dancing late into the next morning. Men in tails and white bow ties. Girls in tight dresses, cropped hair, the appearance of flat chests forced on them by the flapper fashion... Hedonists, every one of them. Free from the horror of war, mindless in the never-ending party that raged across London.

They liked him in the supper club with his shoulder-length hair and the black beret that never left his head. The black opera coat that opened to a velvet maroon. The patent leather shoes. The smile. The soft look of perfect happiness. A man in his own world wrapped in his music. The room so full of cigarette smoke a man with a long knife could cut out a piece and take it home... Christopher was not the best piano player in London. It was his charm the patrons liked. His familiar smile of recognition. One raised, laconic hand from the keys that never changed the music. Always recognising a face when it came again. Making the diners welcome. Sophisticated. The man about town, the gal who had been around: Christopher made each of them feel special. To know Christopher Marlowe at Clara's was a mark of distinction. Old customers brought new friends. To show them. To feel a cut above the rest... Christopher knew it was only a pose but it did not matter. They all liked it: the recognition.

After the sets, he moved among the tables talking to the rich. If he was mocking them, it never showed. If he liked a girl, it never showed. The man paid the bills. Booked the tables. Christopher made the man feel proud of his gal even if the gal flirted with the piano player with the affected upper-class accent they all thought was put on for their benefit. They called him Christopher. Never Marlowe as they would an equal. In the restaurant with its small dance floor, he was their friend. Outside they would have cut him dead in the street...

Once, at a table sipping a vintage glass of French wine, the party insisted he sit down and drink with them, and they were talking about his father. In all, Clive Madgwick was a big man in the City and liked to throw his weight about.

"Sorry, old chap, to talk shop. Boring really. You wouldn't know of course. Wish I could play the piano. You wouldn't like the life in the City." Drunkenly the man paying the table's bill that night waved at the smoke-filled room. "I think the rest of the band are coming back again, old chap. Jolly good."

Christopher was being dismissed.

That night he had smiled more than usual. The truth, indeed, came from the mouths of drunks and babes. It made him very happy in his soft cocoon. It was always nice to know a little more than the other man, he told himself when the party left later in the evening, his right hand rising to them laconically from the keys. Only just that once did he look the departing patron straight in the eye, frightening the wits out of him with a parting look of mockery... The man had never come back again but the gesture had been worth it. Rather like spitting in the eye of his poor old father who would pass his son in the street with the rest of them... How often in his new life had Christopher been looked at by the rich but never seen?

Despite the attic, the long hair like Lord Byron's, the beret, even the company of unpublished poets, the only one who had seen through his façade was Clara. Sometimes Christopher caught her looking at him. In those looks spoke irony and a secret to be kept. An air of faint, amused approval. Of how the world so often stood people on their heads. Christopher was sure she had once been a smasher, when the light played at an angle through the smoky room and magic made her young again.

"Are you going to Clara's after the show?" they would ask.

"Couldn't get a table."

"I'm so sorry, old chap. Such a bore not being able to get a table at Clara's. Next time give me a ring and I'll see what I can do."

To Christopher Marlowe, they were all snobs. The whole lot of them. Strangely he never once regretted not being part of the City... Well, maybe once, he always contradicted himself. When Brett Kentrich, star of *The Golden Moth*, looked straight through him with nothing more than a smirk. And when he began playing the piano, she smirked again. Not a word. Not even a look in his direction but Christopher knew it was for him. 'You can't even play the piano,' the smirk had written all over it.

Every time Brett came into the supper club, always creating a stir, he tried to catch her eye without success. Well, he thought, some success. Always the smirk when he started to play.

They were the sole occasions he did not want to be the anonymous piano player with the long, Byronic hair.

Only once, when an old army friend sat at her table, did he contemplate dropping his guard. For a brief second, Christopher thought, Barnaby St Clair had recognised him. The look of recognition then puzzlement followed by a shake of the head. The dugouts in the trenches had had the same smoke-filled look in the flickering light. Guttering candles and wooden boxes. The same cacophony of sound. In the brief eye exchange, both of them had flashed back into the war. Then the spotlight came on the piano player, chasing away the ghosts.

Christopher remembered staying at the piano that night, not moving among the tables. There had been too many dead men in the room.

At the end of September, when the leaves were falling in Green Park opposite his four-storey townhouse, the Honourable Barnaby St Clair paid a second visit to Clara's and this time he was sure. The piano player was Captain Barrington Madgwick of the Royal Dragoon Guards. Mentally stripping the long hair and black beret, replacing the headgear with a tin hat, it was the same man he had last seen on the Somme in 1916. Barnaby had been on a short visit to the Western Front from Palestine where he had spent most of the war. There was talk of the Turks confronting the allies with trench warfare. He had returned to the Middle East with his major and a long report that had never been read as the Arab revolt, led by Colonel TE Lawrence, was by then underway. The Turks had better things to think about than digging trenches in the sand. Barnaby had been a young subaltern not long out of Sandhurst military college.

By the age of twenty-six, Barnaby had made more money playing the London Stock Exchange than most city workers made in ten lifetimes and was still not satisfied, gambling again and again with good inside information he gleaned on the social circuit. His borrowing at the bank, known only to himself and his bank manager at Cox and King's, was always at the limit. He told himself he had the Midas touch... With the courage of youth, he never saw the consequences or the point of converting the gambling profit into solid property without a mortgage. The money was not what made Barnaby excited. It was the game. The adrenaline pump from winning. The hollow void of fear at the thought of losing. If he had ever taken the time to think about himself other than selfishly, he would have blamed the war for his malady. The war had been exciting. Fear and greed went hand in hand in peace and war. Wars were fought for conquest. Barnaby could have analysed it all the way back to the basic human condition born in the slime of evolution.

Anyone that got to know Barnaby found the veneer of civilisation was just a cover. None of which mattered at the start. He was rich, young and charming. Aristocratically good-looking from an ancient line that traced straight back to the invasion of England by William the Conqueror.

On the surface, he was everything everyone wanted him to be. Women found themselves fighting for his attention. He was their knight from the glory of war and they desired him.

By coincidence, his party to Clara's included Brett Kentrich who had come and gone sexually in his life by that first time Barnaby visited Clara's and thought he recognised Barrington Madgwick through the blue fog of cigarette smoke and the cacophony of sound.

"You know that piano player keeps looking at you, darling?" he said to Brett for something better to do. He was bored. There was nothing new for him among the women as he cast his eye around the supper club. Brett had been a brief conquest to get his own back on Harry Brigandshaw. To try and make himself feel better about Harry marrying Tina Pringle. The fame of actresses was two a penny for Barnaby St Clair. Barnaby knew that Harry, before he went back to Africa, had put up Brett in a smart flat, buying the lease for her as a way of assuaging his guilt at the gap in their ages. Sleeping with Harry's mistress had been a brief catharsis. Harry had won the only woman who had ever got under his skin. Tina Pringle was to Barnaby the one that got away. The mistress he wanted in a flat of his own. To use as he wished. There was something special about wanting the same girl from the age of five, even if she was old Pringle's daughter who looked after the two trains a day at Corfe Castle railway station.

"Do you ever hear from Harry Brigandshaw?" he asked, ignoring his own question.

"Didn't he marry your girlfriend?" asked Brett, sweetly. "And no, I don't go for piano players even if they are good-looking. A girl has to think ahead in this life, Barnaby."

"How goes the show?"

"Full. Every night. It's becoming a bore."

"He's very rich... Or rather, he will be one of these days. His father is Clive Madgwick, the shipbroker... Ah, you've heard of him, darling... I met him during the war in slightly different circumstances. I did hear on the grapevine he had refused to go into daddy's business but this is ridiculous. Playing the piano in a supper club. How common."

"You really can talk rot, Barnaby."

"Ask Clara. You come here regularly... Ask Clara."

"Why on earth would I be interested?"

"The way you smirk at him."

"You really are a bastard, Barnaby."

"No I'm not but Harry Brigandshaw really is a bastard... Did you know Harry was once my brother-in-law? He was married to my sister Lucinda before she was killed... Clara! There you are. Come and talk to us, darling. I have a little scandal for you."

Clara was smiling. It was her job to smile.

"How did you catch such a rich piano player? Barrington Madgwick, the heir to the Baltic Shipping Exchange."

"Don't be silly, Mr St Clair. That man at the piano is Christopher Marlowe."

"Ask him to join us at the break. I think he would like to meet Miss Kentrich... Please ask the wine waiter to give him my card."

Barnaby was enjoying himself. He liked making people squirm. First, he intercepted the piano player's look at Brett. Looked at Brett patronisingly. Then back at the piano player, this time with a smirk. Then Barnaby wagged his finger and turned back to the duck breast on the large plate in front of him. Suddenly he was hungry. He liked enjoying himself at other people's expense. He was still smiling as he fed pieces of the flesh into his mouth.

BRETT WAS STILL LOOKING at the piano player. She had learnt the first night she slept with Barnaby he never made a joke. Her mind went back to that night.

"SORRY, darling, that was just to get at Harry. I hope you'll write and tell him. She belongs to me."

"Who, Barnaby?"

"Tina Pringle."

"Oh, you mean the new Mrs Brigandshaw. Shame on you, Barnaby, for being jealous. Jealousy is so pathetic... No, I'll get a taxi. And by the way. By my standards, you are lousy in bed."

"So are you."

"Tit for tat then." Brett had been smiling. She had found the Honourable

Barnaby St Clair's weak spot. The insult had been worth having... The rat wanted Harry Brigandshaw's wife. "Poor old Barnaby," she had said as she slammed the door to his bedroom in Piccadilly. Downstairs she had called herself a taxi, and on leaving looked up at Barnaby framed in the third-floor window. She gave him a wave. She had long lost count of the number of men she had taken to bed. To Brett, it was just recreation. Harry had been nice. Convenient. The man who had put money into the musical so they would give her the female lead. The flat in Regent Mews was nice. The trouble was, she was as raging jealous of Tina Pringle as Barnaby St Clair was of Harry Brigandshaw.

"HE'S GONE," she said out loud coming back to the present in Clara's, her mind still swimming in memories of Harry Brigandshaw.

"Not really, darling. He's coming over."

Brett was crying.

"What are you crying for?" asked Barnaby.

"Spilt milk... Please excuse me, everyone. I'm tired. The show took it out of me tonight... Good night, Mr St Clair, I really do hope we don't meet again." She was smiling sweetly again. The actress in control.

"I say, old chap, what did you say to Brett?" she heard a drawling voice from behind. Then she was out of the smoke-filled room.

Clara had brought a taxi to the kerb outside on the road. Clara was good. Brett thanked her.

Inside the taxi on the way to her flat in Regent Mews, she began to cry again. Vividly, she remembered singing 'Greensleeves' to Harry Brigandshaw on the balcony of the flat where he had asked her to sing something.

"Driver, no. Take me to the Ritz... I don't want to go home."

Being the toast of the London theatres had changed nothing. All the men had changed nothing. Always when she went home the flat was empty however many people were there. Harry had always given her so much, wanting so little in return.

"Brett, you're an actress. The African bush is no place for you. I'm a farmer. Colonial Shipping belonged to my grandfather. London and big business have no place for me. I'm an African with a white skin. I could never live my life here any more than you could live your life on Elephant Walk. I know because I'm so much older. I know, Brett."

At the Ritz, Brett gatecrashed a party of theatregoers eating supper after a show. She knew one of them... They welcomed her with open arms. Even with all the new introductions, she could still hear Harry's words ringing in her head... And why did he always bring up their age difference? Age had nothing to do with it. Damn Tina Pringle getting herself pregnant. The announcement of the marriage had been in the *Times*. The announcement of Anthony Brigandshaw's birth had been in the *Times*. She could add up. The bitch had seduced Harry on board ship and got herself deliberately pregnant.

"Are you all right, Brett?" a man asked.

"Of course... Come on and dance. I love the Charleston."

Once again, she was brimming over with false smiles.

CHRISTOPHER MARLOWE HAD LOOKED at the small white card with the Honourable Barnaby St Clair's name on it and had gone cold all over. On the card were his real name and an invitation to join the table. St Clair was smirking at him and then looking at Brett. She was more beautiful than ever before. He wanted to tell her he had watched her show six times from the gods, way up at the back of the Drury Lane Theatre. Once a week Clara gave him a night off. Once a week Christopher stood in line at the theatre door to buy the cheap ticket. Six times, he had been lucky. Six times, he had watched her all evening through opera glasses never taking his eyes off Brett.

She was so young. So vibrant. So full of life. Alive like no other person he had seen... His obsession grew with every performance of *The Golden Moth*. All the women night after night at Clara's paled in comparison.

Clara was looking at him with a funny look. The set was finished. Christopher stood up, his legs out of control. He found himself walking shakily across the empty dance floor towards the table. Halfway across, Brett got up abruptly and turned her back on the table. St Clair was leering at her.

Changing direction, Christopher walked through the tables to the staff bathroom. The bathroom was just through the kitchen door. For some reason that had only occurred once before in the war, Christopher was sick.

"You all right, old cock?" asked a male steward.

"Something I ate."

"Not at Clara's."

"Weren't you serving at the Brett Kentrich table?"

"Right up close to her, I was. Right up close. A real peach."

"Why did she leave in such a hurry?"

"Heard her tell some bloke she hoped she'd never meet him again. I think she was crying. You never know with actresses. They can turn it on and off. The bloke was cocksure of himself. Like he was enjoying himself at her expense. Liked to have punched him one but can't do that at Clara's. Never get another job in London. Blokes like that aren't worth it anyway... You ever see her show?"

"Six times from the gods."

"Then you know what I'm talking about. She's a real peach... You got a bit of it on your trousers, cock. Better wipe it off and wash your face."

"Thanks."

"Place is packed solid tonight."

When the man left the room, Christopher recognised what had made him sick. Cold fear. Not of being killed this time. Of being rejected.

As HE WALKED BACK to his piano, ignoring St Clair, Christopher realised Brett Kentrich knew his real name and wondered if it made any difference. He knew what she thought of his piano playing. That much he knew.

THEY WERE PACKING up the instruments when Clara called him into her office.

"What was that all about, Christopher?"

"What, Miss Clara?" he said innocently.

"The card. St Clair gave it to me to give to the waiter. He knew you during the war."

"Sorry, Miss Clara. It made no sense to me."

"Said you were a captain."

"Oh, now that's absurd."

"That your father is chairman of the Baltic Exchange."

"That really is absurd. Would I really be playing your piano if my father was that rich?... What regiment am I meant to have been in?"

"The Royal Dragoon Guards."

"A case of mistaken identity, Miss Clara. You need a large private income to be an officer in the Royal Dragoon Guards."

"Don't you want to tell me, Christopher? I won't bite."

"Not really."

"What are you running away from?"

"We are all running away, Miss Clara. Mostly from ourselves. It's the nature of life."

"You're obviously educated. Well spoken. And playing my piano. Why?"

"Don't believe everything said by Barnaby St Clair. He has a bad reputation."

"So you do know him?"

"Only his name on the card you so kindly told the waiter to give to me."

"You are an enigma, Christopher Marlowe."

"Thank you, Miss Clara. I'll take that as a compliment... May I go?"

"Of course... And don't be late on Monday."

They were both smiling at each other. Very gently, Clara covered Christopher's right hand that was resting on the back of the chair. A gesture of compassion his mother had never done once in his life.

"Do you have any children, Miss Clara?"

"He was killed during the war."

"I'm so sorry... There were so many, with so little point. It rather changes a person's view of life."

THE NEXT DAY the supper club was closed. It was a Sunday. The seventh day for rest and going to church. The theatre was closed. It was Christopher Marlowe's one night off.

The war in France had blown away any idea he had had of religion. The very idea of two opposing armies praying to the same God for deliverance was absurd to Christopher. One side or the other was going to die.

The last Sunday in September was beautiful. A day for Christopher to walk in the park, or better still take the train into the English countryside to smell the flowers and feel the reason for him being alive. If there was a Creator, Christopher found him in the countryside, not in a man-made building with man-made music to condition his mind. He did not sing praises to his Creator. He let the birds do that. They were better. Every one of them he had ever heard could sing in tune.

The ritual on a good day was the same. Christopher retrieved Gert van Heerden from the box room where Gert lived without a window: the poor man was becoming a wreck. A stage manager without a stage to manage, all he could afford was a shilling a week for the box room that gave him a mattress to sleep on with a foot of room to the right for his few possessions.

They walked to Waterloo station across Hungerford Bridge where Christopher bought them each a third-class return ticket to Ashtead station, to the small village where Christopher had been born. There was no chance of their meeting his family as none of them ever took a train on a Sunday. Sundays the family went together to St Giles church in Upper Ashtead, the other side of the village to the railway station.

Off the train, they walked down the platform to the footbridge and climbed up over the railway lines. In front were Ashtead Woods with some of the oldest oak trees in England. Behind, across the common, was the village pond. Always Christopher imagined the cricket field. He could just see the elm trees that surrounded the village cricket ground. He could imagine himself as a boy and a young man, playing cricket. Like everything else in his life, he liked playing cricket but was not very good. They put him in to bat at number nine and let him field on the boundary just because they liked having him in the team. Once he caught a ball on the boundary to everyone's surprise. Mostly he daydreamed, not even conscious of the game played, just the ambience he loved of village cricket.

"It's such a civilised game," he told anyone who asked what he was doing. "If the rest of the way we lived was so civilised we would all have a wonderful life. If the ball is going to the boundary, the fielders stand back and appreciate a fine shot. They never chase after the ball. Village cricket is not competitive. Just a game to be enjoyed by everyone."

Sometimes, from the top of the footbridge with the wind in the right direction, when they walked back to catch the train on a late summer's evening, Christopher thought he could hear the *chock* sound of the bat hitting the ball and he was sad. The cricket and the woods were the only things he missed from his years of growing up before he went to war.

They had packed their picnic in the attic in Christopher's room off Shaftesbury Avenue before setting out for the train. The picnic basket was the only thing Christopher had ever stolen from the house where he was born.

Just before going to work on Saturday was the time to buy from the barrow boys who lined the Portobello Road touting their wares. Fruit and vegetables that were not going to last until Monday were sold off cheap on Saturday afternoons. Mostly the two of them lived off vegetable soup from a big pot for the rest of the week. A few bones and leftover vegetables made a grand meal every day. The big pot, boiled up on the one gas ring next to the gas fire kept them healthy. The snag was the pervading smell of boiled cabbage. Sometimes they managed to sweep up fresh herbs with the leeks and turnips. They called the concoction Royal Soup fit for a king.

Gert van Heerden was an inveterate optimist. One day he was going to stage-manage a grand show. To Gert, the idea of the grand show was more important than the money. If Clara needed extra kitchen staff when someone went sick, Christopher took Gert to the supper club. It paid the rent on the box room and chipped in for the vegetables. Like Christopher's father, Gert's was very rich.

The family lived near Stellenbosch in the Cape of Good Hope in a beautiful Cape Dutch farmhouse that had been in the van Heerden family for ten generations. Gert had attended Stellenbosch University where he studied literature in Afrikaans. There were some beautiful Afrikaans writers, he told his English-speaking friends. Herman Charles Bosman was a classic. All his characters were so real they walked out of the pages. The theatre came with the books. Gert would like to have written plays. He had tried many times and failed. He could picture the set as clear as anything but could never tell a story. Most of his writing was devoted to describing the sets. He went to all the plays put on in Cape Town, hanging around backstage after the shows. He was stage-struck by the sets. On one show, they asked him to help.

The show was out from England touring the colonies. Cape Town was the last leg. When the company went back to England Gert tagged along, forgetting to go back to university. His father had given Gert an allowance for his last year at Stellenbosch which paid for his ticket. He wrote to his father from London.

His father wrote back saying an education could be found in many places, and that now Gert was working for a living he did not require an allowance. Nearly all the van Heerden family wished him happiness. There were many van Heerdens. One or two more or less made little difference. The grape harvest had been good on the farm that year. All was well in the valley. The mountain was still beautiful. They all looked forward to seeing him again when he came home. Only Uncle Johan mentioned the Anglo-Boer War. He had cursed Gert for living with the enemy. Uncle Johan had been drunk at ten o'clock in the morning and none of the family had taken any notice.

Gert was twenty years old the previous March when he moved into the box room next to Christopher Marlowe. They had become good friends. The one thing Gert van Heerden was best at was being happy. Whatever he did amused him. In everyone he met, he found something to like. When he was freezing cold in the box room, he thought of the sun and how nice it would be to be warm again. All the girls wanted to mother him. When he staged his first show, he was going to find a larger room. Even that was not an overwhelming matter. Once he was asleep, his dreams took him far away. To Africa. To his room on the second floor in the barn-like family home. The room with a view of the duck pond. The blue hills far away. The blue sky puffed with white clouds. The smell of wattle drifting into his room of the morning, the window open... Asleep in the box room he could see all these things. Three pairs of socks and sleeping in his overcoat in the first months took him into summer and the trips with Christopher Marlowe down to Ashtead Woods and the picnic under the oaks.

The picnic basket was as grand as anything Gert had ever seen. A large wicker basket with little straps inside to hold the plastic cups and saucers, plates, the two large thermos flasks, the glasses for wine, the knives and forks, the salad spoons. They took it in turn, every two hundred yards, to carry the grand prize onto the train and into the woods.

"Luncheon is served," was the ritual phrase, always spoken by Christopher Marlowe. Then they set to on the hard-boiled eggs, cracking open the shells, making the egg sandwiches.

It had been a perfect day. They had eaten every morsel of food, drunk every drop of tea, and it was time to go home. Neither had spoken for a long time. Reluctantly they got up from the moss floor beneath the oak tree. The picnic basket was packed. Light to carry. Trees, brambles, bracken turning brown. The sound of silence.

"If we don't go now we will miss our train."

"The countryside of England is beautiful," said Gert.

"Come on. You can carry the basket onto the train."

"The bird calls are different. Strange for me to hear a bird and not know its name."

They walked the narrow path out of the woods. On the bridge over the railway lines, Christopher Marlowe stopped. A woman was standing on the platform.

"Oh dear," said Christopher.

"Barrington! Come down immediately."

"I say. That woman seems to be calling us," said Gert.

"Barrington!"

"It's my mother."

His mother was wearing a small green hat with a long green feather. She was dressed for church. Evensong had been over for an hour. Christopher could hear the train coming up from Leatherhead. Something had to be wrong.

Squaring his shoulders and forcing a smile, Christopher led the way down the iron stairs. He could see the white smoke from the locomotive. He could hear his hobnailed boots on the iron steps. The light would fade in an hour.

When they reached the platform, the train was pulling in. No one was getting on or off. The train was returning with weekenders who had gone to the sea. Standing between the slowing carriages and his mother, he could see the few passengers on the train were tired. Some were asleep. A few looked out of the windows at Ashtead station with little interest. The iron wheels on the iron rail squeaked and ground to a halt.

"Hello, Mother. This is my friend Gert van Heerden. He's from South Africa."

"That's my picnic basket."

"May I keep it, Mother? We went for a picnic in the woods. How did you know I'd be here?"

"The stationmaster told me at the beginning of summer. Your hair is far too long and that beret looks ridiculous."

"I live a different life."

"Not anymore."

"What's the matter, Mother?"

"Your father is dying."

The guard blew the whistle. Christopher had the carriage door open. Gert climbed in with the picnic basket. The locomotive puffed impatiently.

"I have to go. This is the last train up to London."

"Come home, Barrington."

"Christopher!" said Gert. "The train is beginning to move."

"Why does he call you Christopher?"

"Where is Father?"

"At home. He wants to see you. Ralph is somewhere in Africa. Please, Barrington. I'm begging you. He's not as hard as he sounds. He's your father."

"How long?"

"A few months. It's cancer, in his throat. He finds it difficult to speak."

"I have a job. Commitments to people. You can call me at Clara's if it gets worse. The famous place where I play piano."

"*You're a piano player?*"

"Yes, Mother... What does he want me to do?"

"Take over the business."

"I know nothing about shipping."

"You knew nothing about war. You have a good brain. You will learn the business in five years. Uncle Wallace can run the firm until you're ready."

"Uncle Wallace is a fool. He is also a drunk. Goodbye, Mother."

"Will you come to us, Barrington?"

"Of course."

They were still looking at each other, mother and son, as the train pulled out of Ashtead station. Only when his mother was out of sight did Christopher slump back into the long carriage seat. There was no one else in their compartment. Christopher felt a lot older than his thirty years.

3

JUNE 1924 – CLARA'S SUPPER CLUB

The Honourable Merlin St Clair, Barnaby's older brother, put down the *Times of London* on the breakfast table in the bay window of his flat in Park Lane. According to the paper, the German mark was now worthless after the French marched into the Ruhr to extract coal and timber as war retribution. Ordinary people in Germany were jobless and penniless, he read.

"Will we ever learn?" Merlin said aloud to himself as he stood up and walked to look out of the window.

Hyde Park was green, the long winter having given way to a pale summer. On the other side of Park Lane, people were walking in the park taking their constitutionals. The sun came out briefly. The windows were open onto the Sunday traffic. Merlin thought it was going to rain. As usual.

Turning back to the round breakfast table, Merlin read the article a second time. It was small. On the third page. As if Germany was no longer of consequence. An ex-corporal of the German army was said to be rabble-rousing. Haranguing the destitute crowds. Telling them what they wanted to hear. That blood did not come out of a stone... Merlin had put down the paper again and was letting his own mind ramble, adding to the brief story in the paper. Giving it flesh. Seeing the human consequence. The suffering. A man with nothing had to steal. To feed his family. To fight was the basic instinct in man's survival.

Smithers, his man of many years, came into the lounge. Merlin had sat down to breakfast at exactly nine o'clock. Bacon, eggs, one sausage, one kidney, one spoonful of kedgeree. Always exactly the same every day of his life. A man of regular habit. A confirmed bachelor of forty years, well content with his lot in life.

As a young man before war broke out, he had made his fortune buying armament shares. He had fought through the war without a scratch and never had to work another day in his life. The guns, made by Vickers to kill, had made him rich.

"There's going to be another war, Smithers."

"With who, sir?"

"The Germans."

"Surely not, sir."

"Mark my words."

"I surely will, sir... Are you out to lunch, sir?"

"And dinner."

"Very well, sir."

Without further words, Smithers cleared the breakfast table and left the room.

Merlin stood again in the bay window and stared down into the park. He had too much time to think. To brood... Putting Corporal Hitler's name out of his mind, he thought of his daughter. He was going to have lunch with his mistress and his daughter. Over in Chelsea. For dinner, he was going to the club... The perfect Sunday.

With his mind clear of ugly thoughts, he smiled down at the people in the park, mentally wishing them all a very good morning. He was about to turn and start his day when Harry Brigandshaw walked across the road towards the grand entrance to Merlin's block of flats. With him was his wife who had once been Tina Pringle.

"What on earth is Harry doing in England?" He had spoken louder than his habit.

"You called me, sir?"

"Better make a large pot of tea. Harry Brigandshaw and his wife. You remember his wife. She was Tina Pringle in those days... Oh, don't be silly, Smithers. None of that look. I got over my infatuation with Miss Pringle before anything went wrong. I wonder if Barnaby knows she's in town?"

"I hope not, sir."

"So do I."

"I'll go and make the tea. Mr Harry knows his way up in the lift."

"You'd better go down to the foyer. The new man on the door won't recognise Mr Brigandshaw... Now, this is a pleasant surprise."

"As you wish, sir."

. . .

THEY HAD BEEN friends for many years. The good memories were coming back as he waited, hands behind his back as he stared across at the park, seeing none of it, only the memories in his mind. They had been good times. All of them before Lucinda had been killed. Harry had been up at Oxford with Robert, the brother between himself and Barnaby. Robert had brought Harry down to Purbeck Manor in 1907. It was at Purbeck Manor that Harry learnt his father was killed by an elephant and had gone straight back to Africa... The memories flooded in... Harry meeting their sister, Lucinda. She must have been no more than fifteen... Elephant Walk. Yes, he remembered Elephant Walk. Sailing out to Africa on the SS *King Emperor* with Harry and the rest of them... A cold shaft of pain cut through his chest at the memory of Lucinda's murder at the end of what had been such a pleasant journey. They had just been married, she and Harry. The man coming up in the lift had briefly been his brother-in-law.

Merlin could hear his front door being opened from the outside by Smithers using the latchkey. He turned from looking out of the window as they came into the room. She was just as beautiful. She and Harry were smiling. Smithers closed the lounge door to go out and make the tea.

"Congratulations upon your marriage," said Merlin, not able to keep his eyes off Tina. Once, long ago it seemed to Merlin, they had driven down into the country for lunch at the Running Horses at Mickleham. He and Tina.

"And our son," said Tina, giving him a look. The look, Merlin thought, was even a trifle smug.

"A son!" He wanted to ask how old. When they were married? That bitch!

"We called him Anthony. He's a year old."

"Congratulations, Harry. My word... How good to see you. Mother and Father will so look forward to a visit. Robert is quite the famous author now. His books let him walk where the loss of his foot won't let him travel... Oh, goodness. I'm gabbling. So good to see you." She was looking at him with a quizzical stare, enjoying his embarrassment.

"You really think Lord and Lady St Clair will receive Tina Pringle through the front door?" she asked Merlin sweetly. Her father lived in a railway cottage not far from the St Clair estate. Tina herself had been born in the cottage, socially as far away from Lady St Clair as the moon.

"Of course, Tina. They have known you all your life. Barnaby brought you into the Manor when you were five years old."

"Children from very different backgrounds are acceptable, Merlin. Up to a certain age. Seven or eight. How's Barnaby?"

"Richer, I rather think. He has a magnificent townhouse in Piccadilly, opposite Green Park. Four storeys... Does he know?..."

"Better not tell Barnaby," said Tina. "Not on purpose... We are going down to Dorset with Anthony. My parents want to meet their grandson."

"Maybe Harry can slip away to see my parents. Robert will insist. Harry, you and Robert were up at Oxford. Wasn't it through you he found his American publisher?"

"Always the diplomat, Merlin... Am I wrong or is the iris of that left eye of yours darker than the last time we met? The right more piercing blue. You haven't done the trick of wearing your monocle and peering at us through your dark eye, trying to look sinister."

"The left eye is coal-black. Like my... Ah, Smithers, how'd you make a pot of tea so quickly?"

"Keep the kettle on the hob, sir. Gently boiling."

"Splendid. Put the tea tray down."

"Like who, Merlin?" said Harry sweetly. It was his turn to dig up the English class system that made him laugh so often. In Africa, an Englishman was an Englishman whatever his social background.

"No one you know," said Merlin.

Harry was smiling at him gently. Harry, Merlin thought, knows about Genevieve. About his daughter born to his mistress, with whom he was lunching at twelve o'clock.

"We've known each other a long time, old friend," said Harry. "Congratulations."

"I'll pour the tea, thank you, Smithers," said Tina, enjoying watching the game. Everyone knew about Merlin's daughter. Even the fact she had two different coloured eyes like her father.

"Thank you, madam," said Smithers equally aware of what was in play.

"Come and sit down," said Merlin. "Both of you. I want to hear everything... Smithers! One more thing, cancel my appointment for today. This man spends too much time in Africa. We will lunch together."

"Not today thank you, Merlin," said Harry.

"Dinner tomorrow night, maybe?... You'll be my guest. It's not easy to get a table at Clara's. You do have time now for a cup of tea? I don't get many welcome visitors calling off the street."

THEY HAD COME over to England from Southern Rhodesia by rail and ship. Harry had wanted to fly the Handley Page to Cape Town. Tina was quite happy to make the flight in an open cockpit. The problem had been Anthony who had been bad enough in the railway compartment and on board the ship. He couldn't yet walk but could move at great speed on all fours.

"Next time we leave our son with my mother," Harry had said.

"Nonsense, Harry. My parents want to see their grandson. Why can't we live in London? We're rich enough. I love Elephant Walk but it's so isolated... I haven't told you but I'm pregnant again. The doctor in Cape Town confirmed. Can't I have this one in England, Harry? We're English, for heaven's sake."

Harry sighed inwardly. There was a price to pay for everything. Even his children.

"Africa is in my blood."

"No, it's not. Not a drop of it."

"Are we arguing, Tina?"

"The way Tembo looks at us sometimes, I'm sure he wants the lot of us to go home and leave Africa alone."

"Tembo is a loyal servant."

"He hates us. For making him a servant. For us being what he can never become."

"He's far better off. Being a nomadic herdsman is no fun in a drought. Only now are the African people multiplying. Ninety per cent of the children never survived into adulthood before we gave them modern medicine."

"They give me the creeps. Always outwardly subservient. Always watching. You don't see what I see in their eyes. The same hate by the poor for the rich, however many crumbs fall their way from the master's table. My family have been servants to the rich for generations. And I don't like it."

"My mother and grandfather would never live in England again. What about Madge and the children?"

"Let them stay if they want to. We can go out on visits. Now with the flying boats, we'll be able to fly out in five days. We can have both worlds. I just want a permanent home in England where I know we really belong. Where our children will be safe. It's all right living permanently in North America or Australia where the people around you are your own stock. Not African or Indian. Or any one of the Asian colonies for that matter. Harry, I know, I came up from the lower classes and know how it is to always be looked down upon. In the long run, they'll want to throw us out of Africa."

"We are going to bring in many more Europeans. Hundreds of thousands of them. Like South Africa."

"That will make it worse."

"Nonsense, Tina. It will make everyone prosperous. Never to have to worry about food or shelter. There will be British law and order. That's what people want the world over. They want stability. They want to know where their family's next meal is coming from. No one will ever go cold or hungry on Elephant Walk. Or in any British colony if I can help it. It's our duty."

"What about a man's pride?"

"Pride goes before a fall, Tina. You can't sustain a family on pride alone."

"Can't we have a home in London?"

"I'll think about it, darling."

"When?"

"When we dock at Southampton."

"We dock tomorrow. I'm so excited."

"Then tomorrow it shall be."

"Good old England. I can't wait to set foot on shore. I never thought I would be, Harry, but I'm homesick. Being pregnant again, maybe. Having Anthony. Africa didn't seem so difficult when I was on my own. Now the children being safe is more important than anything else."

"I'll think about it tomorrow."

"You're such a darling."

"I know I am." Harry was smiling at her fondly. Sometimes he forgot there were two of them.

"This one is going to be a daughter. January next year, I think. I want to have lots of children. Don't you think Anthony looks like you, Harry?"

"The spitting image. Now let's go to the bar and celebrate."

"That English nurse is very good with Anthony. That's what I want for him. Not one of Tembo's umpteen wives. You grew up in Africa, Harry. You understand their language. Their culture. They are always talking about me behind my back and when I catch them I can't understand a word. Mostly Tinus has to tell the servants what I want them to do. My interpreter is a seven-year-old boy for goodness sake."

"Who will right now be missing us terribly."

"Not me, Harry. You. You and your aeroplane. The boy adores you."

"Remember, those children don't have a father. On Elephant Walk, we are one large, extended family. Can you imagine young Tinus living in England?"

"No, Harry," said Tina miserably. "Why is life always so complicated?"

"Not complicated. Challenging. Don't you like a challenge?"

"Not all of them."

.   .   .

CHRISTOPHER MARLOWE HAD FINISHED the fourth set at Clara's the following night when Barnaby St Clair walked into the supper club with a crowd of people who had come from a theatre show. In the party was Brett Kentrich. Her own show had finished an hour earlier. Christopher gave her a long wonderful look before she saw him staring at her. She sat down at a table. She was smiling her bored 'I know I'm a star' look but none of that mattered to Christopher. To him, she was just beautiful. Quite beautiful.

Surreptitiously he adjusted the wig that he wore at work in the evenings. The wig had been made from his own hair eight months ago. Christopher was Christopher Marlowe at night; the bohemian with the black beret and the long hair who played the piano in a supper club. During the day he was Barrington Madgwick in his late father's office, learning the trade; going through each department of the shipping company; learning the pitfalls and profit of the Baltic Exchange. He had sold only half his soul to the devil.

Brett, looking around the diners, gave her bohemian admirer one last look. Christopher was sure she enjoyed their exchanges. It was what kept up his hope. That and the musical he was writing for her. *The Golden Moth* could not go on forever. She would need something else to play. Except that the musical he was writing was not very good. Christopher was bad at believing in himself.

The trumpeter was writing down the music when Christopher played the next song to him at the end of an evening and the guests had all gone home. Sometimes a drunk or two were still at the bar. The trumpeter had played in the London Symphony Orchestra and could read and write music. Some of the songs he said were quite good. Usually, he changed them a little to make them better. The trumpeter could also play the piano. Journeymen, the both of them, or so they both thought of themselves.

"You are a lovesick fool," Danny Hill had said to Christopher more than once. "If it wasn't so damnably romantic I wouldn't waste my time."

"You are a gem, Danny. A rare gem. God in heaven will reward you. Now, please play that back to me again. If I could only sing in tune I would sing the words."

"You really are a mess."

"I'm afraid you are right."

"She's here," said Danny, sitting back on his stool, bending to pick up his trumpet from where he had left it on the floor. Danny opened the valve at the end of the instrument to let out the water from his spittle, blowing through the mouthpiece.

"I know," said Christopher miserably.

"Aren't you too old to behave like a lovesick calf?"

"You are never too old, Danny."

"Thirty-one years old." Danny was shaking his head. The other members of the band were joining them. The trombone player was slightly drunk as usual. Clara gave her signal to the band. Christopher ran his fingers over the piano keys to get everyone's attention on the bandstand. They had a fixed routine. A list of music. It never changed, night after night. Once Christopher had suggested something new, a current hit from *The Golden Moth*. They all gave him a queer look. The best thing any band could follow was a strict routine, to avoid mistakes as much as possible.

The band struck up a tune. The crooner crooned into the microphone. Diners got up to dance. Brett stood up with one of the people at her table. Christopher was playing with his head turned, not looking at the piano. He had played the tune so many times there was no need to look at the keys. Another late party was winding through the tables to the only one left in the room. The girl in front of the new party caught Christopher's attention. If anything, she was prettier than Brett Kentrich. Certainly sexier, though not Christopher's type, he assured himself. All the men were watching her glide between the tables towards the one that was empty. The girl had short-cropped brown hair with a suggestion of red hovering among the curls. The strap under her red dress, dictated by the current flat-chest fashion, was fighting a losing battle under the smooth silk of the material. An older man was following close behind the girl, his right hand lightly resting on her left elbow. The man looked confident, his eyes moving around the diners, watching over his girl. The man at the girl's elbow had the concentrated stare Christopher had seen so many times during the war. The tall man with the sunburnt face had been in the war. The man had killed many times. Christopher was sure of it. The sunburnt skin suggested to Christopher the man had fought in the desert. With Lawrence in Arabia.

The party had reached the edge of the dance floor, almost at the empty table where Clara was hovering, waiting to greet her late guests. They had to be important or Clara would not have kept the table so late. Into Christopher Marlowe's vision flowed Brett Kentrich on the arm of Barnaby St Clair who the previous year had tried to unmask him in front of Clara. Barnaby was leering over Brett's shoulder in a way that made Christopher want to hit him in the face. Deliberately, Barnaby turned his dancing partner to look at the table where Clara was seating the new guests. Brett looked bored, much to Christopher satisfaction. Brett was no more than twenty feet from the piano. Brett's face turned into a look of great excitement. The girl in the red dress waved at Brett, taking the smile off Brett's face. The older man caught sight of Brett and his face lit up the way

Brett's face had lit up with excitement. The man moved towards the dancers on the floor but there were other couples in the way. Barnaby St Clair seemed to know the older man giving him a wave. A man wearing a monocle behind the older man stopped in his tracks. The tableau froze for a moment before Brett broke free and walked off the dance floor on her own. She was almost running.

Christopher turned back to the keyboard wondering what the palaver was all about. Sadly, he thought, it had nothing to do with him. When Christopher looked back again, the older man with the concentrated stare was following Brett out of the room, running after her. From Christopher's angle of sight on the piano stool, he could see Brett was crying. The girl in the red dress was looking livid; she did everything except stamp her foot. Christopher went on playing the piano. He was not sure whether to be sad or happy. Not that it would matter. He and Brett together were nothing but a dream.

BARNABY ST CLAIR had felt a surge of raging jealousy at the sight of Harry Brigandshaw's right hand resting protectively on Tina's elbow. He had known for some time they were married. He had done his mathematics when the birth of Anthony was published in the *Times*. She had caught the wealthy Harry Brigandshaw by getting herself pregnant. Only his lifelong training to always give the appearance of being a gentleman stopped him from causing a scene. Then he remembered the girl he was dancing with had once been Harry Brigandshaw's live-in lady, and sometime friend of Tina. Instead of going mad, he took revenge, turning Brett to look at Harry with his hand lightly resting on Tina's elbow.

It had all gone better than he had hoped, leaving him with a big smirk on his face. He was still smirking as he walked across the dance floor to his brother Merlin and the only girl in his life who had ever meant a thing to him. Probably the only person. From the earliest memory of his life.

Tina's face watching Harry run out after Brett was indeed sweet revenge. The girl was showing panic, something he had never before seen on Tina's face, even the first time he threw her in the river when they were six or seven years old. Not even when he yanked her pigtails for which he received a stinging slap in the face. In that second his Tina knew her Harry still loved Brett. The girl who still lived in Harry's Regent Mews flat. The one whose career had been made spectacular with Harry Brigandshaw putting money into *The Golden Moth*. Her angel behind the impresario, Oscar Fleming.

By the time Barnaby reached the table, he was laughing with happiness, his eyes sparkling with satisfaction.

"I say, Merlin, where's old Harry going? Hello, Tina, old gal. How's married life? Congratulations on becoming a mother."

"You don't want to sit down, do you, Barnaby?" said Merlin.

"Of course I do. Harry was our brother-in-law for goodness sake. He's been away for ages. I'm sure he'll be back in a tick. Darling Clara, be a dear and ask one of your stewards to bring us a bottle of champagne. Heidsieck Dry Monopole should fit the spirit of the family reunion. My goodness, Tina, weren't you wearing a red dress in Meikles that day I borrowed ten pounds from that chap Bowman? Red suits you. Definitely suits you."

"You never gave back the ten pounds." Tina was glaring at Barnaby.

"How thoughtless of me. Doesn't the chap work for Harry in Africa? Now that is good luck. I can give you the ten pounds and you can give it to Bowman. I'll make the cheque out to cash. Clara, darling, a pen? A gentleman always pays his debts. How remiss of me. How are you, Merlin? So nice to see my brother for a change. How are the mater and pater? Haven't had a chance to get down to Dorset for ages... Oh, good. Here comes Harry. Didn't I say he'd be back in just a tick?... Harry, dear chap. How are you? So good to see you. Took the liberty while you were away of ordering a bottle of bubbly to celebrate. Come and sit down. The food here is excellent."

"And how is Brett, Harry?" Tina asked Harry icily.

"She's crying, I'm afraid."

"So would I be if I'd been dumped."

"It wasn't like that, Tina."

"No. It probably wasn't, the way you looked at her on the dance floor."

"Tina! Darling! No scene." Barnaby was grinning and licking his lips at the same time.

"Shut up, Barnaby."

"Why don't you stamp your foot, Tina? You used to do that as a child when you couldn't get your own way."

"I also kicked you in the shins."

"Children, really," said Harry, taking control. "I'm very sorry, Tina. Of course, I was pleased to see Brett. It won't happen again."

"I should hope not."

"The meeting was an accident," said Merlin, putting the monocle back in his eye from where it had fallen on the cord onto his chest. He glared around at the people looking at them. The sight of the one coal-black iris made one woman actually shiver.

"I'm sure that chap at the piano is Barrington Madgwick, Clara. The chap I told you I met during the war." Barnaby was busy changing the subject, still enjoying himself immensely.

"At night he is Christopher Marlowe. During the day he's Barrie Madgwick." The worst thing that could happen in her supper club was a bad scene. Clara was happy to sacrifice Christopher for a diversion.

"How extraordinary. So I was right after all... I think I'll go and find Brett and bring her back so we can all be civilised."

"That would be good of you, Barnaby," said Harry. "Tina, would you go and help Barnaby? Brett is in the powder room. You two I remember were once friends, something our marriage must not change. Any more than you and Barnaby having known each other all your lives... By the by, Barnaby, my wife is expecting our second child."

"Oh, that is wonderful," said Merlin. "We'll make tonight a real celebration. Will the others at your table mind if you and Miss Kentrich join us, Barnaby?"

"Why ever should they, Merlin?"

"You should still make her excuses. Where are your manners, Barnaby? You must come round to the flat more often. Goodness me, we only live around the corner from each other."

THE SET WAS JUST over when Clara told Christopher she had told Barnaby St Clair his real name. She had her reasons. Running a successful business that entailed people drinking alcohol required good information about the patrons. Making certain that enemies were not seated at tables next to each other was just one of them. Clara had been appalled at the sight of Barnaby St Clair turning Brett Kentrich to look at Harry Brigandshaw holding the one-time Tina Pringle with the questionable social background. She had never seen Harry in her life before in the flesh but she knew the story. She had seen photographs. Of the chairman of Colonial Shipping. Of the girl who had once been Tina Pringle promoting herself in *Tatler*.

"If we don't do something, Christopher, those two women are going to scratch each other's eyes out. Make it look as though you are doing your rounds and head for their table. You know exactly which one I'm talking about. If needs be, stay there all evening. Just keep the peace. The band can play without you. No, tell Danny Hill to take over the piano if he sees you are not back at your stool for the start of the next set. Please, Christopher. This time I need your help. Talk about the army. Brigandshaw was in the Royal Flying Corps. The man with the two-colour eyes is Barnaby St Clair's brother. Brigandshaw was married to their sister before she was killed. Use all your charm, for goodness sake. A shouting match will be bad enough. A brawl, a disaster."

"How do you know all these things, Miss Clara?"

"There's more to this business than dishing up the food. Or playing them familiar music. Or giving them the smarm."

CHRISTOPHER HAD WATCHED Brett come back dry-eyed, her head high, the consummate actress once again. She had stopped at her first table, kissed the girl on both cheeks who had been sitting next to her, and gone across to the table that Clara thought might cause all the trouble. Brett was smiling when she sat down next to the older man. All the men had stood up when she and the girl in the red dress came back. Barnaby had come back alone earlier. At that point, Christopher had imagined the incident was over.

Christopher moved between the tables greeting the patrons. The patrons liked being greeted by someone from the band. It was all part of the smarm... Then he made his move.

"I say, aren't you the Honourable Barnaby St Clair? Back in '16 in France. You were over with your major to look at trench warfare. From Palestine. That was before Lawrence raised the Arabs in revolt against the Turks. I was a captain in the Royal Dragoon Guards in those days. Glad to see you made it through the war. Barrington Madgwick. I'm sorry, don't you remember?"

"What on earth are you doing playing the piano?"

"We all have our foibles. Here they know me as the bohemian Christopher Marlowe. During the day I work at my late father's office in the City. Father was chairman of the Baltic Exchange before he died. I hate the City."

"Don't blame you," said the older man. "Come and sit down with me. Harry Brigandshaw. My foible is running a farm in Africa when I should be running Colonial Shipping. My grandfather started the business. So you know Barnaby? This is Miss Brett Kentrich who I am sure you recognise. This is the Honourable Merlin St Clair. Their father's Lord St Clair of Purbeck. I was married to his daughter Lucinda before she was killed. And now, the most important person in my life and the mother of my son. May I introduce to you my wife, Mrs Tina Brigandshaw? Are you allowed to drink champagne while you are playing the piano?"

"Fact is, the trombone player is already drunk. Plays his best music drunk. Goes with playing music. You have to be drunk to play all night."

"By strange coincidence, I've met your brother, Ralph. Flew over him when he was camped on an eyrie overlooking the Zambezi River valley. Gave him my books on geology when he visited Elephant Walk. Had a chap from school with him. Keppel Howland, as I remember. They went off into the bush looking for diamonds. Never heard another word. The world really is small. From a cave overlooking the Zambezi to a supper club in London... Miss Kentrich plays the lead in *The Golden Moth* at Drury Lane."

"I know," said Christopher, smiling at her. She had made up his mind smiling back at him. He was finished playing the piano for the evening. "Excuse me for a moment. I have to change. Danny will be playing the next set for me. We swap around."

When Christopher Marlowe came back, he was Barrington Madgwick. The wig made from his own hair had gone along with the black beret. He was wearing evening clothes like the rest of them. No one in the supper club recognised the young man about town joining the table as the piano player. Brett was smiling again. The crisis was over. Clara gave Christopher a small wave, unseen, from the back of the club. The evening flowed on smoothly. Christopher marvelled at the power of money. Brett Kentrich smirked at Christopher Marlowe. Ignored his longing looks. She was smiling at Barrington Madgwick with his inherited money, and patting the empty chair next to her, the chair the steward had pulled out for him from the table. The nasty taste in his mouth must have shown in his eyes. She was now looking at him as a mother would look at a child.

BRETT LEANED her mouth close to the man now seated next to her. She knew exactly what Clara had done. And why. She was now feeling better after the first shock of seeing Harry. Most relationships ended in disaster anyway. It was just that theirs had been over before she had wanted it. The fact Tina Pringle was a first-class bitch and money-grabber had only added fuel to her flame of rejection.

"I've known who you are for months, Barrie. You're quite famous in musical circles. Not many with old money enter into our profession. They consider it beneath themselves. Maybe a few well-written sonnets published privately and bound in leather to relieve their artistic frustration. Having too much money and not enough to do must be such a bore."

"I'm not a very good piano player."

"Does it matter? It's what other people think of you that counts. The snobby crowd here love Christopher Marlowe, the piano player who writes poetry in an attic as most of them think. Talking down to a half-starved bohemian makes them feel so much more superior. People like to feel superior to others, haven't you noticed?"

"I do live in an attic."

"I'm so sorry. Not now, surely?"

"Oh, yes. I prefer the people."

At that moment, Barrie Madgwick wished he was Christopher Marlowe back sitting on his piano stool. There he was real. Here he was being forced to play a part.

"I'm sorry," she said, "I've hurt your feelings."

"You didn't mean that sarcastically, did you?" He had heard the changed tone of her voice.

"No, I didn't, Christopher."

"Maybe we have more in common than we think."

"I hope we do. Now, here is not the place to find out. I'm very tired. Mentally more than physically... They look good dancing together, Harry and Tina don't they?... Be careful of Barnaby St Clair. I don't know much about his brother. Please see me out of the club before they all come back... Did you know the woman dancing with the brother with the different coloured eyes is a whore?"

"She was sitting at your table with Barnaby."

"Doesn't change the fact she is a whore... No, I've changed my mind. They're all coming back. Running away would give that bitch a victory. Be a dear and get into deep conversation with me. I'm sure you don't want to talk about the war. Neither do the others. The ones who did the fighting never do... Harry was a famous fighter pilot... You and I talking quietly so they can't hear will give a much better impression. The bitch will hate that. I'm too tired for verbal sword fighting. Believe it or not, running around the stage singing all night knocks the stuffing out of you. Even when they do clap madly... Who do I talk to? Christopher or Barrington?"

"Just imagine the wig and the beret." Christopher managed to put on a small smile.

Brett laughed. It was the first time Christopher had heard her laugh. A genuine laugh. It came from deep down in her throat. More like a healthy chuckle between old friends. As though something had tickled her funny bone.

THE MOST ABHORRENT thing in Merlin St Clair's life was the chance of a public scene. He would do anything to run away, including dancing with Millie Scott who had been sitting at the actress's table where she barely belonged. Merlin had met her years before when she was eighteen and dancing at the Hippodrome at the start of the war. She had long legs and walked like a queen. It was in the days when Merlin liked to send flowers backstage to pretty showgirls. The idea had grown during the war when officers back on leave had little time to spare and associating with the lower classes didn't seem to matter at the time. The chance of later embarrassment was far less than being killed on the Western Front. Some of the girls even said they were doing their bit for the war effort.

To escape his current predicament, Merlin had gone across and formally asked Millie Scott to dance, bowing with his right hand held up behind his back. Shortly before, he had watched Harry go off to dance with his new wife. The man who was once the piano player and now Barrington Madgwick was sitting down next to Brett Kentrich. She was talking into the man's ear. Manners and good behaviour seemed to be a thing of the past. With great fear in his heart at an appalling scene about to happen with himself at the centre, he had made his escape. Now all the dancers were going back to their tables. Barnaby was nowhere to be seen but that was nothing unusual. The strange success of his brother's business, so far as Merlin could see, was based on Barnaby's many social contacts. Brother Barnaby was probably working the room. Being his charming self. Trawling for information that could make him more money on the stock exchange.

Depositing Millie Scott back at her table with a formal bow, and receiving a funny look from Millie that asked what was going on, Merlin went back to the table he had gone to so much trouble to secure, the table that was meant to be just for the three of them. If only Barnaby had gone to another of his many haunts, the nightmare would not be happening. Then he saw his brother in conversation with the man Merlin knew to be a banker in the City. He changed course and leant towards his brother, close to the ear on the opposite side to the banker.

"Stay away from my table, Barnaby," he hissed.

As he walked away, he heard Barnaby say to everyone at the table so that he could hear, "Message from the mater... You all know my brother Merlin." He was turning around and smiling at his brother as he said it.

Merlin turned swiftly after giving his brother a flash of hatred. He didn't care if anyone saw. Whenever anything happened to change Merlin's placid life, it was caused by Barnaby. What Barnaby had been doing with Tina Pringle in the first place was beyond his comprehension. In his bad temper his own infatuation with the now Mrs Harry Brigandshaw was quite forgotten.

"Barnaby sends his regards, Harry," he said back at the table, "he will not be joining us again tonight."

He could think of absolutely nothing to say to the piano player. So far as Merlin was concerned, once a piano player, always a piano player.

MILLIE SCOTT WATCHED the performance between the brothers and cursed her naivety. If she had only been a whore for the last ten years instead of kicking up her legs in the chorus line, she would have had something more to show for it instead of the sordid bedsitter off the Bayswater Road. She had slept with more men than she could count as she liked to sleep with men, but, more fool her, had never taken a penny despite what everyone else thought. There had been hope with the impresarios that it would lead to better things back when she was very young. Now at the age of twenty-eight all she still had were legs that went all the way up to her armpits, as she liked to tell everyone, and nothing else, not even her startlingly good looks which were fading. Every night she had to look in the mirror to put on her make-up. The eyes in the same old face were tired. The bloom of youth had gone.

"You think she'll get back with Harry?" she asked of the girl next to her.

"Not a chance. He's married with a kid," said her friend Blanche. They were both in the same predicament and understood each other.

"At least she's got a free leasehold flat off Regent Street for the next sixty years. And a red car."

"How do you know these things, Millie?"

"I listen."

"What was all that about with the Honourable Mr Nibs, Merlin St Clair?"

"I have no bloody idea."

"Who's the bloke with high and mighty Brett?"

"I have no bloody idea."

"The piano player you came to drool over has gone for the night. Must be sick. The trumpeter's sitting down at the piano to play."

"Just my luck. You ever had the feeling, Blanche, you just can't win?"

"Every day is a new start."

"Bloody optimist... Where are all the men at our table tonight? Bloody hen party."

"Don't swear. You know I'm religious."

"Sorry, luv."

. . .

DANNY HILL WAS an opportunist who took his chances knowing they were few and far between. He had put each of Christopher Marlowe's songs on sheet music. He had written the score separately for trumpet, trombone, piano and clarinet. The words to the songs he had added for the crooner, Harvey Lyttleton. Everyone in the band except Christopher Marlowe could read music. All the members of the band were in on the plan, waiting for the opportunity to play Christopher's music at Clara's. Whether the diners were sick of the same music every night, Danny was not sure. The band certainly were, even if the familiar tunes brought the couples onto the dance floor which is what Clara said it was all about.

Having been warned by Clara to take over the piano at the start of the previous set, Danny had used the short intermission to hand out his sheets of music to the band. He had also had a word with Clara. Clara had agreed. Any distraction to calm the flashing looks between the St Clair brothers was worth trying. At the worst, nobody would listen or dance.

The crooner was an old hand at working an audience. Happy to have a chance to sing a new song he had read the words through three times during the interval. Being able to read the music he could hear the tune in his head.

"My lords, ladies and gentlemen. May I have your attention? Some of you may have noticed our new man at the piano. Please welcome Mr Danny Hill, a man of many talents. Mr Christopher Marlowe will be playing the piano here again tomorrow. I'm now going to sing for you a song he wrote especially for the inestimable Miss Brett Kentrich who is graciously among us tonight. Please give a hand to Miss Kentrich. Fact is, Christopher has written a whole raft of songs. He has also written the book for the musical he calls *Happy Times*... Take it away, Danny. Ladies and gentlemen, for tonight only on the piano, Mr Danny Hill."

AT FIRST, Brett was livid. Harry was looking at her with a quizzical smile. Barnaby had gone off to another table, leaving her with a virtual stranger. Now the man with two names was playing a trick on her.

"Now I understand the change of persona. What are you up to Christopher, or is it now Barrington?"

"I had nothing to do with this." Christopher was white as a sheet.

"Then who wrote this song?" Brett was whispering nastily.

"I did."

"Why did you write it for me?"

"Only in my imagination, Miss Kentrich. You wouldn't even look at me, remember?"

"Is there a whole score?"

"It's not finished. I'm so sorry. You can get up and go. I will walk you out and find a taxi. This is the worst moment of my life."

Danny was first playing the tune through on the piano. Halfway through the clarinet began to speak. The crooner began to sing the love song. Everything went quiet in the supper club.

Christopher was sure the quiet was embarrassment and went red in the face. He half got up from his chair and was pulled back by Brett. Harry Brigandshaw had stopped talking to his wife and was listening intently to the song. Couples began to move onto the dance floor, swaying on the spot to the soft haunting music. Christopher waited for it all to be over so he could make his escape and never show his face back at Clara's. He had never heard Harvey sing with so much concentration, which was strange. The man was a hack. The trombone player seemed to have sobered up. Christopher caught Clara looking at him. She was smiling. He was too tense to smile back.

At the end, Harry Brigandshaw led the applause. Everyone stood up except Brett and Christopher until Christopher remembered he was Barrie Madgwick for the night. Sheepishly, he got up with the rest of them and clapped his own music. Harry Brigandshaw, he thought, was smiling like a lunatic. His wife had a queer look on her face as if she had just found something she wanted. The moment was quickly over. Danny was playing Brett's main song from *The Golden Moth*, a song familiar to everyone in the room.

"If it wasn't a setup, how come you had evening dress ready to put on?" Brett was still furious.

"Being the managing director in training at Madgwick and Madgwick, clients ask me to dine with them. They don't want to complete long contracts with my Uncle Wallace who is a drunk and a fool in most people's opinion. This is not the first time Danny played piano. Despite what Harvey Lyttleton had to say, I play the first two sets as Christopher Marlowe and duck out to dinner as Barrington Madgwick. I have never accepted the invitation to the shows except once when the show the clients were seeing was *The Golden Moth*. I've watched *The Golden Moth* six times from the gods as Christopher Marlowe when I lived off the earnings of a piano player. I also have a suit in Clara's office to change into if the evening goes on too long. I play my songs so Danny can write them down on sheet music. We have argued into the mornings over the songs. Then I go straight to the office in the City instead of going home to my attic to change."

"You are a romantic fool."

"What Danny Hill says. But I like it."

"Now I'm going home."

"Don't you want to sing my songs?"

"What on earth for?"

Harry Brigandshaw had been listening to every word. "Because if the rest of them are as good as the first one," said Harry, "I will back *Happy Times*. The same way I gave Oscar Fleming money to put on *The Golden Moth*. My wife says that song was a hit. It's her idea for me to back another show for you, Brett."

"Really?"

"I just love that song," said Tina. "Harry says we'll have to stay in London for a while to tie the ends up."

"You want the flat back?"

"I don't think Harry would do that," said Tina sweetly. "We'll buy ourselves a townhouse. Somewhere in the West End. Don't you think that's a good idea, Harry? We can't stay in a hotel, week after week. Think of little Anthony. Can you read music, Miss Kentrich?"

"Of course."

"Then why not sing Christopher's song tonight and bring the house down? I have a friend at the *Tatler*. Barry Jones will be over here in a taxi before we finish supper. You'll have supper with us? Just the five of us. Barnaby is off making money at another table. A new song from the new show and so romantic. The *Tatler* will gobble it up."

Brett relaxed, smiling at Tina. Of course, she thought inwardly excited, the girl doesn't want to live in Africa. London was more exciting. Brett began to smile... If Tina stayed in London, so would Harry. She put out her hand and covered Tina's lightly where it was resting on the white damask tablecloth.

"Go and give Barry Jones a ring, Tina. We'll wait for him. I'd have oysters tonight if there was an R in the month. But it's June. I'll begin with caviar. I'm starving. Merlin, you were so clever to bring Harry to Clara's. Before the food comes, I'll sit in Clara's office and read through the music. You won't mind me being away from the table for a while?"

"It's really a duet," said Christopher, still not believing his luck.

"Then I can sing with Harvey Lyttleton. He has a lovely voice. Not even bad-looking." She was looking at the band and slowly running her tongue above the upper lip, careful not to fudge her lipstick.

Brett Kentrich was once again in a good mood. Behind Tina's back, she gave Harry a sweet smile. The poor man had no idea what was really going on.

. . .

TINA LEFT the four of them alone to make her phone call. She had used Barry Jones before, to launch herself into London society when she came back to England from Johannesburg on the back of her brother's money. Albert Pringle had first made money from a whorehouse, before legitimising himself by buying a gold mine. The gold mine had launched the Serendipity Mining and Explosives Company with shares in the company quoted on the Johannesburg, London and New York Stock Exchanges. Albert Pringle was what the newspapers liked to call a Rand Baron.

Barry Jones was pleased to hear from her, even said he was dressed in his pyjamas. Tina explained what she wanted Barry to hear at Clara's.

"I'll be right over, darling."

"You'll owe me one for this."

"I probably will."

MERLIN, having no idea what was really going on, walked across and asked Millie Scott to dance. Barrie Madgwick and Harry were in a huddle. Tina had gone off to phone her friend at the *Tatler* magazine. Brett had disappeared with Clara. He felt spare. Left out. Which he thought unfair seeing he was paying for the evening. His only consolation was Barnaby keeping away from the table.

While Merlin danced with Millie Scott and told her what was going to happen for something better to say, he was thinking of Esther and Genevieve. Yesterday's lunch with his real family had been perfect. His daughter had brought him his comfortable slippers. Esther had listened open-mouthed to everything he had to say. Before he left the little flat in Chelsea, he had agreed to give them all the little things they had asked for. Even Esther's friend Joan from Lambeth, who had stayed for half an hour, had not changed his mood. Genevieve had said she liked Aunty Joan and that was good enough for Merlin.

"If your friend from Africa who was married to your sister is going to put up the money for this new musical, could you ask him to ask Oscar Fleming to find me a part? I'm sick of kicking my legs up in the chorus line. So is my friend Blanche. Just for old times' sake, like. We'd some good times you and I back then when the war started."

"Of course I will, Millie. What are friends for?"

"You are my friend? Now that is nice."

To Merlin's acute embarrassment, the silly girl began to cry.

4

JANUARY 1925 – DINNER AT BERKELEY SQUARE

*T*here was one thing Ralph Madgwick finally understood. He could not do without money. By the time he reached the entrance to the offices of Madgwick and Madgwick in Billiter Street down from Aldgate Tube station in the City of London, he was flat broke.

Ralph and Keppel Howland had worked their passages by stoking the boilers in the bowels of the ship all the way from Durban to England, their only pay, their food and passage home. They had both been too proud to cable their families for money. Too proud to admit failure. They looked like what they were: stokers off a tramp steamer from one of the ports of England. They were both shivering in the freezing cold. Neither had eaten for two days. They were unwashed and probably smelled, though neither could smell their own dirt.

With all the reading in the world, finding diamonds somewhere in the African bush was but a dream. Sixteen months after leaving Elephant Walk, expecting to make a quick fortune and a triumphant return to their families in England, they had shot an old elephant with tusks so large the poor beast was pulling them along the ground through the dry bush. The rains had yet to break. The bush was tinder dry, the nearest waterhole miles away. Ralph shot his last elephant with sadness and compassion. He rather thought they both felt the same. At the end of their tethers. Nowhere else to go.

The tusks were huge and heavy on the backs of the packhorses.

Weeks later they rode into Salisbury with their tradable goods only to find the new Southern Rhodesian government under Sir Charles Coghlan had passed a law requiring hunters of big game to have licences. The tusks were confiscated. For the first time in their lives, despite all their education and family background, they were unable to purchase goods or pay for a place to stay. They still had their horses and guns; small game to eat did not require a licence.

They left Salisbury behind on the long journey down Africa, first through the border town of Messina in South Africa from where they journeyed on to Durban, living off their guns and passing through the towns as quickly as possible.

Their eyrie on the Zambezi escarpment where Harry Brigandshaw had first spotted them from his converted Handley Page bomber was as far away as heaven.

"I'll just have to throw myself on the mercy of my father when we get home," Ralph had said to Keppel. "What will your father do?"

"Kick me out again. Going back to the Isle of Man just isn't on my cards. What will your father do?"

"First he'll gloat. Then tell me I'm useless. He might even just try to box my ears. Then he'll give me passage to Australia and tell me never to blight his house again."

"Doesn't he like you?"

"My father doesn't like anyone... How about your father?"

"Only when I do what I'm told."

AN EAST WIND was blowing through their tropical clothes, the bush hats as out of place as themselves. They had yet to see the sun since landing at Bristol from the freighter. Ralph hesitated before pushing into the revolving door. Both could see it was warm inside.

"Why didn't we go to Barrie?" asked Keppel, hunching his shoulders.

"Barrie's a piano player. Barely enough money to keep himself alive. Inside there is the lion's den."

"If he kicks us out?"

"Then we go to Barrie."

"If we had only brought the guns we could have shot ourselves and had done with it. I'm sure I have frostbite on two of my fingers. I can't feel them."

"Here we go, Keppel. Together. We have each other."

"That's all I need."

They both tried to laugh as they crammed into one compartment of the swivel door. Suddenly thrust inside, it was blissfully warm. Both of them stood slightly out of the door's way. They were trying to get warm. Their teeth were chattering. From somewhere in the building came the smell of coffee and freshly baked bread.

"Oh my God. You said it was a shipping company, not a coffee shop. Only Lloyd's was meant to be a coffee shop."

"Both the Baltic Exchange and Lloyd's started in coffee shops. The shop around the corner must be making a delivery to the boardroom. They do that when Father has important guests... This is getting worse."

"Shall we run?"

"Not until I get warm."

A pretty girl who had pushed through the swivel door took one look at them and giggled. Then she went across to the lift.

"Which floor, miss?" asked the man sitting on the stool inside the lift. Ralph and Keppel could just see his shape.

"Fifth floor, Maxwell."

The concertina door to the lift clanged shut. The lift clanged into gear and began to move up. They watched the girl's feet disappear upwards until they were gone.

"Father's office is on the fifth floor," said Ralph. "Come on, Kep. They've cut the wire. We're going over the top."

MAXWELL THOUGHT he had seen everything during the war. Were it not for the public school accent, the man's voice of authority, he would not have allowed them into the lift. The two men wanting to go to the fifth floor, the executive suite, were filthy and dressed in long cotton trousers and shirts with short sleeves. Neither had a coat. Their smell of unwashed bodies brought back to him the trenches. Then, even the officers looked much like the two standing rigidly, looking up, waiting for what looked to Maxwell like their execution. Maxwell found it difficult to tell their age. Both had full facial hair. The one who had asked to be taken to the fifth floor had the small finger missing from his left hand.

The missing finger had made up Maxwell's mind. Both men were shivering, trying hard to control themselves under scrutiny from another rank. Maxwell was sure both men had been junior officers.

"Here we are, sir. Fifth floor. Executive suite."

"Thank you, Maxwell. Is Mr Madgwick in his office?"

"Yes, sir. Good luck, sir."

"We'll need it."

Wanting to see more of what was going on, Maxwell refrained from closing the concertina door. He waited before taking the cage down again.

Miss Prescott, who had come back from ordering the coffee and rolls for the boardroom, was no longer giggling.

"Can I help you two?" she said nastily. Keppel took another look at the girl's face and decided she was no longer pretty despite the good legs. "You may take the lift down, Maxwell," she said. The shaft of the lift rode up next to the spiral staircase. A glass-domed roof overhung the lift and the five flights of stairs.

Ralph gave her a cold look. He disliked people who looked down on the less fortunate.

"Yes, you can. I would like to see my father."

"Do you have an appointment?" Instinctively, Rosie Prescott knew that all was not what it appeared to be. Her answer gave her time to regain her composure. Then she smiled broadly.

"You are Ralph Madgwick, aren't you?"

"Yes, I am. This is Captain Keppel Howland. How did you know my name? Now may I see my father?"

"Your missing finger. You lost it during the war. Your father was very proud of you... You don't know? We've been trying to make contact with you for over a year. He's dead. Your father died of cancer a year ago last week... I'm so sorry."

"Is my Uncle Wallace in his office?" His father had never been proud of him. He was hallucinating. They were still on the ship, shovelling coal to keep the steam up in the boiler. Keppel had him firmly by the elbow.

"Steady, old chap."

"My father is dead!"

"Yes, sir. Do you want to sit down on the couch? The delivery boy from the shop just brought coffee up to the boardroom. I'll go and get some for you both. Oh, dear me."

"And the fresh bread," said Keppel, taking control. "We haven't eaten for a couple of days. Uncle Wallace can wait... Goodness, I rather think I can feel my fingers again... What is your name?"

"Rosie Prescott."

"Rosie Prescott, you are a saint... Now, a dash of speed, my dear."

"Of course... Take Mr Madgwick to the couch."

Only then did Maxwell put the lift into gear to take it back to the ground floor. He had been right. He always liked being right. Officers, the pair of them.

"You all right, Ralph?" whispered Keppel.

"Poor Dad. My poor mother. Now we'll have to go down to Ashtead." To his own great surprise, Ralph Madgwick began to sob: he had never even liked his father, let alone loved him. A boy told to call his father 'sir' was not inclined to affection, to Ralph Madgwick's way of thinking.

THEY WOLFED down the hot rolls and butter. The girl with the good legs had come back quicker than either could have hoped. They both now thought she was pretty, especially when they drank the hot coffee that had been spooned liberally with sugar. After the second cup of coffee from the pot, they stopped shivering. They told Rosie Prescott their story. She went for more hot rolls and coffee. The rolls were wrapped in a white napkin to keep them warm.

"Come this way," she said, smiling. Ralph put her age at around about thirty.

IN FRONT OF UNCLE WALLACE, on the Jacobean desk in the mahogany panelled office that before had been Ralph's father's, was a balloon glass full of brandy. The small antique clock over the mantelpiece said five minutes to ten in the morning.

Uncle Wallace had a smooth face with bright red cheeks and a monocle that covered his left, glass eye. Uncle Wallace had been a full colonel during the war. The day he quite unnecessarily led his regiment over the top waving a swagger stick at the German trench some hundred yards away, he was drunk, or so the less friendly witnesses were heard to say afterwards. The brigadier, appalled at so senior an officer leading an infantry counter-attack, had put the colonel up for the Victoria Cross. Uncle Wallace and his regiment had chased the Huns out of their front-line trench. The living then rested, eating German sausage that hung on the walls of the enemy entrenchment. Everyone said it was a pleasant change from tinned baked beans and bully beef. The colonel, now only seeing out of one eye and ignoring the blood oozing from his left socket, looked for and found the German officers' dugout where he opened a bottle of good German hock. By the time they got him back to the British lines, he was gibbering.

The brigadier sent him back to England and settled with the War Office for a Military Cross. Uncle Wallace was immensely pleased. He was equally pleased with the glass eye and the desk job at the War Office. Going back on active duty was never mentioned again.

"Come in, my dear nephew. And you must be Mr Howland? Please sit down. My word you are a sight for one sore eye... Ah, still the pinkie missing. Well, it would be. Like my left eye, they don't grow again, what!... Come and sit down, nephew, and let me have a look at you... Miss Prescott has told me about your predicament... Will the Savoy do? My tailor will be told to call on you. Splendid tailor. The Grill Room in the Savoy is excellent. My driver will take you to the hotel... Your poor father. Why I'm in his office, of course. Senior partner now. Barrington, I'm afraid, is up at the Dale Street office in Liverpool... Wasn't I meant to be in a meeting, Miss Prescott? Never mind. They don't want to see me anyway. Postlethwaite will cope. Jolly good chap, Postlethwaite. Fact is, I don't know a damn thing about shipping. As the grandson of the owner, there never seemed any point... What are you going to do for a job, young nephew?... Ah. Good. You'll work for me. I'm sure we can find you a desk."

"What's Barrie doing in Liverpool?" asked Ralph alarmed.

"Works for us now after your poor father died. Grooming him for senior partner so I can get out of this office... Want a drink? Suppose it is early."

"So he sold his soul to the devil?"

"Only half his soul. Queer chap, Barrington. Still lives in an attic and plays the piano at night in an appalling supper club. Wouldn't be seen dead there. Writing a musical. Damnedest thing. It's Barrington who says he only sold half his soul to the devil. With you, young Ralph, back in the living he may have a new chance to buy back the other half. He'll like that. Now off with you."

Uncle Wallace, at ten in the morning, was more than slightly drunk.

Working on the principle that it never paid to argue with a drunk or a fool, they followed Miss Prescott out of the senior partner's office. Ralph was smiling.

Even in the brief moment of the cold outside as they dashed across the road to the senior partner's Rolls-Royce, neither of them shivered.

"Barrie and I underestimated that old fox," said Ralph, resting luxuriously on the leather seat at the back of the car. It was blissfully warm in the sealed compartment.

The chauffeur slid back the glass window above the driver's seat and smiled at them.

"Where to, sir?"

Ralph gave the driver the address of his brother's attic room off Shaftesbury Avenue. Miss Prescott had been politely told to leave off telephoning the Savoy and the tailor. They both thanked her for the coffee and bread rolls and sending for the car.

That night, Gert van Heerden took them to Clara's to wash dishes. They were both by then wearing Barrie's clothes. Clara paid them by letting them eat as much as they wanted standing up in the kitchen at the end of their shift. Ralph had told Keppel free stays at the Savoy came at a price.

THREE DAYS LATER, weary and cold, Christopher Marlowe let himself into his attic room. It was Saturday evening. Clerks at Madgwick and Madgwick did not travel on company time. Christopher had left the Dale Street office with his suitcase and gone directly to the Liverpool railway station. The company worked until one o'clock on Saturdays. At first, his mind did not register the change. He was too late to go to Clara's. Christopher wished to climb into bed, get warm and go to sleep. He had had to stand in the third-class corridor all the way to London.

Realising something was wrong he walked out again and banged on Gert van Heerden's box room. Gert was the only other person with a key to his room, so he could boil up the vegetable soup on the one-ring gas stove. There was no reply to his banging.

Back in his attic, Christopher found the source of the new smell. The room smelled of paraffin. Behind the old couch he had picked up in a second-hand shop for five shillings, he found a cylindrical paraffin heater that was two feet high and giving out heat. The curtains in his room were drawn. The room was warm. Christopher opened his cupboard to put away his overcoat to find his clothes gone. Not only his clothes, his two spare pairs of shoes that were necessary to change into as most nights coming home his shoes were wet and took two days to dry out. He pulled open the two lower drawers. His shirts were gone. Instead, he found a strange outfit neatly folded. He pulled it out. The outfit of shirt and long trousers was made from lightweight linen. The colour was khaki. There were bad stains under the armpits but the shirt had been washed. Under the first outfit in the drawer was another exactly the same. On the hat rack next to the cupboard hung two large hats with wide brims.

Christopher picked one off the hook. The inside of the hat was stained black from sweat. Below the hats on the ground were two pairs of old boots. There was someone else living in his room. Banging around in the drawers, Christopher found nothing else missing.

Hunger was dominating his wish to get into bed and sleep. The matches were still in their place on the shelf above the large pot that stood on the gas ring. Christopher pulled off the heavy iron top and looked inside, fearful he was going to have to go to bed hungry. The pot was full. Christopher put his finger in the rich stew. The stew was still warm. When he licked his finger, he could taste the meat. Taking a plate from the shelf, he helped himself.

There was just the right amount of herbs and salt. He ate a second plate of stew, got into his bed in his pyjamas and fell asleep, too tired to fathom out his new predicament.

CHRISTOPHER WAS HALF WOKEN from a bad dream at three o'clock in the morning by someone opening his door: it was never good to sleep. The dream and reality were still part of each other. The German bombardment had stopped, bringing him wide awake. The German infantry was about to attack his trench. In his dream, he jumped out of bed and was looking for his tin hat when the single light bulb in the attic room came on. Two men with long hair down to their shoulders were grinning at him. All Christopher could see, other than facial hair, were eyes, dirty foreheads and noses. Behind them, grinning, was Gert van Heerden.

"I let them in a couple of days ago," said Gert. It was said as if Gert had done him a big favour.

The two men in front of Gert were wearing his clothes. The one with familiar eyes was carrying a full bottle of whisky.

"It's the prodigal bloody son," said Christopher, throwing back the blankets to find his room still warm.

The other man was looking in the stewing pot.

"He had a go at my stew," said Keppel Howland with satisfaction.

"Don't I know you?"

"You should. Spent two summer holidays at Ashtead."

"Keppel Howland!"

"Have a drink, Barrie," said Ralph, offering the bottle of whisky.

"Christopher."

"Christopher?... Uncle Wallace said you were working for the old firm. I assumed..."

Keppel Howland, with a cold plate of stew in his hand, watched the brothers hug each other, something neither of them would have done before the war. The war that had changed everything in all their lives. Keppel Howland wondered how much different their lives would have been without the Great War... There were many things he wondered about.

KEPPEL AND RALPH were sleeping on the thin carpet on the floor. It was one thing to borrow a man's clothes; quite another to sleep in his bed. They had bought blankets and the paraffin heater with the fifty pounds delivered to the attic by Rosie Prescott. The driver of the Rolls-Royce had known where to go. Inside the envelope she handed Ralph on their first day in the attic was a note from Uncle Wallace and ten white five-pound notes. None of them had ever seen a five-pound note before. They were very large and had to be folded in four to fit in Ralph's wallet. The message was simple. No questions. No threats. No arguments at him turning down the Savoy and the best tailor in Savile Row.

FROM ONE SOLDIER TO ANOTHER.

THERE WAS NO SIGNATURE, just the note and the money. Rosie was looking around the cold, bare room. The curtains of the one big window were open. On the outside ledges of the small, book-size windowpanes, snow was half an inch high.

"He lives like this?"

Being nosy and with specific instructions from Uncle Wallace, she took the lid off the pot of the one-ring gas stove.

"Just vegetable," she said in disgust.

"What about the strings attached?"

"There are none. He made me go to his bank for the money. Something about a finger being worth more than fifty pounds."

"Was he drunk?"

"He never gets drunk, Mr Madgwick. Sips just enough brandy through the day to keep himself smiling. He prefers the country. Horses and dogs. That kind of thing."

"Good old Uncle Wallace," said Keppel Howland.

"You need a heater in this room," said Rosie Prescott, holding her arms together across her chest. "It's like an icebox in here... What are you going to do?"

"When does my brother come back from Liverpool?"

"Saturday night."

"We'll be working Saturday night."

"Doing what?"

"Washing dishes at Clara's. She feeds us."

"Didn't you two get an education?"

"The best. We were at school together with Malcolm Scott. Malcolm was blown to pieces when I lost my finger."

Rosie moved off to look out of their attic window at the snow-covered roofs of the houses.

"Always the war," she said. "It must have been terrible." Then she shuddered but not from the cold.

"Makes people do strange things they otherwise would not do," said Ralph quietly.

"Like living in an attic when you have more money than you can count."

"Did Barrie inherit my father's money?" he asked.

"You both did. Provided you run the company. All Mr Madgwick receives now is the salary of a junior clerk. When he has been through all the departments they will make him senior partner."

"Poor Christopher."

"Who?"

"My brother. When he lives here, he calls himself Christopher Marlowe. It was going to be Will Shakespeare but that was too obvious. He wants to live like an artist even if he doesn't have the talent to be one."

"Then what's all this about a musical he is writing for Miss Brett Kentrich, the star of *The Golden Moth*?"

"That's news to me. We've been in the African bush for a long time. As far as the Skeleton Coast in South West Africa looking for diamonds."

"You didn't find any?"

"Not one."

"Then you will be coming to work at Madgwick and Madgwick."

"First my brother... Please thank my uncle for me... Very much. I'd write a note but..."

"He doesn't have any children of his own, Mr Madgwick. I don't know why."

"There will be a reason. We just don't know it. You or I, Miss Prescott."

"The driver is waiting downstairs."

"Then you must go."

THEY WERE ALL TOO tired to drink the bottle of whisky.

"It's just wonderful to see you, Ralph."

"You too, Christopher."

"I must go back to sleep now. This time I won't have bad dreams. We'll get some old mattresses tomorrow from somewhere."

"The floor's fine. We've slept far rougher than this in Africa... Sleep tight."

Before Ralph could turn off the one light, his brother was gently snoring. Within a minute he and Keppel were asleep under their blankets on the floor.

It snowed heavily during the night unbeknown to any of them. Ralph dreamt of the eyrie on the escarpment overlooking the great Zambezi. The leopard was outside eating the remains of the buck. The leopard was smiling at him with soft yellow eyes, growling contentedly in the bottom of his throat, but it was difficult to tell if the big cat was male or female. Alfred had retreated to the back of the cave, the big fire he had stoked with wood between himself and the leopard.

ALL THREE OF them woke with the sound of Gert van Heerden banging on the door. All three of them had had a better night's sleep.

"I had some change left over from the meat, Christopher. Rolls and butter with strawberry jam. How does that sound for breakfast? Get up! It's ten o'clock in the morning."

They were all ravenously hungry, smiling at each other as they ate, Gert watching them.

"I dreamt of a leopard," said Ralph.

"Male or female?" asked Gert.

"I don't know."

"That's a bad sign, dreaming of our animals. It means you'll want to go back again."

The paraffin heater had run out of fuel during the night. Keppel finished his breakfast and got up from the floor to fill the small tin tank at the bottom of the heater with paraffin from a bottle.

"When there is so much space in the world, why do we cram ourselves into cities like London?" he asked, screwing the lid back onto the small tank.

"Then why did you come back?" asked Christopher.

"Because it's home. The Isle of Man is my home. Now there's a place without too many people. And a raw wind off the sea. The ancestors call to us from all their pain of survival. Do you know in the Island when a house is abandoned we never knock it down? The little people come to live in the ruins. The little people who came before us, long, long ago... I'm going home, Ralph. Whatever my father says. He saved up all his pennies to send me to a good school. I let him down. Oxford. He wanted a son up at Oxford. No one on the island he knew had a son up at Oxford. Then I lied about my age and ran off to war and here I am on the floor of a London attic. All that money spent on my education and not a penny given back in return. In Africa, I imagined finding a handful of diamonds to give him but that was not what he wanted. A son at Oxford. A man of letters. An educated man... It makes you wonder."

"You can still go up to Oxford," said Christopher.

"How? Who pays for it? Anyway, I'm too old to go back to school. The war destroyed more than flesh and blood. It destroyed dreams. Here I am at twenty-three and nothing to show for it."

"There are foundations who put soldiers into Oxford. We'll find one. Maybe Madgwick and Madgwick could set up a foundation. You fought for King and country."

The war hovered in the air for a moment.

"It was just Da's dream," said Keppel. "He didn't even have enough money to support me for three years at Oxford. There are only so many sheep you can run on a thousand acres of hard ground."

"What did you want to read at Oxford?" asked Christopher.

"English literature. Then I can be a writer."

"You don't have to go to Oxford to become a writer," he said smiling. "Why don't you write some stories about Africa and see if we can sell them to the newspapers?"

"Do you think I can write about the Handley Page?" said Keppel to Ralph.

"The pilot was a famous fighter pilot during the war."

"Why don't you ask him?" said Christopher, smiling broadly.

"He lives in Africa."

"I have an invitation to dinner on Wednesday. With Miss Brett Kentrich. I'm sure he'll be happy to invite you two as well."

"What are you talking about?" asked Ralph.

"Harry Brigandshaw. The night he agreed to finance *Happy Times* he said you stayed with him on Elephant Walk. It was the kind of strange coincidence that made him want to finance another musical... He's a strange man. Such a mixture. A hard-headed man of business one minute and a dreamer the next, a lover of the African bush, of Africans and their traditions. He tells me Africans see everything in the future through dreams. That they believe in omens. Harry flying over you two outside your cave on top of the Zambezi escarpment was an omen. Meeting the brother of the same man playing two parts was an omen as it is what he does himself. Harry believes in omens. He believes we are given directions and just have to follow them whether we like it or not, brother Ralph."

"What are you saying?"

"I'm saying nothing. It's for you to decide. Your own destiny as well as your duty to family and country. To the people before you who made it possible for you to be alive and here and dreaming about your leopard."

. . .

ON THE FOLLOWING TUESDAY MORNING, Christopher Marlowe went straight to the office from Clara's. He had taken off the black beret and the wig made from his own hair and changed into a business suit. Christopher was both tired and elated.

They had played through all the music from *Happy Times*. Danny Hill, now officially music director for *Happy Times*, had kept the band playing until breakfast time when Keppel Howland and Ralph Madgwick brought out the bacon and eggs from the kitchen with Clara's blessing. They were all involved in the production, physically and emotionally, including Clara.

Harvey Lyttleton had sung all the songs for Christopher's brother, back from Africa with his friend. Gert van Heerden, employed by Oscar Fleming to stage direct the musical on the instructions of Harry Brigandshaw, had vividly described the sets that were being painted in a studio just south of Wembley.

Christopher had started their evening with two drunks still at the bar. The tables were empty and cleared away by Ralph and Keppel who were employed every night to wash the dishes. January was a busy time for the London theatres and the supper clubs that fed the patrons after the shows finished. With snow and slush on the streets, a warm theatre or a full restaurant was the place to go for those with money. Money, as Ralph Madgwick had found out on arriving destitute at the port of Bristol, was the commodity everyone had to have, rich and poor, if they wished to survive. The two drunks had a paid-for full bottle of whisky that rested on the bar. After the first song from *Happy Times* that Christopher played out for his brother on the piano, the drunks loosened their starched white evening shirts at the collars and quietly settled in for the night. Danny Hill on the trumpet and William Blake on trombone filled in the brass sections. The clarinet player had had to go home to a sick wife. After the first song had been played through, once by Christopher and the brass section, Harvey Lyttleton began to sing. Very soon, the busking became professional. For the two drunks left at the bar, for Clara and the three waitresses who had stayed behind, the magic had begun and the magic went on all night. All of them were the first in the world to hear the full score of *Happy Times*. None of them moved until it was all over, the chattering only began with the rich smell of bacon and eggs.

Keppel Howland had been seen to have tears in his eyes when he went off to cook everyone's breakfast. Even at the age of twenty-three, he knew. All the reading in school, all the long hours in the school library, the Shakespeare plays he took part in as a schoolboy in the speech hall, told him what he heard and imagined was a musical that would last down the years, giving pleasure to so many.

When they went their separate ways into the cold London January morning, they were all light of heart. It was still snowing. There were no taxis. Nobody cared. Not even the now sober drunks who had found a good breakfast in front of them without being asked.

Gert, Keppel and Ralph walked arm in arm back to the room off Shaftesbury Avenue.

"Can't you just imagine what it will sound like with a thirty-piece orchestra in the pit?" said Gert. "Just imagine the power of the music."

THE NEXT DAY, the Wednesday, twenty-three people sat down to dinner in the dining room of Harry Brigandshaw's new house in Berkeley Square. The house was four storeys high and sumptuous. Tina Brigandshaw had made sure of that. Having money to Tina meant one thing: showing it off. Having given birth to her daughter on the second day of the year, she was again able to fit into her evening gowns. Before the dinner party began, she had fed Beth and handed her back to the nurse. Each of her two children had an English nurse to look after them. It was the way Tina always thought motherhood should have been. The pleasure of children without the pain. The nursery was in the attic, far up at the top of the house. Her children were to be seen and not heard. After the excitement of Anthony and catching Harry Brigandshaw, which she had cemented solidly with the birth of Beth, she found children boring. They always wanted something. Tina admitted to herself she was a taker, not a giver. The one thing she had never done in her life was fooled herself. Or so she thought.

The dinner party was a joint celebration. The most important aspect to Tina was the London house in the heart of Mayfair, not far from the flat leased by Merlin St Clair, and the townhouse lived in by Barnaby St Clair. She had arrived in London society despite the impediment of her birth. The new child, her re-entry into society after the birth, the celebration of *Happy Times* being fully cast, the new Colonial Shipping airline that would fly passengers in seaplanes down Africa in five days – all was secondary to Tina. They were Harry's, not hers to celebrate. She was no longer Tina Pringle from the railway cottage near Corfe Castle in the county of Dorset. She was Mrs Harry Brigandshaw, the young and voluptuous wife of the chairman of Colonial Shipping who, if she had anything to do with it, was going to live the rest of his life in London, making money and just maybe amusing himself in the theatre. Africa, for Tina, was going to stay a long way away.

Having used Brett Kentrich and the man who sometimes called himself Christopher Marlowe to keep her husband from running back to the boring African bush where he wanted to go, she was happy to invite them to dinner, safe in her new house and being his wife. Ex-mistresses and men who wrote silly musicals instead of running the family business had no chance of upsetting her future. She had traded her youth and looks for a treasure house beyond her wildest dreams and no one was going to take it away.

The twenty-fourth invited guest had still not arrived and Tina began to seethe. Showing off to the others meant nothing in comparison to showing off to the Honourable Barnaby St Clair. Then the note was brought in on the silver tray by the butler, Engelbert. The note was offered to her husband. Harry read the note and frowned, his only physical display of something unpleasant. The butler removed the twenty-fourth place setting at the table leaving an unsightly gap. There were now eleven men and twelve women sitting under the crystal chandelier. For Tina, it was a slap in the face, something Barnaby had given her most of her life. No one mentioned the missing guest. Everyone knew from the place setting name, written in Harry Brigandshaw's own hand, who had insulted the hosts by withdrawing at the last moment.

NOT FIVE MINUTES AWAY, Barnaby was enjoying himself immensely at the bar of Clara's. It had to be Clara's to make sure Tina found out. There was no pleasure in insulting someone unless they felt the pain. The girl that had been in his life ever since he could remember had married out of her class to make him look a fool. Everyone in London knew she had been his mistress. By sending his regrets at the last moment, he had shown his friends what he thought of Mrs Harry Brigandshaw. What he had forgotten in his jealousy was that by insulting Tina he also insulted Harry. Harry who he had always taken for granted. The grandson of a self-made rich man. Not the son of an ancient baronetcy. The St Clairs were aristocrats. The Brigandshaws were not. Sometimes his friends sniggered about Colonial Shipping in his presence, knowing his sister Lucinda had been married to Harry before she was killed.

The conversation Barnaby had had at the same bar a week earlier began to play through his head.

"The old man was a bloody pirate, did you know that Barnaby? No offence to your sister, of course. Us aristocrats have to marry money wherever it comes from. Once we make the money respectable, it's as good as old money. A pirate. What has England come to?"

"His maternal grandfather is a baronet. Old as the St Clairs, I'll have you know."

"That's my point. Had to marry his only daughter off to the eldest son of the Pirate. Manderville was broke. Surely you know the scandal after that. The daughter was already pregnant by the youngest son who had been banished by the Pirate to the colonies. Came back and put a ladder up to his brother's wife's window and carried her back to Africa with her son. Harry shouldn't have inherited Colonial Shipping. He's a bastard. Did you know that about your brother-in-law, Barnaby?"

"You're a bastard, Donald."

"No, I'm not. The bastard is Harry Brigandshaw who married your tart with the big tits... Go on. Take a swing. I'll have the story around London in five minutes... That's better. Now, let me buy you a drink and I'll give you the low-down on AV Roe so we can sell them short. Those seaplanes of theirs will never fly down Africa. I have it on good report. The fuel tank isn't big enough and who is going to sell them high-octane petrol in the middle of Africa when they run out of fuel, even if the chief aviator is the Pirate's illegitimate grandson? They can only take ten passengers. A big ship takes thousands."

Danny Hill was sitting in at the piano for Barrington Madgwick who still called himself Christopher Marlowe in the evenings and never gave Barnaby any inside information on the public companies listed on the London Stock Exchange. Barnaby put it down to shell shock from the war, poor chap. The man was obviously dotty. All that inherited money and still playing the piano. Writing musicals. There was no telling other people's taste.

Barnaby got up from the bar and walked off towards the people sitting at the tables. He wanted everyone to see him. Everyone knew he was invited to the Brigandshaw dinner party. With luck, Tina would hear he was at Clara's before the evening was out. That he was not taken sick from seafood poisoning. If he had seen Harry Brigandshaw frown back at the Mayfair house he would not have swaggered so much. Made the insult so public.

AT THE DINNER PARTY, Harry was more hurt than annoyed. The St Clair family had had a special place in his heart ever since going down on holiday from Oxford with Robert St Clair in '07 when he had met the fifteen-year-old Lucinda St Clair for the first time. The two girls who would have been sitting on either side of Barnaby had moved next to each other. Harry walked down the table between courses and briefly joined his chief pilot.

"He's going to come a cropper one of these days."

"What you say, Harry?" asked Ignatius Bowes-Lyon, not realising Harry had sat down in the empty chair.

"Sorry, Iggy. Just thinking aloud. Barnaby is jealous of Tina. His way of showing it. All he's really done is make a fool of himself in public."

"Barnaby?"

"St Clair. The missing man who should be sitting in the empty chair. And Tina went to so much trouble to get everything right. So soon after Beth... You ready for the first flight, Iggy?"

"Of course. Forget St Clair. People who behave like that are not worth worrying about."

"You don't know him then? He gets around."

"I'll make a point of keeping away... I had confirmation today of all fuel stops on the route. We'll land north of the Victoria Falls on the Zambezi River exactly five days after flying out of the Southampton Solent. You are sure, Harry, there's enough clear water on the Zambezi? The Nile, Lake Victoria and Lake Nyasa are easy."

"The test flights landed on the river a dozen times. I've flown over it low in the Handley Page another dozen times. We just have to watch any unusual floodwater coming down from upriver in Angola. I have it monitored. There's more calm water on the river for you than at Southampton. Just hope it is not blowing a gale in the Solent. What a splendid first commercial flight. England to the Victoria Falls. Makes my heart flutter. Opens up southern Africa to the world for the first time."

"You won't come with us?"

"Love to but Tina put her little foot down with the new baby."

"I like the new house."

"Not a bit too gaudy, Iggy?"

"Not at all. Just right. Your wife has perfect taste."

"I'll fly again with you one day."

"I know you will. Thank you again for the job. Life for me has not been so easy after the war."

Ignatius was a diplomat. Harry Brigandshaw had been his CO in France during the war when they flew with 33 Squadron of the Royal Flying Corps. Ostentatious would have been a nice word to describe the crystal chandelier that hovered over his head at the long dinner table. Whoever painted the garish pictures that hung around the room menacing the guests, should have been taken out and shot. The paintings of Pablo Picasso, Ignatius Bowes-Lyon could just understand when he pinched his sensibilities. The legion of imitators that painted big, oval eyes in the cube-shaped faces had, so far as he could see, made a mockery of art. They certainly made fools of those who paid good money and hung them on their walls.

Ignatius looked up at the one face that had been following him all evening and shuddered, picking up his napkin to dab his mouth to cover up the tremor going through his body. Somewhere someone in an expensive London art gallery was pulling his leg.

"They are bloody horrible," whispered Harry in his ear. "Just don't tell my wife. That one that made you shiver winks at me of a morning when I'm trying to eat my breakfast."

Ignatius gave his old CO a queer look of sympathy. When he glanced around, Mrs Brigandshaw was watching him. He was quite sure she knew what they had talked about. Sometimes money produced more problems than it solved. Attracted the wrong people. He gave Mrs Brigandshaw a broad appreciative smile. She was a good-looking woman. What people did with their money was none of his business. He was a pilot and once more flying aeroplanes. Nothing else mattered in his life. Harry Brigandshaw got up and walked away... The girl sitting next to him on the other side was smiling at him. When she had come to sit down at the table, he had seen the long legs that went up to heaven.

"You don't remember my name?" she said smiling.

"Of course I do, Miss Scott."

They had first had drinks in the lounge before going in to supper. Someone had introduced them, he as the chief pilot of African Airways, and she as a leading member of the cast of the musical *Happy Times*. Iggy guessed she had been in a chorus line with such long legs.

"Call me Millie," she said.

"Maybe we can go out to a club for a drink later."

"I would like that, Mr Bowes-Lyon... Are you related to the Earl of Strathmore and Kinghorne?" asked Millie Scott, repeating what she had been told by her friend Jane who was sitting opposite her at the table next to the South African who was stage directing their show with the first name that sounded more like a girl's. Millie had once had a friend called Gertrude that called herself Gert.

Ignatius was not sure what to say to Millie Scott. He liked chorus girls. They were usually uncomplicated.

"I'm the current earl's third cousin once removed."

"Can you explain how cousins get removed?"

"Not really." They were laughing together. He was right. She was uncomplicated.

. . .

MILLIE SCOTT WAS THINKING how lucky she had been meeting Merlin St Clair during the war. She looked again at Merlin across the table and smiled. To pull her leg, as she knew his trick from old, he made a point of putting the clear glass monocle in the eye with the coal-black iris and looked across at her. Millie raised an eyebrow in the direction of the one empty chair on the other side of Ignatius Bowes-Lyon. Merlin turned the dark eye on the chair, his good humour vanishing.

CHRISTOPHER MARLOWE CAUGHT the interplay between Merlin St Clair and Millie Scott, putting away the exchange in his memory bank. Those two knew each other better than they said. No wonder Millie had been given a part in the show. The girl with the long legs looked better than she sang. Idly appraising Millie as she chatted to the pilot who was going to fly down Africa the next week, Christopher wondered if the girl could play comedy. There was one thing still missing in *Happy Times*: not enough laughs. A pretty girl with long legs that could make the audience laugh was what he wanted... An idea began to take shape in his mind. Another scene between the songs... Too much of anything in a musical made an audience grow restless. He had to keep their attention. Always.

Brett Kentrich had been sat in the chair at the top of the table next to Harry Brigandshaw who was sitting in between Brett and his wife. Brett was sure Tina had put Harry in the middle deliberately. On her right was Oscar Fleming, the impresario who was staging *Happy Times* with Harry Brigandshaw's money at the Globe. *The Golden Moth* was to carry on at Drury Lane with a new leading lady, a common practice in the London theatres according to Oscar Fleming to stop a smash hit from growing stale. Brett was sure Tina Brigandshaw knew she had had a brief affair with the elderly impresario soon after Harry Brigandshaw left her to go back to Africa. With Harry out of his chair and down the dining room where she had watched him with the chief pilot of African Airways, she was face-to-face with her adversary.

"So nice of you, darling, to put me in between Harry and Oscar."

"Quite the rose between the thorns," said Tina, equally sweetly.

"I love the paintings around the room. Are they painted by a friend of yours?"

"I don't know any painters the way you do, Brett. I try not to mix with bohemians."

"You should, Tina. My word you should... Is this chandelier the largest in a London private house?... Of course not. I saw a larger one when I was presented to the Prince of Wales at Fort Belvedere. He is such a patron of the theatre... Have you been presented at court?" asked Brett, knowing perfectly well she had not. Her own invitation to Fort Belvedere had been after meeting Edward when he came backstage at Drury Lane. The Prince of Wales had an eye for every pretty girl. Their picture together had appeared in *Tatler*. "Did you see our picture together in *Tatler*? It was so nice getting there without your help, Tina. How was Barry Jones? This time I'm afraid he was not the photographer."

"I will ask Harry to have me presented to the King."

"It's not that easy."

"It will be for Harry. You would be amazed at how much money can accomplish."

"That much I can see."

"Then you like our house?... How strange life is. If things had gone a little differently, you might be me... How is the flat in Regent Mews? Once I rather had an idea of a flat over a stable. Gives such a rural feeling in the heart of London. Of course, all the stables are being turned into garages for all the nasty smelly cars. Rather negates the point. I much preferred the smell of horse manure."

"I don't remember ever smelling it... Come and sit down again, Harry. I've been having such a nice talk with your wife. The butler is hovering. Is he Austrian? So difficult to find an English butler these days. He wants to serve the next course and is waiting for you to sit down next to me again. I was saying to Tina how nice it was for her to put me between you and Oscar. Tina's going to be a great society hostess."

On the other side of Brett Kentrich, Oscar Fleming theatrically stroked his pointed grey beard. He was quite sure before the end of the evening the two girls would scratch out each other's eyes. He was looking forward to it. Catfights for Oscar Fleming were fun... Then he turned his thoughts to the recurring problem that kept coming back into his mind. How to get the voluptuous Mrs Brigandshaw into his bed for a few nights without upsetting Mr Brigandshaw, the money man. Usually, he never contemplated fouling his own backyard. But for Tina Brigandshaw there just had to be an exception in his life. She had more sex appeal than the rest of the girls in the room put together... Such a shame, he thought, giving Brett Kentrich another look. Brett was so pretty and still so young but once he had had them, they were no longer of sexual interest to him. Part of man's quest to plant his seed as far afield as possible, he told himself without guilt. Nature's way of cooling off desire so the male would hunt again somewhere else. Nature was marvellous he thought, smiling broadly to himself as he tucked into his food. Oscar Fleming looked around the room with the eye of a connoisseur.

There were exactly five women in the room, including Tina Brigandshaw, that he had not taken to bed... "What did women see in middle-aged men?" he asked himself smugly. Well, middle-aged men at the very end of their middle-age. At fifty-nine, Oscar Fleming never told anyone his true age... He was as bad as the women, an idea that pleased him immensely.

A new course was put in front of him. He began this time to eat politely. Brett was looking at him disapprovingly. The damn girl could read his mind.

"You're going to be a sensation in the new show," he said to her, putting down his knife and fork. The frown left the brow of his leading lady. Flattery never failed. People were so easy to manipulate. He had known all his life that all you had to do was to tell people how wonderful they were.

SEATED between two of the prettiest showgirls he had ever seen, Keppel Howland was enjoying himself. He had not sat next to a girl since leaving England to go to Africa, if he discounted Mrs Brigandshaw, who spent too much time springing into his thoughts which Keppel knew was a sin. She was married. He should not have looked at her sexually on Elephant Walk. He should stop letting her catch his eye down the dinner table; that made him flush, much to her amusement. He just hoped she was unaware of the arousal taking place under the table. Which he doubted, especially when she licked her lips the second time around which everyone at the table must have seen.

Keppel had watched poor old Ralph all evening trying to unsuccessfully catch the eye of Miss Brett Kentrich. Whenever Keppel looked from Ralph to Brett, Brett was looking at Harry Brigandshaw. No one had told him but something was going on there so far as Miss Kentrich was concerned.

The two girls on either side of Keppel were both trying to engage him in conversation, which would have been better for Keppel if they had – anything to stop the acute arousal under the table. He supposed the girls were interested in him because of him being invited to the sumptuous dinner party, something he had never seen the like of in his life before. Just as he was getting control over himself, the girl on his right with the classic name of Poppy, put her half-gloved hand on his knee and sent his hormones screaming. Having not been with a woman since leaving England, Keppel knew he had better do something about it before he had a problem in public. The touch of the half glove on his knee, that covered the girl's palm, was far more erotic than if she had stood in front of him naked. As he looked up from his plate for some kind of deliverance, he caught Mrs Brigandshaw looking straight at him.

Mrs Brigandshaw then looked daggers at Poppy. Was there nothing the woman couldn't see in his face that did not make him feel stark naked?

In a desperate attempt to regain control, Keppel thought of that morning when Christopher had taken the three of them to the barber and then to Moss Brothers in Regent Street to hire Gert, Ralph and himself evening clothes. Slowly, he forced away the feel of the glove. His newly shaven fresh face returned to its normal colour and the starched shirt started hurting him again around the stiff collar.

"Did you scrub your face or something?" Poppy asked, perplexed.

"Can you believe it? Coal dust, Poppy. It ingrains itself into the skin. Right deep down in the skin after three weeks of constant contact."

"What on earth are you talking about?" The girl affected an educated accent, which mattered nothing to Keppel with his Manx accent, a blend of Irish and Lowland Scot.

"Shovelling coal into a hungry boiler all the way from Africa to England."

"Tell me." The hand had been removed from his knee. She was looking at him like a schoolteacher just told a lie by a difficult but favourite pupil. She was sucking her tongue, pursing her lips and her eyes were smiling at him all at the same time. She was not bad-looking after all.

Keppel Howland started to concentrate. He wanted that silk half glove on his knee again when he was not wearing his trousers. Smiling at her, he thought to himself a man could always hope.

FROM THE BOX room next to the attic off Shaftesbury Avenue to the dining room in Berkeley Square, made Gert van Heerden want to laugh. From a diet of reheated vegetable soup from leftover pickings on the Portobello Road of a late Saturday afternoon to a seven-course supper waited on by white men was absurd. He knew his father in the luxury of the Stellenbosch estate would be drinking wine far superior to the French wine that had gurgled from the bottles into fine glasses down the length of the table. He would have enjoyed the irony. Gert even thought his father and mother would enjoy a first-night performance of *Happy Times* even if their son had not been the stage director. Sitting at the splendid dinner table next to the beautiful Jane under the sparkling crystal chandelier, Gert made a mental note to himself to invite his parents to the premiere, scheduled for the end of March. Gert was sure his new real boss, who was not Oscar Fleming, would arrange a suite on the SS *Corfe Castle* from Cape Town to London where the ship docked not far from the Globe Theatre. The idea of his mother flying up Africa in a ten-seater seaplane never crossed his mind: his father was going to have enough trouble getting her on a ship. His mother spoke barely a word of English. In a musical, such as *Happy Times*, that did not matter. She would appreciate the songs and his sets. Well, he told himself, sipping the white wine that had been served with the duck course, he would give it a try. Throughout his life, getting his mother off the farm had been a constant problem.

"My flowers and garden are not in Cape Town," she would complain in Afrikaans. "The view of the mountains is better from the farm. If I leave for a day, everything will fall to pieces. You all go and enjoy yourselves whatever you want to do and I'll stay here... Now, run along. I have things to do, Gert."

Smiling at the old conversation with his mother in her old gardening clothes, he had not heard what Jane had said to him. She was sitting between himself and Christopher Marlowe, who had used some of the fifty pounds from his Uncle Wallace that morning to smarten them up. Refusing to let them cut off his long hair, having seen what the barber had done to Keppel Howland and Christopher's brother Ralph, he now wore it in a luxurious ponytail down his back. He was in the theatre. He could get away with a ponytail, in the same way as Oscar Fleming who, when Keppel glanced across the table at him, looked like some French count out of a bad French farce. Despite having been given his job by Fleming at the instruction of Harry Brigandshaw, he found it difficult to like the man. He had watched the impresario coveting Harry Brigandshaw's wife. To Gert, that was not nice. Chorus girls, Brett Kentrich, maybe. Not a man's wife. In different circumstances, he would have taken the man to task. Made a fuss and forced a duel to protect her honour. She was the most beautiful woman he had ever seen. Punched the old boy on the nose like a typical overbred Englishman... His job being more important than anything else in his life, he refrained from giving the man even a glare.

"Do you speak another language?" Jane asked him again.

"Only English in England and Cape Town away from the farm. On the farm, only Afrikaans, where my Uncle Johan would have me shot for a traitor if he heard me speak English. He had fought in the Anglo-Boer War. When drunk my uncle brings out his gun with the notches of dead Englishmen cut into the stock."

"How dreadful!"

"You English shot a lot of his friends. Put his wife and children in a concentration camp where they died of diphtheria."

"How absolutely awful. I'm sorry. You tend to forget the suffering of the other side when you have just been through a war. Now, as Christopher was just asking, do you think Millie Scott could play comedy? She can't sing."

"Why not? I mean the comedy. Give it a try. Yes, I rather think she could. I suppose Christopher will write another scene and want another set made. He's right on one thing. The show needs some laughs. Sentimental love songs, however good, can be too much of a good thing if there is nothing in between."

"Thank you, Gert," said Christopher, leaning forward so he could talk across Jane Tamplin at Gert, "I'll remember that."

"It's my pleasure."

"How do you feel in a starched shirt and white tie?" asked Christopher.

"I want to get inside and scratch."

"Maybe I could help later on," said Jane innocently.

The idea of trying to get tall Jane into the box room with him and the dog made him want to laugh aloud. The dog had been introduced halfway through the winter to keep him warm. Better than any hot-water bottle.

"Thank you, Jane," he said in banter. "I'm sure you'll be a great help."

"You're welcome."

Secretly Gert smiled. He was only a prude when it came to married women and especially Mrs Tina Brigandshaw. Showgirls he liked. All of them. One of the reasons he tried to dispute with himself as to why he joined the theatre in the first place.

WHEN RALPH MADGWICK followed the rest of the guests into the withdrawing room after the best dinner he could remember eating, he was slightly drunk. Most of the guests finished half the glasses of wine. New wine glasses were filled to the top with a different wine for each course of the meal. Having been deprived of anything so good for so long, Ralph had finished each glass, even drinking the sweet muscatel that had been served with the pudding, a trifle rich in fruit and sherry. Smiling to himself and anyone else, Ralph knew he had consumed over a bottlesworth of good wine... A footman put a balloon glass of brandy in his hand while saying if he wished to smoke a cigar, he should join the men in the smoking room on the other side of the hall. Forgoing the pleasure of cigar smoke for the more important company of a bevy of showgirls, he headed into the withdrawing room where his brother was seated at the grand piano, the top of which was up and ready to play. Like his friend Keppel Howland, he had not had a woman for a long time. His face was itching from its first shave in over a year, something he was happy with. There was a price, Ralph knew, for everything. The man he had looked like in his Uncle Wallace's office would have stood not a chance with even one of the ladies in the room. Like Keppel, he concluded the girls thought him rich by the fact of being at the dinner. Girls liked rich, young men. He had always known that. The trouble for Ralph as he looked around the drawing room was which one to pick. They were all pretty. Getting prettier. Foolishly, he could not make up his mind and flitted from one to another, like a reformed drunk in a bar who had just gone off the rails and was testing all the bottles. Slugging down a shot of the brandy he was meant to sniff, Ralph made his way around the flower-decked room until he came face-to-face with Tina Brigandshaw where he stopped.

"You look wonderful," he said.

"Thank you, Ralph," said Tina before moving across to the piano where her adversary was about to sing.

Only when Brett Kentrich had finished singing her third song, Ralph Madgwick realised how he could have any woman he wanted in the room. He was on his third large liqueur brandy and was happily drunk, swaying gently on his feet and grinning at everybody. All he had to do was accept Uncle Wallace's offer. Learn the business. Go to the office in Billiter Street every day in a suit.

His friend Keppel Howland had him firmly by the elbow and was moving him through the room to the double doors that opened onto the hall and the way out. His friend's grip was like a vice.

Within two minutes, Ralph and Keppel were in a taxi heading for the attic off Shaftesbury Avenue.

"Where'd you get the money for the taxi, old chap?" Ralph slurred.

"Your brother."

"Good old Barrie or whatever he wants to call himself... Did you see all those women?"

"I did."

"Why didn't you bring some with us?"

"They don't like cold attics in winter."

"Didn't you light the heater?"

"Out of paraffin in all the rush of dressing ourselves up."

"It'll be better than a cold shower."

The old friends who had been to school together and through the last years of the war began to giggle.

"There'll be another time," said Ralph.

"There had better be... Do you know her name was Poppy?... Did you see Gert? I'm afraid that Jane is too long for the box room. She won't fit in. He'll just have to move."

"Wow. Am I drunk? Thanks, Keppel."

"What friends are for, old boy. At least the Hun isn't going to throw a whiz-bang in this trench. We're safely home... Out of the cab, Ralph. Christopher said he would be another hour. Poor chap's head over heels in love with Brett."

"Wasn't Mrs Brigandshaw looking smashing?... Hey, it's cold out here!"

5

MARCH 1925 – THE CUCKOLD

The train from London was ten minutes late. Old Pringle, stationmaster, booking clerk, railway porter, looked up the line hopefully. He wanted to go home, put on his slippers and sit in front of the log fire. He could smell his wife's cooking in his mind. Wednesday was baking day: bread, cake, pie. On Sunday, he had shot and skinned a buck rabbit that had hung in the shed until he cut it up before going to work in the dark that morning. Tending the flower beds that stretched on both sides of the waiting room was most of his job until the summer when the trippers came down for their holidays. The white heads of the snowdrops were moving in the wind outside. The east wind was bitter, the only warmth inside the waiting room around the fire.

No one was waiting to get on the train to Swanage. If the train had not been late, he told himself, he would have been walking home by now in his big overcoat that had been his winter companion for twenty years. Irritated by the delay, he went outside to look up the track, pulling the overcoat's collar up to his ears.

On the knoll stood the ruins of Corfe Castle a mile away, knocked down by Oliver Cromwell. He stood looking at the ruins while he listened for the train.

"Why do people always knock everything down?" he asked himself.

For the first time, he noticed a daffodil that had fought its way out of the hard soil in the last of his small flower beds.

Old Pringle often looked at the ruins. He knew his history as it had affected the Isle of Purbeck, a jut of land out to the sea, not a real island. The Pringles had been in the Isle of Purbeck since time immemorial... Cromwell had cut off the head of his king before knocking down Corfe Castle. The third Baron St Clair had gone out with his king against the Roundheads. When the monarchy was restored they built Purbeck Manor down the river, seven miles from the castle ruins. The Pringles had known the St Clairs for all those centuries. As servants. Never as equals.

"About time," he said rubbing his cold hands. He could hear the train. The sound bounced off the ridge of hills that ran down the spine of the Isle of Purbeck.

The hot, yellow crust of the rabbit pie came into his mind and he smiled.

IN THE TRAIN bringing him home from seeing his English publisher, the Honourable Robert St Clair, Barnaby's elder brother, had the carriage all to himself. He wanted to scratch his right foot, which was impossible, as it had been blown off when Private Lane was killed in November 1916, changing Robert's life forever. Why a foot itched that wasn't there, was for Robert one of life's mysteries, according to Mrs Mason, the Manor's old cook.

He was thirty-nine years old. *Keeper of the Legend* had been reprinted eleven times since the war. Three later books had not been so successful in England. In America, all four had been what his American publisher liked to call 'bestsellers'. He rather thought the term was more for their advertising. No one ever said how many books had been sold... He had an adequate income anyway even if he rarely left Purbeck Manor. Mostly he stayed alone in his second-floor bedroom with a good fire. In summer, he liked to walk the countryside until the stump of his leg in the artificial limb hurt and the pain became greater than his pleasure. He had many chosen places to stop, sit and think. Robert thought a lot about his life that had been, never his future. He had been out of England twice, once to fight in France with the East Surrey Regiment as a lieutenant until he lost his foot and the War Office discharged him from the army as no longer of use. That was nine years ago, he said to himself as his railway carriage slid into Corfe Castle station.

Robert smiled at the familiar sight of old Pringle in the same old coat. The train was late. The engine up front puffed to a stop sending sulphur smoke all the way down the three carriages. Robert could hear a door open from another carriage. The heavy door must have swung back and hit the side of the coach. There was another passenger getting off at Corfe Castle. Robert put down the window and looked for the open door. A woman with a large hat that hid her face was trying to pull a pram out of the compartment. The step was in the way. The pram canted dangerously. There was a baby tucked up in the pram that lurched forward, stopped by the reins that tied it securely inside. The pram was the most elaborate Robert had seen in his life. Another child was somehow tucked under the woman's right arm. The toddler was screaming with fright as it stared down at the gap between the train and the platform. Robert pushed open his door in a hurry and put his hat on his head. Then he stomped up the platform to the rescue. He could not remember when he had last gone to help a woman in distress. Then, with the east wind whipping tears from the corners of his eyes, he remembered. It was Africa, his sister Lucinda, on Elephant Walk. When a snake had chased her out of the cottage where they stayed with Harry Brigandshaw after he and Harry came down from Oxford in 1907.

The girl had the pram out of the carriage now and on the platform. She had her back to him.

"Can I help you?" he called out. He was still twenty yards away. The stump of his right foot was beginning to hurt.

THE ONE THING Tina Brigandshaw knew she should not do was to introduce a servant into her mother's house. She had left both nurses in the Berkeley Square house and bitterly regretted her decision. She had half-dropped Anthony on his head out of the train, catching one leg as he screamed, dangling his head a foot from the edge of the platform. Beth was being held attached to the pram by the harness. Two of her blankets had fallen out of the pram, one down next to the rails where it was going to stay. The blue dress down to her ankles, that had looked so good at Waterloo station when Engelbert saw her onto the train, was caught in the front right wheel of the pram and was pulling at her bodice. The wind took her hat clean off her head.

To surprise her mother, who had not seen Beth, she had decided to go down to Dorset on the spur of the moment. In a pique. The day after the opening of *Happy Times*, Harry had flown from Southampton in the last commercial flight of his seaplanes to visit Elephant Walk.

They were poles apart, she and Harry. She had been a fool to let herself get pregnant the first time by mistake, let alone the second by intention. As she struggled to offload her two children from the train, the idea of ten children was the furthest from her mind.

Tina knew she was at screaming point. Then, at last, her father came to his senses and was running down the platform to help. Another passenger off the train was hobbling towards her calling out an offer to help. The man himself was not familiar, only the voice, Robert St Clair, Barnaby's brother... Tina stamped her foot on the ground as though to free herself from Barnaby, but also her blue dress from the small spokes of the wheel. It was all Barnaby's fault. If he had only married her in the first place.

"IS THAT YOU, TINA?" asked her father, now recognising her without the hat.

"I don't know who else it is." Involuntarily, she had gone back into the Dorset brogue, which made her more annoyed.

"Can I help?" said Robert. "Good Lord! It's Tina Pringle."

"No, it isn't. It's Tina Brigandshaw... Dad. This is your granddaughter, Beth, the reason for this fiasco... What's wrong with your leg, Robert?"

"Lost my foot in the war."

"Sorry. I forgot. Why I left both nurses in London is ridiculous. I wanted to impress Mum. How she ever brought up eleven children on her own I have no idea... Dad, grab Anthony before he falls down that gap. Quick, for God's sake. Your damn train's going off again."

Robert began to laugh.

"What are you laughing at Robert?"

"I'm sorry, Tina. I just never imagined you like this."

"Neither did I... Leave that blanket where it is. My husband can afford another one. Now, someone go and phone for a taxi. We can give you a lift to the Manor. The idea of pushing the pram all the way home has gone right out of my head... Can someone get my hat before it blows onto the track?"

ROBERT DECLINED THE LIFT. He had his own plans. The idea of his mother coming face-to-face with Lucinda's replacement and Harry's two children was not worth the chance. His mother would have behaved perfectly but the sight would have hurt her inside. Losing a son in the war and Lucinda in Africa had made his mother prematurely old. Sometimes the girls visited Purbeck Manor. Not very often. They had their own lives. Other problems to think about. Parents were there, safe at home.

Old Pringle had saved the hat. The family had all driven off in the only taxi in Corfe Castle. Robert had quietly told the man to come back. It was better that way. He had told Tina his mother was meeting the train with the car. Tina had piled the two screaming children inside the taxi. The driver had let down the lid of the boot to make a platform with strong chains holding it in place. Robert had then helped the driver strap the pram into the back of the car.

He watched the car and pram disappear into the village. Then he followed slowly down the road to the Greyhound. It was opening time and Robert needed a drink. Often he drank on his own in the bedroom. A few stiff drinks made him sleep, so he could write well in the morning. A bad night's sleep was bad for his writing.

He had told the driver where to find him when he came back from the old railway cottage beside the brook. It was a pretty cottage. Comfortable. Robert smiled happily to himself as he thought of Mrs P seeing her new grandchild for the first time. In those big arms, the child would be gurgling happily in no time at all.

As Robert reached the Greyhound and went inside to the warmth, he wondered what it would have been like to have children of his own.

The driver of the taxi found him half an hour later. Robert had managed two drinks in the private bar.

When he reached Purbeck Manor in the dark he did not tell his mother Tina Brigandshaw was visiting her parents at the railway cottage. Or the children. The Manor house was very cold. For some reason, the kitchen stove had gone out. Robert cut doorstops off the bread from the bread bin and made himself a cheese and pickled onion sandwich. He took his supper up to his room. He had laid the fire the previous day before going up to town. Robert put a match to the newspaper. The fire caught quickly. When the flames were high enough, Robert turned off the light and sat down in his big armchair by the fire to warm up. He had put the plate of sandwiches on the small table next to the chair along with the bottle of brandy and the glass. He liked to drink the brandy in a crystal glass with a small amount of water.

Content with his own life, Robert began to think of the new book he had outlined to his publisher. He knew the characters in the book would become his best friends.

It was how it worked. Why he liked writing. Fame and fortune were nothing in comparison to the comfort given by his friends, the friends that would live with him in the small bedroom for two or three years. For as long as it took to finish the book. In winter in front of his fire, in summer with the big window wide open to the scent and sound of the English countryside Robert loved so much.

The old house groaned in the east wind. Somewhere a shutter had come loose. As a child, he thought the Manor house was haunted. Now he enjoyed the thought of the old souls walking the corridors where they had lived as flesh and blood centuries before. It gave him a real connection to his ancestors who had fought so hard to keep what they owned in the family. Frederick's son would inherit the Manor and the title. Robert's mother thought of Frederick as her eldest son after Richard had died. There had been something wrong with Richard when he was born. Frederick had died in the war leaving Penelope with Gwen and young Richard. Frederick had named his son after his elder brother who had died at the age of thirty-one. Young Richard had just turned eight years old. His mother had never brought him to Purbeck Manor since Frederick was killed. She cried a lot from the war. If anything happened to young Richard, Merlin would become the eighteenth Baron St Clair of Purbeck. It was lucky Gwen was a girl so she could have no pretensions to the title. The eldest male inherited. Then it was his turn without children. How strange would it be if Barnaby then inherited the title? If he had married Tina Pringle? If Anthony had been Barnaby's son, not Harry Brigandshaw's?...

Robert put two more logs on the fire and waited for the flames to show him his empty glass and the bottle of brandy. The crystal glass began to glow, reflecting the flames in the grate. Robert poured himself a refill. Got up with difficulty and splashed in some water from the water jug he kept on the dressing table. The curtains in the bedroom were drawn tight, moving only slightly with the wind blowing hard on the outside of the windowpanes. Robert could hear a branch of the elm tree tapping on the window... Later, Robert fell fast asleep in the armchair. He had taken off the artificial foot when he first sat down in front of the fire.

When he woke in the night, the fire had gone out. The room was cold. Robert climbed into bed by hopping to it on one leg. He was soon sound asleep with his dreams. So often, he dreamt of faces he had never met and wondered why in the morning.

BACK DOWN THE river that some called a stream and some called a brook, Tina Brigandshaw woke with the dawn in the old bedroom she had shared with her sisters. There was one room in the railway cottage for the girls, one for the boys. The three-tiered bunk beds rose right up to the ceiling. They had all been made by her father when he was a young man. Growing up so closely surrounded by her sisters had given her family a closeness she missed. The older girls looked after the younger girls.

Same with the boys in their room. They were all packed too close together to quarrel. Growing up had been the best time of her life. With

Barnaby. Growing up with Barnaby visiting from the Manor nearby every day during the school holidays.

She knew where she was immediately. It was the smell of the room. Her children had been put to bed in the boys' room where her mother had slept the night.

"You need a good night's sleep, Tina. I'll look after them." Her mother had been smiling. What was a blessing for her mother was a chore for Tina. Tina first thought of Barnaby when she woke. It was the evocative smell in the room. Then she remembered her children. There was something wrong with her, she told herself. A lousy mother. Always but always thinking of herself, Tina thought most people thought of themselves more than others. The ones who said they didn't were liars. Sad but true. Part of life.

Tina got up from the bottom bunk bed and went to the window. The curtains she tried to open stuck on the uneven wooden pole as they always did. Outside, the vegetable garden looked bleak from the winter. None of the fruit trees had any leaves. From the boys' room, Tina heard Beth begin to cry. The sound grated on her nerves. Then the crying stopped. Tina opened her bedroom window. A thrush was calling in the morning cold. Looking out from her first home, Tina wondered where she belonged. The contrast of the Berkeley Square house and the railway cottage was extreme. There was something nice about the railway cottage now the baby had stopped crying. The thrush had a good voice. Tina asked herself why songbirds never made a harsh sound. There was no other sound than the bird. Her other home in Africa could have been on the moon. Only then did she think of Harry, somewhere over Africa, flying back to the farm he called home.

"I don't have a home. Not a real home." The thrush stopped calling at the sound of her voice. "Oh, Barnaby, why did we love each other so much as children?"

The sound of small running feet drowned out her own voice.

"Mummy, Mummy! Come see bunny rabbit Grandda found for me."

The boy spoke well for so young a child. Her day had begun. Putting on a brave smile, Tina opened her childhood bedroom door to her son. The rabbit was only a few weeks old. Too small for her father to kill and skin. The long ears were laid back on the grey fur. Anthony was gently stroking the long ears with his small hand, holding the rabbit in the crook of his other arm. The small wild animal looked at Tina with a terrible fear in its eyes. The nose was twitching. Tina wondered how many brothers and sisters the rabbit had left in the burrow. Wondered whether the mother had missed this one small pulse of life.

"He's very beautiful," she said to Anthony. "Be gentle with him. After our breakfast, we will take him back to his mother. Back to the burrow."

She picked up her son still clutching the rabbit and walked with him down the rickety wooden stairs to her mother's kitchen and the morning smell of frying bacon.

Beth was in the pram, next to the cooking stove. Her father had gone to work. Her mother looked happy doing what she liked to do best. Cooking for her family.

"Sleep well, Tina?"

"Like a log. I can't tell you how nice it is to be home."

Only when Tina sat down at the scrubbed white kitchen table made from elm, with Anthony and the rabbit on her knee, did she realise what she had said: the railway cottage was the only real home she had ever had.

"Do you mind if I stay a few days?"

"Stay as long as you like... When is Harry coming back from Africa?"

"I don't know... He wants me to take the children back to Elephant Walk."

"Then you must take the next boat."

"But I don't want to live in Africa."

"That has nothing to do with it. You and your children live where your husband wants to live. Anyway, you'll be better in Rhodesia. Harry told me there isn't a class problem among whites... You've married above yourself, Tina. Despite our Albert employing Miss Pinforth to teach you to speak proper, they'll never accept a working-class girl in them posh places in London... You're better off in Africa."

"I hate the place. I want to live in England."

"Then you shouldn't have married Harry... Or that Barnaby St Clair."

"What's this got to do with Barnaby?"

"Everything, I should think... Before you eat your breakfast, feed the baby. I'm surprised she didn't wake for her feed in the night."

"Feed her here?"

"Why not? I fed you here, and the others."

"What if someone comes?"

"There's nothing nicer than a mum feeding her baby. Beautiful it is... You do have some milk?"

"Plenty... It's leaking out. My blouse is wet already."

"Then feed Beth. It's her milk... Here, give me Anthony and the rabbit."

. . .

BARNABY HAD HEARD from Merlin that Tina had gone down to Dorset to visit her parents. He knew Harry was on his long flight out to Africa. The stock market was still going up. Barnaby had borrowed more money from Cox and King's bank against the increased value of his shares to buy more shares. He had also mortgaged the new shares to the hilt. Barnaby felt pleased with himself. His share portfolio was as long as his arm.

He had not visited his parents for over a year. The snub of Robert being in London to see his publisher, and not staying with either of his brothers, had been noticed by everybody. Robert was annoyed with them, it seemed. Merlin had not gone down to Dorset for months, obsessed with his bastard daughter who could twist her father round her little finger. Always aware of appearances, the opportunity to visit his parents as a dutiful son and be alone with Tina was too good to be missed.

WHILE TINA WAS FEEDING Beth next to the stove sitting on an old wooden chair watched by her mother, Barnaby was standing at Waterloo station waiting for the morning train to take him down south. He would have to change trains in Guildford but it was still better than taking the car. Instead of walking the seven miles to Purbeck Manor direct he would take a slight detour and visit Mrs P. Anyway, old Pringle would be at the station in Corfe Castle. Barnaby had his excuse. There was no reason why the parents should suspect he knew Tina had gone down to Dorset. Merlin had said her decision was taken on the spur of the moment. Lucky for him Merlin had gone round the previous morning to Berkeley Square to find Tina about to go to the station. Barnaby suspected Merlin was still sweet on Tina. Everyone was. Barnaby liked his women to be wanted by everyone. It kept up his interest, having something the others wanted. Between the bastard child and Tina in London, Barnaby considered his brother a mess. A good example of never believing a man for what he looked like. For all his appearances as a stuffed shirt, his brother preferred common girls. Showgirls like Millie Scott with the long legs.

"Poor old Merlin," Barnaby said to himself as he got on the train. "No wonder he never got married."

The thought of putting horns on Harry Brigandshaw by sleeping with his wife gave Barnaby a surge of pending sexual pleasure. It was barely the start of spring but they would find a place in the woods despite the weather. The more dangerous the better. Lucky he had gone round to see a disconsolate Merlin in his flat soon after his brother had come back from visiting Berkeley Square. What luck. It was all luck. Like betting on the stock market except it always went up. CE Porter was sure the bull market was going on forever. The war was over. There was peace. Everyone who was anyone was making money. Labour was cheap with so many men back from the war still looking for jobs.

"Money for old rope," he said to the empty first-class carriage. Barnaby took out the *Telegraph* from his briefcase, turned to the financial pages and began to read. After the *Telegraph* he would read the *Economist*. After the *Economist*, the *Wall Street Journal*... Another good reason, other than Tina Brigandshaw, not to drive the car however much he enjoyed driving. Barnaby had just bought himself a Bentley 3 Litre that went like the wind.

"Good," he said again to himself. All but four of his shares had gone up. The price-earnings ratio was ridiculous but who cared. It was what people paid for the share that counted. Every day he was making himself another fortune. "Money for old rope." The idea of working for a living had never once crossed his mind. Even in the army, he had fiddled the books in the officers' mess when he was put in charge of the accounts. They had found out and demobbed him early in Cairo at the end of the war. Nothing more. The army did not like a scandal. Barnaby was of the opinion he could get away with murder if he ever wanted... And Harry was a long way away. With luck, Harry would not come back to England. He and Tina would have the best of both worlds: she a rich marriage and a fine house, he his mistress to visit for as long as he liked when he liked without one iota of responsibility.

When the train arrived in the afternoon at Corfe Castle station, it was raining. Even the best of plans, Barnaby admitted, had sometimes to be changed. Old Pringle rang for the taxi. Amazing, he thought, the railway station had a telephone! Old Pringle seemed pleased to see him. Strangely, the old man mentioned nothing of Tina's visit to her parents. Showed him the snowdrops in the rain. The lone daffodil. Despite the discomfort, Barnaby had walked down the platform in the rain, his train had gone on to Swanage. He hoped old Pringle would mention his daughter. Make a visit to the cottage less unexpected.

"How's Mrs P?"

The old man was pointing at the lone daffodil bravely blooming in the rain, the soft yellow colour washed with rainwater. Barnaby had his umbrella up. Old Pringle was letting the rain run off the peak of his railway cap. He was wearing an oilskin over his uniform, the type they had worn in the trenches during the war.

"Everything all right at home?"

The old man ignored him again. They walked back to the waiting room. Barnaby stood in front of the fire. Pringle went off into the ticket booth.

When the taxi finally arrived, Pringle had gone. Barnaby thought there had to be a back door to the ticket booth.

"She's there," said Barnaby inside the taxi to what he thought was himself.

"Who's there, sir?"

"Tina Pringle."

"Mrs Brigandshaw now. Married some rich man in Africa. Two young kids. Drove her yesterday. Pram near fell off the back of the car."

"Are my mother and father at the Manor house?"

"And Mr Robert."

The suitcase packed by his man Edward was in the back seat next to him. His briefcase was on his knees, his hands resting comfortably on it.

"How long's she staying?" he said innocently.

"You old friends?"

"Her husband is a friend of mine. He was married to my sister Lucinda before she was killed. He met the new Mrs Brigandshaw in Africa. Coincidence, really. Her brother Albert lives in Africa."

The driver looked relieved. He was looking back at Barnaby through the rear-view mirror. Barnaby smiled at him, pleased with his dissimulation. He had put the driver right off the scent.

"She didn't say," said the taxi driver.

The rest of the journey to Purbeck Manor went in silence. They took the high road. Down below, Barnaby could see the small river. He would take a walk back down the river when the rain stopped.

The surprise and pleasure on his mother's face when she saw him standing in the hall made Barnaby feel guilty. Old Warren had opened the side door in the big Gothic front door to let him in. The sound of the knocker had echoed through the old house. Old Warren was bent, his hands twisted from arthritis.

"No cows to milk?" Barnaby had said as a question. Warren was his father's cowman.

"Can't no more."

Then Barnaby's mother was coming down the spiral stairs to find out who had hit the knocker on the old oak door with such force.

"Barnaby! What a lovely surprise. Robert and your father will be so pleased. Come on in away from the rain. The house is so cold in winter."

"I have tried many times to come down," lied Barnaby.

"You must be so busy. Merlin should come down more often. He doesn't have a job or a wife. Come into your father's study. We keep a fire going all the time in there these days. It's cosy. The room is small. Your father is down with his pigs. He won the second prize for Hector the fourth at the county fair. Drove himself and the pig all the way to Swanage."

"Was the pig in the car with him?"

"Oh, no. They made a big box on bicycle wheels and towed the pig behind the car. Made quite a sensation when he arrived. I'll ask cook to make some tea. Are you hungry?"

THE WORD HAD REACHED Mrs Mason five minutes before she was asked to bring tea to the study. She and Old Warren had been friends all their lives.

"What's he doing here?" asked Old Warren for something better to say.

"Haven't you heard, Mr Warren?" After all the years together at the Manor, they still called each other Mrs Mason and Mr Warren. Old Warren looked perplexed. 'He understands cows better than people,' thought Mrs Mason. To Mrs Mason, Barnaby St Clair arriving at the Manor out of the blue was definitely not one of life's little mysteries.

"She's here," she said. There was so little to talk about in the servants' quarters at the Manor. She was going to draw out the scandal as long as she could. "Have a cup of tea?"

"I don't mind if I do."

"She's married now, you know. Two little ones. The taxi man told the postman who told little Mavis who told me. Pram near fell off back of car."

Old Warren knew the game. It was warm in the maid's sitting room next to the kitchen. There was an old leather armchair next to the coal fire. The fire was glowing in the half dark. The room was below the one high, long window that was level with the ground outside. He warmed his hands, waiting for Mrs Mason who had gone off to make the tea. With luck, he could make the conversation and the tea last half an hour, and maybe she would bring him some of her plum cake with the walnuts on top. Then he heard little Mavis in the kitchen next door asking Mrs Mason to make tea for Lady St Clair. The door was still half open. Mavis wanted scones for Mr Barnaby. Warren smiled to himself as he settled back in the old leather armchair. It was getting better. The scones would need warming up in the oven and that would take time.

Only Mrs Mason could ask him into the sitting room. He was an outside man. With luck, they would forget him. The idea of later being brought hot scones with butter and strawberry jam made his mouth water. He had no idea what Mrs Mason was talking about. It was the last thing that mattered on his mind. He had forgotten if or why Lord St Clair had sent him up to the house. Often when he went up to the house and came back again to the pigs or the cows, neither of them could remember why he had gone up to the house in the first place. Both he and Lord St Clair were quietly losing their minds. To Old Warren, it was one of the pleasures of old age. He could remember things that had happened far back in his life. It was what he had just done that he often forgot. Like whether he had left Lord St Clair at the pigpens or the cowsheds. Then he slowly remembered. He had been teaching a young lad from the village to milk the cows. The boy had been hurting Daisy. Daisy had kicked over the tin bucket twice. He had gone up to the house to get some ointment to put on the cow's teats. The boy would have stopped milking the moment he left the shed. Daisy had not been so full of milk to make her uncomfortable.

WHEN MRS MASON brought him tea and scones, Old Warren was fast asleep in front of the fire. She smiled at him and sat in the high-back chair on the other side. Whatever he had come up for, he had obviously forgotten. Little Mavis, who was not little anymore, had gone off to dust the dining room just in case the room was going to be used. Barnaby was Lady St Clair's favourite. He had the charm to stop people seeing through him. Mrs Mason had known otherwise from when he was a small boy. There was always a bad one in a litter. Sometimes the bad ones were difficult to see. To Mrs Mason, those were the most destructive. Anyway, she told herself, it was none of her business to interfere. When she looked again at Old Warren he was smiling at her, eating one of the scones. She decided not to tell Old Warren any more. It would do no good.

AFTERWARDS, in the thick woods, not far from the railway cottage, they said it had had to be telepathy to meet as they did on the path by the river, drawn by a force to each other beyond their known sensors. They had rutted like two animals caring for nothing but their own satisfaction. When it was over, Tina felt utterly miserable. From blind ecstasy to misery in ten minutes. She began to cry.

"Don't cry now," said Barnaby. "It's too late... You were always mine. Always. You can't stop yourself any more than I. The power of nature. Wipe your eyes and pull down your dress in case someone comes. Better still, off you go. No good being seen together."

"You're a rotter."

"Look who's calling the kettle black. You are the one who is married with two children."

Tina had slapped him hard across the face. It made Barnaby grin at her. The ground was wet from the earlier rain. Her mother would see her wet dress. Her mother would know the moment she found out Barnaby was at the Manor. Her mother would find out. It was the one social pleasure for the servants to tell tales about people they worked for.

"Don't fight it, Tina. We'll be better off in London. Why did you walk out alone? Our minds must have told each other. We are part of each other, part of the same person, you and I. We always have been."

"Then why didn't you marry me?"

"You know perfectly well why I could never marry you, my Tina. I am the son of a lord. You are common."

"Does it matter?" Tina's teeth were chattering from cold and fear.

"How naïve can you be? Never marry out of your station. People don't like it. My family would look down their noses. Yours would think you had got above yourself. You'll see with Harry. Well, it won't matter if you become my mistress. He'll throw you out of his life with a good allowance."

"And my children, Barnaby. What about Anthony and Beth? Who gets the children? Oh, no. I'm going back to Africa. This will never happen again, Barnaby St Clair."

"You'd better get the green sap of spring grass off the back of your dress. Dear oh dear. Why do we fight the inevitable? Like the Germans. They are going to do it again. All this National Socialism. Another word for pride. They want their pride back that was taken at Versailles by the French. Lloyd George said in 1919, the terms of surrender at Versailles demanded by the French were so severe we will have to fight the war again in twenty years' time at three times the cost. Another world war in 1939!"

"What are you talking about?"

"That's my point, Tina. We come from different worlds. Very different worlds. This, right here, it's the only world we understand together... When are you going back to London?"

"Tomorrow morning."

"I'll have to stick around a few days I suppose. What a bore."

"Why did you come down?" asked Tina, knowing perfectly well.

"To do this, Tina. Wasn't it fun?"

"Do you hate me so much for marrying Harry?"

"Not anymore... Oh, and you won't go back to Africa. Not after this. Far too good wasn't it?" Tina had stopped shivering. She wanted to go. She could not move. Her dress was still hitched up. The juices in her loins started flooding all over again.

"Come here, my Tina. I want you again... And again."

She had no power to stop him. The desire for satiation was too strong. Forgetting the consequences, Tina Brigandshaw lay back on the wet new grass, accepting him.

When it was all over, she dressed carefully and left the wood. They had not spoken again. At the railway cottage, her mother was in the kitchen getting supper ready. Tina went upstairs and changed before going down to her mother. Her father had yet to come home from work.

"Did you enjoy your walk?"

"Lovely. When the rain stopped, the wind went down and the sun came out. Almost spring. That smells lovely. I'm so happy."

"You changed your dress."

"From the trees. It was wet from the long grass."

"You didn't take your raincoat?"

"Of course... Where are the children?"

"Sleeping in the boys' bedroom. I put them down an hour ago."

ROBERT HAD SEEN his brother go for a walk when the rain had stopped. Robert had been standing in his bedroom window, his mind wandering. At first, he could not make out who it was. Barnaby appeared round the corner of the house on the path that led to the river and then all the way to Corfe Castle.

Saddened by his younger brother not coming up to say hello, he was about to call out when he saw there was something furtive about the way Barnaby looked around before walking away from the Manor. As if he did not wish to be seen. Strapping on his artificial foot, Robert went downstairs to find out what was going on. He found his mother in the drawing room from where she could see a part of the path that led down to the small river. She was white as a sheet, staring out of the long sash window. All the windows in the drawing room went from waist-high to almost the ceiling. There were pulley ropes to help pull them up.

"Was that Barnaby I saw walking down to the river? What's brought him home all of a sudden? Nobody told me he was here."

"It's her. He's gone to see her."

"I'm sorry, mater. Don't understand." Robert himself had also gone white, understanding all too well.

"Harry's new wife. Mrs P's daughter. I've just had a message from Mrs P and was looking for Barnaby but he has gone. The moment the rain stopped. The two of them must have an arrangement... Poor Harry. If that madman Braithwaite had not killed Lucinda this would not be happening... That girl has some terrible power over Barnaby."

"You think it's her fault? I doubt it. Barnaby never does anything he doesn't want to do. If I was writing it into a book, I'd say Barnaby was jealous of Harry... You do know, Mother?... Tina and Barnaby started a long time ago."

"We're too late."

"We have all been too late for a very long time."

"But he is such a nice kind boy."

"That's what he wants us to believe. We all judge other people by the way we behave ourselves. There are good and bad people."

"Are you saying your brother is bad, Robert? I won't have that."

"I'm sorry. I said too much. I saw Tina at the railway station. I don't think she knew about Barnaby coming down. She had her children. I'll run after Barnaby and stop him from doing anything silly."

"You would not get within half a mile." Robert knew his mother was thinking of his missing foot.

"I suppose not... Then we must hope my brother knows how to behave himself. Obviously, Mrs P doesn't think he does or she would not have sent you a message. All we can do is pretend nothing is going to happen. That nothing does happen. Harry is in Africa. Flown out on one of his seaplanes. I didn't tell you about his wife because I thought it would make you upset, having Lucinda's replacement down the road with Harry's children."

"Don't tell your father. He thinks the world of Barnaby."

"Don't worry, Mother. Barnaby will have to go to the railway cottage. Mrs P won't let them out of her sight."

"What if they arranged it with Harry being in Africa?"

"She told me Harry was in Africa. Why would she do that if she was up to something with Barnaby? She knows Harry is my friend."

"Thank you, Robert, I feel a lot better. How's the new book going?"

"They are talking to me. The characters. It's begun. Written down on the first page is today's date, the 29 March 1925."

TWO HOURS LATER, there was a knock on Robert's bedroom door. Everyone knew in the house that when he went to his room to write he was not to be disturbed. An interruption chased his characters out of his head. Often for the rest of the day, the scene he was writing lost forever.

Cursing he would have to start the first page over again, he went to the locked door and turned the key. The only light in the room was over his writing desk. When he opened the door, a jaunty Barnaby was standing outside. He smelled of crushed grass and damp earth. The light from the lamp on Robert's desk was turned in a way that shone the light at the doorway. In the annoyance of being disturbed, Robert had knocked up the angle of the lamp. Even someone less attuned to the reality of people's minds behind their outward façades would have understood. Over the years of writing, Robert's skills had improved. He most always saw past the face to the truth. The truth now was glaring at him.

"You really are a scoundrel, Barnaby."

"What are you talking about, brother? Oh, sorry to disturb the genius." He was smirking at Robert. A self-satisfied smirk.

"You know perfectly well. I introduced Harry into this family. To Lucinda and by extension from our family, I introduced Harry to Tina."

"I don't know what you are talking about."

"Tina was on the train with me yesterday. I helped her with the pram. With Harry's children."

"How noble of you. Just what has that got to do with me?"

"I can smell her now. Her perfume. And your clothes are wet."

"It's raining, Robert. Raining again. Rain makes people wet."

"She didn't know you were here, did she?... Good. At least Tina was not part of your plan... You are jealous of Harry. Of everything Harry has ever done. He is ten times the man you are... Mrs P sent Mother a note, telling her to prevent you from seeing Tina. Mrs P had been told of your sudden arrival at the Manor."

"You really are a frustrated old bachelor stuck in the middle of nowhere. You are the one who is jealous. Jealous of me... Go back to your scribbling, brother. I came up to say sherry is being served in the drawing room. Mater and pater. A family reunion. I left you alone as long as possible... Oh, and if you think I would make Tina commit adultery you're wrong. It is a sin. Harry is also my friend. I went for a walk. If Tina is in Corfe Castle, it is the first I heard of it. The perfume you smell is Mother's if you smell anything that isn't part of your imagination."

"How did you find out Harry had gone to Africa and Tina to Corfe Castle? Someone in London will tell me. How about Merlin? I'll give him a ring now we have a phone you did not use to warn Mother of your generous visit. And, Barnaby, I do know the smell of our own mother's perfume."

"Mind your own business, Robert."

"It is my business. Harry is my friend. And yes, I am a frustrated old bachelor. But that has nothing to do with what you have just done.

Remember one thing, Barnaby. If you can get away with doing wrong, that no one else may find out, you still have to live with yourself."

Barnaby turned his back and walked away, laughing uncontrollably. At the end of the dark corridor, he turned back to his brother still standing in the light of the doorway.

"You really are a fool, Robert. Living with the thought of Tina, especially Tina with her clothes off, is the best part of my life. You would think so too if you ever had the chance. Don't be such a sanctimonious hypocrite. There is far more to life than being stuck in a room writing stories about imaginary people. Real people have flesh and blood. Like me. Like Tina. We feel. We feel the ecstasy of life when we come together. Something you will never understand however many books you write. You have only one life, Robert. Enjoy it while you still can. Use some of your money from the books. Get out of here. Start living your life. You are my brother. Don't look at me and my faults. Look in the mirror at your own. We all have them... Now Mother and Father are expecting us. No more of this conversation downstairs. It's been going on for all eternity."

EARLIER THAT DAY on the Sunday at twelve o'clock midday, one hour ahead of London, Harry Brigandshaw was having the time of his life. The seaplane had flown six feet above the Zambezi River before climbing into the blue sky over the Victoria Falls, the plane drenched in the spray sent up by the falling water cascading over the lip into the boiling water deep in the earth below. Again, Ignatius Bowes-Lyon brought the plane down over the river, the long white wing floats graceful as swans. The heads of the family of hippo had sunk below the brown water to the sanctuary of the riverbed. The landing was clear.

On the third approach, the floats kissed and bounced the water, kissed again, settling, sending a stream of white spray behind Harry's eyes level with an elephant browsing the top of a tree on the north shore of the river. The seaplane came slowly round to face upriver, gently pushing against the flow of the river towards the wooden jetty on the south side. Three black men were waiting to secure the plane with ropes. Harry released his seatbelt. He was home.

Half an hour later, the passengers and crew were standing outside the entrance of the Victoria Falls Hotel.

"One day we'll fly it in less than a day," Harry said to Ignatius. "There'll be an airport here. Not as big as Croydon Airport but an airport in the heart of Africa. This is not over. Financially the airline has been a disaster for us, but it is just the beginning. We've proved it can be done. And remember, AV Roe is working on another flying boat with a hull that can land on water, the wing floats just to steady the plane. Sixty passengers in the same comfort of a train."

"It's disappointing, but I hear you, Harry. When are we flying her back?"

"Two weeks. The train will take me to Salisbury from here where Tembo will pick me up and take me to the farm. I promised my wife not to be away for long. You can't have everything in life, Ignatius. Just some of it, some of the time. Did you see that elephant?... Don't look so sad. You'll still have a job. We'll just have to wait for the right aircraft. Pioneers rarely succeed the first time. Any business venture has to make money. This one at the moment doesn't."

6

DECEMBER 1925 – LOVE IN THE COLD

*H*aving persuaded Uncle Wallace to pay him a salary far in excess of a lowly clerk's, Ralph Madgwick had become quite the man about town. There had been a lot of uncle/nephew talk on the merits of being an English country gentleman. Uncle Wallace, glazed with excitement, had given in. It was irrelevant to Uncle Wallace later that bills of lading were still foreign to his nephew months into the training programme. Uncle Wallace had little idea what they were either, which left Postlethwaite without a case for dismissal. Uncle Wallace put it down to jealousy. Both nephews' salaries were now just short of Postlethwaite's.

"Try and make him learn, Postlethwaite."

"He's not interested. Neither is the brother interested in the company. For goodness sake, Mr Madgwick. Barrington Madgwick is still living in an attic and playing the piano in a supper club."

"Don't for goodness sake me."

"I'm sorry, sir."

"Look. They own half the business. You make a good salary. How about another thousand a year? Don't worry me with the details. I want them competent enough to run the business in two years. Not a day later. I'm not getting younger. Old men don't ride horses. I like riding horses. I like shooting grouse. I like catching salmon. I hate this business. Now, do you understand me, Postlethwaite?"

"Exactly, sir."

Postlethwaite almost slammed the door to the senior partner's office.

There was a fine line between shutting it and slamming it. Uncle Wallace decided to give Mr Postlethwaite the benefit of the doubt.

There was one thing he was sure about. Neither of his nephews were fools. When they had to answer questions from clients, they would find out what they were talking about. They were both well educated. Their minds were alert.

Uncle Wallace, still full of hope, had found just the place to fulfil his dreams in the Lake District, Cumbria. That was where he was going to start enjoying his life. Lots of dogs. Lots of horses. Big log fires. Snifters, lots of snifters. Peace. Peace and quiet away from the City, away from Madgwick and Madgwick and the looks of contempt, hidden admittedly, by Postlethwaite... The man had a wife of thirty years' standing and eleven children!... Uncle Wallace shuddered. Dogs and horses did not talk back. That was what he wanted. A country house full of dumb animals.

Adding to his annoyance, Rosie Prescott knocked on his door and came in without her knock being answered. She was carrying a sheaf of papers. Uncle Wallace's left eye began to water and hurt. Before his secretary could say a word, he lifted the balloon glass that was ready on his desk and drained the brandy. Then he smacked his lips and smiled at her through his one good eye. They both waited for the jolt of brandy to take effect. Then he was ready for business.

"Good morning, Miss Prescott. Make a note to the chief accountant to increase Mr Postlethwaite's annual salary by one thousand pounds. My younger nephew appears to have learnt nothing in the last six months. You do understand. Confidential, of course. The salary increase. The poor chap has eleven children so he won't be going anywhere. My word, that is a terrible thought. What on earth would we do without Postlethwaite?... Do I have anyone to see, Miss Prescott?"

"Sir Jacob Rosenzweig."

"What on earth does he want to see me about? He's our banker. Doesn't he want to see the chief accountant? I know nothing about figures... Oh my God, it's young Ralph again. Last month I sent him as my proxy to celebrate the one hundred and fiftieth year of the founding of Rosenzweig's in Berlin. He must have misbehaved. I'm going to have to talk to young Ralph."

"Mr Barrington Madgwick has again given me his letter of resignation. *Happy Times* is now running full steam ahead at the Globe after a shaky start. Word of mouth... I rather think he does not need his job at Madgwick and Madgwick."

"Don't look so happy, Miss Prescott."

"It's a wonderful musical. I have seen it three times."

"I know. I sneaked in myself twice. Don't tell Barrie or whatever he calls himself... How can a man have two names?"

"From the letter, he only wants one. Christopher Marlowe. He is working on a new musical."

The estate in Cumbria, the dogs and horses, all were fading in front of his eyes. Wallace cursed his luck.

"Why can't a man do in life what he wants to do, Miss Prescott?"

"That's what he is going to do."

"Not nephew Barrington. Myself. No one ever thinks of me."

Miss Prescott left the papers on the antique Jacobean desk, half filled the empty balloon glass with brandy and left the senior partner's office, gently closing the door behind her.

"Poor old bugger," she said to herself outside.

Maxwell, the lift operator, looked across at her. The door to the lift cage was opening. Out of the cage, a tall, thin man was stepping into the executive suite. The man was in his late fifties with a large hooked nose like the beak of a predatory hawk. Both of his eyes were watery. He carried a cane with a beautifully worked silver top. When he smiled at her, Miss Prescott liked the man. She looked at the clock above the lift entrance. It was ten o'clock precisely.

"I'll tell Mr Madgwick you are here, Mr Rosenzweig."

This time Rosie Prescott knocked three times in quick succession on the old panelled door. When she opened the door to admit the senior partner of the London branch of Rosenzweig's, the balloon glass was nowhere to be seen. She had given Uncle Wallace just enough time to drink the contents and hide the glass.

Uncle Wallace stepped around his desk, his most affable self. Socialising was what he was best at.

"What a pleasure, sir. What a pleasure." His right hand was out, the other ready to cover the old man's shoulder to guide him to the comfortable couch in front of the coffee table where they could talk man to man. Uncle Wallace was right. The problem, as he had suspected, was nephew Ralph.

RALPH MADGWICK HAD MET Rebecca Rosenzweig two days after Keppel Howland went up to Oxford on a Madgwick and Madgwick scholarship. It had been part of Ralph's extortionate deal with Uncle Wallace. By then Ralph had escorted a string of showgirls around the nightspots of London. He had an expensive flat in South Kensington on a ten-year lease, paid for by Uncle Wallace along with the furniture. The Kensington Road flat had four nice rooms, quiet enough after the African bush for Ralph to get a good night's sleep. Mostly Ralph went to work when he felt like it. His elder brother had been quite right. The shipping business was boring. From finding the right ship, to shipping and financing the cargo. For some reason quite beyond Ralph's comprehension, the last part of the transaction was called confirming and required a great deal of money. Which was where the old and trusted Rosenzweig Merchant Bank came into the picture, according to Mr Postlethwaite.

Whenever Mr Postlethwaite mentioned the name Rosenzweig, it was as if he had said the name of the King. Very soon after taking up his new duty of learning the trade as soon as possible, Ralph surmised rightly that without the backing of Rosenzweig's money, the firm of Madgwick and Madgwick would either have to find another trust bank or go out of business. The money was lent to Madgwick's to lend to their clients. When all went well everyone made money. If a client did not pay on time, the risk belonged to Madgwick's. If Madgwick's went insolvent, the risk belonged to Rosenzweigs. Ralph thought that like so many other things, the initiated made it look complicated; it was all a lot simpler than it looked.

"It's simple," Ralph had said to Mr Postlethwaite sometime during the summer. "We are lending and then retrieving the bank's money."

"Which is why we require a letter of credit before shipping the goods."

"What's a letter of credit?"

"There are two types..." Ralph by then had turned off his mind to the boring detail. He waited impatiently for Mr Postlethwaite to finish.

"Then my job is to make sure we pick the right clients," he said, getting a word in edgeways. "Clients who will pay their bills and stay in business."

"Something like that."

"Like a classical symphony. Mozart for example." Ralph was grinning.

"What has Mozart got to do was shipping?"

"Nothing. Everything. I can listen to his music with great pleasure without having to know how to compose and write down the music." The line about Mozart had come earlier in the week from Christopher, a line Ralph had liked.

"What are you talking about?" asked Mr Postlethwaite.

"I can do all the shipping business I like without touching one of your letters of credit. Or, a bill of lading. Or, a list to pack."

"Packing list, Mr Ralph. The success of our business is in the detail. Any one piece of detail missing and everything breaks down. Like a long chain attached to that small chair over there. If all the links are properly in place, when I pull the chain the chair comes towards me. A missing or broken link in the chain and the chair stays right where it is." Mr Postlethwaite, Ralph knew from experience, liked a little homily.

"What on earth has that chair got to do with shipping?"

"Like Mozart, you can't listen to the music without all the notes. Without the right shipping documents, the goods stay right here and the money right there and nobody makes any money."

"I only want to listen to the music."

"Thank heaven Mozart did not think that way and despite your advice composed his music."

"I'll have to have another word with my brother on that one."

"I would if I were you. And please listen to me, Mr Ralph. I do not like wasting my breath."

"I'm sorry, sir."

"That's better. Now, an irrevocable letter of credit means that once it has been raised it will not be revoked by the paying bank provided we present to the bank the right shipping documents proving we have sent the goods, that they have been cleared by customs, the railways picked them up from the ship and delivered them to our customer. If all the links in the chain are right we always get paid." Ralph's eyes were wide as saucers.

To Ralph, it was all just like eating soup with a fork. Just when he thought he had picked up something he could eat, it slipped right off again. He had taken out a girl from the cast of *Happy Times* the previous night. He had taken her home at four o'clock in the morning. His head was throbbing, his brain working badly. He rather thought his breath still smelled of booze, despite the peppermints he had been sucking.

"Is there a book on all this?"

"No there is not... Try getting some sleep before coming to the office... What was her name?"

"Blanche Saunders."

"Nice name." Mr Postlethwaite was smiling.

"I'll try."

"I'm sure you will. It's the trying harder we want, Mr Ralph. You can't give orders or supervise orders unless you know what you are talking about. So you can pick out their mistakes. You must have learnt that in the war or you would have lost more than a little finger... And don't be fooled by your Uncle Wallace. He knows a lot more about this business than he lets on. Despite the other day denying knowledge of a bill of lading."

Back then in the summer, Ralph had gone off muttering to himself with the best of intentions. He knew his trouble was just turning twenty-five. Just finding out girls liked him. That in London there were more pretty girls than young men with money to spend on them. Work, right up to the time he met Rebecca Rosenzweig, came second best.

She was small. Brown, smouldering eyes. Tight curled black hair. Lips that made the perfect shape of a perfect bow. Voice with a catch in the lower cadence. A smile that looked right inside him that night they first met at the grand party at the Dorchester to celebrate Rosenzweig's one hundred and fiftieth birthday. That night four weeks ago he had had no idea who she was, or she who he was. They simply fell in love.

They had slipped out of the hotel. The beginning of November. Snow falling in Park Lane. By the time they had run up to Oxford Street, they were hand in hand. It was the consummate moment for them both. They both knew it had changed them forever. The perfect, uncomplicated love. The only reason for being alive.

UNCLE WALLACE HAD LISTENED to the story right from the beginning. He had sat down on the couch. Sir Jacob Rosenzweig had walked up and down the senior partner's office. The pit of Uncle Wallace's stomach was hollow.

"She's nineteen years old, Mr Madgwick. My youngest. Maybe that makes it worse. You may do business with us. You may not live with us. We are Jews. Do I make myself quite clear? Your nephew will never see her again."

"Isn't that up to them?"

"Marriage. The continuance of a tribe. These things are sacred. We do not make the choice. The choice is made for us. A marriage must be among similar people. Same background. Same education. Same wealth. Same religion. Marriage is difficult enough without an inherent impediment. I don't wish to speak with you again on this matter, sir. As a gentleman, I require your assurance. His father is dead or I would have gone to his father. We stop it now. Before we have a disaster. Now!"

"I have little influence over the boy."

"You employ him."

"Somewhat unwillingly. For him, I mean. His brother has just resigned. There is no one else to take over the firm. He will be rich. That is one common factor. He is educated. Another, maybe... Can I interest you in a brandy?"

"At this hour of the day?"

"Myself, maybe?... Since the war. The only thing that relieves the pain in what was once my left eye... Surely, telling Rebecca will be enough? If Ralph calls, you tell him she is out. At nineteen, I mean... You sure you won't have a brandy? Well, I'll just have one myself you see... Nineteen. My word, that is young."

"She has threatened to run away with him."

"Has she... Where to, might I ask?"

"Africa. He wants to take her back to Africa with him."

"Nephew Ralph is going back to Africa? That is a blow. Not a word to me, mark you. He never said a word to me... Africa. That is a blow. If he can't have your daughter here he'll take her to Africa, is that it?... You sure about the brandy?... Very well. Yes, I'll have a word with him. A very strong word. I'll do my best, that I will."

"Our business dealings depend on it."

"They do? Yes, I suppose they do..."

"Good day, Mr Madgwick!"

"Good day, Sir Jacob."

The tall, thin man stalked out of the office leaving the door open. Uncle Wallace watched the lift come up from the couch where he was still sitting. His knees were too weak to get up for the brandy. He had tried to twice. He watched Maxwell open the lift door. The banker stepped inside and turned. They stared at each other for many seconds before the lift went down. Even with the concertina doors closed across the cage, he could still see Sir Jacob's hawk nose pointing straight at him. If the bankers withdrew their line of credit, things would be difficult. Commercial banks were far stricter than merchant banks. Merchant banks did business more with individuals on the shake of a hand. From generations of doing business together. From mutual trust... As Uncle Wallace watched the lift sink, his stomach sank with it, the hollow feeling tinged with fear.

When Uncle Wallace finally reached the brandy bottle, the Cumbrian estate was the last thing on his mind.

Rosie Prescott quietly closed the door. She had heard the raised voices. Rebecca. Ralph. Jews... She had seen the dreadful stare from the lift directed through to the partner's office. It took no more to understand what had happened. Why Ralph had been behaving himself for the last month. Coming clear-eyed to the office on time. She understood. The poor boy was in love. With the banker's daughter. And the banker was a Jew so nothing could ever come out of it. For either of them.

Rosie Prescott left the executive suite for the first time ever in office hours. The telephone could ring. In half an hour, the senior partner would be in no condition to take calls anyway. No one before had ever tried going into his office without going through her first.

Rosie took the stairs down to the floor below.

"Put your coat on, Ralph. We are going for a walk." They had a good rapport, she and Ralph. Ever since the fifty pounds and her visit to brother Christopher's attic when Ralph first arrived back from Africa, dirty, dishevelled and broke.

"What's going on, Rosie?"

"Sir Jacob Rosenzweig. He has just left your uncle's office in a bad temper. It's over, Ralph. I'm sorry. We can go to a coffee shop where I can explain. What on earth were you thinking?"

"You don't think of anything else when it happens."

"I know. Yes, I do know. I was quite pretty myself at nineteen." When necessary, Rosie could hear right through the panelled door to Uncle Wallace's office.

"Did you overhear their conversation?"

"They were nearly shouting at each other. Come on. I want you out of the office. After the coffee, you go home. Don't come back here until Monday. Under no circumstances do you go anywhere near Rebecca Rosenzweig."

"I love her."

"Sir Jacob has threatened to pull Madgwick's credit line. In the millions, Ralph. Trade is good. Everyone is shipping goods. You will sink the whole firm. Your mother, your brother, Mr Postlethwaite, me, all of us... Don't you see what you've done?"

"Talk to me some more over coffee, Rosie. I feel sick... You think he would do it?"

"Oh, yes."

"Just because she's his daughter?"

"No, Ralph. Just because she's a Jewess and you are a Gentile... Come on. Now. Before your uncle comes down. He's drinking, Ralph. It'll be all over the City before you know it if you two have a shouting match... I want you out. Hurry!"

"You are a good woman, Rosie Prescott."

She looked at him again. Properly. She should have known herself better. She was infatuated with Ralph Madgwick. From the first moment she visited the attic. And she was thirty-one years old, Ralph twenty-five.

"There's no fool like an old fool."

"What does that mean, Rosie?"

"Just get a move on, Ralph Madgwick... I like my job and I want to keep it."

. . .

CHRISTOPHER MARLOWE HAD SENT his letter of resignation through Rosie Prescott to Uncle Wallace the moment he saw his brother Ralph was taking the family responsibility to the firm seriously. Christopher thought the trappings of wealth had finally shown his brother the light. He was sad, though glad for himself and conscious that, as he put it to himself, one man's meat is another man's poison.

The firm of Madgwick and Madgwick only needed one senior partner and that was now going to be younger brother Ralph. Christopher told himself he could stop feeling guilty.

That morning when he wrote the letter in the attic before going to work, the first of Keppel Howland's stories had appeared in the *Daily Mail*. Christopher had used his new influence as author and composer of *Happy Times* to pass the story to a friendly reporter at the newspaper. The story was somewhere between journalism and a short story: *Leopard Cave* brought the romantic out in Christopher over breakfast and prompted his letter of resignation. Christopher thought it better not to ask his brother why Ralph had turned over a new leaf. Now that *Happy Times* was playing to full houses and Brett Kentrich sometimes deigned to go out with him, he was not going to look another gift horse in the mouth. He had not inspected Harry Brigandshaw's teeth and he was not going to look at his brother's. He was writing a new musical, though what about he had no idea. There were only bits and pieces. To stop the thought that sent him into a cold sweat that he was a one-show man, he had dashed off the letter of resignation. Now he was committed. To the theatre and Clara's. Forever. Clara's, that was the place to be seen in the West End right now and it had not a little to do with the success of *Happy Times*. He owed that to Clara. He may be able to write songs, he said again to himself, but he was still a lousy piano player.

By lunchtime when he had still not been summoned to the senior partner's office to explain himself and his letter of resignation, he knew something was wrong. When he went up to the executive suite and found Rosie Prescott missing, he was certain. The door to Uncle Wallace's office was firmly shut. Leaving well alone he tiptoed out of the office down the back stairs and went home, where he found Gert van Heerden, Rosie Prescott and his brother Ralph and the story of Rebecca Rosenzweig came tumbling out.

SIR JACOB ROSENZWEIG had also gone home to face his daughter who, when he arrived, was not there. In the winter months, the family mostly stayed in town at their house in Golders Green. The big house in Surrey was left to the servants to look after. His wife liked the theatre and the concerts. It was mostly all she liked but Sir Jacob tried not to think about that. Their own marriage had been arranged for them under the domineering wishes of their fathers. All family business and no love. Jacob and Hannah Rosenzweig hated each other. They always had. From the time they first saw each other after the betrothal. How they had managed to have four children was one of God's miracles. So far as Sir Jacob was concerned he could remember fewer than a dozen times his wife had let him into her bed. Always at her bidding, never at his. The cynic in him wondered if it was the reason why all his children looked different and none of them like his own family except Rebecca. Which, if he was honest with himself, was what the fuss was all about. What Hannah did in her spare time was of no interest to Sir Jacob. He mildly hoped she had enjoyed herself. He certainly had done so with his own mistresses. They had all been paid off and gone their own ways with some of his money. It was what money was for. And power, he added sometimes when he was being more honest with himself.

If only I could tell Rebecca, he said to himself as he searched the empty house. Then he sat down in his study and poured himself a stiff whisky, splashing in some soda from the syphon on the silver tray. Wallace Madgwick's ten o'clock brandy had been too early for him. But not by much. Trying to keep a business and a family together was enough to send any man to drink.

When Sir Jacob poured himself the second whisky, there was one thing certain in his mind. If Rebecca broke tradition by marrying a Gentile it could ruin the bank. Depositors would take their money somewhere else. All of them. They were all Jews. The only thing that kept Jews from obliteration was tradition, keeping together, keeping their faith in their religion, their almighty God. Then he began to think about his visit last week to Berlin and the worries started all over again from another direction. The new upsurge of violent German National Socialism in Bavaria did not include the German Jews. They were going to be the scapegoats as usual. Everywhere in the world, when a country went wrong financially, they turned on the Jews.

The second drink was not as good as the first. His mind began thinking about what he must do to protect the family bank. Even the Paris branch would become vulnerable if Germany re-armed, as Sir Jacob feared they were going to do, Treaty of Versailles or not. The leader of the National Socialists was already pointing at the Jews as if inflation was their fault. Inflation that had sent the cost of a loaf of bread from two hundred and fifty marks to two hundred million. In less than a year! Europe was in a bigger mess after the war than before. The French had not listened. They wanted their pound of flesh. First the coal and timber from the Ruhr. What were they going to demand next? Unless the Europeans learnt to live with each other as one family, it was always going to be a mess. Napoleon. Bismarck. The litany went back two thousand years. Right there, right then, in his armchair in front of the fire in the study, he had a vision. A clear, calm vision he knew to be right. He was going to move the bank to America. To New York. Getting the family into America with so much money would not be a problem. His depositors would agree. He could service his clients in Europe from America where the money was safe.

Excited, Sir Jacob got up from the chair and paced the room. He was right. He knew he was right. If Hannah wanted to stay in London that was her business. Stopping in his tracks at the knock on his door he told whoever it was to come in. When she came through the door he could see Rebecca had been crying. Her eyes were red and listless. Her shoulders were slumped. It must have been snowing outside as there was snow on her overcoat.

"We're going to America," said Sir Jacob, his eyes shining. "America! Isn't that wonderful?"

With absolute certainty, Sir Jacob Rosenzweig knew God had answered his prayers. They and all their money were going to America. His family was going to survive another one hundred and fifty years. He was walking faster around the room.

"Can Ralph Madgwick come to America?"

"You'd better ask him. I'm told everything is different over there."

"What changed your mind, Daddy?"

"A man you've never heard of and I hope you never will. He's written a book called *Mein Kampf, My Struggle*. I had a preview. He hates us Jews. Berlin is full of fear and famine."

"But I love England. I'm English."

"You may be English second, Rebecca. As I am. A knight of the realm. But first of all, we are Jews and always will be."

Sir Jacob was in such a good mood as he smiled at his daughter that he had forgotten his main depositors were still Jewish. That Rosenzweigs was a Jewish merchant bank, in Berlin, Paris, London or New York.

ON THE FOLLOWING MONDAY, the 21 December 1925, Brett Kentrich had agreed to go on to Clara's after the show. She had agreed soon after being told Tina Brigandshaw had given birth to a second son in an exclusive nursing home in Paddington. Having added it all up on her fingers, Brett was not sure whether to sulk or dance the fandango, one of the Spanish scenes in *Happy Times*.

When they all reached Clara's it was full and they sat at the bar. After her first drink, Brett moved among the tables. She had seen Harry Brigandshaw throwing a party at one of the big tables and wanted to say hello, to see his reaction and calculate from his face whether he too had worked out what had likely gone on back in March. The whole of London society thrived on rumours. Harry was either a fool or putting on a brave face. Brett had been told on good report that back in March Barnaby St Clair had chanced to visit his parents at the same time Tina Brigandshaw was visiting hers. The Manor house and the railway cottage were not five miles apart. No one ever said it aloud, the insinuation was far more fun, but everyone who knew them and many who did not were aware of the very different family backgrounds. One middle-aged woman, with a face like a horse, sometimes imitated the sound of a steam train just within earshot of Mrs Brigandshaw, but only when Barnaby St Clair was in the room. Barnaby seemed to like the insinuation, smiling at the horsey face with a smirk. With Harry Brigandshaw away in Africa for the whole of March, the two of them had been seen by Brett exchanging far more than glances. Only when Harry came back at the end of his aborted flying venture did the looks between Barnaby and Tina dry up. Tina, along with others by the look of it in Clara's, thought Barnaby St Clair had given his one-time brother-in-law a pair of horns and a bastard son to go with them. To add spice to the evening and smirks to the socialites' faces, Barnaby himself came into Clara's, large as life, and brazenly walked across to congratulate Harry just as Brett arrived at the table.

"Your usual chirpy self, Barnaby," said Harry Brigandshaw. "How was the show tonight, Brett? Clara, my dear, can you push in a couple of chairs? We all want to celebrate Frank. Frank Sebastian Brigandshaw after my father who, some nasty-minded people have liked to suggest through the years of my life, was not married to my mother at the time of my birth."

"How is Tina?" asked Brett.

"Glad to be free of him and into the hands of a nurse. Just came from the nursing home. Mother and son are flourishing. For tuppence, my wife would have got out of bed and come right here. Young Frank was making a lot of noise. Good lungs. Always a good sign. The most successful people in this world, so I am told, make a lot of noise. Champagne. A cigar, Barnaby? Especially a cigar for my brother-in-law. How are your family? Please give them my regards. Merlin! Dear, dear, where's Merlin on such a night? Clara, my dear, phone the Honourable Merlin St Clair. Bring him over. What a night to celebrate."

Brett plonked down next to Harry. Christopher Marlowe was giving her sheep eyes from the bandstand as usual. Barnaby sat down on the other pushed-in chair two seats away from Harry. Under the table, Harry took her hand. For the first time since meeting Harry, she realised he was drunk. Her best hopes were instantly revived. Tina had her baby. Brett had his hand. It was going to be the happiest night of her life if she had any say in the matter. When Harry left the supper club that night, Brett helped him into a taxi. Then got in next to him and told the driver where to go. Not to the big house on Berkeley Square. To the small flat in Regent Mews. Where it had all begun. She had won even if Harry was past caring. All her pent-up jealousy at Tina Pringle exploded through the long night. In the morning, she was exhausted, full of life, full of joy. Whatever happened in the future could take care of itself.

When she went onstage that night, she sang her heart out. They were indeed *Happy Times*. Without good floorboards, she would have stamped the fandango right through the floor of the stage.

THE STRANGEST PART of it all for Harry was knowing Frank was part of Lucinda. That this was her way from the grave of giving him back their son who died in her womb when she was shot dead by Mervyn Braithwaite on Salisbury railway station. A lifetime ago that would not go away. Haunting him. Knowing Fishy Braithwaite only killed her to get his own back on Harry for something he had not done. He had been a friend to Sara Wentworth, not her lover. It all just never seemed to stop.

What to do with Brett Kentrich was the next problem on his conscience. He had used her. Willingly, but used her just the same. Tina was much easier. She was his wife, mother of two of his children if not the third. Would always remain his wife, even should they live separate lives. Barnaby was Barnaby. Selfish. Self-centred. Conceited beyond the normal meaning of the word. Harry doubted if Barnaby had ever thought of anyone else but himself in his entire life. That was Barnaby, Harry repeated to himself for the umpteenth time. A leopard never changed its spots whatever else it appeared to be doing, appeared to be trying to do to allow others into letting it get its own way. Harry even surmised that Barnaby thought he was the injured party. That he, Barnaby, had found Tina Pringle first... On the boat, there had been no doubt in Harry's mind she was not a virgin. A woman of considerable experience. Like Brett Kentrich. He had recognised the type the first night in his cabin on board the SS *Corfe Castle*, the ship he had named after the ancient family fiefdom of the St Clairs, his first wife's family. Likely Frank was made in Corfe Castle, the haunting coming back again to Harry, never stopping. The circle going on.

He could leave Tina in London with the children and go back to Africa but that was not his way. He always tried to think he faced his problems. Running away had solved none of them in the past. There were five of them to think about, not one, despite what Barnaby would have thought in his shoes... Frank Sebastian. He would learn to love him. Chances were he would be the best of the bunch. Life's irony.

The roads were bad and covered in ice but that did not matter. He still had his 770cc BSA motorcycle stored in the company warehouse, along with his Royal Flying Corps goggles and long leather coat, leather gloves that came up to his elbows, and fur boots that kept his feet warm in the air.

After tinkering for an hour, the engine fired. The tyres he inflated with a hand pump. Dressed for the cold, Harry rode the bike out of London to the north through London into the winter day and the English countryside, the clouds low and grey, ready for snow. With the throttle turned full on the handlebar, Harry roared down the country lanes, shouting at the top of his lungs, driving the stench of London off his skin, out of his mind.

If he killed himself, he did not really care. There was money enough for all of them.

WHEN THEY HAD LEFT Clara's the previous evening, Christopher Marlowe had watched with a sinking feeling. After Harry and Brett left he played the piano worse than usual; distracted. Rumours had been flying for months about Barnaby and Tina. The same Barnaby St Clair he had met in France during the war. Christopher did not like Barnaby and not only for seducing Mrs Brigandshaw when her husband was in Africa. The man had only one thing on his mind: Barnaby St Clair. The fact of Barnaby releasing Harry to pursue Brett had much to do with his dislike that night and the bad piano playing. Even Harvey Lyttleton, the most laconic of singers who rarely spoke a sentence using more than seven words, had raised an eyebrow. Danny Hill, the trumpeter and collaborator on *Happy Times*, gave him a sympathetic smile. Christopher thought Danny must have seen Brett leave with Harry. The other guests celebrating the new birth had stayed behind, making the exit of the star that much more obvious.

The next day while Harry was trying to kill himself on the icy lanes north of London, Christopher telephoned a message to Clara asking Danny

Hill to stand in for him that night on the piano. He wanted to be alone. The attic now boasted two paraffin heaters and was warm as toast. It was beginning to snow outside, the view of rooftops cold and hard. She was never going to take him seriously if Harry Brigandshaw was back in her life. With *Happy Times* becoming a word-of-mouth success there had been hope. Fame and fortune had still left him in the attic. The hair was growing again, the wig left in the cupboard next to the one gas ring that still cooked his food. The black beret was more comfortable on his head without the wig. Barrie Madgwick had finally been left behind. There had been no word from Uncle Wallace. There did not have to be. Both knew the only reason he had gone to work at Madgwick and Madgwick was his guilty conscience for taking so much from the family and giving nothing of himself in return. Ralph would be just fine in the job of senior partner now he was taking his training seriously. The idea of giving Ralph his share of the family business made him feel even less guilty for abandoning the family business.

There were so many girls now. All of them seemed to want a man who had written a successful West End musical. All except the one that mattered. The one he had written the musical for in the first place.

"Why do we always want what we can't have?" he asked the closed window as he stared across the bleak and lonely rooftops.

Then he remembered a task he set himself in the winter months and pulled up the sash window letting in the freezing cold and a flurry of snow. Picking up the box of birdseed from the sideboard, Christopher sprinkled a good layer on the outside sill and quickly closed the window. Within a minute, the pigeons were pecking up the food, ruffling their feathers against the cold. Christopher even thought one of them gave him a wink.

Suddenly a real idea came to him for the new musical, sending him across the room to his small desk where he began to write. This time Christopher was going to write the libretto first and then, with the help of Danny Hill, the music.

On a park bench on Hampstead Heath not far away from the attic of Shaftesbury Avenue, Rebecca and Ralph were sitting in the snow. Neither of them had spoken a word for ten minutes. It was late on the Tuesday afternoon and the light was going. For both of them, it could have been the final darkness proclaiming the end of the world.

Rebecca had written to Ralph at his four-roomed flat to meet her on the Heath. Her father had given permission for her to write the letter. The snow was drifting down, muffling the sounds of London, leaving them alone in a world together for probably the last time.

"What would I do in America?" asked Ralph. He was desolate. "I once looked for diamonds in Africa, did I tell you that? Not one. I nearly starved. I knew how to shoot a gun and that's all."

"Then what about us running away to Africa? How would we live in Africa?"

"I don't care. I just want to be with you."

"Then come to America. Everyone who wants a new life is going to America... Father thinks there's going to be another war with Germany."

"Do you want to go to America?"

"Of course I don't."

"Then why can't we be together here? I'll be senior partner one day now my brother has pulled out. Rich. I'll be rich."

"But you won't ever be Jewish. Father will keep his promise. He says if your Uncle Wallace can't make you see sense, the trust of the last two generations of Madgwicks and Rosenzweigs will be broken. He will stop doing business with Madgwick's. Cancel your line of credit that you use to do business with your customers." She had listened long and hard to her father's tirade.

"We are in love. Doesn't that count?"

"Not to Father. Not to the men who lend money to his bank. It's not just my father, Ralph. We're Jews. We're different. The only thing we've ever had to keep us together for thousands of years is our religion. And Jews are not allowed to marry Gentiles."

"Then why will it be different in America?"

"I don't know."

"I do. Your father knows I can't just up and go. He knows I don't have any money of my own. He knows to marry you I need my job and the prospect of running the firm... When are you going, Rebecca?"

"Next Monday. From Liverpool."

"Oh my God."

THEY HAD SAILED on the turn of the tide from the Port of Liverpool heading far out through the Irish Sea. By lunchtime, the MV *Glasmerden* had passed the Point of Ayr heading towards the Isle of Man. The sea was frozen thirty yards out from the land. Sir Jacob could see in the distance from the upper deck the mountain of Snaefell, the highest ground on the island. They were to pick up more cargo in Glasgow before heading out into the Atlantic, across to the Newfoundland port of St John's. From St John's, they would sail south direct for New York where the ship would pick up cargo and sail back to Liverpool past the south side of Ireland. It was the first available ship to cross to the New World with berths. Sir Jacob wanted Rebecca out of England before anything worse happened in her life. Hannah would follow later. Sir Jacob and Rebecca were the only passengers on the cargo ship and would eat with the captain.

Only out of Glasgow two days later did Sir Jacob realise he was trying to leave the land of his birth for another world.

He had made sure his daughter was on board in her cabin before going up on deck. Rebecca had cried from the time the ship sailed out of Liverpool. She had eaten all her food in her small cabin, taken down to her by Sir Jacob himself. There were moments when he would have changed his mind were they not on the high seas. He just hoped he had done the right thing and not destroyed another woman's life as he had done to Hannah's so many years before. Rebecca was only nineteen. There was the comfort for him in her age. She would get over a young man she barely knew, which was what his hurry had been all about. The less they saw of each other, the fewer memories his daughter would have to forget.

So wrapped up in saving the family name and the family bank from danger, he had never given his own emotions a thought. Until the small ship sailed out into the Atlantic and the British Isles faded far behind. Only then did Sir Jacob realise he was wrong about one thing. He was an Englishman first, a Jew second, not the other way around. The pain of sailing away from what he had known all his life was physical. Making sure which way the wind was coming onto the ship, Sir Jacob Rosenzweig was violently sick over the side, retching and retching until his stomach was empty even of bile and the pain in his sphincter became agony. Even in the sub-zero cold, his face had broken out in a cold sweat. He was going into exile. Running away. The only cold comfort lay in his certainty of being right. Rebecca, he realised as he looked back at an empty, angry sea, was just an excuse. After reading *Mein Kampf, My Struggle*, by Adolf Hitler, Sir Jacob knew Europe was once again going up in flames. That in the flames, the Jews who stayed behind would burn. That the Nazi Brownshirts of the party would soon do more than spit at the Jews. That Hitler's planned way to power was making the Germans hate the Jews, blaming the Jews for their plight. Even the poor Jews. What made one man's struggle any different to others was beyond his understanding.

Sir Jacob got to thinking, blocking out the physical pain that had racked his body. It had happened so many times before in history and no doubt, he thought staring at the running swell of the sea, it would happen again and again. Attila the Hun had been four feet two inches tall, only feeling himself a man when on top of a horse, taking out his revenge on the world by directing his hordes to rape and pillage.

Then he smiled thinly, the cold now intense. If he was wrong about Germany, they could go back again. Back to England. Feeling better with himself, he went down the stairway into the ship in search of a hot cup of tea.

As they were moving out into the North Atlantic, the small cargo ship began to pitch in the long swells. It was the second day of the new year in the year of the Christian Lord one thousand nine hundred and twenty-six.

7

JUNE 1926 – LOVE, OR SOMETHING
LIKE IT

*R*alph Madgwick was on the brink of no return. When he was in the office, it was in body, with his mind elsewhere. Bloodshot eyes. Hands shaking so much he dropped his head to the coffee cup to drink, his right arm locked, refusing to lift the cup to his lips. Rosie Prescott had tried everything over six months and given up. Even the secret letter from Rebecca in New York sent him into a drinking depression. The only difference before Rebecca Rosenzweig and after, was the women. All were whores, amateur or professional. To Rosie, it was as if Ralph wanted to dirty himself as much as possible after the brilliant light from Rebecca had shown him a life worth living.

Since January, Ralph had learnt nothing. The only day that drew any interest from him at Madgwick and Madgwick was the day Rosie gave him his pay cheque. Rosie even thought Ralph saw himself as a martyr. A victim. The butt of a cruel joke.

Christopher Marlowe, still conscious of his own guilt when it came to the affairs of Madgwick and Madgwick, had also given up trying to talk sense into his brother. There had never been any logic in his life in arguing with a drunk or a fool. To that, he had now added a brother in the throes of unobtainable love.

Without Mr Postlethwaite, the company would have fallen apart. The more nephew Ralph went into decline the more Uncle Wallace drank in the office, the cloud of depression right over his head for all to see. Either someone persuaded the girl to come back to England from America in open defiance of her father, or the next generation of Madgwicks would never take over the firm, sending, as Uncle Wallace put it succinctly to Rosie Prescott, four generations of hard work down the drain.

It was in the course of one of Uncle Wallace's bouts of despair that Rosie came up with the answer, or at least so she hoped.

"Send Ralph to America," she said in the senior partner's office. "Open an office in New York. Our correspondent in Manhattan makes a fortune doing our business for us. Let us do it ourselves. Make the profit for ourselves. Many of our clients have subsidiaries in America who will happily do business with us. That will be in addition to clearing their shipments from England to America."

"But Ralph knows nothing about shipping."

"He will learn fast with the right incentive. Say eighteen months of dedicated hard work right here in London, with America as his reward. Rebecca will be twenty-one with the legal right to make up her own mind. Sir Jacob can then say to his fellow Jews, it was all beyond his power."

"He'll disown the child. I know Jacob."

"Even better. They won't need Rosenzweig's money. She'll have been thrown out of the Jewish community. Problem solved for Sir Jacob Rosenzweig."

"It won't work, Miss Prescott."

"At least Ralph will know his shipping at the end of eighteen months' hard work. Better to let Ralph think he has a chance of fulfilling his dreams. Often the journey towards the dream is better than the dream itself. At least it will stop Ralph from drinking. Make him nice again... I can't stand it any longer."

"What's the matter, Miss Prescott?"

"Nothing, Mr Madgwick."

"Then why are you crying?"

The door to the senior partner's office closed with a distinct bang. Not a slam, Uncle Wallace thought, just a bang. He stared at the closed door for a full minute. Only then did it click in his half-sozzled mind.

"I'll be damned. She's in love with him. What a combination for the future of the firm. And the future of me." Uncle Wallace was smiling.

For the first time in months, Uncle Wallace saw horses in his mind. And dogs. Gundogs. Hounds following the hunt... He could hear the sound of the horn, the baying of the dogs. See the fox racing away over the fields and hedgerows of his own country estate.

"By Jove," he said, "I think she's got it. Nothing wrong with a nice piece of bribery, come to think of it. Not when it comes to a young lad who is an extortionist... The things a man has to do to get the best of both worlds."

From outside at her desk where Rosie Prescott was feeling sorry for herself, she heard the distinct sound through the closed door of the senior partner whistling out of tune.

TINA BRIGANDSHAW KNEW she had done the opposite of the right thing by telling Harry Brigandshaw the truth. While what was being suggested to Ralph Madgwick dawned on him as the best bit of bribery he had been offered in his life, Tina was contemplating the wreck of her own in her room on the third floor of the Berkeley Square house.

She no longer shared a room with Harry since the ill-fated flight down Africa. Having quarrelled violently over Tina's wish to stay in London and thinking the flaunting of her body during the day would break down Harry's resistance, Tina had moved into her own room. It was her only weapon, which had always worked before.

But, by the end of the first month in separate bedrooms after his return, Tina had been gripped by a cold fear. Only the once had she managed to get him back into her bed, knowing only too well that by then it was too late. She was more than two months pregnant with Frank, the spawn of a leering seducer who had caught her in the woods, turning their deadly attraction to his will. Laughing at her in public afterwards. At least until Harry had come back from his extended trip to Africa and given Barnaby St Clair a look of cold anger that had put real fear into Barnaby St Clair. People who had killed consistently in battle were still killers. Tina had looked from one to the other, seeing in herself what Barnaby saw. Knowing then she knew no more of her husband than the surface. And only the surface he wished her to see.

Without sex with her, had Harry gone back to Brett? In private husband and wife said not a word to each other. Only in public did they talk normally for the sake of appearances. He was two people: the affable older man of the world when they were out with friends, a cold, distant monster when alone. A monster with a will she was unable to break.

BACK IN MARCH 1925, after Harry and Tina quarrelled over his sudden plan to go to Africa, Harry left Ignatius Bowes-Lyon at the Victoria Falls Railway Hotel. Their nine passengers dispersed, going their several ways further into Africa with their journey home booked for them later on the SS *Corfe Castle* that would sail them back to England. Harry himself had taken the train on the narrow gauge railway to Bulawayo where he had spent the night in the Cecil Hotel, boarding the next train to Salisbury the following evening. Harry had a sleeping car all to himself, waking up to the dawn: a beautiful, red and crimson African dawn that drew the bush out of the night, the long elephant grass moving in the morning breeze in waves.

Harry had been awake from the first rays through his open window, tasting the morning scents of the new dawn. They were still twenty miles from the capital of the newly self-governing colony of Southern Rhodesia. There was game on both sides of the train as the engine at the front slowly pulled the line of carriages through the veld. Harry stood looking out the window smiling like a small boy with his first toy. He was truly home. Twenty miles the other side of Salisbury was Elephant Walk. Tembo was meeting the train with the car at Salisbury station. By breakfast time, he would be home.

So overwhelmed by the thought of seeing his mother and sister, his grandfather and Madge's children, he had forgotten to think of Tina and his own children back in England.

"If you could just see this, Tina... Everything will be fine when I bring you and the children home. This is our home. Africa. Here is space. Space for a man's family. Here is living away from all the damn people who want to steal and tell tales. It's here we'll grow old together in peace."

The intention was a two-week stay on Elephant Walk with Harry returning to the Victoria Falls for Ignatius to fly the empty seaplane back up Africa over the lakes and the Nile River.

THE DOGS HAD CHASED around the garden as if the devil was after their tails. Flowers from the round beds that circled the msasa trees that scattered the lawn right down to the Mazoe River flew into the air, torn from their stems by the ridgebacks, the bitch leading the mayhem in front of the two dogs. The cat on the windowsill of the main house stopped even trying to look asleep with her eyes open. The tame Egyptian geese had gone off honking to the river where they flew round and round making as much noise as the dogs. The two tame giraffes looked across from their paddock next to the farm buildings and kept staring. Everyone on the farm, black and white, was smiling despite the previous year's drought. It had decimated the cattle, limited the maize crop to three bags to the acre, and produced a Virginia tobacco so off-type the buyers in London had said they would not take the crop after receiving a sample sent by Jim Bowman on the instructions of Sir Henry Manderville, Harry's grandfather.

The only crops that had grown in profusion were in the vegetable gardens close to the Mazoe River and watered by Sir Henry's combination of windmills, gears and pipes. The river was still flowing but would likely stop before the next rains in October.

The first job Harry did after taking up young Tinus his nephew in the Handley Page for a flip to stop him pestering, was to look for a dam site upriver from the farm.

His grandfather began to explain the problem.

"One year it rains too much and the water leaves Rhodesia down the Zambezi River for the sea in Mozambique. Useless to man and beast. The next year there is little rain and most of the smaller rivers dry up and stop flowing. We must have dams, Harry. Big dams. To survive. With our medicine and a constant supply of proper food throughout the year, the black population is exploding. In a normal drought year like this, they'd be dying of starvation by September, especially the young children. With the new government stockpile, there will be enough food for everyone. But not in five years' time if we don't increase production with irrigated water. When you go back to London, Harry, send out an engineer. My bit of amateur irrigation isn't enough for a grand scale... When are you going back?"

"Two weeks was what I said to Ignatius. Tinus is already in a state of hypertension. When I go back, he is going to go wild. He misses his father and I miss my children and Tina doesn't want to live in Africa. I'll stay for a month. A compromise. Then we fly out of Victoria Falls all being well. The planes we have now are too small for commercial purposes. We need much larger seaplanes. More like flying boats. It'll work one day... I know a chap from Birmingham who is a good engineer. He was involved with the construction of the causeway connecting Singapore with the Malayan mainland. He may yet get a knighthood for getting the road across that swamp. A few dams in Africa will be a holiday in comparison. Now, let's sit down under that tree and you can tell me everything that happened while I was away... How are you?"

"Getting old, Harry. I'll be seventy-five next year. No man lives forever."

"Don't talk like that."

"I've been in Africa over thirty-five years. Been in Rhodesia ever since Cecil Rhodes started the country. Almost as long as you and your mother."

"Any regrets?"

"None. Look at the place. Look at Elephant Walk."

"Why can't women be happy wherever they are?"

"Maybe she will be one day."

"We had such a row."

"I'm sorry, Harry."

AFTER FRANK'S BIRTH, Tina had told him the truth on a bench in Berkeley Square not far from the front door to their house. Anthony, who had turned three the following year, had walked off with his nurse in pursuit of a butterfly that he could not catch. Eighteen-month-old Beth was fast asleep in her pram under an elm tree. Six-month-old Frank was in the nursery back in the house.

It had been one thing to suspect it was Barnaby. Another to know. Harry's first instinct was to get his gun and go shoot Barnaby St Clair. Strangely, he was proud of his wife for telling the truth, confirming what in his heart he already knew. That Frank was his first wife Lucinda's nephew, not his son. He had asked Tina a direct question. Usually, the husband was the last to find out. Harry outlined the dates. Their two months apart when he flew with Ignatius to Africa. His return in late May. Frank's birth on the 21 December the same year. Six months after they had made love, that once. That one time before he saw Barnaby leering at his wife, turning his desire for Tina to nothing.

"Are you sleeping with Brett?" she had asked Harry.

"Once. The day Frank was born."

"I'll move out."

"You don't have to, Tina. You and I now know the truth. Only we know. Barnaby cannot be certain. If we had shared the same bed just before I left with Ignatius, Frank could have been mine. Think of the children. It was all very well being a bastard like me in the wilds of Africa where nobody cared. Quite another in London. I hate keeping up false appearances but there is no choice. What we have to do from now on, Tina, is make everything look normal when anyone else is around."

"The servants know."

"Know what?"

"That we sleep separately. They also can count on their fingers."

"Do you want to go and live with Barnaby?"

"Do you want to go and live with Brett?... Barnaby won't have me. Not with the children."

"With Frank? Not with Anthony and Beth."

"Not even with Frank. He'd laugh in my face."

"He would not laugh in mine."

"You don't know Barnaby. I've known him all my life. I just never could get him out of my system... Am I evil, too? He's evil, Harry. He only ever thinks of himself. Unless you threatened to kill him, he wouldn't care less what you said. And he knows you won't kill him because of Lucinda. Because of his family. What are we going to do, Harry?"

"Nothing, Tina. Absolutely nothing."

Harry had got up from the bench and not looked at her since, not even in public.

IN THE SMALL bedroom that was now her prison, Tina began to sob. Since sitting on the bench in Berkeley Square it had been the longest month of her life. He had not hit her. Not shouted at her. Not spoken to her. Harry had done nothing. Absolutely nothing.

THE NEWS HAD REACHED them from India the previous day.

Robert St Clair had finally taken Barnaby's bad-tempered advice. He had bought the lease of a flat near Merlin, in Stanhope Gate. The royalty cheques from *Keeper of the Legend* had been invested in good quality shares since the end of the war. Robert was a rich man by anyone's standards. Living at home and investing his money had turned the worth of his first novel into fifty thousand pounds and the cheques were still coming. Trying to spend some of the money had proved just as difficult as writing the first book. Mostly because he could not see the point of being in London in the first place. Living at home in Dorset where he had been all his life except for the war years was what he most enjoyed. For weeks on end, no trace of the sound of man would emanate from the old Manor house to disturb the peace of the woods and fields that had been in his family for eight hundred and fifty-six years. To Robert that was the true way of life for a man. Not in the small flat without animals, the sound of strangers all around, dodging the snarl of traffic in Park Lane on his way to walk each day in Hyde Park, the foul smell of man-made engines that always brought back the horrors of the war. These were strange exchanges for his lost tranquillity. In three months he had written not a single word; his consolation was seeing things to write about in a time some distance from his present.

Most days he visited Merlin, old bachelors happily chewing over the long ago.

Their mother had phoned from Purbeck Manor. A letter had come from Penelope, who was living with her parents in India. She was the widow of

Frederick, the eldest of the St Clair brothers, killed in action in France 1917. Richard, the heir to the St Clair barony and Frederick's only son, had died of typhus at the age of eight, leaving Merlin heir to the barony.

"You know what this all means," said Robert, looking out from Merlin's favourite breakfast alcove over Park Lane into the green trees of Hyde Park on the other side of the road.

"That Penelope is in misery. I've been trying all day to write her a letter of condolence. It's not easy making words have real meaning."

"That I know, Merlin... Apart from poor Penelope."

"What apart from poor Penelope?"

"You will have to get married."

"I'm forty-one. Don't be ridiculous... Why?"

"Barnaby will inherit the title."

"Not if he dies first."

"Then his eldest son will inherit."

"He doesn't have a son."

For a full minute, there was an awkward silence as both brothers stared out the window.

"If I die first you will inherit the title. Why don't you get married, Robert?" said Merlin nastily.

"I'm forty."

"Not quite but so what."

"I only have one foot."

"Good God, Robert, don't tell me you're a virgin?" Merlin had put the monocle in his left eye for a better effect.

"It's not that bad."

"I'm glad to hear that."

"I'm quite happy as I am."

"So am I."

Esther, his mistress, and Genevieve, his daughter, hung in the air.

"You don't have any children, Robert."

"What's that got to do with it?"

"A lot."

"We can't let Barnaby's bad blood taint the title."

"Where'd you think he got it from?"

"How should I know?"

"He's exactly the same blood as you and I."

"Nonsense. A throwback. Something one of our ancestors did years ago they shouldn't have."

"Then you had better find a wife as well, Robert. To make sure."

"Don't be silly, old chap. What do I know about women?"

"Then why did you come up to London?" said Merlin, giving him a lecherous look. "I'll help you, Robert. I know lots of very nice girls from very nice families who would love to marry a famous author with only one foot."

"What do I say to them?"

"Would have thought that the least of your problems."

Robert looked at his brother. Merlin was actually having a giggle at his expense.

"How are Esther and Genevieve?" said Robert spitefully.

"Why don't we go down to Clara's for a drink and dinner and talk about women? You'd better go home and change. Clever of you to get a flat within walking distance."

"Where is Clara's?"

"You mean you've been in London three months and not been to Clara's?"

"I'll help you with the letter to Penelope tomorrow."

"That will be a help. I hate writing letters. Poor little Richard... Do you remember him before they took them off to India? Her father was in business out there. Or something."

"Not really. All small boys look pretty much the same."

BARNABY ST CLAIR sat thinking about women while his brothers made their marital plans. His view was over Green Park from the second floor of his townhouse at the top of Piccadilly, not far from where Piccadilly met old Park Lane. Most of the townhouses were exclusive men's clubs where women were not allowed. Ironically, just up the road from where he quizzically gazed into the tall green elms on the other side of the busy road, was the new Royal Air Force club, founded by Lord Cowdray. Barnaby knew Harry Brigandshaw was a member of the club. His neighbour, so to speak.

The stock market was still rising steadily. Had been doing so for weeks so there was no need to contemplate the risks in making his money. Barnaby owned a little over five million pounds of mostly ordinary, voting shares in companies listed on the London Stock Exchange. All were pledged to Cox and King's bank in Pall Mall to secure Barnaby's four million pounds overdraft. When he sold shares, which he did on negative information gleaned from his social connections, he took a taxi to the bank himself to retrieve the share certificates of the companies he had sold. He did not drive his Bentley 3 Litre on short journeys. The share certificates were then hand-delivered to his stockbroker in the City by Edward, his valet. Only Barnaby and his bank manager were ever to know the shares were pledged.

Every month Barnaby paid the interest on his overdraft exactly on the first of the month. His borrowings were never allowed to exceed eighty per cent of the current value of the shares. Usually, the dividends were sufficient to service the loan. Of late, with the share prices reaching too high in relation to the dividends they paid, Barnaby was forced to sell a few shares to realise his paper profit in order to pay the interest on his overdraft.

The mortgage on the four-storey townhouse was in a separate account at the bank, the interest again paid on the first of each month. Barnaby hoped he had lulled his bank manager into a false sense of security, making good money for his bank without doing any work or taking any risk. Unless, of course, as Barnaby often thought to himself in his occasional black moods, the value of his share portfolio dipped more than twenty per cent before he could offload the shares.

What the bank manager had never worked out, and hopefully never would so far as Barnaby was concerned, was his habit to sell large numbers of shares short that he did not own, or buy large blocks of shares and sell them again before his stockbroker required payment, forty-five days from the date of the original share transaction. Even Barnaby sometimes shivered at the potential downside of these transactions when for a few days his liabilities could exceed his assets if the shares he was betting on went the other way.

The trick, Barnaby knew, was to sell his entire portfolio at the right time, pay off the bank overdraft and the mortgage with the proceeds, and live the life of a gentleman for the rest of his life with more money in the bank than a man could spend in five lifetimes. The problem with that, as he told himself on many occasions after recovering from one of his black moods, was what to do with himself when he took away the fear and joy of his highly addictive gambling. He was not thirty years old until the coming year. He would be bored to tears living in the country. He disliked chasing animals around fields on horseback. He saw little point in all the effort and discomfort of shooting birds in the rain. If he fancied a nice cock pheasant for his supper, as he did when the poor birds were in season to be shot, he ordered one ready cooked in a restaurant, far away from having to take the half-dead bird from a large dog's mouth and wring its neck. Some of his friends had such strange primal instincts he wondered what being a gentleman was really all about.

Women were Barnaby's prime source of interest after gambling all his money on the stock exchange, and there were very few women in the country without facial resemblance to horses or dogs. He had even met one in Dorset who looked like the family parrot brought back from Sarawak by her grandfather in the middle of the previous century. Horsey women to Barnaby were sexless. Which meant they were no good to him at all.

Ah, women, he thought again, bringing his mind round in a circle to the subject that rarely left his conscious mind. Why did some women make him want them more than others? Why did some women want him more than some other men? Why did the very odd women, like Tina Pringle, never lose their attraction even minutes after sex and others send him straight off to sleep? Why was he still not free of a woman he had known all his life while others, who had warmed his bed night after night for weeks, were long ago forgotten? Even their names.

It was not love, he was sure of that, as he stood close to the open window with his binoculars to look at a woman who had appeared in his line of vision across in the park. Love was a word for lust invented by polite people. Barnaby smiled at the thought. The words even had the same kind of sound. Hybrids of the same original meaning back in the primal slime.

"Not bad," he said out loud to himself. "Just not worth chasing after across the road. Women! When will I ever get enough of them?"

Tina of course was silly, he told himself. She could have had a flat all to herself, really good sex when she needed it, all the security in the world to eventually grow old in comfort, and none of the screaming brats all of whom were only interested in what they wanted for themselves.

Now he was at war with Harry Brigandshaw over the girl he still thought of as Tina Pringle. A war Barnaby knew could get ugly if he went anywhere near Tina again, despite both of them knowing who was the father of young Frank.

Poor Tina. She had the worst of both worlds. More than once, he was tempted to give her a ring and tell her what a fool she had made of herself. Except there were Harry and Frank, a fear of death and a total lack of any wish to shoulder any kind of fatherly responsibility. Like the cuckoo, he preferred his offspring to grow up in someone else's nest.

"For goodness sake," he told himself, picking up the binoculars from the half-moon table. "I don't even like children. Not even my own."

Idly, looking up at the next young woman across in the park, Barnaby wondered if there was something wrong with himself. Something missing... Then he smiled, put down the field glasses in a hurry, ran downstairs to his own front door and out into the traffic where he dodged the cars in his hurry to cross the road and go for a walk in the park, the one he had seen from the window well worth the chasing.

.   .   .

THAT NIGHT CLARA had people standing at reception waiting for a table or a seat at the bar. Waiters were running everywhere with trays of drinks and plates of food. Clara was exhausted. Every night except Sundays for weeks.

"There are times like tonight I'd sell the place lock, stock and barrel, buy a cottage in the country and live out the rest of my life as a recluse."

"Why don't you?" said Christopher Marlowe, smiling. "Sell the whole damn thing."

"You'd better get back on the piano... That was Barnaby St Clair and some new girl. Both his brothers he isn't talking to are at the bar. All we need now is Harry Brigandshaw and his charming wife... Or Brett Kentrich."

"Brett's right behind you, Clara."

"Oh my God... Miss Kentrich! What a pleasure to see you."

"You look harassed, Clara... Have you got a table for us?"

"No booking?"

"You know what it is in the theatre... Was that the Honourable Barnaby St Clair I saw going in? Can't we join his table?"

"Not tonight. Quite specific."

"A new one?"

"Said he met her this afternoon in the park."

"Man's incorrigible or just maybe something worse. Just do your best, darling. Hello, Christopher. How are you?"

"How was the show tonight?"

"One of the screen sets fell over during the interval. Your friend Gert van Heerden lost his temper again. He's in love with Jane Tamplin but she won't go with him back to Africa."

"Gert's not leaving England."

"Then she's using that as an excuse. Poor chap doesn't have enough money... You'd better go and play the piano. The band's coming back."

"Can we have a drink later?"

"Let's just see how it all turns out."

"It never does, Brett."

"Life usually doesn't... Is Harry here?"

"No, he's not."

"Damn. He's avoiding me... I went to so much trouble to stop him going back to Africa."

Christopher was going to say he had gone to a lot of trouble writing *Happy Times* for Brett and walked away instead. She was not interested in him. Plain to see.

When he reached his piano stool and struck a chord, he was not sure if writing his new musical had any point. Doing anything in life was pointless if it wasn't to be shared. Even *Happy Times*. She had sung his songs, spoken his lines but they had not really shared it together. She was the actress. He was the writer. He had tried so hard. Even Harry wasn't interested in her anymore, the irony not lost on Christopher.

He smiled first at Danny Hill who had picked up his trumpet, then at Harvey Lyttleton at the microphone who was going to sing the first song from Christopher's new musical to test it on the aftershow diners. They began the new set as they had done so many times before. The black beret was firmly on Christopher's head, the hair no longer down to his shoulders. The song was a love song. The words for Brett Kentrich. As he played the background to Harvey's crooning, Christopher watched Brett and one of her party being shown by Clara to a stool at the bar. She had not even turned round to listen so he could wave. She was talking animatedly with the man escorting her to the bar where Millie Scott was sitting with Merlin St Clair and his writer brother from Dorset, the author of *Keeper of the Legend*. If the brothers were still at the bar when the set finished he would go and talk to them. By then Brett would have been shown to a table. She didn't want to talk to him. He'd be thick-skinned not to have seen that at reception when she arrived from the Globe Theatre. There had been no sign of Oscar Fleming, the lecherous old impresario, in the party. Even Oscar Fleming, so it was said, had had an affair with Brett Kentrich… If only he could find other women attractive. The more she brushed him aside, the more he wanted her. It was becoming an obsession that dominated every facet of his life. Even being a bohemian had lost part of its attraction. Apart from having a roaring success on the West End stage, nothing was working in his life.

To add to Christopher's disquiet his brother Ralph arrived at reception with another tart he had picked up somewhere. From the stage, he could see through to the reception desk over the heads of the dancers.

"Poor old Uncle Wallace. Even bribery hasn't worked."

It seemed his brother was back to his old tricks, staying out late getting drunk and not going to work in the morning… Ralph was right. America was a long way away and eighteen months was a lifetime. Poor Rebecca. Poor old Jacob Rosenzweig. He'd dragged his daughter to America under false pretences… Anyway, Christopher told himself when Harvey had finished singing his new love song to only mild applause, he was not going to go back to work in an office. Under any circumstances. Never. Whatever his mother said and pleaded. He was his own man even if he was without Brett Kentrich.

The rest of the set, Christopher played without any concentration. Danny gave him more than one frown. His heart wasn't in it after Brett left the bar to join a table.

There were no new tables available. Her party had split up. She and the man who had gone with her to the bar had been invited to the Ramsbottom table. Clara must have asked them. He could just imagine the fawning conversation. The dumbstruck silence of the three daughters. Mrs Ramsbottom talking nineteen to the dozen in her broad Yorkshire accent.

They were regulars at Clara's when they were staying in London. Mr Ramsbottom was in coal. Mrs Ramsbottom called him Mr Ramsbottom. He called her Mrs Ramsbottom. No one had ever found out their first names. The girls were called Hermione, Clarissa and Portia. None of them was married.

He always went to their table when they came in. They were so grateful for the attention. The girls were brought down from Yorkshire three times a year each to find a husband. They had never yet come to Clara's with escorts. Mr Ramsbottom was rich. Mrs Ramsbottom was always hopeful. She liked the chinless wonders for her daughters with upper-class accents. Mrs Ramsbottom was a social climber. Had told Christopher her daughters would only be allowed to marry gentlemen.

Many of the so-called gentlemen came into Clara's to look at the actresses and dancers who came in after the West End shows had finished playing. Mrs Ramsbottom had never considered Christopher to be a gentleman. Gentlemen, the type he supposed she wanted for her daughters, did not play the piano in a supper club. Even a very high-class supper club.

Christopher always relaxed and smiled in her company. Mrs Ramsbottom was a straightforward kind of person. When Clara told her in front of him he had written *Happy Times*, she had given out a good Yorkshire bellow of a laugh.

"Don't be daft. Our Christopher here is a piano player. Had he written *Happy Times*, would he play your piano, Miss Clara? I like that one! Good show, it was. Me and Mr Ramsbottom seen show three times. Going again I should think. Our girls like it. What a nice bit of rubbish, Miss Clara. No offence, Christopher. I like you. But I have a secret. You're a lousy piano player." The third laugh was even louder than the first two.

"I suppose if I told you my father was chairman of the Baltic Exchange, you wouldn't believe that either?"

Christopher remembered the conversation word for word. He had been enjoying himself. The girls had liked his show. That was more important to him.

They relaxed with him and laughed heartily at his small jokes. He was not a potential husband. They could afford to relax. Even in the presence of Mrs Ramsbottom. Christopher had the feeling the girls would be a lot of fun away from their parents.

He was now watching them dumbstruck. Brett was a big name. Her escort did not have any chin to talk about. Mrs Ramsbottom was in full flight.

When the set finally came to an end with Danny Hill wearing a distinct pained expression for his benefit, Christopher worked his way through between the tables on his way to the bar and the two St Clair brothers. He had checked that Barnaby had not joined them... Mrs Ramsbottom was right about one thing. He was a lousy piano player. Especially tonight.

So as not to make himself more miserable than he already was, Christopher gave Brett and the Ramsbottom table a wide berth. Mrs Ramsbottom had tried hard to attract his attention. She obviously wanted to show off the star of the musical stage that now graced her table. Even to Christopher. Having a big star at your table was no good to Mrs Ramsbottom unless everyone saw what was happening. Christopher had found it difficult not to break out into a broad smile as he avoided eye contact with Mrs Ramsbottom.

"Hello, Millie. Merlin. Did I sound as bad to you as I did to myself?"

"Worse, Christopher. Please meet my brother Robert, the author."

"Why I came over... Sorry, that did not sound quite right."

"Shall I go and ask Brett to join us?" said Millie in mock retaliation.

"You stay right there, miss, or I'll never write a funny line for you ever again... I've read *Keeper of the Legend* twice, Robert."

"I've seen *Happy Times* twice," said Robert. His missing foot was itching as usual. "Barnaby told me to come up to London. I was hibernating in Dorset. Writing all right but hibernating. I'm glad I came up to London."

"Barnaby's in the club," said Christopher.

"Leave him where he is," said Merlin. "Millie, move across the one seat so the two authors can have a good chat. You look very nice tonight, Millie."

"Why, thank you, kind sir."

"I mean it."

"I know you do, you old fool."

"What's that meant to mean?"

THEY TALKED TOGETHER for half an hour. There were few other authors. Both had seen or read the other man's work. There was a bond between them.

Robert told Christopher about the death of eight-year-old Richard. About their quest. About Barnaby being unfit to inherit the title. It was difficult for Robert to explain himself without denigrating his younger brother in front of someone who was not a member of the family.

"Poor Harry," said Christopher. "Everyone in London talks about Barnaby and Tina behind his back. What you are saying is by no means news to me. I first met your brother in France during the war. He was in the trenches on a fact-finding mission from Palestine. Allenby thought the Turks might resort to trench warfare. That was before TE Lawrence raised the Arab revolt and attacked the Turkish supply lines changing everything. You can't fight trench warfare without a solid supply line. Sorry, old chap. I forget. Teaching my grandmother how to suck eggs. I heard about your foot from Merlin."

"Better to lose a foot than a head."

They both tried to laugh. The laughter had a false ring to it. Christopher looked away. Instinctively he looked for Brett. She was getting up from the Ramsbottom table with the chinless wonder. The pair moved off between the tables towards reception. Brett was going home. Mrs Ramsbottom looked distinctly crestfallen, which gave Christopher a good idea. Danny Hill was sitting in for him at the piano, doing a far better job. Christopher had managed to signal him from the bar when the new set had been due to start. Now the small dance floor was crowded. The band was trying the new song again to make it more familiar. The polite clapping when it came to an end was stronger the second time. Christopher gauged the increased applause professionally. It was important. He could write as many tunes as he liked but if the public did not catch on to them, want to hum them, they were no good.

"They liked it better the second time," said Robert, smiling.

"How did you know it was mine?"

"Had your signature all over it. Come on, I'm a writer. We all have a distinct fingerprint."

"You do want a table so you can eat tonight?" asked Christopher. "Some friends of mine would be happy for you and your brother to join their table."

"She's just left, you mean."

"You saw that too?"

Robert was giving Merlin, deep in conversation with Millie Scott, a fond look. "There will have to be enough room at the table for Millie... One of those three girls is quite pretty."

"They are from Yorkshire."

"Ah. Now I see the plot."

"He's rich. Very rich. Old yeoman Yorkshire family. Salt of the earth. Land in the family for generations. Sheep, lots of not very profitable sheep until they found coal, lots of coal, under the ground. Unlike some other countries in the world, in England the landowner owns what's under the ground as well as what's on top of it."

"You don't have to tell me, Christopher. She's pretty. Trouble is I'm too old for her."

"You are a bachelor, Robert, so never too old. Anyway, so many of the young chaps were killed in the war. Chaps that would be running after those three girls right now. For Mrs Ramsbottom, a husband with even an Honourable in front of his name is a good catch. For you, it's much better to have a young wife if you are going to have one... Prepare Merlin and Millie, I'll approach the Ramsbottoms... Oh, and they think of me as a lowly piano player not fit for their offspring."

"But do they know you are in love with Brett Kentrich?"

"You really don't miss anything."

"That's my job. I'm an observer. Then I write it all down and call it fiction."

PORTIA RAMSBOTTOM WONDERED if it could get any worse. Two old men and a middle-aged woman were being introduced to the table by the piano player who wasn't playing the piano for the time being. Portia was bored. Had been all evening. The show they had seen had literally sent her to sleep. The star of the West End stage had been so full of herself, Portia was only too happy to see her go and take the sycophant: the man had positively drooled over every word from the great Miss Kentrich. The man escorting the star had had a round face with big round ears and eyes like a puppy dog.

Portia turned her bored attention back to Christopher Marlowe.

"May I present Mr and Mrs Ramsbottom with their charming daughters Clarissa, Hermione and Portia? Miss Millie Scott, the comedienne for *Happy Times*? They tell me it is showing nightly at the Globe. With her are the Honourable Merlin St Clair and his brother, the Honourable Robert St Clair. Their father is the seventeenth Baron St Clair of Purbeck in the county of Dorset. Merlin here is the heir to the barony. So kind of you to ask us to sit down, Mrs Ramsbottom. Ladies and gentlemen, please take your seats. Unfortunately, I must repair to my work and play the piano or Mr Danny Hill will be claiming my wages from Miss Clara... So nice to have spoken to you all."

Portia's eyes bugged in amazement. The piano player her mother was so impressed by was not only bad at his music, he was behaving like a pompous ass, the little wink he gave her at the end of his dissertation an insult to her intelligence. Why were there no young good-looking men in London, as her mother was always promising her? At least in the Yorkshire countryside she was not bored as she was in London.

To add insult to injury, the freak with the two-colour eyes was putting a monocle in his dark eye to have a better look at her. When he turned the dark eye on Clarissa, Clarissa giggled, making Portia want to kick her under the table. Their mother was fawning even more than over the Kentrich woman. Portia sighed and sat back in her chair to be miserable.

The brother with two ordinary eyes had been put into a chair next to her. There was something wrong with his leg. He had difficulty getting his right leg under the table. She was nineteen years old, she told herself, sitting next to a man old enough to be her father, with a gammy leg and likely not a brain in his head. She doubted if he had ever read a book after leaving school. It was horrible. Perfectly horrible. Portia began to sulk.

"Sorry," said Robert. "It was Christopher's idea. And by the way, he did write *Happy Times* along with the tune they are now playing for the third time this evening."

"I like it."

"So do I. Now, can we try and be friends? I also live in the country. In Dorset. Something of a recluse. My younger brother dragged me up to London."

"There's another one?" said Portia in horror before she could control herself.

"I'm afraid so. He's the scallywag in the family. What are your interests, Miss Ramsbottom?"

"I read a lot. There isn't much else to do on the Yorkshire moors. I'm going to be a writer... Are you sure about the piano player?"

"Absolutely."

"Then what's he doing here?"

"He likes the atmosphere. He always wanted to be a bohemian. You want to be one of the Brontë sisters? We all want to be something other than what we are."

"Would you like to dance, Mr St Clair?"

"I can't, Miss Ramsbottom. And I did see your mother give you that look. You didn't have to suggest a dance."

"Why can't you dance with me, Mr St Clair?"

"Because my right foot was blown off by the Germans during the war."

"I really am sorry."

"Better than blowing off my head. All my brothers went through the war except the eldest, Richard, who was retarded and died young. Frederick, the next brother was killed in the war. His only son Richard has just died of typhus. Why the two old bachelors are out looking for wives. Have you heard of anything so ridiculous? Both of us are old enough to be your father. It was Christopher's idea. Something about all the young men who should be escorting you girls are now dead or married. Sorry. Now, which is your favourite book?"

"*Wuthering Heights.*"

"If only we could all write as well as Emily Brontë."

"They came from our part of the world."

"I know."

"Do you read books?"

"Sometimes... The other problem was the lack of a table. Write it down later as an experience. Two old codgers. Fact is, we weren't too bad before the war. Why Millie Scott over there is still in love with my brother."

"Is she his mistress?" whispered Portia.

"She was. He has another one now. The first one, actually. She went off and married a corporal during the war."

"Why isn't she with the corporal?"

"He was blown to pieces by a shell... Esther and Merlin have a daughter. Genevieve. He dotes on her."

"You are pulling my leg, Mr St Clair?"

"I wish I was."

"Tell me some more. Lots of some more. Then I'm going to make it all into a story and write it down when I get back to Yorkshire." For the first time since getting to London, Portia realised she was no longer bored. Forgetting the rest of them at the table, she prodded the man on to tell her his stories. Even between mouthfuls when his food came along.

"You're starving, aren't you?" she asked.

"Not in the direct sense of the meaning. But yes, I rather think I even forgot my breakfast. I have my own flat here in London on my own."

"And no mistress?"

"No mistress, Miss Ramsbottom. Not even a glimmer of hope. My brothers are the ladies' men. When they gave out charm, I was left on my own."

"I find you charming."

"Then what has happened to the old bore you were thinking of when I sat down?"

"How did you know?"

"I'm an observer. Of human nature. Not difficult when you get to know people. You can read their inner thoughts in their faces. All the real truths behind the mask."

"I want to know."

"You'll have to live a little longer."

"Where did you learn to read faces?"

"In the war. In the trenches. Everything the men thought about was an open book when you looked at their faces. The ability to read faces can sometimes be a curse. You learn things you don't want to know. Many things in life are better not spoken about. Our innermost secrets. If we already knew each other for what we really are, life would be a bigger disaster than it already is."

"Can I see you again, Mr St Clair? After tonight?"

"It will be my pleasure. But am I not so old?"

"You can love a man's mind as well as his body."

"I don't think I ever thought of that. That is rather a nice thought. You see, minds unlike bodies never grow old. My mind still thinks I am young. Only when I look in the mirror do I see grey hairs... But back to the stories."

"You are a wonderful storyteller."

"Why, thank you, Miss Ramsbottom. That is a very nice compliment."

BRETT HAD GONE HOME to the loneliest flat in the world. Everything reminded her of Harry: it was after all Harry's flat in the first place. Before he had deserted her and gone back to his damnable Africa, the last place in the world she ever wanted to go. Just the thought of a creepy-crawly sent shivers up her spine.

It wasn't a bad night standing on her balcony looking down on the mews. London around her was quiet. Mostly asleep, something Brett knew would be impossible for her even if she tried. The show brought her alive. Took a long time after the curtain went down to stop the adrenaline pumping through her body.

The family from Yorkshire had been just dreadful, the mother treating her like someone so marvellous, every word she spoke like a pearl of wisdom, which was all a lot of rubbish. Why did people behave like that when all she did was sing on a stage and talk a few words in between? She had felt like letting down her façade, telling Mrs Ramsbottom a few choice words on the subject of bodily functions and ending with her dead mother's favourite, 'we all look the same under a bus'. Brett hated being fawned over.

Made her put on her duchess act she had badly learnt in drama school. If nothing else, her grand performance in Clara's had annoyed the youngest daughter. The poor thing had not been impressed.

Brett would have gone home earlier were she not so hungry. Always after a good show, she was famished. To eat she needed a table and an escort. Poor fellow was another besotted idiot. If only her mother had taught her to cook and not spout lines out of bad plays and make her go to drama school. Brett knew she could not properly boil an egg. Either it ran all over the eating spoon or it was inside the shell as hard as nails. Toast, always, burned in her toaster. Her mind was elsewhere. She was domestically hopeless... Maybe her mother, as usual, had been right. She would have made a lousy housewife.

"I'm twenty-three years old and a bloody mess."

Having said that very loudly she looked down and hoped her neighbours were fast asleep.

Brett went back through the French windows into the bedroom she had shared with Harry and had a good cry on the bed. She felt sorry for herself. She had everything everybody else wanted. Nothing she wanted herself. She wanted Harry.

With the curtains blowing in the breeze from the open balcony doors, Brett finally found herself in the land of sleep. She was in Africa. The head of a large lion was looking at her from the depths of long, brown grass. Cold yellow eyes. The tail swinging and thrashing the grass. Ready to pounce.

Brett woke half an hour after falling asleep in a cold funk. The French window was banging. The room was dark. There was no one else in her life to turn to.

Only when the daylight came up through the closed French windows did she fall into a peaceful sleep that lasted right through to lunchtime.

Brett was hungrier than she had been after the show when she had gobbled her food in Clara's and run for the door.

For the first time in weeks, Brett pulled out her frying pan and fried herself an egg. She placed the funny-looking egg on a slab of bread, slammed another chunk of bread on top and ate hungrily, her improvised sandwich tasting perfectly delicious. Having finished she fingered up the spilt part of the yoke from her kitchen table and licked her finger.

Today she was going to phone Harry. Even if the bitch answered the phone, she promised herself.

"Why is it always worse in the middle of the night when everything is quiet?"

Brett Kentrich was feeling better.

. . .

AT FOUR O'CLOCK in the afternoon when Brett was phoning his Berkeley Square house and getting only Engelbert, the butler, Harry was sitting down to afternoon tea at the Royal Air Force club. He had waited downstairs five minutes for Ignatius Bowes-Lyon and left a message with the hall porter at the Piccadilly entrance. His friend was late, something unusual for a man who prided himself with always being on time.

Harry was more bored than usual with the day-to-day routine at Colonial Shipping where his managers did most of the work and took all of the decisions. Harry liked to delegate and then watch what he delegated. Two men could never do the same job properly. Many of his people were specialists and knew more about what they were doing than Harry. Harry supervised the overall direction of the firm founded by his grandfather: the old hands in the firm still referred to him as the Pirate behind Harry's back, the same old hands who thought of the young man from Africa running something he knew little about as something of a joke. The demise of the seaplanes had given them satisfaction and more than one look at Harry said 'we told you so'. Harry was quite happy to make mistakes and cut his losses before they really cost money. Fortunately, the shipping line that served the whole of Africa was making good profits and 'Harry's Folly' as he found out it was called, after his last trip back with Ignatius from Africa, was written off against income from the ships.

Harry had taken a table in the alcove on the first floor where the club's restaurant overlooked Green Park. It was five minutes later that Ignatius Bowes-Lyon joined him. There were two other members taking tea at separate tables. They both glanced at Ignatius striding through the room and went on with their tea. Ignatius was a tall man with the comfortable look of an aristocrat.

Harry looked up from his tea and smiled. They had been through a lot together in the war, he and Ignatius.

"Scones are fresh and the strawberry jam quite perfect. Never could make strawberry jam in Africa. Mother tried for years. Said it was to do with the fruit growing too quickly in the hot sun."

"Sorry I'm late."

"What kept you, Ignatius?" It had been a joke with them for years, Ignatius Bowes-Lyon's fetish for punctuality. In everything else, he was a normal male: drank too much when encouraged, told borderline jokes that brought down the house, even in female company. It was only his large fob watch and keeping his promise on time that kept him apart from everyone else. In the Royal Flying Corps he made his point by leaving the bar if his promised drinking companion was more than five minutes late, leaving the poor chap to drink on his own.

To Harry's surprise, Ignatius now looked flustered.

"Something wrong?"

"Not at all. Chap with the first taxi had a flat tyre," he lied. "Had to wait for a growler. Anyway, here I am... You think we can go down to the bar for a drink after tea?"

"Why ever not? What we do when we come to the club. The club bar opens as usual at five o'clock."

"Taking English tea at four o'clock is so civilised."

"Ten past four, old chap."

"Sorry, Harry."

"Think no more of it... You got something on your mind, Iggy?"

"Course not. Whatever gives you that impression?"

"You are fidgeting with your table napkin. You only did that at breakfast time, before we flew on dawn patrol."

"Am I really? I didn't notice."

'The bloody man can see straight through a brick wall,' thought Ignatius. 'Am I that obvious?'

He was sweating. He knew that. After walking up Piccadilly to the club on a summer afternoon instead of taking a cab. Which if he had done would not have found him in his present predicament.

Not far down the road from the club, as he was taking his constitutional by walking on the pavement instead of opposite in the park, which would have made him late by crossing the road into Green Park, he had seen a taxi stop outside the townhouse belonging to Barnaby St Clair. Before he could stop or hide, he had almost bumped into Harry's wife as she jumped out of the taxi and ran for the steps that led up to Barnaby's front door. She had seen and recognised him but not stopped in her flight. Barnaby himself had opened the front door. He had had to be watching from a window for his paramour. The front door had opened and quickly closed on Tina, Barnaby taking a swift look at the street. Like a thief.

Ignatius Bowes-Lyon's dilemma was whether to tell Harry. To be the teller of an appalling bad tale. To Ignatius, soliciting another man's wife was as bad as anything he understood. The chap was a rotter. Unless the meeting of the wife with the brother-in-law was a normal, prearranged visit. Harry would then think it odd him not mentioning bumping into Tina, who in innocence would tell Harry she had seen him walking down Piccadilly. Ignatius knew he was caught between the devil and the deep blue sea.

Ignatius had hurried off into the park to think out his problem, making him late, and still not providing him with a solution other than to say nothing.

When he thought that through, eating his tea, he knew nothing said by Tina would remove his predicament. Except he would then know for certain the Honourable Barnaby St Clair was a cad.

Ignatius took out his fob watch and looked at the time. He could barely wait for the bar to open downstairs.

ACROSS IN HYDE PARK, which could be seen from the Park Lane entrance to the club, Robert St Clair was sitting on a bench in the shade of a tall silver birch, unaware of Ignatius Bowes-Lyon's predicament caused by his brother. Robert would have taken off his prosthetic foot were it not for the need to take off his trousers to get at the straps as he did in the woods around Purbeck Manor. He had walked across from his flat, as was the daily habit that would bring him later to have drinks with Merlin at six o'clock. Neither man ever drank before six. It was another good habit. To Merlin, anyone who drank before six in the afternoon was a drunk.

The book was going badly. In fact, he had to admit, it was not going at all. Three months of wasted time that would have been better served in Dorset, working in his room. Except he was enjoying himself. He had had a jolly good time in London and never once felt lonely or bored.

"You deserve a rest. A rest will make the next book a real humdinger if only I could think of what to write."

Robert felt a small shaft of fear slice into his mind. What, he asked himself, if there were no more books? What would he do for the rest of his life? In panic, he got up from the bench overlooking the Serpentine and almost bumped into Portia Ramsbottom walking the other way all on her own.

"I say, what an extraordinary coincidence. It's Miss Ramsbottom, isn't it? Do you live around here?"

"No, and it is not a coincidence. I took a taxi from Brown's Hotel. You said last night you were a man of habit. That you walked from your flat every day to the same park bench overlooking the Serpentine in Hyde Park. At six, you join your brother for drinks. You may think me a forward little hussy but I do so want to be a writer. You can tell me so much. Your stories last night were spellbinding. You would never have wanted to see me again as you think I'm still a child. Can I sit down next to you?"

"I'm standing up," said Robert, who began to laugh.

"What's so funny?"

"When I do my plot thinking in Dorset," he said, forgetting he had deliberately not told her he was a writer, "which I do sitting on a series of conveniently fallen trees, I take down my trousers and remove my right foot. If you see what I mean. The straps won't undo with my trousers on. Let's both sit down. We are in public so it is still quite appropriate. Well, not the bit about removing a man's trousers. If you see what I mean?"

"For a man who is a writer and told me so many good stories in Clara's last night, I do believe you are tongue-tied, Mr St Clair." They sat down on the bench and both began to talk nineteen to the dozen.

FOR THE FIRST time in three months, Robert was late visiting Merlin. When he finally reached the Park Lane flat and went up in the lift, it was a quarter past six. Smithers, Merlin's man, opened the door to the flat.

"Mr Merlin is in the lounge with Miss Scott. How are you, sir? If I may be so presumptive you look very chipper today, Mr Robert... Please go on in."

Merlin, to Robert's surprise, did not mention he was late.

The first whisky tasted very good. With it came the first shadow of an idea for a book.

"Hello, Millie. How are you?" he said to her for the second time.

"You're chipper today, Robert."

"Just what Smithers just said."

Only after the third whisky an hour later did it dawn on Robert he was being naïve. How did she know he was a writer? He had not told her the night before. He had spoken of Christopher writing *Happy Times* but not about himself writing books. *Keeper of the Legend* was not even mentioned... They must have all known. Why they let such a young girl into a taxi without a chaperone. The young girl he had swooned over in the park was not interested in the old man. The parents must have thought him harmless with his grey hairs. Portia the girl had no interest in Robert the man. It made him go cold at the thought of his assumption. His stupidity. His vanity. Portia Ramsbottom, the aspiring writer, was interested in the author of *Keeper of the Legend*. The man of letters. Not the man. Not the man, he repeated to himself to make the point clear in his mind.

Millie Scott was looking at him with a peculiar expression on her face.

"What's the matter, Robert? Someone walk over your grave?"

"Not really. Just as bad. Far worse, in fact. I just made a fool of myself back in the park."

"What did you do? Drop your trousers?" She was indeed a good comedienne, Robert thought sarcastically. He had told them both his habit in Dorset. Millie had thought it funny. Merlin had frowned.

"Worse than that. I exposed my mind."

"To a young girl? Her name would not by any chance be Portia?... She wanted to meet you again, you idiot. Smile, Robert. I told her where you sit in the park. The exact branch. I told her you write lovely books. Don't be silly, Robert. She's interested in you, not your books. She told me so last night when you were off chatting to Clara. I set you up. Just hope her mother and father don't find out she was hobnobbing with a man who takes off his trousers in the woods to think... So what she's nineteen? My father was twenty years older than Mother. Without him, I wouldn't be here and I wouldn't have grown up among one of the rare happy marriages of life... You can give me a kiss on the cheek when I leave... Now, Merlin, I must go. The curtain goes up in an hour."

"Smithers has called a taxi."

"Why are you always so thoughtful? Maybe one more drink. I don't have to go on till the second act. I'm funnier a bit tiddly... That's better, Robert. You look chipper again. Don't they all say life begins at forty, which Merlin tells me you will be later this year?"

Only when Millie Scott finally left in a hurry to get to the theatre, did Robert put two and two together. Millie Scott had been in his brother's flat since the previous evening. She was holding a small overnight bag that likely held the dress she had been wearing in Clara's.

The front door closed. They both watched out the window in silence. Millie came out of the building with Smithers who opened the taxi door, handing in the small overnight bag.

"You old dog, Merlin. You've got two mistresses!"

"I'd like to marry her, Robert. We get on so well together. Have done for years and years."

"Then get on with it."

"Oh, I couldn't. She's a dancer."

"Won't be the first time one of our family married an actress."

"You think not?" Merlin said quizzically. "Let's have another drink."

"Why ever not? I feel marvellous. Tell you what, I'll take you out and buy you supper... I've got a new book coming, did I tell you that?"

AT THE END of the month, Ralph Madgwick called in for his cheque. It was ten o'clock in the morning and quite possible he was still drunk. He had brought a girl home from his last port of call in an unlicensed bar near the

Chinese quarter in Soho. They had sat up drinking in the flat, both drunk. Ralph had passed out in the chair with a hazy vision of the girl making her way to the door, clutching a one pound note she was going to use to get a taxi back to her own room somewhere in London. Ralph had no idea of her name. He had lost the first girl he had started off with somewhere along the way. Her name was Agatha, a prim and proper lady, unaware at the start of the evening of how badly he could behave. He had not tried hard to keep her. There was in his drunken memory a friend from the army who had taken her away who was a first-class chap. It was not Keppel Howland as it could not have been. Keppel was up at Oxford working hard and had never, to his knowledge, liked prim and proper girls. It must have been the challenge of converting a prim and proper into a slut that had made him take her out in the first place. He was, Ralph told himself, undoubtedly getting worse if that were possible.

Giving Rosie Prescott a leery smile, Ralph put his hand out. The door to the senior partner's office was closed. There was no sign of Uncle Wallace, who mostly came in an hour or two before lunch. The early start, even an early drunk start, was to avoid his Uncle Wallace while he executed the one and only important task of his month at Madgwick and Madgwick.

As usual, by the end of the month, he was broke. The first task after payday was to go round his friends and pay them back what he borrowed in the last week of the month. They thought him a good chap and did not mind he would be back with them in the last week of the new month. They knew about his cheque. They knew he would pay his debts.

Rosie was looking at him sadly. She was shaking her head.

"No pay without work this time, Ralph. Order of your Uncle Wallace... What about your agreement?... Don't you love her after all? Not even one day this month did you do any real work."

"But I don't have any money. Fact is, I owe the chaps ten quid, or was it twenty? Got a list if you want to have a look?"

"Your breath smells of whisky."

"I'd run out of brandy in the flat... What am I going to do, Rosie?"

"Sober up and do some work. Was eighteen months so long a time for someone you profess to love?"

"Yes... And I don't like America."

"You've never been there."

"She doesn't write. She has not written in weeks. Rebecca does not love me anymore."

"Her father stops her, likely. I would if I saw you now and the girl was my daughter."

"Not a penny?"

Rosie shook her head.

"I'm going home. Didn't get paid for today so I shall go home and sleep. The chaps will have to wait. Could you lend me five quid, Rosie?"

"No."

"What on earth am I going to do? I liked being rich. The girls liked me being rich."

"Find a way to get a letter to Rebecca. Tell her about the offer. Of going to New York in eighteen months. Then come to the office sober, on time and not smelling like a brewery... Do some work, Ralph!"

"Do I really smell like a brewery? How positively terrible... Why are you crying, Rosie?"

"Because you are such a damn fool."

"The war wasn't nice, you know."

"Oh, Ralph! Stop blaming the bloody war! It's over. Has been for eight years. Just grow up... Please!"

BACK IN HIS South Kensington flat paid for by Uncle Wallace along with the furniture, with Rosie's last words ringing in his ears, Ralph had a look at himself in the bathroom mirror. His eyes were red and puffy. There were red blotches on each of his cheeks. His hair was too long and all over the place.

"Where the hell were you last night, Madgwick?" he asked the debauched face in the mirror. The eyes were sad. He felt sad. He had no idea what to do. He felt sick. The sickness was alcohol, not food deep in his bowels. He was broke. In debt. No friends to speak of. Christopher had given him a lecture and told him to go to hell. His mother would throw him out of the Ashtead house. Keppel was up at Oxford. The idea of catching a train to Oxford to pour out his woes came to mind and left. He did not have the train fare.

"They've got you by the testicles this time," he said sadly to the mirror of himself. "She's right. The bloody war's long over... Nice girl, Rosie. Make someone a good wife... And she's right."

Before he could change his mind, he went to the liquor cabinet and took out the bottles one by one, pouring their contents down the kitchen sink. Then he went to bed and fell asleep on his stomach where he lay all day and most of the night. When he finally got up off the bed, his mouth felt like the bottom of a parrot cage. In the kitchen with the light on, Ralph drank pint after pint of water. Back in his bedroom, he lay on his back thinking of the leopard cave and Alfred tending the early morning fire in the mouth of the cave. He even thought he could hear the cry of the fish eagles down in the Zambezi River valley.

Next thing Ralph knew it was morning. In London. The traffic was moving outside. Someone was cooking bacon in one of the neighbouring flats. The smell of coffee came in with the bacon through the window he had left open day and night.

Ralph was more hungry than he had ever been before in his memory. In his kitchen, he found a tin of baked beans and an old, stale loaf of bread. There was an onion in an empty fruit basket one of the girls had left behind. They were the only ones who ever cooked. He found a bottle of olives in olive oil. Put oil in the frying pan and fried the onion, finally tipping over the open tin of baked beans that had cut his hand in the opening. Soaking slices of stale bread in olive oil on a breakfast plate, Ralph poured over the cooked mess and sat with the full plate at the kitchen table where he ate without looking up.

"That's the best meal I've ever had."

With the change he found in a trouser pocket in the cupboard, Ralph took the Kensington Tube, changing twice before reaching the City where he walked to his office and up the stairs to the third floor and sat down at his desk. Mr Postlethwaite looked at him amazed. Ralph smiled, his eyes crystal clear. It was half-past seven in the morning, an hour before Madgwick and Madgwick opened for business.

"I'm sorry, sir."

Ralph, for the first time since coming out of the army, told himself he was now ready to do some real work. After all, they had him by the testicles.

8

OCTOBER 1926 – FALLING LEAVES

*G*len Hamilton, the new editor of the *Colorado Telegraph*, looked at the unopened envelope on top of the morning mail. Somehow, the handwriting was familiar. An old, comfortable familiarity from a long time ago. He had replaced Matt Vogel the month before, Matt retiring after thirty years with the paper. The stamp on the envelope was without the name of a country, the head of a man in one corner.

"Why didn't you open this one, Freya?"

"Marked private."

"Then what are you waiting for?"

"To see what's in the letter."

"Then it won't be private."

"Only if you tell me what's in it."

"Have I ever told you how infuriating you can be, Freya?"

"All the time."

"How long have you been my personal assistant?"

"Oh, ten years, I think... Come on. Open the letter. It's from England."

"How do you know? The stamp?"

"Turn it over."

On the back was the name and address of the sender: Robert St Clair, Purbeck Manor, Dorset.

"He wrote *Keeper of the Legend*," said Freya.

"I know. I met his brother-in-law during the war. Was at the Salisbury railway station when Braithwaite shot her. And Tembo later shot Braithwaite... You remember?"

"The fighter pilots. We had it all over the paper. Weren't you trying to investigate another of Braithwaite's victims during the war? Sara Wentworth. Harry Brigandshaw was married to Robert's sister, Lucinda. Come on! Open the letter. Must be important. I met Robert when he came to America after Max Pearl published his book. Didn't you send Max the manuscript?"

"So that's it. You fancied Robert."

"Poor chap only had one foot. The other was blown off in the war."

Getting nowhere, Glen opened the letter. Inside was another letter sealed in an envelope addressed to a Miss Rebecca Rosenzweig. The handwriting, Glen noticed, was not that of Robert St Clair. There was no return address on the back of the envelope.

Glen read the short letter from Robert and smiled, putting down the letter on the pile of opened mail. To Freya, standing in front of the desk, the letter was upside down. Slowly, still smiling, Glen turned round the letter so Freya could read.

In the silence, Glen listened to the tick of the clock on his office wall while Freya read the three paragraphs. Then she smiled.

"Such a romantic. Such a romantic. Doesn't waste words. He wants you to go to New York, find this Rebecca girl and give her the letter from her lover without the father finding out. Robert thinks the father has been stopping Ralph's letters reaching Rebecca for months... There's much more to this than meets the eye."

"Most probably." Glen was giving Freya a queer look.

"When are you going, Glen?"

"I'm not. You are. You are going to find Rebecca and give her the letter from Ralph Madgwick. It will give you an excuse to write back to Robert and suggest he again visits with us in Denver. We can arrange a bit of a book tour. Or he can come out for the young lovers' wedding."

"You are so clever."

"That's why they gave me Matt's job when he retired. Now run along. You have a job to do."

"How do I find her?"

"Her father is a prominent Jewish banker, as you read in the letter. Go and see Max Pearl. He's Jewish. The way your eyes flashed at the idea of inviting Robert, I think you'll find her. Now on your way."

"Can I go now?"

"Wasn't that what I just said?"

"To New York?"

"To New York, Freya. All the way to New York. The newspaper will pay your train fare and expenses. Everyone in the world loves a romance."

"You can't publish her name!"

"We give them false identities. It'll still sell newspapers. We'll syndicate right around the world. There were some newspapermen in Salisbury, Rhodesia, I met after my visit to Elephant Walk, Harry Brigandshaw's farm. Did the same thing and made a name for themselves. Most of the best stories in the world start at provincial papers and spread."

"What happens if the father finds out we're promoting a match between Jew and Gentile?"

"Hopefully by then it'll all be too late and we can all go to the wedding... You do like weddings, Freya?"

"You are yanking my chain again!"

"Probably... Best of luck."

Glen was still smiling when Freya left his office with the letter to Rebecca clutched in her hand. He was remembering. The couple brought together by the *Rhodesia Herald* were happily married and living on Elephant Walk. The man, Jim Bowman, was the tobacco manager, the nurse, Jenny Merryl, the paper had searched for, was running a clinic for the local black people. The *Herald* had done a series of follow-up stories that was syndicated around the world.

"Simon Haller. That was the newspaperman's name. Now he should come to America. Whoever said travel opened the mind was right."

Glen was smiling and thinking. Even if they did not get a great story out of thwarted love, the expenses of Freya Taylor would be paid by the newspaper. After all, he was the editor of the newspaper. There had to be some perks.

"I can't do that, Freya," said Max Pearl to Freya Taylor three days later. They were in his office just off Broadway. "Rosenzweig. He's big. She's been introduced to every eligible young Jew in New York. If I interfere, they throw me out of the synagogue. You any idea what that would do to my business, Freya? Tell you what, for coming all the way from the great state of Colorado, I'll give you dinner at 21. All those celebrities. How does that sound? Robert is such an old romantic. Thinks life is like one of his books."

"She hasn't married one of the young eligibles?"

"I didn't hear so. No. She hasn't. The story about Rosenzweig bringing his daughter out of England to America is well known. Made him a hero among the Orthodox. Smoothed his American banking licence and residence. I would think with near certainty he's been intercepting her mail and censoring the wrong ones from England by dropping them in the fire."

Freya was looking at the portly Max Pearl sitting candidly behind his desk with his plump hands in view, the tips of the fingers joined in manipulative contemplation. He was bald with a black ring of hair just above his ears.

"They love each other," said Freya, pleading. "Doesn't that mean anything?"

"They'll get over it. Everyone gets over love. Usually when you are married to the bitch. Everyone, Freya. Everyone gets over love. It's a temporary insanity designed to make young men get married and before they hate each other have kids. Religion and society like nice little ordered families."

"You're a cynic, Max Pearl."

"I've had three wives."

"I'd love to have dinner with you."

"That's my girl... Tonight? I can swing a table. Some very famous writers on my list, including Robert St Clair... He owes me another good one."

"We all do, Max."

"What you mean by that?"

Freya was smiling. Men were so simple.

"At least you could tell me where Rebecca lives. Has she got a job? Where does she go? I won't mention a word to anyone."

By ELEVEN O'CLOCK THAT NIGHT, Freya had drunk a bottle of wine. She was enjoying herself. A sleuth reporter on the job. Max Pearl was as tight as a clam when she brought up Rebecca. By then it did not matter. The speakeasy was full and Max knew everyone. The co-owner of 21, Jack Kreindler, sat five minutes at their table drinking some of the wine that would have cost Freya a month's salary. Later, Ernest Hemingway sat at the table talking to her and ignoring Max Pearl. He was in his late twenties. Freya liked writers. She had just read *The Torrents of Spring*. She told Hemingway she had loved it. Freya liked writers who told the truth, she said. He invited her to his small room at the Brevoort. Max intervened and Hemingway went off to look for another iced daiquiri and another woman. Freya watched him go. Life was good for a young, successful man like Hemingway. She wanted Ralph Madgwick to be successful and Rebecca to have her one and only love forever. There had to be more to love than parting... The drink, Freya knew, was making her sentimental. Max was a dear but both knew she was not going to bed with him. She had found out one thing from Max that she thought came out by chance. Sir Jacob Rosenzweig had been interviewed by the *New York Times*. The financial editor had done the piece on Rosenzweig. It was enough for Freya.

Before she drank enough to have a hangover the next day, she asked Max to take her back to the hotel.

"It was a very lovely evening, Max." She meant every word.

"Maybe again sometime?"

"I'll ring you the moment I get back to New York."

In the years to come, she was to always remember meeting Ernest Hemingway. And whenever she thought of Hemingway, she thought of Max Pearl.

AT NINE O'CLOCK THE next morning in the offices of the *New York Times*, Freya Taylor learnt what she wanted to know. By then she had worked out why Glen had sent her and not gone himself to New York. She always wore sexy clothes. Always had the attention of men. Unlike Ralph and Rebecca, she had never been in love. By the time the financial editor took her down the history of the Rosenzweigs, she doubted she ever would. Love was for the very young. Before all the disappointments.

"They are German Jews. Two hundred and some years ago, the bank was founded in Berlin. Fifty years later, a branch of the family bank now run by Baron Evelyn Rosenzweig, opened in Paris. Sir Jacob runs the London affairs of the bank. Or did until he came to New York. We did the interview as a follow-up to Sir Jacob being granted a banking licence in the state of New York... How is Glen Hamilton? He deserved Matt Vogel's job. What's Matt doing with himself in retirement?"

"Fishing salmon up in Canada. The usual."

"He'll be bored in a week."

"He was... Did any of Sir Jacob Rosenzweig's family come to America?"

"Only one of them. A daughter. Hannah, I think her name was, stayed in London with the older children. Sir Jacob said he was moving his money out of Europe before this Hitler chap gets his hands on it. The grapevine says it was more about the young daughter. The Jews don't like their children marrying Gentiles, so I hear. Like to keep the race pure. Don't we all?"

"Does the girl work?" Freya had been about to use Rebecca's name and just stopped herself in time.

"I have no idea. He bought a luxury four-storey house overlooking Central Park where he lives quietly with the daughter. They say he only mixes socially with Jews... All this bit about Germany going down the drain is a lot of hogwash. We beat them good and proper. They won't get up again. Why should they? He's a good speaker, Hitler, I'll give him that, but that isn't enough. The Germans are good people. I should know. My family came over from Bremen, in 1793... Are you doing anything for dinner tonight, Freya?"

"I'll give you a ring. My schedule is tight."

"Why do you ask about Rosenzweig?"

"We at the *Colorado Telegraph* think you are wrong about Hitler. We think he's going to plunge Europe into a second world war."

She had had to think of something.

Five minutes later, she was down in the street and heading for the telegraph office. As she might have expected from a secretive banker, Sir Jacob Rosenzweig's telephone number was not listed. What she had seen in the office she had just left was a photograph of the man. The editor had found her the newspaper's article on Rosenzweig Bank. She had the back copy in her handbag. The article had described the banker as an aristocrat: a tall, thin aristocrat with a nose like a hawk's beak. The kind Freya thought of as predators. She hoped above all, in her quest to further one true love, she did not meet the man. Men like that gave her the shivers.

Freya also had in her handbag a pair of opera glasses that could fit into the palm of her hand. She headed for Central Park in a cab and found a bench. In the *New York Times* office, she had glanced down the long article only taking in the photograph with Sir Jacob Rosenzweig at the centre of the page.

The leaves were falling in the park. For the first time since arriving in the financial capital of America, she was conscious of the sound of the birds. An old man behind her at the side of the broad street was feeding his horse from a nosebag keeping one eye on the passing pedestrians for a fare. The old horse was still locked in the shaft, the buggy ready. Freya made up her mind to take a horse and buggy ride around the park if she found out what she wanted and luck was on her side. Once she found out where the Rosenzweigs lived, she could keep an eye on the entrance through her small binoculars.

The article she read did not give the address of the Rosenzweig apartment where it said the banker lived with his beautiful daughter but it did give the name of the fashionable block overlooking Central Park. Sir Jacob lived in an apartment, not a house. Freya Taylor's heart began to beat faster. She got up and walked across the grass to the pavement sending a squirrel up an elm tree, flashing its tail in alarm. The old man had finished feeding the horse. The old horse looked at Freya with doleful eyes that spoke of old age and pain. The horse was quite content to stay where he was.

"Do you know where to find the Abercrombie apartments? They say it's rather small." She gave the old man her best smile. He seemed as little interested as the horse. Her luck had run out: there must be hundreds and hundreds of apartment blocks overlooking Central Park. Even the ones stuck a bit behind would claim they overlooked the park when it came to talking to friends.

"Don't need me and old Nell for that, lady. You look right across the road you see the Abercrombie over there." The old man was pointing. "Sometimes I pick up on that side of the road. I keep the feedbag tied to the iron rail this side. She doesn't eat enough. Likes a beer at the end of the day."

"The horse?"

"Sure, the horse. Holds her head up sideways so I can pour the beer from the bottle down her throat. We both have one. Then we go home. Slowly."

Freya took the newspaper from her bag. It was folded at the Rosenzweig article. She found a dollar bill. With her thumb holding the bill next to the photograph of the banker, she showed it to the old man.

"You've seen this man?"

The old man removed the dollar bill from under her thumb and put it in his pocket. The horse had stopped looking at Freya. Freya put a second dollar bill under her thumb.

"You know what his daughter looks like?"

Again, the dollar bill was removed from under her thumb. Freya put the newspaper back in her bag.

"With Nell fed, you can wait the other side of the road?"

"That's right."

"Take me to the other side of the road where we can wait. You point out the girl, you get fifty bucks. No girl, twenty bucks. Old Nell here will give you a kiss with the beer at the end of the day. I'll even give you one if you point out the girl."

"What's she done?"

"Fallen in love. An Englishman. Her father doesn't approve. I want to put this letter from him in her hand. To make sure the father doesn't lay his hands on it. Then I'm going back to Denver."

"You came all the way from Denver to give a girl you don't know a letter? Lady, you're nuts. Get in... Come on, Nell. See how good you are today working your way across the traffic. Most people are good people, lady. They like horses. Give us room. I can smell that fifty-dollar bill as if it were right under my nose. She walks out every day to the park at eleven o'clock. That's in half an hour."

"How do you remember?"

"She's pretty. Real pretty. What's her name?"

"Rebecca."

"Pretty name. Real pretty. On Sundays, she walks the park with the old man in the paper. Eleven o'clock. Always took him to be the father."

HALF AN HOUR LATER, Freya was walking behind Rebecca towards the pedestrian crossing. People up ahead were waiting for the policeman to signal them across when he stopped the traffic.

Earlier, Nell had managed to cross the road and stand outside the Abercrombie. Freya had waited in the buggy. The old man had put up the top as much to make her less conspicuous as to keep out the autumn rays of the morning sun.

When the girl came out, even Freya knew it was Rebecca without being told. The small, dark girl had the most beautiful brown eyes Freya had ever seen. Full of sadness. She gave the old man the fifty-dollar bill, hoping it would not lead to her own crucifixion. She would not have anything to show for the expense in the form of a chit.

"Real pretty."

"Real pretty," Freya had agreed.

She had to walk quickly to come up close behind Rebecca to stand with her and the others waiting to cross the road. The policeman was wearing white gloves. Freya turned and smiled at Rebecca. The brown eyes smiled back and then the girl turned to look at the crossing that would take her into the park. The girl had a book in her right hand, a light cloak over her shoulders.

"Rebecca! I have a letter for you from Ralph."

"Who are you?" The voice was husky. No wonder Ralph was smitten. Freya quickly gave Rebecca the letter. The policeman had stopped the traffic. They were all about to walk.

"I hope it works out," said Freya.

"Walk with me into the park."

"Better not. Your father."

Freya turned as the pedestrians began to stream across the wide road, towards the calm of the park where the leaves were falling in the gentle morning breeze.

She walked back past the old man and the horse. Neither had moved.

The old man did not look at her. Further down Freya hailed a cab and went to her hotel where she packed her bags. The cab was still waiting downstairs and took her to Grand Central Station where she caught the first train that would take her back half across America to her home. She had never felt so sad in her life.

In the train, Freya decided not to write to Robert St Clair. They were older now. Too much older. Trying to make old embers spring to life had never worked before.

Sir Jacob Rosenzweig came home to Abercrombie Place at seven o'clock that night. He was tired and irritable. He had reached the new office in Wall Street at seven o'clock that morning. With all the undercurrents of fear among the Jews in Germany, many were trying to get their money as far away from Adolf Hitler as possible. The bank was swamped with work: the decision to open a bank in America was the best he had made in his life. The British knew as well as he did there was a terrible chance of another war with Germany. The way Sir Jacob read the news was the people in Whitehall were frightened. Some were calling for rearmament. In the British Parliament, they were trying to sweep the problem under the carpet, ignoring the warnings. Civil servants in Whitehall usually knew more than most politicians who only wanted to talk about the good news to keep themselves in office. The senior civil servants stayed in their jobs whichever party ran the government, unlike in America.

Within ten minutes of reaching home, he knew there was something wrong with Rebecca. She was keeping something to herself. Almost bursting with excitement to tell him. Putting aside all the problems of Europe, Sir Jacob smiled at his daughter. They were comfortable on their own. No Hannah to incessantly nag him and make him irritable. The apartment at Abercrombie Place was a small haven of peace. Somewhere in the Bible, he had read it was better to live on the roof than inside with a nagging wife. That was when the houses in Israel had flat roofs. Those old writers knew what they were talking about, he told himself.

The whole evening and the next day Sir Jacob waited for his daughter to tell him what was going on. Then it came to him like a bolt of lightning as they were taking their walk together in Central Park. It was the best part of his week. Somehow, despite all his efforts to stop it, his daughter had received word from Ralph Madgwick in England.

"Is he here in America?" Sir Jacob asked his daughter. He could feel his temper rising. He had enough problems for one man.

"No, Father. He's coming in a year's time."

"How do you know?"

"A girl gave me a letter in the street from Ralph yesterday."

"Who was she?"

"I don't know. She walked away when I crossed into the park. She knew my name. I'm sorry, Father, I should have told you yesterday."

"The one thing you did not do to me, Rebecca, was lie. You have never lied to your father. Just never lie to me. There are enough problems in my life without being lied to by my family." Rebecca had put her hand lightly on her father's elbow. The gesture always calmed him down.

THE VOYAGE to America on the MV *Glasmerden* had been the worst journey of his life. The small cargo ship had rolled and pitched its way across the Atlantic to the port of St John's in Newfoundland where the captain had been taken sick. They had waited a month in the freezing cold port for a new captain they were told was being sent to them from Liverpool. None of the other officers had a master's ticket. Even the cod fishing boats stayed in port most of the time. The sea was frozen around the coast and gales lashed the shore. It gave them both the time to recover from the debilitation of chronic seasickness.

When the new captain finally arrived and took the ship out of the harbour, father and daughter both had a great fear of the swells. The gulls' calls over the head of the departing ship were like cries from hell. The new captain was a man of few words at the dining table. There was some animosity with the ship's engineer that was felt by everyone on board though no one said a word aloud. Five days later, after first hugging the shore of Nova Scotia and then America, the ship sailed into New York harbour.

They were moored at an obscure dock where the dockers were on strike. The crew had to carry their baggage off the ship into a shed that had more open doors than a barn. The cold wind whipped through the shed where Sir Jacob waited two hours for a man from customs to look at his luggage. Having packed in a hurry before leaving his home in London, there were only five suitcases between the two of them. The man, who seemed to double up as an immigration officer, had taken Sir Jacob and Rebecca's passports. The strike had produced a lot of bad tempers.

"Here you are, Jake," said the man giving him back their passports. Sir Jacob bridled and looked at the man. There was no malice in the man's words. "What kind of name is 'sir'?" asked the American.

"It's a title. I'll have you know I am a knight of the realm."

"We kicked all that out long ago, Jake. Welcome to America. Your daughter? Good. We need some good-looking broads in New York. My brother says some of the trash that arrives here should be thrown back in the sea. What are you doing in America, Jake?"

"I've come to open a bank."

The man gave him a different look.

"Better open the bags. What you got in there to open a bank, Jake?"

"I have a bank in England."

"You have a bank in England and you travelled on that rust bucket out there on the quay? Lucky to get here. Go on then. You're free. Do what you like. Start a bank. Everyone does something when they come to America, Jake."

"It's Sir Jacob, my good man."

"Not in America, Jake... Have a nice day."

The man winked at Rebecca who giggled. Even if her father was unaware of it, the man from customs was pulling her father's leg. At that moment, Rebecca knew she was going to like living in America.

THE LETTER from Ralph Madgwick was in the handbag Rebecca took with her to the park. It was the only English habit she had not left in London. Without her little bag, she felt naked. The idea of anyone snatching her bag on Hampstead Heath had never crossed her mind.

Rebecca had read the letter many times after first sitting down on a bench in the park. She was far more interested in reading the letter and wondering how the person knew who she was; the American woman who had put it in her hand just before the policeman waved them across the road.

Having now told her father she had the letter, her dilemma was letting him read what it said. He would have either to lie to her or admit to destroying so many of Ralph's letters. She had only stopped writing when Ralph stopped writing back, thinking men fickle. There had been two letters from Ralph and then silence. Both had been waiting at the bank in Manhattan her father had given as their forwarding address.

Once Rebecca wrote back after the terrible voyage out from England, she gave Ralph the address of Abercrombie Place. The porter at the reception desk downstairs took in all the mail. There were only ten apartments in the block. Like a men's club, her father had explained, the mail was only handed by the porter to the owner of the flat. As Rebecca had never been inside a men's club she always let her father collect the mail.

Now it was clear from the letter in her bag that dozens of Ralph's letters had never reached her hands. For two months, Ralph had written to her every day. Rebecca was not sure which would hurt her father most: not being shown the letter, or knowing she knew he had destroyed so many letters. If he had only told her at the time he was not going to let her read Ralph's letters, she might have understood. She was not yet twenty-one. Her father had complete authority over her affairs. Thinking Ralph had forsaken her had made it all so much worse. Two men she loved, fighting over her love.

With a supreme effort of will, Rebecca kept the letter from Ralph tightly in her bag, while gripping the bag on her knee where she sat next to her father on the park bench, the people scuffing at the autumn leaves on the ground with their feet as they passed by the bench.

SITTING NEXT to his daughter on the bench, Sir Jacob knew perfectly well the letter he wanted to read, so he would know how to take countermeasures to prevent a catastrophe, was in his daughter's small bag she was fidgeting with on her knee. If the boy was coming to America then likely he was being sent. Sir Jacob knew Ralph had no money to speak of that he could call his own.

They sat in silence for a long ten minutes, each waiting for the other. Then Sir Jacob got up, having made up his mind to drop the matter from all future conversation. A year was a long time. There were many more girls in London who would catch Ralph's eye. If neither brought up the subject of the stolen letters, the matter did not exist. He could still stop Ralph's future letters reaching his daughter.

"Come along, my dear," he said brightly. "It's a beautiful day. I feel like a good long walk after being cooped up in the office all week. Tell me what you have been doing?... The new flowers in the flat are so beautiful. You arrange them so well... Where do you get them from, my dear?"

"A nice little florist I found, Father. Yes, a nice long walk will be just what we want. The brown and red colours of the leaves are so beautiful at this time of the year. They say it gets very cold in January in New York. We were lucky to arrive at the end of February. My friend in the flower shop tells me the worst of the winter is over by the end of February. Let's make the best of a walk while we can."

.   .   .

When Rebecca wrote back to Ralph the next day, she gave the name of her friend at the flower shop, along with her friend's home address. Her friend Maryanne knew all about Ralph Madgwick. They were both the same age with almost the identical problem, except that Maryanne was a Christian and her boyfriend, Shaul, a Jew.

When Maryanne had finished reading the letter from Ralph, there were tears in her eyes.

"He sounds so lovely. All those months will fly by like the rushing of the wind. They always do when you are in love. Rebecca, I'm so happy for you. So happy. It tells me all will be well with Shaul after all. This is America, the land of the free. You just see. We'll all be best friends. Have apartments next to each other. Our children at the same schools. Aren't you excited, Becky? I'm so excited. Come back at my lunchtime and we'll go for coffee... I love your Ralph already."

"Fifty bucks!" said Glen Hamilton to Freya Taylor in Denver on the Wednesday. "You gave an old man with a horse and buggy fifty bucks!"

"Fifty-two to be exact. A buck for recognising the photograph of Machiavelli, a buck for telling me he knew what the daughter looked like and fifty bucks for pointing her out."

"Thought you'd be gone a month."

"Now you tell me. I was enjoying myself. Max Pearl looks like a friendly pudding but he's better company over dinner than most men I've seduced."

"You seduce men, Freya?"

"Always. Had a chance with Ernest Hemingway but Max spoilt the fun. He went off with an Italian-looking girl with a face right out of Botticelli. Max said the girl was Legs Diamond's girl. Max knows everything and everyone. Legs Diamond was due back in New York the next day. Jack Kreindler who owns the joint told Max he was going to tell Ernest. Before he got himself killed... You ever been to 21, Glen?"

"All the time I'm in New York. Did you seduce Max?"

"Don't be ridiculous. Just because a man's good fun you don't have to take him to bed."

"You must be sick of trains."

"It was beautiful. Clickety-clack across the heart of America. All these new aeroplanes are going to take the fun out of long-distance travel. All the autumn shades of brown and red. All the leaves on the trees ready to fall. Fall is the most beautiful time of the year in America."

"You going to write and tell Robert St Clair?"

"No, I'm not. Old embers don't burn bright. It was years ago. Why do we always think of things that happened to us years ago are so much better than what is happening to us now?"

"Write out a chit for the fifty-two bucks. I'll sign the expense."

"Are we going to write an article?"

"Of course you are."

"I'm not a journalist. I'm your assistant."

"Now you are a journalist. Part of the time. Put it all in. The policeman with white gloves. Meeting Hemingway. The Botticelli girl. The Machiavellian father. All of it except Legs Diamond."

"Won't he recognise the Italian?"

"The Legs Diamonds of this world don't read. You'll have a monthly column. A pseudonym. How about 'Juliet'? Each month you will tell our readers of a lover in distress. A love story to cut to the heart. You, Freya, are going to lighten all the women's hearts in Denver. Maybe, just maybe, far beyond. Love is the only thing in life worth having, did you know that?"

"How long have you been married to Samantha?"

"All my life... Well done, Freya Taylor, newspaper reporter... Now leave me alone and let me do some work... You sure about Robert?"

"Absolutely."

"You don't like him anymore?"

"Of course I do, he's a writer. And a very nice man."

"Out you go."

"I'm gone."

GLEN SAT at his desk smiling to himself. Then he picked up the handset of his telephone. The operator answered.

"Put me through to telegrams. Thank you...I want to wire England. The address is Purbeck Manor, Dorset, England... Yes, just that. Last time I heard the house had been where it was for hundreds of years. In the same family. Send it to Robert St Clair. Message reads: '*Letter of love delivered to safe hands, stop. When are you coming out again to America, stop. Freya Taylor sends her love, stop. Glen Hamilton.*'"

Glen was still smiling when he put down the telephone receiver.

"One good deed deserves another," he said happily.

Only then did he get down to doing some work.

'Clickety-clack. Clickety-clack. She really is a good girl. Positive jewel,' he said to himself. 'Poor old Max Pearl. All that money and nothing to show for it.'

. . .

THE TROUSERS WERE off the prosthetic foot with the leg straps resting on the ground among the golden leaves. Across the pond in Dorset, the autumn leaves were falling just the same.

The new book was writing easier in the country with no interruptions to Robert St Clair's mind. Sitting on the fallen tree thinking through the plot was quite comfortable now his foot was off and resting on the ground. Robert had walked from the Manor house to the same small wood where his brother had fathered Harry Brigandshaw's young son, Frank. Only Barnaby, Tina and the trees knew what had happened back then.

It was a perfect autumn afternoon with the leaves falling from the trees all around him. It all made Robert feel so much at home. So much an intrinsic part of it all. They had been around, the same old trees, so long. Many of the big old gnarled oaks had grown from the earth before the Norman Conquest. The symbiosis of centuries, the giant trees sheltering the moss below and all the small life that lived in them. Insects. Birds. Squirrels. A bat or two. To Robert sitting on his log, it was all it meant to be, an Englishman at home in his wood, content at peace, the storyline of his new book running in and out of his mind. Never once did he try to think. Pictures of the people popped into his head and began to talk, telling Robert what to write.

So often, he had tried to explain the process to Portia. He was her mentor. Just her mentor. There was nothing else despite the wishful hopes of Millie Scott. The girl had only just turned twenty. Still twenty years his junior. Robert had now turned forty. The start of middle age. His mother had told him on his birthday it made her feel old. Little comfort.

London had grown too hot. Too stuffy. Too full of people all talking at him at the same time. All with their own agendas. The break away from Stanhope Gate had been good for stimulating his mind despite his grumbles. Man liked company. Robert knew that. It was just so nice to get away again and keep the company of wild animals that never interrupted all the thoughts rushing in and out of his mind. He was happy and that was good. The horrors from the war had mostly left him. Even his right foot, the one that was missing, left in France, had stopped itching in his mind.

Neither he nor Merlin had found themselves wives. They were both far too set in their ways to try something new. Getting to know another person was better done when young. Merlin was comfortable around Millie Scott. There were no surprises. Even being milked by Esther and his daughter

Genevieve for every material comfort they could think of, was comforting in its regularity.

They were all creatures of habit, like the pair of squirrels he had been watching for an hour stashing away the acorns in a hole beneath the one big above-ground root of the great oak tree that gave Robert shade from the autumn sun. They were grey squirrels not indigenous to the island. The tree rats with their curly furry tails were increasingly problematic as they were bigger and stronger than their red cousins were. Robert sighed. Even among nature's beauty lurked the pain of life. The good for one making the bad for another.

Robert heard a dog-fox bark from somewhere in the wood. It was time to go home. The day was going. Time to make the first fire of winter in his room.

His mother had said there would be muffins for tea, dripping in fresh farm butter. Gently, Robert pulled on his artificial foot, tightening the straps. It was not really so much an inconvenience. Then he pulled on his trousers.

Smiling, Robert got up and without the help of a stick began his walk home to the Manor, making his way beneath the falling leaves. The pigeons were calling to each other from all over the St Clair acres. His father's cows sitting in the field by the small river, chewing the cud, took no notice of him as he passed. The smell of field and woodland was swirling all around him. The soft scent of flowers. The rich smell of the grass broken by the cows. The smell of cow dung sweet in the gloaming at the end of an English autumn day.

In the kitchen, his mother gave him the telegram delivered in its brown envelope from the post office in Corfe Castle village. Robert read Glen's words and smiled.

"Freya loves me," he said to his mother, giving her a small kiss on the cheek.

"I thought it was Portia... What was that for?" She had touched her cheek with her right hand.

"I felt like it... Is Father back from his darling pigs?"

"In the sitting room. The fire's going. He's waiting for the pot of tea and the muffins."

"So am I."

"The boy said the telegram was from America. Is there anything wrong?"

"Nothing at all. Cupid struck right where he was wanted."

"You are talking nonsense again, Robert."

"Not all nonsense is nonsense, Mother dear... Believe me."

"Are you going to America now?"

"Probably. Yes, I rather think I shall take a trip on the RMS *Olympic* to America. To Denver, Colorado to be exact. Why not? I'm forty. Life begins at forty. Of course, I will need a train for the last part of the journey from New York."

"Now you are just talking rubbish... Robert, please carry the tea tray."

The old cook Robert had known all his life had been sent to her room to rest. Robert picked up the laden tea tray and took it to his father.

GERT VAN HEERDEN, the stage director of *Happy Times*, answered the knock on Christopher Marlowe's attic door. Christopher was away in Ashtead, a duty visit to his widowed mother. This time Gert and Christopher had not gone walking in Ashtead Woods. Somehow, there was something missing from the time of their poverty when a vegetable soup with three shin bones cooked on the single ring was luxury itself.

Gert had let himself into Christopher's room looking for some of that magic. There was none there. Just an attic room with the one big window looking out over London roofs. In comparison to then, they were both now rich. Christopher was certainly rich. Because Gert still lived in the same old building off Shaftesbury Avenue, he spent only half his wage from Oscar Fleming, the impresario and producer of the show. He did have a larger room on the same floor, this time with a window. The box room where he had lived with his dog in poverty was a box room again, full of junk. The dog still slept in his bed when Jane Tamplin was not staying the night, the dog miffed when turfed onto the carpet. Jane loved Heinz 57, but even Jane drew a line at three in a bed when one was a dog. Heinz 57 was so faithful to Gert, he poured emotion and love out of his eyes. The dog had big eyes, big, floppy ears and a long snout. No one Gert had asked could tell him which of the many breeds made up the dog's ancestry.

A small boy was standing in the doorway when Gert opened the door. Gert was due at the theatre in two hours; it was only a short walk from the attic. The boy was holding out a small brown envelope. A telegram.

"You Christopher Marlowe, mister?"

"Yes," said Gert, taking the envelope. Telling a small lie was easier than having to explain. The boy waited. He was looking expectantly at Gert. Gert found a penny in his pocket and gave it to the boy.

"Thanks, mister."

It was the first time a telegram had been sent to Christopher. Gert opened the envelope. He could hear the boy go off down the stairs whistling, the stairs creaking as the lad went down.

. . .

LETTER DELIVERED TO REBECCA. I AM GOING TO AMERICA ON
RMS *OLYMPIC.*

GERT SMILED. The sender had not bothered to sign his name. Maybe, Gert
thought, famous writers were not required to sign their names to telegrams.

Gert's first instinct was to go and tell Ralph Madgwick. Ralph would be
at the offices of Madgwick and Madgwick now he was behaving himself. It
had been Christopher's condition for asking Robert St Clair to send the
precious missive to Glen Hamilton in America. Even Harry Brigandshaw
had known Glen Hamilton during the war. The world according to Gert's
view of it was smaller than everyone thought. A man at the theatre had
delivered a verbal message from Gert's mother in Cape Town only the other
day. She had still not made a trip to England despite his father's suggestions.

"What if the girl doesn't want to write back?"

Hearing the voice of his master, Heinz 57 looked up at him with
enquiring eyes.

"Walk?" said Gert. The dog always wanted to go for a walk.

The whole dog wagged. They went out of the room, leaving the open
cable on the small table. Christopher would guess he had opened the
envelope. At least it was not a crisis. Christopher could decide later whether
to tell his brother the news. Love had as many changes as spots on an
African leopard; when it came to love, he told himself going down the old
stairs with the dog following behind, it was better not to interfere.

Down in the street, the broad leaves from the plane trees were falling on
the pavement. All were red.

"Would you like to go and live in Africa?" he said to the dog. The dog,
with its leg up against the mottled trunk of a plane tree, took no notice. Jane
wanted Gert to go back to Africa. She was always asking him when he was
going. She had heard from someone his father was rich. Before, she did not
want anything to do with Africa or a permanent relationship... Love really
was for the birds. Poor old Christopher still swooning over Brett Kentrich
the star of the show and Christopher getting nowhere. As Gert understood
it, Harry was paying Brett visits. Like he used to do. He had, so they told
Gert, paid for the flat off Regent Street anyway.

Idly kicking the leaves, Gert wondered what his Uncle Johan would say
to him bringing back an English girl. His Uncle Johan hated the English.
Likely, he would show Jane his Boer War Mauser rifle that Uncle Johan

notched seven times, each time after shooting an Englishman. Maybe it wasn't just love in life that was so bizarre. One day he was going to properly direct a musical and not be told what to do every time by Oscar Fleming. Largely all Gert did was paint the sets and keep them moving smoothly between scenes during the performance. Poor old Christopher. Even Oscar Fleming had had an affair with Brett Kentrich. Once women knew a man really wanted them with no eyes for anyone else they treated them like dogs. Worse than dogs. Gert had Heinz 57 on a long lead. The dog was sniffing at everything. Far better off than Christopher Marlowe. The moment Christopher found someone else and was no longer interested in Brett, she would come running after him. It was the way of things. People always wanted what they could not have. Rarely appreciated what they had.

As he walked the dog, Gert was trying to think of a way of taking out another girl in the chorus line, the irony of his own thoughts lost completely on him. Her name was Sylvia and she had very large breasts.

Gert had to bring his mind suddenly into the present. Heinz 57 was trying to wind the lead around a lamp post. Gert shortened the lead and kept a firm grip on the dog.

His mother would tell him to make his mind up once and for all and settle down. In Africa. In the Cape of Good Hope. Thinking of that for a second, Gert found he was homesick, making him stop suddenly in his tracks and half throttle the dog. He could see the Cape Dutch farmhouse in the Franschhoek Valley as clearly as if he was seeing his family home through his own eyes. It was spring in the Cape. The trellised rows of vines were just beginning to bud. Behind the barn-like farmhouse, he could see the mountains in his mind's eye. They were blue and very beautiful.

THE MADGWICK BROTHERS had left Murray Court in Ashtead on the Sunday morning just when the sun was coming up. It was the day after Gert had opened Christopher's telegram from Robert St Clair. The brothers, nine years apart in age and looking nothing like each other, had filled their haversacks with sandwiches and walked the mile from the family home to the level crossing half a mile from Ashtead station where Christopher and Gert in the old days stepped off the train from London with the Madgwick family picnic basket. Christopher would have brought the basket finally restored to his mother, but the brothers intended to walk the woods and out the other side as far as Chessington Hall. Carrying the basket that far would have been awkward. It was the first time the siblings had gone into Ashtead

Woods alone together. Growing up, a man of eighteen and a boy of nine were poles apart.

By the time they walked into the woods, Christopher was thirty-four and Ralph turning twenty-six on the 11 November. Ralph had celebrated the armistice that ended the war with Germany on his eighteenth birthday in France. By then he had lost his small finger to a German shell fragment. After that, with Christopher a captain in the Royal Dragoon Guards, the brothers had more in common. By the time they sat down under one of the oldest oak trees in England, they had a lot in common, particularly Madgwick and Madgwick, the family shipping and confirming house, which up till then neither had wanted to join with any conviction. Now Ralph was going to catch the eight-ten train to Waterloo the next morning. Life had changed for both of them.

"You think she got the letter, Christopher?"

"You got my name right!"

Christopher had done his best getting Robert St Clair to write to his old friend Glen Hamilton in America asking Glen to deliver Ralph's letter into Rebecca's hands. Now it was in the lap of the gods.

Christopher let the question hang in the air. The leaves were falling from the trees. The moss was springy and soft under his bottom. The tea from the flask was just how he liked it.

Christopher looked across at his brother who was looking miserable. No one who did not know them had ever accused them of being brothers. Christopher was dark-eyed, dark-haired and slim from years of food deprivation in the attic room off Shaftesbury Avenue. He was slim and willowy tall. Posing as a poet had been easy. All bohemians were meant to be slim and slightly consumptive so when they died young their poetry would live forever. Why they wrote the poetry or painted the canvases knowing the shortness of life. Ralph was very different. He was thickset. Well built. Blond. More blond after he came back from Africa where the African sun had seemed to bleach his hair almost white forever. His eyes were blue, his hands practical.

"Did you like Africa?" asked Christopher, sipping his tea from the plastic cup that unscrewed from the top of the thermos flask.

"Sitting up there on the edge of the Zambezi escarpment was like being God until Harry flew his aeroplane out of a clear blue sky one morning. Imagine that. A converted wartime bomber in the middle of Africa. There we were with Alfred looking down over the shrouded valley of the most exciting river in the world. Thinking about it makes me want to go back but that's all over now... Why do we see that one woman and love her so much?... It wasn't lust this time. Love. You know we have only kissed each other gently on the lips. She'll write, won't she? It was the same for both of us. It had to be. There was so much feeling. You can tell me, Christopher... Why is there just one woman who is so different from all the rest?"

"I've never even kissed Brett."

This time Ralph stayed silent. He was again thinking of Africa, wondering what had become of Alfred and the family of leopards. Keppel he knew was still up at Oxford. They had drifted apart. Africa and Rebecca drifted in and out of his mind.

"Strange how people so close just drift apart," said Ralph.

"You think I'll just drift apart from Brett?"

"I was thinking of Keppel Howland. In the hols, he goes to his family in the Isle of Man. We don't even write. All those years at school together and then in the army... You think I could ever drift apart from Rebecca?"

"Our parents did. Except when we were around I don't think they spoke to each other apart from the trivial. Most married people end up talking trivia. Did you know in the end they had separate bedrooms? Now Mother is so lonely she is beside herself... We were lucky, you and I, to be given life. Poor Mother had so many miscarriages. No wonder it sapped their love. Could you hate someone for doing that? For giving you the wrong seed or having the wrong womb to bring the child to term?"

"You know a lot about giving birth."

"Mother was telling me. Like a floodgate. I just sat and listened while she cried. Maybe we should try and get to know her better."

"I've never really spoken to Mother," said Ralph, "not about anything important. Like feelings."

"Neither had I... I hate coming down to Ashtead."

"Poor Mother."

"There's a price to pay for everything."

"Did you ever think of me as a brother when I was a child?"

"Not really... There could have been a whole tribe of us. All those brothers and sisters dead before they started life."

"That would have been fun. One of them might have really liked being a shipbroker living in Surrey and catching the eight-ten train to Waterloo every morning for fifty years. Living in a row of expensive houses. Suburbia."

This time they both lapsed into silence. Neither wanted to talk about their responsibilities to the firm. What other people called their duty, like going to war. The price they were obliged to pay for their privileged births. Their education at an expensive school.

Eventually, they got up and walked further into the woods, comfortable in each other's company. Christopher rather thought he liked his younger brother after all. Ralph during Christopher's early life had been a pest. He had called his brother the sprog just to see him get annoyed. To make him go away. Ralph was then always hanging around his elder brother, complaining he was bored. As if it was Christopher's job to keep Ralph amused.

"What are you smiling about?" asked Ralph.

"You. I think if I called you a sprog now you would knock me up that bloody tree... Do you think I am being selfish? Not joining the old family firm?"

"You have a great talent."

"No, I don't."

"You make thousands of people happy watching your show. That's a talent. A lot of people just make other people miserable. They come and see *Happy Times* and smile for weeks. I know. People have told me that many times."

"That's the most beautiful compliment I have ever received."

"Leave Madgwick's to me. I have no talent except for chasing showgirls and that gets boring in the end. It always ends up just the same. They all merge into each other. Meaningless. Pointless. Pointless for everyone."

"Maybe you'll grow to like being a high-flown executive. Some people like power. To them writing a silly musical would be a complete waste of time. They want money. Lots of it. And power."

"I never thought of power."

"Think of it, Ralph."

"Making money just to be powerful!"

"That's the stuff."

"How positively awful."

"Then think of providing lots of people with jobs. Linking the world by trade, not through force of arms. Helping lots of people through their lives who like being told what to do. Do you know, underneath most people like to be told what to do in a safe job with a weekly wage? That way they don't have to think."

"Have I told you about my leopard cave where we lived in Africa? The three of us: Keppel, myself and Alfred? Alfred was a black man we picked up as a guide in Salisbury. That's the capital of Southern Rhodesia."

"No, you haven't. Then I had better sit down again."

"Please do. I'm going to have a sandwich."

"You've only just had your breakfast."

"Then, I want to hear all about the new show you are writing."

"Then I had better have a sandwich."

They were both laughing when they took off their haversacks and put them under another tree where the moss was growing thick. A rich green moss covered in autumn leaves. When they got down with their backs against the broad girth of the oak tree, a rabbit was watching them from out of the bracken on the other side of the bridle path that would lead them out of the woods, half a mile down the tunnel through the trees.

"Do you really think most people don't want to think?" asked Ralph.

"Bertrand Russell says most people would rather die than think. And many of them do."

"He's a philosopher. They like saying things that sound interesting. To impress."

"You are probably right... It may not even have been Bertrand Russell."

RALPH FOUND the telegram from Rebecca under the front door of his South Kensington flat when he went home from the office the following evening. The day at the office had been boring as usual. He thought he had learnt something for the long task ahead of him, which was something. He had put the information in a separate part of his brain. Where he had stored information to survive the war in the trenches. The other parts of his brain he kept for the more important matters. If there wasn't anything more important than survival, which Ralph hoped with all his heart there was, then there wasn't any point in going through it at all.

"I love you, Ralph," it said. Four small words that meant more to Ralph than surviving the war or running Madgwick and Madgwick.

His depression lifted. The year would not be long. Intense happiness flooded his entire body.

"There's going to be a point to it, after all," he said clutching the telegram and shutting the front door with the back of his foot. The brown envelope he had ripped open had floated down onto the wooden floor where it stayed.

9

APRIL TO MAY 1927 – LOVE ON THE BANKS OF THE RIVER

Stella Fitzgerald was happily aware of being a first-class bitch. She had come to London in the spring for the summer grand tour of Europe. Provocatively attractive or dominantly beautiful as the moment required, she had cut a swathe through upper-class English society. Stella was twenty-two years old and from Boston, her father spinning money on Wall Street the way Barnaby St Clair played the stock market in London. The spring of 1927 in London was a hedonist's paradise with the money dance becoming ever more frantic as the stock markets of the world went up and up.

Old Patrick Fitzgerald, Stella's father, ran liquor from Canada across the border into the States hoping the fools who called themselves politicians would not change the law of prohibition. The American government banning the sale of liquor had been, for an Irish nationalist with balls, the laugh of the century. From trade unionist, to managing the union's pension fund, to a bootlegger richer than half of Ireland in one lifetime, was the old man's boast when he was drunk. His son, Stella's brother, was already a small-time politician with better things in mind for the Fitzgerald family. Seamus was going to make the family name really big in America. Stella, according to her father's instructions was to marry well. In Europe. To the eldest son of a duke if she could find one. The idea of sending money to Ireland to fight the damn British and his daughter to England for him to buy into the British aristocracy, was sweet irony to his peasant's ears. It was his revenge twice over for being born poor with only his wits to get him through a material world.

The three pillars of her father's life were Money, Power and the Catholic Church, in that order, Stella always told herself in the brief moments of self-appraisal.

"Every damn wop's a duke in Italy looking for money from a woman. There are French dukes. Belgian counts. Spanish dukes. German princes. None are any damn good. Don't mean a thing, my darling girl. The only throne that lasted was the throne of England. That's the one I like. The one with meaning. My daughter a duchess married to a British duke. Now that's sweet thinking. Then we'll see our Seamus. Him a rich American out of Yale. His sister a duchess invited to Buckingham Palace... You only have one life, my darling girl. One life. Like your father out of the bogs of Ireland, make the most of it. We're going to build a dynasty to rule the Anglo-Saxon world. The Fitzgeralds. People are going to remember us. For generations, my darling girl."

"Why did you wait till you were thirty-five to marry, Father?"

"The poor marry the poor. The rich marry the rich. Your grandfather was the richest Irishman in America. Luckily, your mother was born the last of a large Catholic family. For his eldest daughter, the old bastard would not so much have looked at me then. The trade union movement made me rich. When you control a pension fund worth millions, people do you favours. Including your grandfather when he wanted to borrow money. Often the rich look richer than they are. For the moment. Whoever lent money to a poor man, may I ask?... My daughter, the duchess. Now off with you to Europe. And, daughter darling, don't you even think of money. You'll have whatever you want. The best of everything. Remember, the Fitzgeralds of Boston are rich. You tell them that. Money always talks. The rest is up to you but the good Lord up there in heaven tells Patrick he has his money on the right filly. It's all a game to me, my darling girl. Life's a game."

THE PRIZE INVITATION to the spring balls was the May Ball at Nuneham House, the seat of Lord Harcourt, on the banks of the River Thames four miles south of Oxford. Lady Harcourt, daughter of an Anglo-American banker, had been approached personally by the American ambassador to the Court of St James. Stella had promptly received her invitation at the Dorchester where she was staying in London, a stone's throw from Merlin St Clair's flat in Park Lane. The rest of the invitations to the May Ball had been sent out weeks before.

"Oh, Daddy, you really are good," she smirked with the heavily embossed invitation in her hand. Stella had been in London for exactly ten days. The ambassador's private secretary had telephoned Stella at the hotel the previous day telling her the invitation was on the way.

There had been men all over the place giving her attention, one of whom would be asked to escort her to the dance. The invitation read:

MISS STELLA FITZGERALD and Partner

THE MAN HAD to be the right class but sufficiently realistic to allow Stella freedom to do what she wanted at the ball. She wanted an escort, not a partner. A man with predatory instincts like her own. Someone with his own reason for wanting to be seen at the best of the spring balls. Racking her brains for less than a minute, Stella began to smile. The young man with the rich man's wife as his mistress. The perfect ice-cold escort with the very charm of the devil himself. Her father would indeed be proud of her choice. Barnaby St Clair was a man after his own heart.

They had met the second night after Stella arrived in London with so many introductions arranged by her father she had not known where to begin. The man she phoned who invited her to the dinner party was her father's investment man in London, CE Porter. That was the man's name and no more. He was arrogant, too old for her, and probably a crook if he did business with her father. He was only the means to an end.

"He knows them all in London, my darling girl. You won't like CE Porter but he'll take you where you ought to go. If he tries any tricks, slap his face or whatever you young girls do to unwanted advances these days. Use him. He uses me for information that I rather think he sells to his aristocratic clientele. When I know an American company is going to announce a big rise in dividend, I tell CE Porter over the transatlantic telephone. We both make money, my darling girl. The buying orders come to Wall Street from London. My friends never suspect I divulge their secrets. A man in control of the union gets told these things. Everyone knows only insiders make money on the stock market. Better than betting on a ringer at the racetrack. Not what you know but who you know. Old as the hills but still as true as the day that little saying was born. Didn't I tell you people are wicked?"

They had gone to a supper club called Clara's after the old woman who ran the place. CE Porter had said that to be seen at Clara's was to arrive in

London society. To get a table without Clara's permission was apparently impossible.

There were ten to dinner that night after the show, her first night out in London that had started the meteoric rise in the number of invitations flooding into her hotel. It was lovely. The scandals just poured out of their mouths, the cattiness to Stella's taste. From the moment CE Porter picked up what he misguidedly thought was his prize at the Dorchester Hotel, Stella was never bored. There were three taxis full of well-dressed young people outside the entrance to the hotel. The taxis took the party on to the Globe Theatre. After the show, a light, pleasant musical that asked no one to think, they had gone to the supper club where they stayed half the night. It seemed most of the party had seen *Happy Times* at least once before.

Now, with the invitation in her hand that had been handed to her with the others at reception, she went up to her room where she telephoned the Honourable Barnaby St Clair and asked him to escort her to the May Ball at Nuneham House.

"How do you know I don't have my own invitation?"

"Because if you had, you would have let me know."

"I like you, Miss Stella Fitzgerald from America. I have a brother who has gone there. Sailed on the RMS *Olympic* from Southampton dock to New York. Manhattan. Must be months ago. Maybe I should go to America."

"What are you talking about, Mr St Clair?"

"I'd love to go to Oxford. With you. Especially with you."

"I said escort."

"We'll see, my most beautiful lady from Boston. Did CE Porter give you my number?... Yes, I thought he did. Your father is one of his valued customers. I do business with Porter. It now makes sense. We will have to stay in Oxford for the night or somewhere. Does Lady Harcourt know you are inviting me?... Good. Don't tell her. Her late husband was an acquaintance of Harry Brigandshaw's. Now that would be a giggle."

"What are you talking about?"

"When you've been in London ten years you will understand."

"I'll book my own hotel in Oxford."

"Won't you tell me which one?"

"Of course not. What's your brother doing in America?"

"Book tour. He writes books."

"Not Robert St Clair? Goodness me, there's more in the family than an old title you might one day inherit if the old bachelors don't find wives."

"Who told you that?"

"You did, Barnaby. The first time we met. In Clara's... I loved *Keeper of the Legend*... How old is he?"

"Forty."

"That is old... Do you know, I rather think we understand each other. How is Tina?"

"Don't be catty. I did not tell you that."

"Everyone else did. Why doesn't Brigandshaw take a gun and shoot you?"

"He was once my brother-in-law."

"Oh, that really is the devil being wicked."

"Maybe not a hotel. I have a friend with a large house a little further down the river. We were in the army together in Palestine during the war. Just hope he has forgotten my little indiscretion. Probably. Everything comes into a better perspective when you get older. He's in import and export. Made a fortune since the war. Has to be dodgy."

"Were you dodgy, Barnaby?"

"In retrospect, not at all. Very minor. Borrowed fifty quid from the mess funds. Was going to give it back for goodness sake. What does a gentleman do when he can't pay his mess bill at the end of the month? The war was almost over. Then they wanted everything to add up right. Sort of balance the mess books. Got me out of the army without having to wait too long when the war was over the following week."

"What did they do to you?"

"Absolutely nothing. I was an officer and a gentleman."

"What happened to the fifty quid as you call it?"

"No idea. Colonel probably paid with his own money. Wasn't a bad old codger for a chap who had been in the army all his life... We'll go down on the Friday. Make a weekend out of it."

"Won't your friend mind us using his house as a hotel? Will he have an invitation?"

"No. Definitely not. Give me your telephone number. I will see what I can do, Miss Stella Fitzgerald from Boston."

"Is your brother in New York?"

"No. Denver, Colorado wherever that may be."

"Midwest. Good skiing."

"You have skiing in America?"

"Maybe you should go. Do you good."

. . .

WITH THE PRIZE invitation three weeks ahead, Stella changed her schedule. Paris, Rome and Berlin were put off to the middle of summer. She was having too much fun in London. Spring was in the air and Stella Fitzgerald was wondering to herself what it would be like to lose her virginity. Looking at the calendar, the weekend of the May Ball would be just right. She was a good Catholic girl. Using a contraceptive had never entered her mind. Thinking back on her father's instructions, the last thing she wanted in life just then was a husband telling her what to do.

She was after all twenty-two, far away from home, and curious as to what all the fuss was about.

CE PORTER'S expression was one of mild amusement. They were in his office in the City discussing Patrick Fitzgerald.

CE Porter had grown to like Barnaby St Clair even after Harry Brigandshaw made him give the profit on his sale of Colonial Shipping shares to Barnaby. CE Porter had arranged the earlier public listing of Colonial Shipping on the London Stock Exchange and had tried to allocate himself a large block of shares at list price through nominees in five separate banks, until Harry found out. The man had morals when it came to making money, which CE Porter felt quite shocking. He had met Barnaby on the SS *King Emperor* on a trip back from Africa.

CE Porter had never been a man to hold grudges for very long. Especially when Barnaby kept giving him good information about the market gleaned by Barnaby on his social round from gullible executives working for public listed companies. They now split the proceeds of their dealings from reciprocal insider information in half as much as either of them could tell what the other one had done. CE Porter always knew there were as many games involving cats and mice in the City of London as those involving bulls and bears. What CE had never found out was Barnaby having to give his father the profit from the sale of the Colonial Shipping shares, a way for Harry to give his then father-in-law money without being embarrassing.

"Her father has pretensions of grandeur... Oh dear, Barnaby. You didn't tell Stella that if Merlin and Robert stay unmarried, your children will inherit the title?"

"I rather think I did... She's invited me to the Harcourt May Ball."

"How on earth did an American get an invitation? I've been trying to get one of those from Lady Harcourt for years. Just ignores me... Must have been Patrick again, the old fox. He wants his daughter to marry a duke and make his daughter a duchess. Came out of the bogs of Ireland."

"Have you met him?"

"Once. Quite enough. Slit your throat for money while smiling into your eyes. Charming man. We do business together."

"Rather gathered that was how Miss Fitzgerald found herself at Clara's."

"You don't have to like the people who make you rich. Can't think he'll like a lowly baron for a son-in-law. He wants his own son to be president of America. Would try himself, except they don't allow the foreign-born to be head of state over there. Hates the English. Rumour has it he funds the Irish Republican Army along with half the Irish in Boston. They rattled tins in the worst bars in Boston to fight the cause. Don't blame them really. We were stinkers in the potato famine. Didn't raise a finger. Richest empire in history did nothing when the Irish were starving just across the Irish Sea. They've hated us since the time of Richard the Second. That just put the cherry on top... So she invited you to be her partner at the Nuneham Park Ball of Lady Harcourt."

"Escort was her word. You start with a barony and work your way up. She's very pretty. Do you know how many dukes there are in England other than the royal dukes?"

"He'll settle for one of those."

"The British would never allow an American to marry into the Royal Family."

"Probably not. She'll be very rich when he dies. He's old. Married late. Waited to get rich and then married a rich man's daughter. Another Irishman. There are far more Irish over there than in Ireland. You should use your charm on Stella. You look rich enough, Barnaby, even if you do owe the bank a fortune."

"How did you know about that?"

"I know everything. You'll be staying with Hayter down the river, I presume? Poor old Hayter. Had his legs blown off. The war was less kind to some of us. At least he made himself rich sitting in a wheelchair. Poor chap won't be going to the May Ball even if it is just upriver. Hates looking at other people having a good time. Do you know what he does, Barnaby? When he sees a world shortage of a commodity looming, he buys as much as he can lay his hands on, waits for the price to go up and sells. Doesn't even have a warehouse. Good contacts around the world. They feed him information round the clock. Clever chap, Hayter. Mind you, he does have a lot of time on his hands sitting in that wheelchair all day long looking down the slope at the river. Riverglade will be beautiful in the spring. All those trees on one side of the house and all the daffodil lawns down to the river on the other side. Lucky chap. Doesn't have to stare at the walls of a flat like me when I meditate... Doesn't he know you nicked fifty quid from the mess fund in Palestine? Surprised if he'll let you stay."

"He's not as straight as he seems. Has the habit of creating rumours in the commodity market just before he sells. Creates his own shortages."

"Do you have proof?"

"Yes, I do."

"Does Hayter know you have proof?"

"Yes, he does."

"Then enjoy your weekend with Stella Fitzgerald at Riverglade. Maybe I'll come down for the weekend. Hayter's a first-class friend of mine. How's Tina Brigandshaw?"

"Fine, thank you, CE."

"Never did manage to get her into my bed."

"If you even try, CE, I'll kill you."

"Poor old Harry."

"She was mine long before she even met Harry. All our lives. She's mine."

CE Porter was about to say, 'so was Frank', and then thought better, swallowing the words just before they were spoken. The look from the piercing blue eyes in the tanned face first scorched in the Arabian Desert, he rather thought was no idle threat. CE Porter shivered as if someone had walked over his grave.

"But please come to Riverglade. Bring one of your girls. You have enough of them now you are so rich."

"I've always been rich, Barnaby. Which is more than you are. One of these days you may wish to swap me your Tina for getting you out of a mess."

This time Barnaby felt the cold shivers.

"She doesn't belong to me to swap," he said in the moment of brief panic as he looked into the abyss.

"Oh yes, she does... Now, what information do you have for me that can make us money? I'll have to say, I don't like the feel of the markets. Everyone is too complacent. There's going to be a crash. A real crash, Barnaby, that'll put half the world as we know it out of work."

"What would you buy instead of shares?"

"Farmland. Not only in England. In Africa. Far away from the crash. Food is food whatever monetary price we give it and everyone has to eat or they die. Farmland. A nice large piece to live on, while the rest of the world picks up the pieces. You then buy the right shares cheap with the cash you left in the bank."

"You talk as if it is going to happen."

"So is another war with Germany. That chap Hitler is dangerous. He has the Germans listening to him. The rich, what's left of them, and the poor. After the markets crash right down to the bottom, buy shares in companies that make guns. Or tanks. Or aircraft. That's how your brother Merlin made himself rich. He bought Vickers-Armstrong shares just before the last war."

"He lost out on the stock market boom. Kept all his money in government bonds."

"Maybe. If the stocks end up worthless he won't have lost out on anything despite how much they might be worth now. Remember that when you dream about your bank overdraft backed by your signature and those entirely worthless share certificates in the bank safe."

"I'm listening, CE."

"So you should be. We are friends, aren't we?... Do you know Felicity James? I'll bring her to Riverglade. You never know, I may just be able to wangle a late invitation to my first ball at Nuneham Park. They have fairy lights in the trees right down to the banks of the river so I am told. Beautiful if it doesn't rain. I'll have to use Cuddles Morton-Sayner of course. Felicity will like the May Ball. Do her standing in society a lot of good, I should think."

"Whereabouts in Africa?"

"Rhodesia of course. Some of the best farmland in the world. Ask your old brother-in-law. No. Maybe not. He wants to take Tina and his children back to Africa as far away from you as possible... Or so people say. The ones I know. The ones I talk to. They don't like you, Barnaby. A man's wife is sacred ground whatever you did in the past. She married Harry, not you. You can't have your cake and eat it even if you think you can... Why didn't you marry her?"

"Her father's a railway porter for goodness sake. What would people have thought?"

"They don't think anything less of Harry. His mother's family are just as old as yours. His grandfather's baronetcy goes back to William the Conqueror."

"He can't inherit."

"Neither can you if either of your brothers marry and have male children. The days of being a snob are over, did you know? Right down there underneath all your shit, you love the girl. I saw it in your eyes just then when you were threatening to kill me."

"I know," said Barnaby very softly.

"What did you say?"

"Nothing, CE. Nothing... Did anyone ever tell you, you know too much for your own good?"

"Every woman I declined to marry."

"Why didn't you marry?"

"Never met the right one. You have to know a girl all your life to be sure. They put on façades until you marry them and only then show you what they really are and turn into exact replicas of their mothers. Can you think of any of the mothers you would want to live with? Most men marry perfect strangers when you think about it. Meet a girl one year and marry her the next. Chap I know who was going back to Sarawak after home leave from the Colonial Service met a girl one Friday and married her the next. Has a Chinese girl and a family in Singapore but that doesn't count I suppose."

"How did it go?"

"Don't know. They are in Kuching."

They both began to laugh, the tension drained out of their conversation.

"We'd better have a bite of lunch together," said CE Porter.

"That would be nice."

"We'll go to the Cavalry Club. They let me in again after I apologised to the club secretary for talking shop. We English do have some strange rules."

"How nice of them. It's next to the Royal Air Force club where Harry's a member."

"You just can't leave it alone... It's a nice day. Take your brolly and your bowler and we'll walk to the Tube station. Be one of the plebs. From Piccadilly Circus, we'll walk up Piccadilly to the club. Take a taxi back, of course. All the trees are in leaf in Green Park. Every man should take a walk every now and again... I don't like having to use the services of Cuddles but there isn't any other way. Can't have you going to the May Ball with Stella Fitzgerald all on your own. Her father told me to keep an eye on the gal he calls his darling girl in that delightful Irish accent. I do like an Irish accent. That's one thing."

"Oh, darling, I'm up to my eyeballs. Anyway, there are no more invitations for the May Ball at Nuneham Park. Like gold, CE. Like gold."

"How much gold, Cuddles?... Do you want cash or tips on the market?"

"Cash, CE. Definitely cash. When the ball is over the price of the shares won't matter to you."

"How much cash, Cuddles?"

"Fifty pounds."

"That's extortion."

"Would you like to ask Lady Harcourt yourself? She considers you anything but a gentleman."

"The Honourable Barnaby St Clair is going."

"How on earth did he manage that?"

"An American lady with a rich father and influence asked him to be her escort."

"Does she know about St Clair?... That may be an idea. I'll ask around. That is, if any respectable gal would want you as an escort, CE."

"I want to take Felicity James."

"Poor Felicity. Could there be a nice side to you, CE? Give me twenty-four hours. You are rich. That much is on your side. And charming when you wish to be... Do you remember all those years ago before the war? When my father was rich and the empire ruled the world? When all the colours in England were so bright? Boating on the Thames. The Derby at Epsom... Then the war and Father. My poor mother. I do, do my best. Rather like pushing out the barrow so to speak if you see what I mean, CE. I just sell social favours instead of apples and pears to make a living. Maybe if I had had more than a tutor and a home education I might have done better. Even then, a woman doesn't stand a chance. Certainly not a poor woman past her prime who has to make her own living and support Mother. Maybe everything will change when all women over twenty-one get the vote."

"Are you going to the Harcourt Ball, Cuddles?"

"Of course. After Father shot himself, they all feel sorry for me."

"Take me, Cuddles."

"Is this a cash transaction or a favour?"

"Both. And you won't have to ask Lady Harcourt for my separate invitation. We'll spend the weekend at Riverglade to be near. Hayter will invite us. I help him in business. The charming Barnaby St Clair will be in attendance with the American... Now that's an idea. For you to chaperone Stella Fitzgerald for the season. Maybe a thousand pounds for the season for all the right introductions. Her father wants her to marry the eldest son of a duke and that costs money."

"I should think so too... Twenty-four hours. I'll have to tell Lady Harcourt who I am bringing. And St Clair, now I know."

"That was the idea, Cuddles. These Americans don't know the form. Would you like me to phone her father in Boston?"

"Would you, darling?... Do you really want to go with me, CE? Or is it just business?"

"I want to see you, Cuddles. We had a lot of fun."

"Yes, we did."

"Getting the vote won't make the slightest difference."

"You don't think so?"

"Women will just vote what their families tell them to vote. You can't have two people running the same family. They fight like cats and dogs."

THE LAST THING Harry Brigandshaw had wanted was an invitation to a dance, to talk polite small talk to people he had no wish to know and sleep in a strange bed. If he was going to talk about anything, it was farming in Africa, which left the locals looking at him with blank, very uninterested faces that Harry quite understood. London trivia left Harry with a vacant look.

For some reason, the invitation had come to the office for Mr Harry Brigandshaw and partner and not to the Berkeley Square house for Mr Brigandshaw and wife. Harry's first instinct was to drop the invitation in the wastepaper basket. Instead, Harry shoved it in the drawer of his desk and put the May Ball out of his mind where it would stay forgotten until just before the dance when he would send Lady Harcourt his regrets for himself and his wife.

He had made no mention of the invitation to Tina. They were talking to each other, for the sake of the three children, otherwise, they were living apart. Harry did not have to have his wife followed to know when she saw Barnaby. He knew. The same way Tina knew when he visited Brett Kentrich at the Regent Mews flat. They were simply living separate lives mostly in the same house. Life went on. Thankfully the children, or so he thought, were too young to notice anything was wrong. The servants knew as the servants always knew. One of the prettier chambermaids had even given him coy looks which Harry ignored.

Even his desire to go back to the farm in Rhodesia had been squashed, as he would never then see his children, the most important three people in his life. Harry had trained his mind never to think of Frank as Barnaby's son. His life had become one long charade anyway. For Harry, there was no solution. Divorcing the mother of his children was out of the question.

He had even thought of going down to Dorset on his own to explain his predicament to Tina's mother and father but could see no way they could possibly help. They believed their daughter was in a good marriage with a rich man. The truth, like the truth always did, would hurt. If he had thrown the happiness of his life away having a blistering affair with Tina on the boat, the consequences of what was now a disaster should neither be visited on the children nor their grandparents. He had made his bed in the owner's cabin of the SS *Corfe Castle* in September 1922. If the only good that came were the children, he was happy. Even when he wanted to wring Tina's neck in his fits of jealousy when he knew so well she had again been with Barnaby, he thought of the children he may well have never had. After Lucinda's death, he had had no wish to marry again and would certainly not have done so were Tina not pregnant from their affair on the boat. Life was never straightforward. Never had been. When Brett asked him about the invitation, he even smiled.

"You didn't really think I could take you as my partner, Brett?"

"Why not?" sulked Brett.

"I'm married."

"Are you going?"

"Now I think I'll have to. With Tina. To squash any rumours the invitation to me and partner might have made. Those society folk have tongues like vipers. I always have to think of the children... How on earth did you engineer the invitation, Brett?"

"Cuddles. Cuddles Morton-Sayner."

"Who on this earth is Cuddles?"

"She sells social favours."

"Is she a whore?"

"I suppose in a way. She prostitutes herself. If we go together, everyone will know your marriage is only kept alive for the sake of your children. We can go out together again in public even if you won't get a divorce and make an honest girl out of your Brett... Harry, you do realise how much I love you? I'll throw up my career and go with you to Rhodesia."

"And be miserable. No. Absolutely no to both requests. Frankly, I think we should stop seeing each other."

"If you do Harry, I'll kill myself."

"You're being dramatic."

"Try me."

CUDDLES MORTON-SAYNER HAD ALWAYS LIKED the analogy of pushing out the barrow when money became tight. Everyone, she thought, had something to put on their barrow to sell. Everyone could make some money if they put their mind to it and often it was fun. If some thought arranging social favours was beyond the pale, it was better than begging or letting an old mother starve. Cuddles looked at her occupation as an exercise in public relations. People needed doors opening in their private lives as much as their business lives. An introduction that proved successful in business was rewarded with a monetary commission. She was no different to a stockbroker who pointed out the right share, using his knowledge of business and accounting. If she were ever to print a calling card, it would read:

MISS PRUDENCE MORTON-SAYNER, Public Relations Broker.

EVEN IF HER friends had called her Cuddles ever since she could remember, it did not have to carry over into her business. She was providing a service. She expected some respect. If some people respected CE Porter and Barnaby St Clair in business, what was wrong with her, she asked for pity's sake? She was good at her business. Very businesslike. Which was why she drew up a contract for the American from Boston that had to be signed before she would waste her time on the daughter... The son of a duke!

"If I find the little tart the eldest son of a duke, I want a damn sight more than a thousand pounds. With no quibbling. A legal contract between me and the father, a father with more money than sense."

So there it was now. In neat columns. A duke. A marquess. An earl. A viscount. A baron. A baronetcy... And the one thousand pounds retainer payable on signing the contract... She told herself she was only cuddly by name, prickly by nature. She liked that idea.

When she saw CE Porter, she told him to wire the whole contract to America to save time.

"If you do this and pay for the telegram, if Fitzgerald signs and you have your American lawyer's confirmation of his signature on a typed copy of the contract, I will take you to the May Ball at no cost. How does that sound?"

"Perfect. I'll get on with it right away. I'll ask Hayter to invite us to Riverglade for the weekend of the ball."

"So Fitzgerald will sign it?"

"Of course he will. What does he have to lose?"

"A thousand pounds. Plus ten thousand pounds if I put her in line to become a duchess."

"Just make sure his darling girl doesn't get herself pregnant. American girls are a lot freer than our young girls. Keep an eye on her. She's pretty."

. . .

"WE ARE GOING to the May Ball at Nuneham Park next month," Harry Brigandshaw told Tina, the first time for weeks she had been addressed by her husband about anything other than their children. "We are staying the weekend at the Swan on the river. I'll be visiting my old college. The professor who taught me geology is still a don."

"Why are we going? You hate dancing."

"Brett engineered the invitation which came to me and partner. I will not have this town talking behind my back. To squash any more rumours we are going together."

"Why don't you take Brett?"

"Because she is not my wife! Our children will eventually have to go to school. Children can be just as nasty as adults. They called Mervyn Braithwaite 'Fishy' at school, because sideways-on his face resembled the head of a codfish. Why he became obsessed. Became a killer. Why he killed Lucinda."

"Are we going back to Lucinda again?... I'm sorry, Harry. My father works for the railways. I don't see what the children have to do with Fishy Braithwaite."

"What if the other children say their mother is a whore when they go to school? Our children will be on the defensive for the rest of their lives. People can be very nasty to each other."

"Then you had better stop visiting that flat in Regent Mews you are so fond of."

"Keep away from Barnaby, I will keep away from Brett. We are married. For better or for worse, remember... I was going down to Dorset to talk to your parents."

"You keep my parents out of this."

"Then we shall go back to Elephant Walk where people don't have the time to say nasty things about each other's private lives. Where people do not feed off other people's pain."

"I hate Rhodesia."

"You should have thought of that before you got yourself pregnant on the boat."

"You men make me sick. Don't you know it takes two people to get a girl pregnant? That you might have had something to do with the problem? You didn't exactly run away."

They both stood glaring at each other in the lounge of the Berkeley Square house. Both had spoken quietly making the words sound even more venomous. Neither had wanted the servants or the children to hear them argue.

"Damn that bloody Barnaby St Clair," said Tina, wanting to cry she was so frustrated.

"Don't swear. The children will hear and copy you."

"What are we going to do, Harry?" This time Tina had spoken normally.

"I have no idea."

"I'll need a ball gown. The fashions change."

"That is the least of my problems."

"Don't you want a divorce?"

"No. We do not divorce our wives... The children."

"Always the children."

"Yes, Tina. Always. Maybe time will temper the jealousy."

"Are you jealous?"

"Aren't you?"

"Then you do still have feelings for me... What a mess."

"Just keep up appearances. That is all you have to do. At the ball, we will show the world a loving couple."

"What I hate most, Harry, is the silences between us."

"So do I. How do people's lives get into a mess like this?"

UNCLE WALLACE MADGWICK had known Lady Harcourt for more than thirty years. The kind of old friends made through associations to events long past. Their lives had crossed at balls, weddings, funerals, the Golden Jubilee of Queen Victoria. They had never really known each other as people but that did not matter. They had gone through lives parallel to each other, always in sight of each other at regular intervals. The only time Lady Harcourt had made a social visit to Uncle Wallace was during the war in the London hospital they had sent him to after losing his left eye in France. The lady worked through the war for the Red Cross. It was the one and the only intimate moment they had had together when she had looked down at him in the bed and said, "Oh, Wallace, I'm so glad they did not kill you."

Uncle Wallace's invitation to the May Ball had come to him as a surprise, bringing back a flood of memories from the long years that had made up his life. Of course, he had no intention of going to a dance but it did give him the excuse to telephone Lady Harcourt for a natter about old times that had lasted half an hour.

"You must come, Wallace. It'll be the last time. This year is the last ball I shall throw at Nuneham Park."

"Gout. I have unbearable spasms of gout, which requires sitting in a comfortable chair with the afflicted foot on a small stool to stop the blood rushing. There is nothing more painful than gout. Anyway, you won't have time to talk to old friends. You'll be far too busy. I'll just be another old codger in a uniform smelling of mothballs. All the youngsters will keep well away from me in case I tell them stories and bore them to tears... It's been a lovely chat. Looking back, we had happy times... Can I send my nephew instead?"

"Of course you can. I'll change the invitation list from Colonel Wallace Madgwick MC to Colonel Madgwick or nephew in case you change your mind."

"The boy can tell me how it went in detail. I can then enjoy your ball without all the pain in my foot."

"Maybe we can again speak on the phone without being interrupted so many times by the exchange. Six minutes would never have been enough time."

THE IDEA in Uncle Wallace's mind was to send young Ralph to the ball with Rosie Prescott as a reward for Rosie keeping his nephew in line at the office. Uncle Wallace knew Rosie had an eye for Ralph, which would stop all the nonsense of Ralph going to America next year. If nothing else, Uncle Wallace was an optimist when it came to his living in the country far away from all the bickering of the human race.

"It's not that I don't like people, just that I have grown tired of them. I'm sixty-three, Ralph. I deserve some peace."

"Let me think about it."

"There's a good boy... How are you getting along with Postlethwaite?"

"Famously. I'll be going to America next year, don't you worry."

"I do, Ralph."

LEAVING HIS ANSWER LATE, intentionally, Ralph told his uncle he could not be unfaithful to Rebecca by taking Rosie to the ball. Ralph made his point a week before the date of the May Ball in the senior partner's office.

"Why don't you give the invitation to Christopher?... I mean Barrie."

"Do you think he would want to go?"

"Yes, I do, Uncle Wallace. Indeed I do."

"Then ask him for me... How's his new musical coming along?"

"Famously."

Uncle Wallace suspected something was up when Ralph left his office whistling.

"Sorry, Rosie," Uncle Wallace heard his nephew say to his secretary in the outside office.

"That's all right, Ralph. I'm happy for Rebecca."

Rosie Prescott, it appeared by the tone of her voice, had become resigned to her fate as a spinster a long time ago.

Uncle Wallace sighed. A bachelor was respected by society. A spinster they felt sorry for. How could the two be anything but the same, he asked himself?

THE WORST PART of the day for Douglas Hayter was watching the rowers on the river in the mornings. During the school holidays from boarding school before the war, come rain, sun, hail or snow, Douglas had taken the slim craft out of the boat shed onto the river dressed in a singlet and shorts and sculled a mile up and down the Thames before breakfast. He had tried three times without his legs, each time falling in the water. He could not balance the boat however hard he tried and swimming without legs left him floundering. If he had fallen out of the boat in the middle of the river, he would likely have drowned which seemed to Douglas a little silly after having survived the war even with stumps.

The morning of the May Ball that was to take place at Nuneham Park just upriver, Douglas was sitting in his wheelchair at Riverglade. He was looking down on the river that ran at the bottom of a long slope of well-cut lawns the gardener had cut specially for the guests who were due to arrive soon after breakfast. Douglas liked the smell of cut grass and the look of the clumps of daffodils that dotted the lawn as far down as the river. If anything, he was excited at the thought of guests and some new faces to relieve his chair-bound boredom. He had tried artificial legs but the stumps were not long enough. Even the lone sculler out on the river was rewarded by his wave rather than his frown. Douglas for once was in a good mood.

"Beautiful day for the dance, Douglas," came floating across the water and up the slope of the lawn to the veranda where he was sitting. The early morning was still. Not a breath of wind.

"Good morning, Dale. Who are you taking?"

"Martha Abbot."

"Have a lovely time. I have guests who are going. Isn't it Lady Harcourt's last May Ball?"

"I rather think so. Parts around here will never be quite the same."

Douglas watched and envied his old friend moving smoothly over the calm water, bending, pulling, dipping in the oars until the trees and a bend in the river took Dale Jarvis out of sight.

"Damn," he said. "Damn. Damn. Damn."

Swearing made him feel better. He was alone so no one would have heard. A flotilla of swans came into view, swimming with the flow of the river. They were all big, majestic birds. The cygnets would come later, he hoped, at the end of the spring. It was why he had gone into business to protect Riverglade, as after the war and the death of Douglas's parents in a major car accident, the estate was quietly falling down from disrepair. Riverglade and the river were all he had. When Douglas restored the old house with loving care, it was well worth having. A solace for the loss of his legs and the end of life as he had known it, back then when he was eighteen years old and a German shell blew him almost in half.

STELLA FITZGERALD THOUGHT Douglas Hayter was the most beautiful man she had ever seen in her life when he turned and smiled at her from his wheelchair on the lawn.

They had all driven down from London in Barnaby St Clair's Bentley 3 Litre, Stella unaware of the extent her father had employed Cuddles Morton-Sayner to look after her affairs. The top of the car had been down all the way with Barnaby driving fast, fear and exhilaration making them shout above the rush of the wind as they sped through the English country lanes.

The four of them had arrived after breakfast as they were expected. Soon after her first glimpse of Douglas Hayter that burned into her mind, the men had gone off to talk business. Douglas had smiled at Stella only the once, a soft, longing smile full of pain and deep understanding that had also sent a sexual shaft of feeling straight to her groin. He was just beautiful sitting helplessly in his wheelchair with the rug over his knees hiding the lack of his legs. CE Porter had told her how Douglas had lost his legs when he was not much more than a boy, before the car drove out of built-up London and the rush of the wind stopped conversation.

"He lives all alone with the servants at Riverglade which he treats like a mistress, lavishing love and money on the house the way he would have done on a wife."

"Is the poor man impotent? Many rich men who lose their legs marry and have children."

"He's too proud. I don't think he has ever looked at a woman in his life."

"Oh, you mean he's like that?"

"Not Douglas Hayter. Were it not for the war, Douglas would have got his rowing blue at Oxford."

"What's a blue, Mr Porter?" Stella was already bored and just making conversation.

"Someone who has rowed in the Oxford and Cambridge boat race. Goes back a very long time. I have no idea where the blue originated except both universities wear blue. Cambridge light blue, Oxford dark blue. That must be it."

"You did not go to university, Mr Porter?"

"Trinity, Dublin. Despite my English accent, I am Irish."

"Why you do business with my father?"

"Yes, it is... You'll like Douglas. Frightfully good chap."

"With whom you do business?" Everything, wherever she went, seemed to be about money.

"Yes, I do. The three of us. Bit like an old boy network but it isn't. We all went to different schools."

The conversation came to an end when Barnaby picked up speed.

On the back of the Bentley, strapped to a wide metal rack, was a large trunk containing the girls' ball gowns neatly packed on trays so they would not be crushed or creased.

Stella was impressed with Barnaby's handling of the car even though she thought he drove too fast once they were in the open lanes. He was a good driver, perfectly handling the big motor car with the big bonnet strapped down across the middle with a thick leather belt. Stella had never seen such a leather belt before. The separate large and round headlights rested on the front wings of the car. Barnaby had told her when they drove out of his garage behind his house on Piccadilly that he liked to clean the car himself. In the strong sunlight of the new day, the back of the polished chrome headlights shone back at Stella like two beacons of wealth and power, steady as rocks in front of her as they hurtled through the trees on either side of the lanes.

Only after lunch did Stella find herself alone with Douglas Hayter away from the house, fifty yards from the river.

"Can I push you down to the river, Mr Hayter? The water looks so beautiful."

"I can push myself, thank you, Miss Fitzgerald. I still have my arms. I hang from a bar for fifty pull-ups every morning... Do you know you are the first American girl I ever met? Come on. I'll race you to the water but you are going to have to run... Mind the daffodils!"

. . .

WATCHING from the house through the bay window of the sitting room, Barnaby found himself mildly jealous, not that Hayter could do anything to spoil his weekend, poor chap. He could feel as much as hear Stella's shouts of glee as she picked up her skirts and chased after the wheelchair that was going at an alarming speed directly at the river. Next to him, CE Porter took a quick look at the French windows that were open onto the wide veranda with intermittent steps down onto the manicured lawns. At the last moment like a rider galloping a horse, Douglas Hayter spun the wheelchair back to look up at Stella still racing down the lawn. Barnaby this time clearly heard Douglas Hayter laugh. Unable to stop herself from running down the bank, Stella fell into the wheelchair standing firm on the lip of the riverbank.

"Strong arms," said CE Porter, relaxing from the moment of tension. "That takes real strength to hold the wheels. He was a damn good rower before he lost his legs. I thought both of them were going straight into the water."

Striding to the open French window, CE called down to the two locked together in the wheelchair, their bodies pressed hard against each other, Douglas Hayter unable to take his hands off the wheels. "You two all right?"

For a long moment, nothing happened. The two stayed entwined. Then they watched Stella slowly extricate herself from the wheelchair.

"I think she stayed there longer than she should have done," said Barnaby nastily.

"You can't be jealous surely, old boy? He doesn't have any legs."

"You don't need legs to make love to a woman."

"She's a well-brought-up American and certainly a virgin. So is Douglas. He told me in confidence some years ago, poor chap. Must be dreadful... You are talking rot, Barnaby. And we had better stop. Here comes Cuddles."

"Did you see that?" she said. "Just like lovers. Fell right into his arms."

"His arms were holding the wheels," said Barnaby, heading for the French windows.

"Then they really were very close. How romantic... No, Barnaby. Leave them alone. That poor man deserves a little happiness no matter how short the time. Why don't we all go for a walk? The other way. She'll be quite safe. It doesn't look like that poor man could even get himself out of his chair to go anywhere."

TWO MILES downriver on the opposite bank of the River Thames, Christopher Marlowe and Brett Kentrich had arrived at Ferry Cottage. In his pocket was Uncle Wallace's invitation to the May Ball. Oscar Fleming, the impresario who had staged *Happy Times* mostly with Harry Brigandshaw's money, had lent them the cottage he had bought as his retreat from London more than twenty years ago. Not only that, but he had lent Christopher his car which he never used when he was living in his flat in town. Christopher would have liked to ask Brett if she had visited the cottage before with Oscar Fleming but decided a row wasn't worth the asking. The moment they arrived at the cottage he knew what the answer was anyway. Brett knew her way around far too comfortably. To get Brett to come with him to the May Ball was his biggest triumph since seeing her for the first time in Clara's when he was just playing the piano for a living.

Ralph had been the one to bring him the invitation to the theatre and the one to suggest he take Brett as his partner. To Christopher's great surprise, Brett had jumped at the idea of going to the ball. She had then asked Oscar Fleming for the keys to the cottage and the loan of his car. Despite a considerable bank balance from the money Christopher had received as the co-author with Danny Hill of *Happy Times*, he had still not bought himself a motor car or moved out of his attic room. He and Danny were now wealthy in many people's terms but to them, it made no difference. They liked living the way they had always been living. Playing in the band at Clara's, Danny playing the trumpet well, Christopher playing the piano not very well, everyone, including the customers who liked Christopher's habit of sitting with them at the tables between sets, forgiving him the occasional mistakes on the piano.

Ferry Cottage was right on the water with its own enclosed boat shed. Christopher's first job was to try to start the engine of the wooden-cabin boat Oscar Fleming left locked in the shed. Doing exactly what he had been told to do, priming the carburettor, cranking the starter handle this way and that to build up torque, the petrol engine fired with a powerful noise and a cloud of blue smoke before settling down to a steady purr.

That night they were going to chug upriver warm inside the closed cabin and dressed to the nines. On the other side of the river, they would moor the boat at the Nuneham House jetty and walk up the path to the ball. It was perfect. Far better than taking the car and parking far from the great house that stood majestically on the hill just above the river.

To Christopher's great joy, Brett was in the best of spirits, giving new hope to his old desire. Here he was, alone with his love, a new set of rather dashing evening clothes waiting for him in the boot of the car. Alone with the prettiest girl in the world. Were Christopher able to sing, he would have sung a song from his new musical before deciding Brett's first hearing would better come from Harvey Lyttleton, the crooner in the band.

"Why are you so happy, Brett?"

"Need you ask? I love going to such a grand ball. This is the pinnacle of the spring season. Some people would just kill for an invitation don't you know?"

"Do you know some of the guests?"

"I don't think so."

"They'll all know you."

"Now isn't that nice? Let's take the ship upriver and have a look where we are going tonight. Didn't they tell you to always make a reconnaissance in the army before making an advance? There's a big light on the front of the ship for when it's dark. When you go home."

"They call them boats when they are this size, Brett. Boats... The way you said that last bit suggests it will only be me going home to Ferry Cottage."

"Of course not, darling. What I meant was you will be driving the boat."

"Do you mind being alone with me for a night?"

"Why should I? No one will see us out here. You're not going to bite. Oh, Christopher, I'm so looking forward to the ball. To see all the important people... You do know how to dance?"

"Just not very well. Mother sent us to dancing classes. Ralph is very good. Yes, going with a famous actress is going to be fun."

"Come on then. Let's go and have a look. There is a lovely riverside restaurant where we can have lunch. I'm starving. Then we can come back and have an afternoon nap to be bright-eyed and bushy-tailed. Then dress for the dance. I have a new dress just for the occasion. It's going to be a sensation if it all stays together. A bigger sensation if it doesn't."

Brett put her right hand over her mouth and giggled.

"Take her out on the river, captain," she said uncovering her beautiful mouth so he could see it again. "I'm ready. Do you have any idea how lucky you were to get tickets?"

Besotted, Christopher helped the one and only love of his life down into the boat, every nerve in his body tingling at the feel of her touch.

THEY TALKED to each other all morning, Stella sitting at the foot of the wheelchair on the grass. The last of the April showers sent them scurrying for cover under a tree. After the rain, Douglas took off his tweed jacket and spread it on the lawn over the wet grass. Stella watched his every graceful move despite his impediment, the perfectly chiselled face concentrating with a smile, the long curls of brown hair dropping forward as he bent, the powerful arms in complete control of the jacket as Douglas spread it open for her on its back.

"I'll get your coat."

"I'm not cold. I don't like taking the rug off my knees in company. Or where my knees should be. I'm afraid the Germans did a good job cutting off my legs. The stumps are too short to attach anything. I'm working on a motorised chair which will be fun. Give the old arms a rest."

"Do you hate them?"

"Not really. We both did the same things to each other. For the life of me, I don't know why. They were building a fleet to challenge the Royal Navy, which might have challenged our control of the seas giving access to the colonies, as well as the trade routes. Why we had to sit in France opposite each other dug into the ground for four years shelling each other, is a mystery. When my legs went I came back to Riverglade. On a still night with the wind coming from the southeast I could hear the guns. I still can, which of course doesn't make sense. Now sit you down again and tell me all about Boston. How you learnt to sail. The Irish and English are islanders, Stella. Our lives have always been about water. The rivers that lead to the sea. The sea, master and mistress. We have so much in common you and I... Oh, this is lovely. A beautiful day by the beautiful river with a beautiful girl who can talk and think. Riverglade means so much to me. Isn't life ironic? Were I all in one piece, you would be going to the ball with me tonight."

"What about Barnaby?"

"I'd have picked a fight and knocked him down. No, dear old Barnaby, who isn't really dear at all, would have accepted the inevitable. He thinks I'm crooked in business. Why do we always judge other people by how we treat the world ourselves? He thinks I manipulate commodity prices instead of researching meticulously from all over the world. Then you can see the future shortages and surpluses. I had to do something to save Riverglade after my parents died in a motor car smash. People say fortunes are made and lost in three generations. My great-grandfather made the family fortune. He was a sea captain. A merchant captain and gentleman, though they said he was probably not a gentleman. Quick fortunes are never made in a gentlemanly way. The *Cormorant* was more a privateer than a merchant ship. Heavily armed. It was during the wars with Napoleon. Any shipping was fair game if they flew a flag that was at war with Britain. No one counted the swag when they came back to home port. People steal from others to get rich. Man's done it since he came out of the slime. Darwin gave it a polite term: survival of the fittest. Back in the early days, it was simple rape and pillage. His only son, my grandfather, spent most of the money and my father finished off the rest. Great-grandfather built Riverglade. He liked to be beside the water even in his old age when he could no longer go to sea... Now that's enough of me and my family. Tell me all about yours, Stella."

"Mainly pushing other people out of the way and taking what they wanted, I suppose. Father now runs contraband whisky from Canada down to the States."

"Good for him. It's a stupid law."

"He won't admit it to me but people get killed in that kind of illegal trade... Like Barnaby and CE, he uses the information he gleans as a trade union leader to make money on the stock exchange. At least that is legal."

"Probably not for long. It's a swindle if you think of it."

"He's in politics mainly through the union. The unions and politicians are closely linked in America. My brother is going to be the president of America. You have to have political power to bend the rules to your own advantage, so my father proudly tells me. I still love him very much."

"Sounds like Great-Grandfather... And you sailed Massachusetts Bay in a yacht while I sculled the River Thames... Have you ever been in love?"

"My father wants me to marry the eldest son of a duke. He wants his daughter to be a duchess... Let's go down the towpath and find out what there is at the other end." Stella felt almost sick with the pain of longing.

"I'd like that... You will let me see you in your ball gown before you all set off for Nuneham Park?"

"Of course, Mr Hayter."

"Douglas. Please. We British are not all stuffed shirts."

SLOWLY THEY WENT OFF TOGETHER DOWNRIVER. From a clump of trees high up beside the road above Riverglade, Barnaby watched them go. This time he found himself even more jealous of the cripple.

DOUGLAS HAYTER, quite unaware of Barnaby and his animosity on the hill, turned the wheels over and over slowly with his hands. Stella was telling him all about Boston. About her sister in a convent and her brothers. About the new world that was America.

Douglas listened sadly, building up his own pain he knew very soon was going to hurt more than the loss of his legs. At first, he thought she was just being nice to a man with no legs. At that moment Douglas knew he should have turned around and gone back to the house where everything was calm and familiar and let them all go off happily to the dance. He always had work to do. He should take himself off to work instead of memorising Stella as she walked, talking softly, always smiling, mostly smiling at him. Given so much time to think on his own, Douglas knew the girl was just as beautiful on the inside as on the out.

By the time they turned around to go back for lunch, Stella found herself thinking she had not been her usual, spoilt little bitch even once. If the feeling inside her was being truly happy, she had never felt it before. Why, she asked herself, was love so sudden?

THE SWAN HAD BEEN Harry Brigandshaw's favourite watering hole during his student days at Oxford. They had arrived in time for lunch having spoken not a word on the journey from London in the car. Harry would have liked to ride down on the motorcycle except for the evening clothes they would change into for the ball. Instead, he had taken a pool car from the office as he did when he needed transport out of town. Owning another vehicle when he wanted to go back to Africa was an unnecessary expense. Like his mother had told him from a child, Harry never liked to waste money.

"Throw away a stale loaf of bread and one day you'll want to eat it. Don't be mean in life, Harry, just don't waste. There are a lot of hungry people in this imperfect world."

Whenever Harry indulged himself, he felt a tweak of guilt. Which was why they were staying in the Swan instead of some posh hotel covered in chrome.

The Swan, right on the River Thames, was as beautiful a spot as Harry had ever known. The very sight of the place melted his animosity along with the wrong reason for going to the May Ball. Smiling at Tina for the first time in a long while, Harry decided they were both going to have a good time and his old tutor at Oxford could wait.

"Twenty years and nothing has changed. I'll show you around Oxford if you don't mind a walk. I miss my long walks in the bush with a gun for protection more than I realised."

"I'd love that, Harry. Thank you for smiling. Life is so short. We have so much you and I that is good together. I'm just so sorry. So, so sorry."

"Did you buy a new gown?"

"Oh, I did."

"You'll knock them dead... They have a steak and kidney pie in this place that puts the food at the Savoy to shame. And rough cider. We'll both eat in the bar with the students if they'll let us. The official word is no women in the bar but we broke that rule most of the time."

"What was her name?"

"What was whose name?"

"The girl you brought here to break the rules."

"I can't remember."

"I'll bet you can."

"Carol Lambert. A complete tease. Everyone tried and everyone failed."

"I'm glad."

Harry put his hand on his wife's elbow as they went through into the bar. The place was raucous, full of young people who had been too young to be in the war. Sprinkled among the students were the pretty girls.

They both smelled the steak and kidney pie at the same time.

"I'm starving," said Tina, praying Harry's good mood would continue through the day.

"Come on. They'll think I'm a don and make room for us at the bar. You watch. Having an old husband can have advantages."

"You're not old, Harry."

"Sometimes I'm not sure. Today I feel young. There they go. Thank you, gentlemen." Harry smiled at all the youngsters.

"The seat's not for you sir, it's for the pretty girl." He was probably nineteen with a twinkle in his eye Harry liked.

"The pretty girl is my wife. I was here as a student myself."

Harry was about to add the twenty years ago and found Tina shaking her head. She was smiling at him with a look of longing Harry had never seen before. The student got off his stool and gave it to Harry with a smile and a small bow.

"It must have been wonderful," said Tina, smiling at the man. The young man looked flustered. "I was referring to my husband's days at the university."

"They were," said Harry.

"Where are you from, sir? Your accent is a little unfamiliar," said the nineteen-year-old.

"Africa, actually. Rhodesia. I have a farm."

"Wow," said the man.

"Since you gave us your chairs I'd better give you all a drink. In my day, I was pretty near broke most of the time. That probably hasn't changed either."

For some reason Harry could not imagine, it was the best lunch he had had in a very long time. When the closing bell rang in the bar at half past two, Harry thought they had been in the Swan only a few minutes, not more than an hour. Both of them were slightly drunk on the cider when they went outside for their walk. They had made many young friends in a short time. As they walked among the colleges, the buildings with tall spires built centuries before, the history of England was all around them. Harry, comfortable with his English heritage, was happy again they had won the war and hoped the students they had laughed with would never have to see another one.

"So much of England has survived for so long," said Harry.

Tina bit her tongue and kept her mouth shut. It was exactly as she felt. England was familiar, part of her being alive. Rhodesia frightened her. In England, she felt safe. In Africa, there were strange animals, spiders, snakes and people who barely wore clothes.

IGNATIUS BOWES-LYON WAS one of the first to arrive at the ball for the reason he had nothing better to do. He was alone. His partner to be, had gone down with flu the very same day. Or so she said.

His cousin had married the Duke of York, the second son of King George the Fifth, which Ignatius knew was the reason for his invitation. People were impressed with influence when it stretched right to the top. If Elizabeth had not married, he would be sitting in his room in London wondering what to do with the rest of his life. He had come to Oxford more out of boredom than anything else. For something to do, hoping his evening clothes would not look too out of fashion.

What the fuss was all about he had no idea but people were funny. Edward, Prince of Wales was going to be the next King of England not the Duke of York. He had only met his cousin twice, the daughter of the Earl of Strathmore and Kinghorne. Ignatius sometimes said to his few real friends he was so far from the money there was not a penny in sight. Were it not for Harry Brigandshaw's retainer, while the Short Brothers built their flying boat, he would be broke. On the streets. Or off to the colonies where most of the broke aristocrats seemed to finish up trying to impress the colonials with their pedigree. Ignatius often wondered what happened to people like that in the end.

"Probably just fade away."

"I'm sorry, old chap, do I know you?"

"Probably not," said Ignatius to the strange man.

Ignatius wished he had stayed in London. In his one room. Alone. Thinking of a fleet of flying boats with which he was going to conquer the passenger market of the world. In his vision, he saw ships as defunct, except to carry heavy cargo.

The man had turned his back rudely at the rude reply leaving Ignatius not caring less. Strangely, he missed the war. The camaraderie. In the war, Ignatius as a pilot had felt wanted. Not another fading aristocrat without money and a proper job. Just a life to be got through without prospects.

"Why do we always need so much money?"

This time nobody tried to enter his conversation with himself. Ignatius had picked up talking aloud to himself during the war on the dawn patrol. It had kept him alert. Probably saved his life.

Taking another look around to see if he knew anyone, he saw Barnaby St Clair with a girl he had never seen before which Ignatius thought was no surprise.

The old mansion was filling up. The band was playing what the American cousins called jazz. A big band for a dance but then it was the dance of the spring.

Just to get his bearings, Ignatius found the ballroom before the place was swamped with people. No one was dancing. A few like him were looking around a little lost. He took in the high frescoed ceiling, the heavy chandeliers, the slightly uneven wooden floor that would not matter when the five hundred guests packed the dance floor swaying to the music as if they were in a nightclub trying to avoid bumping shoulders with strangers. Balls, to Ignatius, were a bore except for the money Lady Harcourt would raise for the Red Cross.

Ignatius remembered the Red Cross from the war when a Hun had shot him down in flames, luckily behind the British lines where the Germans were trying to bomb the British guns under the umbrella of a rare fighter escort. There had been fifteen German aircraft. Ignatius was alone in the Sopwith Camel on his way home after patrolling the front and being waved back by Harry Brigandshaw after running out of ammunition. With the stupidity and bravado of youth, Ignatius had flown his plane through the German bombers to put them off their aim throwing bombs out of the open cockpits onto the guns not far down below. Ignatius had taken British rifle fire when the German triplane got on his tail. The Tommies were blazing away at the German bombers with everything they had. The gunners had him out of the burning aircraft. The Red Cross had patched him up. He had given Lady Harcourt a cheque for ten pounds that was more than he could afford. It was always good to remember.

Ignatius found a small bar off the ballroom, looking out on the long terrace that ran the length of the house. Along the low wall of the terrace were intermittent steps down to the lawns with large, tall flowerpots on either side bursting with flowers.

Through the trees was the Thames, dark in the valley. The trees were sparkling with fairy lights and couples were standing underneath them, the sight of them making Ignatius feel lonely. Ignatius thought the small room must have been a sewing room for the ladies of the house before it was emptied for the ball. The whole bottom floor of the mansion was open to the guests, with bars and flunkies in some of the smaller rooms. There were tables set with flowers in beautiful vases, waiting for the waiters to bring in the buffet supper they would serve to the guests for most of the night. In some of the rooms were violin players in pairs, playing music in the background. From one room Ignatius heard Vivaldi. Another, Mozart. The pillar at his back kept Ignatius safe as he drank slowly but with the aim of mellowing his rotten mood. Only when he was mellow was Ignatius able to join the small talk, use the polite phrases that meant very little, as was their intention. Ignatius knew he had to be a little drunk to talk to people like that. Not really drunk. He hated being drunk and out of control as they had done in the Flying Corps when bad weather grounded the Germans and the British... Too often, his mind went back to the war where things then had mattered. Where men were real men and said what they wanted, knowing they'd likely be dead by the end of the month. Only during the war years had Ignatius felt so alive.

They were lucky with the night. There was no rain and no sign of it.

Ignatius went to the open window that opened up from the level of his knees. Boats with searchlights were making for the jetty. Women in long, billowing gowns were being helped out of the boats by men in livery, who were holding umbrellas, in case they were needed, as well as hurricane lamps. There was a tall tree at the top of the jetty on the end near to the house with a tall, thin trunk Ignatius thought likely was an elm. The path from the jetty came up to the set of stone steps right in front of his window. One of the beautiful girls walking up the gravel path Ignatius recognised as the star of the musical stage, and had met her, but racking his brains, he just couldn't remember her name. Ignatius only rarely went to the theatre. He preferred a good book on his own now there was no girl in his life... The right girls were not interested in paupers however blue their blood. However nice a person. Not to be serious with.

Ignatius began to enjoy himself speculating on each new guest up the path from the river. The booze was finally making him mellow. They sometimes looked in the room but did not seem to see him with the tall glass in his hand and his back to the round pillar. When he looked up, the pillar rose high through the ceiling, most probably helping to hold up the house.

Some new guests came into the room that was serving as a bar and stood next to the low table covered with the drinks. They looked across at him inquiringly, standing on his own. When he failed to acknowledge the nods of the men they left him alone. The noise coming from all through the house was mounting so Ignatius could no longer hear the cars pulling up on the gravel in front. The building was aflame with light from the clumps of lamps the caterers had somehow positioned on the grass and in the trees.

When there were so many people, Ignatius liked to come early to find a good parking place for his small, red two-seater – the only possession he had ever truly loved in his life. He was pointed back down the driveway next to a yew hedge so when he left he would not have to turn the car around. Ignatius hoped no one had parked in front of him or he would not be able to get out. He was driving back to his London room in the dark for lack of money to stay in a hotel. No one in Oxfordshire had invited him to stay. Not for a long time.

Once again he was asking himself why he had bothered to come and give Lady Harcourt the cheque instead of putting it in the post when he felt a tug at the arm of his jacket. He was so far away in his mind he had not seen the person standing next to him.

"Good evening, Iggy. We might need some help," said Merlin St Clair. "Harry is here with Tina and Barnaby with some girl from America. I had a word with Cuddles Morton-Sayner to find out. To add to the trouble, Brett Kentrich has arrived with Christopher Marlowe and that is certainly not by coincidence. Are you alone?"

"Ah, Miss Kentrich, I saw her earlier and I couldn't remember her name. And yes, Merlin, I am alone. Where's Harry?"

"He's around somewhere. That young brother of mine is a menace. I think he knew Harry was bringing Tina. All we need is a family scene. You'll have to help me keep them apart, please. I can't abide scenes."

"How do we do that with everyone milling around?"

"I have no idea. I can't very well tell my brother to go home now can I? Frankly, we're not talking to each other."

"Are you alone too?"

"Yes."

"How about Miss Kentrich being here?"

"They have understudies, the big stars. Millie isn't exactly a star."

"Could have brought someone else?"

"Robert and I are looking for wives. To stop a brat of Barnaby's inheriting."

"I never thought of that."

"Neither did we until young Richard died. Poor Millie. She would have liked all this nonsense."

"But you said you were looking for a wife?"

"Quite frankly I've no notion where to start or where to look. Millie isn't complicated. Wives are complicated. With so many brothers I never thought it would matter whether I'm married or not." Merlin was smiling, thinking of his illegitimate daughter by Esther the one-time barmaid at the Running Horses in Mickleham.

"Then maybe Robert?"

"He's in America. Been there for months. No idea what he is up to. Never writes letters. Says writing books is quite enough for him. Very inconsiderate. You can't rely on Robert when it comes to that kind of thing."

"Maybe he has found a nice girl in America."

"I really hope so. You will help, old chap?"

"Of course. Harry's my boss."

"I forgot that. Oh, thank goodness. I'm no good at scenes."

CUDDLES MORTON-SAYNER NEVER FORGOT A FACE. The first time she met Merlin St Clair a dog ran away from him squealing with its tail between its legs. The very look of Merlin gave her the shivers. Two completely different eyes looking at her with one through a monocle. She had never been surprised he had never married despite making his fortune on the stock exchange. To Cuddles's mind, no woman in her right senses would choose to wake up every morning and have to look into that face.

When Merlin had asked her who his brother had brought to the dance, she told him a little about Stella Fitzgerald.

"Just an American. She invited your brother."

"How on earth did an American get an invitation to this?"

"Her father's very rich."

"Explains Barnaby. Thank you, Prudence. Nice to see you again, CE."

"He's the only person in London who calls you Prudence," said CE, watching Merlin's receding back.

"Who's Prudence?" said Stella, leaving Barnaby talking business with a drink in his hand.

"Me. That was Barnaby's brother asking who you were."

"Why didn't he ask Barnaby?"

"I have no idea," lied Cuddles. "Over there is Lord Montagu, the eldest son of the Duke of Manchester. One of the oldest dukedoms in England outside the Royals. Someone said Manchester was named after the family and not the other way round. Probably one of those stories... Oh dear, he has that Australian girl in tow. Rumour has it they are getting engaged. Montagu has coffee estates in Kenya. Ginty, the girl's sister, is married to one of the few rich Australian industrialists. Quite beautiful girls." Cuddles smiled. She had changed the subject.

"How do you know so much about people?"

"I never forget a face. Come along Stella, there's a young man I wish you to meet. We can leave Barnaby to talk business. Will you excuse us for a moment, CE?"

IGNATIUS BOWES-LYON FOUND Harry Brigandshaw on the lawn, smoking a cigarette on his own.

"What you doing out here, old chap?"

"Keeping out of the way till the place fills up. My wife has gone to the powder room... Brett is here. With Christopher Marlowe. How do these women do it? She wanted me to bring her but of course I couldn't. She arranged for me to receive an invitation through Cuddles Morton-Sayner. I had no idea. How on earth did Christopher get invited? He hates this kind of thing as much as I do."

"Barnaby is here, Harry. Merlin told me to warn you. With some rich American girl. Probably another client of Cuddles."

BRETT KENTRICH HAD EARLIER BEEN ENJOYING herself watching Harry on the lawn. She knew he had seen her ten minutes before. She had waved over the crowd that was still thin enough to allow her to recognise people on the other side of the room.

Fortunately for Christopher's wellbeing, he had been looking the other way when Brett waved at Harry. Christopher was now basking in the admiring looks directed at Brett. Being her escort for the night made him envied by half the men at the ball. He was smiling back at perfect strangers having yet to see anyone he knew which, when he thought about it, was not so surprising. Except at Clara's, he did not mix with society and then only as the piano player. Christopher had tied his long hair at the back to stop it flopping over his face, giving himself a ponytail... He had never seen Brett look more gorgeous. The new dress showed her ivory skin to the best and went against the current fashion by lifting her breasts. A few of the prettier young girls were wearing the new fashion. Everyone seemed to be coming across to talk to Brett, making his lack of conversation not so noticeable. All Christopher had to do was stand and be with Brett, tending to her needs.

"Sorry, darling, actresses have to be seen. Part of the job I'm afraid. There's a bar over there that really looks nice and it's not yet full. Come on. Follow me."

When they reached the small room, Brett turned around and went out again. Harry was not where she expected him to be. She hoped he had come up into the bar. Then she saw him through the French windows further down on the lawn under a tree where the lamps flooding the face of the old house shone some light. He was smoking a cigarette and talking to a man.

"What was that all about?" Christopher asked, following her.

Brett saw Tina at the moment they walked back into the ballroom. The band was playing. Some of the guests had begun to dance. Tina was looking around, searching for someone. To make Brett's night worse they were wearing similar dresses with Tina's large breasts making Brett's look small. Brett stared at Tina and Tina stared back. There were people in between them. The band was now loud, the trumpets and the trombones in the big band were in full swing. Tina glared and then went white, now looking over Brett's shoulder.

"Hello, Brett," said Barnaby. "How are tricks? Doesn't she look beautiful?" Barnaby was smiling across at Tina full of self-confidence.

"Leave her alone," said Brett.

"Don't you think more appropriately you should leave her husband alone, Brett? Ah, Christopher. Didn't see you at first... Where is Harry?"

"On the lawn talking to Ignatius Bowes-Lyon," said Christopher on his guard. He had also seen Harry under the tree.

"Merlin's here. On his own, poor chap... I think we are all in for a jolly good party don't you think?"

Barnaby began to walk off in what Christopher thought was Tina's direction.

Christopher moved forward quickly and grabbed Barnaby by the arm.

"If you go near that woman, I'll punch you on the nose."

"Don't be silly, Christopher, or whatever you call yourself these days. You couldn't punch the skin off a rice pudding."

Pulling his arm free with a jerk, Barnaby turned to look for Tina who was gone.

"There's going to be trouble," said Brett not unhappily. "He's obsessed with that girl. Thinks she's his property, not Harry's... Shall we dance?"

To Christopher's surprise, they swept round the room as if they had danced together all their lives. When the music finally stopped, they were on the opposite side of the ballroom.

"That was lovely, Christopher."

To Christopher's equal surprise, he even thought Brett meant what she had said.

BARNABY WAS FURIOUS. Were it not bad for business he would have punched Christopher. At the bar, he ordered a whisky which he drank. He could see Harry on the lawn with a man who looked familiar. Expecting Tina to find Harry, he watched the two men on the lawn. He was morose and went back to the bar for another drink. People were filling up the bar. Mostly men, their women in the ballroom watching the dance and listening to the music. Barnaby had his back to a pillar that when he looked up went right through the ceiling. His anger at being told what to do by Brett was building. The whisky was the fifth he had had that night. When he looked again for Tina out on the lawn, the two men were walking further away from the house in the direction of what looked like a jetty in the dark. Then Barnaby saw her. She was walking after the two men, fifty yards behind. He swallowed what was left of the whisky and walked to the French windows. Tina was walking slowly. With hope rising he walked out onto the terrace and down the small flight of stone steps. Tina turned. She must've seen him and began to run despite her long gown. It was the kind of game they had played as children. Barnaby began to run as well, following Tina running right down to the jetty, catching her up all the way.

HARRY AND IGNATIUS heard Tina shout and turned around from where they were standing next to the jetty with boats lined up on either side. They both saw a man running down behind her.

"Barnaby!" said Harry. "You'd better leave, Iggy. This is not your quarrel."

"Harry! Can't you help? Barnaby is chasing me."

BARNABY TOOK the one punch before he knew what had happened. He found himself going backwards between two boats into the water. A frozen Tina had her hand to her mouth. Harry was still coming forward as Barnaby fell in floundering.

When he climbed out, he was alone. A man who was guarding the boats gave him a smirk.

"You look a bit wet, sir," said the man in good humour.

"Mind your own bloody business."

Skirting the big house with all the lights, moving in the dark from tree to tree, Barnaby found his Bentley 3 Litre under the tree where he had parked. The keys to the car were in his pocket where he kept them with his house keys. He never let go of the keys.

Grimly smiling at not being seen, Barnaby drove his car down the long driveway of Nuneham Park, away from the party. He was on his way back to London. His jaw was clenched to stop his teeth chattering. His jaw hurt from the punch but not as much as his pride.

When Christopher and Brett sat down together later for the buffet supper in a room on the other side of the mansion to the ballroom, there was still no sign of Barnaby St Clair. Not long after Christopher had stood up to Barnaby, Brett had seen Tina and Harry come back into the house. They were hand in hand.

Looking at Christopher with new eyes, she thought Barnaby was wrong about the rice pudding. The man who liked to be thought of as a bohemian had straightened his back and seemed to grow six inches when confronting Barnaby. Brett knew he had gone through the war in the trenches as a captain in the Royal Dragoon Guards where conditions were anything but soft. She had a sneaking suspicion the only thing that would have looked like the skin off a rice pudding, had Christopher taken his threat further, would have been Barnaby's face. Under the long hair and soft voice, Brett had seen something else which made her wonder if all those years of war had made Christopher want to change who he had become in the army and live like someone else. The war had disgusted him and what it had made him become. Why he now said so little. Found small talk so unimportant.

Eating first her oysters and then a lobster salad, Brett began to think of Christopher Marlowe, the piano player, in a different light. There was much more to his life than *Happy Times*, musical or no musical. Then she smiled to herself. How often it was the best things in life were right under her feet.

"Why are you smiling, Brett?"

"You would have hit Barnaby?"

"Oh yes."

"And you would have beaten him."

"Oh yes."

For a man who never boasted about writing a long-running West End musical, Brett found the two softly spoken words more chilling than what might have been an ugly night in public that certainly would have reached the papers for both of them, the kind of bad publicity Oscar Fleming would have abhorred and never forgotten in their future careers.

Then it came to Brett as she watched Christopher staring at nothing in the room. The war had made them all killers. Christopher. Harry. Barnaby. Merlin. What she now saw was just the veneer of civilisation. The good manners. The polite talk. Even the way they drawled their speech.

"Was it terrible in the trenches?" she asked Christopher, putting a hand over his where it was resting on his knee half under the table.

Christopher did not reply. Instead, he gripped her hand so hard it almost hurt, making Brett want to cry, not for the pain in her own hand but the pain in Christopher's tortured mind. For Christopher, she saw the war would never be over and now people who knew were talking about another one.

CUDDLES MORTON-SAYNER WAS WORRIED. She was being paid to protect Stella Fitzgerald from social gaffes and find her an aristocratic husband. She had not seen Barnaby St Clair for hours. At first, she had thought with so many people milling around and socialising she had missed him in the crowd. CE was off talking business but came back regularly to see if she was all right. He was her partner for the evening and knew how to behave. Stella had been swallowed up in the crowd more than once for half an hour at a time. The May Ball was a place to meet people as well as dance. The old days of booking a girl for a dance had gone with the war when so many changes had swept through England. Even Lady Harcourt had no longer received her guests formally. People were expected to send her a cheque for the Red Cross in the Royal Mail, which made it easier but not so personal. A payment, no longer a gift.

By the time she had eaten her supper and Barnaby had still not turned up, Cuddles knew she had to do something. How were they going to get back to Riverglade and poor Douglas Hayter who had looked so forlorn when Stella swept away to the ball in all her finery? Douglas had come right out to the car on the driveway in his wheelchair to watch them go. When Cuddles had turned round in the car to look back as the Bentley reached the end of the long driveway, Douglas was still watching them from his wheelchair, the lights of the car shining up the avenue of trees for him to watch their car disappear.

"Where's Barnaby?" asked Stella. The three of them were eating supper together as was expected of them. Barnaby if nothing else was being rude.

Further down the table where people had sat down carrying their plates of buffet supper, Ignatius Bowes-Lyon heard the American accent along with the question. He had finished his supper and was thinking about the long drive back to London. He had drunk little, knowing how far he had to travel. He got up and walked to the other end of the table.

"Mr St Clair has gone back to London, I'm afraid," he said from behind the seated diners.

"Oh, dear," said Cuddles, "Barnaby brought us here from Riverglade in his car. We are all staying with Mr Hayter. But thank you for the information, Mr Bowes-Lyon."

"My own car is a two-seater. I'll ask Merlin St Clair to give you a lift."

"Thank you, Mr Bowes-Lyon. I would like to introduce you to Miss Stella Fitzgerald. Mr Bowes-Lyon is a cousin of the Duchess of York, the King's daughter-in-law. Please sit down, Mr Bowes-Lyon. Are you on your own?"

"Thank you. So nice to meet you, Miss Fitzgerald. Unfortunately, I have a long drive back to London. Despite Elizabeth, I have to work for a living when I can find an aeroplane to fly. I'll ask Merlin on my way out. You'll have to forgive me."

"Is there anything wrong with Barnaby?" asked Stella. She had been annoyed for hours being left on her own by her escort. Being stood up was the kind of novelty Stella did not like.

"I gather he fell in the river and thought it best to go straight home."

"Did anyone push?" asked Stella innocently, full of interest.

CE Porter, sitting on the other side of Cuddles, was snorting with pleasure, the very idea of Barnaby in wet evening clothes tickling his funny bone.

"Was Harry Brigandshaw anywhere near when his brother-in-law fell in the water?" he asked as a matter of fact.

"Funny you should ask," said Ignatius, "I rather think he was."

"Don't worry Merlin for a lift old chap," said CE, smirking happily. "I have many friends at the party... Good old Harry."

When Cuddles and Stella looked at him together with mirth in their eyes, all three sitting at the table broke out laughing as Ignatius bowed to the ladies and left, unable to keep a straight face.

Even Stella knew the rumour that surrounded Tina Brigandshaw without the actual facts ever being spoken. That there was bad blood between Harry Brigandshaw and Barnaby St Clair. Slowly, deliberately, Stella began to have her own ideas for the rest of the evening. Wonderful ideas.

.   .   .

HAD SHE PLANNED EVERY DETAIL, Tina Brigandshaw knew her timing could not have been better. The marital war was over the moment Barnaby St Clair hit the water impeccably dressed in tails, starched white shirt and white tie. The sapphire studs in his shirt front flashed just before he sank on his back beneath the surface. Only she, Harry and Ignatius Bowes-Lyon, halfway up the path towards the house, had seen what had happened. Tina had seen Ignatius spin around at the sound of the crack of bone knuckle on bone jaw, watch Barnaby disappear into the water, and then carry on up the path. She had not seen the man standing inside the door of the small shed that guarded the jetty. Harry had gone across to make sure Barnaby surfaced from the water. Silently he had taken her hand and walked her back to the party.

All evening they kept to themselves, only dancing to the slow numbers, keeping close together. They both knew they wanted to make love more than at any other time in their past. Being fought over by two men had never happened before to Tina. The real luck was Tina being right in the middle of her monthly cycle.

They said goodbye to no one. Lady Harcourt had long left her own party for the quiet of a friend's house. Brett had left with Christopher Marlowe from the jetty. Harry had stood watching them at the French windows in the small room that tomorrow would again be a sewing room when the servants took out the long table that stood in for a bar. Harry was smiling. He did not have to tell her he and Brett were over.

When they reached the temporary car park and found the pool car Harry had borrowed for the weekend, Cuddles Morton-Sayner was leaving with CE Porter and the American girl who had brought Barnaby to the May Ball. There was no sign of Barnaby and no one seemed to care. The car they were all climbing into was a large Austin driven by a chauffeur dressed in a uniform. Merlin St Clair was standing nearby. An old man with a bald head was in charge of the car. Inside the front seat was a woman with blue-rinsed hair. To Tina, passing by, the woman looked miffed.

"Everything all right, CE?" Harry called.

"Never been better. Jolly good party. Not a spot of rain."

"Good night."

"Good night, Harry."

DOWN ON THE RIVER, the wooden-cabin boat that belonged to Oscar Fleming was shining a light fifty yards down the river on its way back to Ferry Cottage. When they reached land, Christopher helped Brett from the boat having first tied it up to the posts next to the boathouse for the night. They went inside and turned on the lights. Brett found the key to Oscar Fleming's small cellar. The key was hidden in a flowerpot in which the flowers had long died from lack of water.

"Red or white, Christopher?" she called. "Better try red or it won't be chilled. Take off your coat and tie. Take the whole damn lot off if you want to. I'm getting out of all these clothes. The moon's due up soon. We can sit on the bench near the water. There are wine glasses in the kitchen and a corkscrew in the drawer."

They drank half the wine wearing very few clothes. Somewhere upriver towards Riverglade on the other bank of the River Thames, the owls were calling to each other. The night was warm and Christopher went for a swim in the river. When he climbed up the grass bank, Brett was waiting for him naked in the full light of the colourless moon. They made love slowly at first on the flat grass at the top of the bank, ignoring a boat going upriver. Neither of them even heard the engine.

AT RIVERGLADE in his bedroom on the ground floor, Douglas Hayter was trying to keep himself awake, listening to the owls calling to each other from the trees. Sometimes, when he was more wide-awake, he called back to the owls, imitating their sound. The owls called back to him as if he was one of their own. On nights when Douglas was unable to sleep, the conversations with the owls went on for hours.

Now he fell asleep.

He woke to the sound of them coming back from the ball. There was something wrong. The car was not a Bentley 3 Litre. Then he heard CE Porter call to someone a cheerful goodnight and the car drove away. Feet crunched on his driveway in front of his house. The front door opened with a key he had given CE Porter earlier in the evening. They were all being as quiet as they could. All was well. The Bentley must have broken down. Douglas fell back to sleep as the owls started calling to each other again. Down on the river, a motorboat was going downstream from the ball.

When Douglas woke again the owls were still calling from far away. The moonlight was streaming through the open French windows into the room that had been the drawing room before he came home without his legs. Stella was standing in the moonlight taking off the clothes she had worn at the ball. Douglas thought she must have walked in through the French windows. The night air was surprisingly warm for the beginning of May.

When she was naked, Stella came to the bed and one by one pulled off the bedclothes. Douglas was lying on his back. Neither said a word. Douglas's only clothing was his underpants. After the army, he had never slept in pyjamas. Stella leaned over him and pulled off his underpants, her large breasts in front of his face. He was rigid with excitement, vibrating with desire. He could see the light of the moon shining through her open legs as she lowered herself. Douglas felt the hard resistance as Stella pushed down, trying to let him inside her body. Then it broke and Stella let out her only sound, a stifled, ecstatic scream. Slowly they made love again, and this time Douglas screamed for himself. They relaxed, holding each other. Soon they were fast asleep with Stella curled up beside Douglas as he lay on his back on the naked bed.

When Douglas woke in the night, she was gone. Were it not for the lack of the sheet and blankets and his underpants not within reach, Douglas would have said it was all part of a beautiful dream. The cold must have woken him. The moon had gone. The night outside the French windows was quiet.

A cock crowed some minutes later from the farm far back on the other side of the river from Riverglade, a farm Douglas had only heard and never seen.

Douglas was smiling as he fell back into a dreamless sleep, calm and satiated.

When he woke into the morning, the house was quiet. On Sundays, the servants took the day off.

Douglas found his underpants on the floor beside his bed, picked them up with difficulty and pulled them on. Then he dressed and shifted himself off the bed into the wheelchair.

The grandfather clock in the hall was at ten past ten. Douglas wheeled himself into the kitchen to make himself a cup of tea. On the small breakfast table was a note from CE Porter.

"Problem with the car, old chap. Taken the train. Nice day for a walk to the station. We'll be back to collect the extra clothes. Wonderful evening. Trust you slept all right."

As he made the tea from the kettle he had boiled on the hob, Douglas Hayter was whistling.

"She'll be back," he said, smiling at his cat.

The cat, as usual, did not bother to even look up at him.

10

FEBRUARY 1928 – FATHERS AND DAUGHTERS

*W*hile Tina Brigandshaw was giving birth to her fourth child in a Paddington nursing home, Ralph Madgwick was moving into his new offices across the pond. The building on the docks was owned by the Blue Funnel Steamship Company of New York and was two storeys high. The ground floor was one vast open-plan warehouse with wire cages full of different cargo. The floor above was offices full of clerks handling all the paper. Ralph's first job had been renting space for himself and a secretary. For many years, Madgwick and Madgwick in London had done business with Blue Funnel in New York.

UNCLE WALLACE HAD BEEN IMPRESSED with Postlethwaite's report of Ralph's progress.

"Being out on his own will likely make him concentrate, Mr Madgwick. You can't run off for advice when something requires immediate attention. Even the telephone won't help at such a distance. Decisions will have to be his own. He does now know the difference between payment by letter of credit and payment by cash against documents. Along with the financial implications. Your nephew has a first-class brain when he applies himself. Can I recommend Miss Prescott goes with him? I've had a word with her. She's quite willing to go to America. Seemed rather anxious as a matter of fact."

"What a splendid idea, Mr Postlethwaite. What a splendid idea. She can keep an eye on him in more ways than one."

"Were Miss Prescott a man, she would have made a first-class departmental manager."

"Oh, well. The new ways of the world haven't gone that far quite yet. Dear oh dear. What a ghastly thought. I've known a few women in my life who love to order people around. How long must we leave Ralph in America before we can give him my job?"

"At least two years, sir."

"As long as that?... I was hoping... Miss Prescott can write us reports of his progress. If they are very good, maybe... If he puts on lots of business for instance."

"If he breaks into American business he may not wish to come back."

"Now that is a dreadful thought. I'll have to die in harness. Did I tell you about my small estate in Cumbria? It really is very beautiful. The house is on a lovely slope..."

Postlethwaite, who had so far been standing hoping the conversation with the senior partner in the senior partner's office would not go in the direction it was now going, sat down. While Uncle Wallace rambled on, Postlethwaite let his mind run through the rest of the problems in the office. Whether Ralph Madgwick went to America and came back again was right at the bottom of the pile. The very least of his worries!

"When can he go?"

"Who, sir?"

"Ralph, of course."

"As soon as it can be arranged, I suppose."

"Excellent. Ask Miss Prescott to come in. I'll give her specific instructions to make sure Ralph comes back to England. Don't want a Madgwick turning into an American, do we? I always remember that bit about the Boston Tea Party. All that tea floating in wooden chests around the bay. Goodness me, everyone has to pay their taxes. Even Americans. How can such a silly thing start such a big revolution? Now if the empire had stuck together as it should have done, Germany would not have gone to war in the first place. They always say families should stick together if they want to get on in life. Why, I was talking to a chap in the club last week who talked of another war with Germany. As if we didn't have enough trouble the last time... Where are you going, Mr Postlethwaite?"

"I have to spend a penny. I have a..."

"Of course. Run along. Nature doesn't stop for anyone."

. . .

THE VIEW from Ralph's office was out over a bleak New York harbour. It was snowing and the ships were shrouded in white. Like ghosts lying silent. Inside, unlike an English office, the two rooms rented by Madgwick and Madgwick were warm: the Americans had installed central heating.

By the time Rosie Prescott made contact with the local telephone company, things to her seemed quite out of hand. The only thing she seemed to have in common with the Americans was the English language.

"Use my phone, lady. Local calls cost nothing in America," said one of the Blue Funnel clerks. In England, a local call cost a penny.

"Thank you, Mr Rossini."

"Alberto. That's my name, Rosie." Back home, people used their Christian names in families. Never with strangers.

"Will they give us our own telephone by the end of the month?"

"In an hour, lady."

"That's unheard of in London."

"Here the phone company's a business that tries to make the shareholders a profit. Quicker they give you a line, quicker they start charging you for calls you make to London, Rosie. Within an hour. Longer than that, you ask your man Ralph to kick his fanny when he comes to put in the line."

"Fanny, Mr Rossini, really!"

"Call me Alberto. Just use my phone and call them."

Inside his office, Ralph was wearing a broad grin when Rosie came in to report progress.

"What are you grinning about, sir?"

"What's this 'sir' all of a sudden?"

"You are now my boss."

"We're in America, Rosie. Call me Ralph. And just for your self-edification, Rosie Prescott, in America the bonnet of a car is the hood, the boot the trunk, and the thing we all sit on a fanny, not a bottom, and certainly not what you were thinking of out there talking to Alberto."

"Are you sure?"

"He's right, Rosie," called Alberto. "The arse in America is the fanny."

"How most dreadfully confusing."

The thin walls of the office partitions had allowed the staff of Blue Funnel to be part of the private conversation. Rosie's shocked, very English reply, brought forth a gale of instant laughter.

"Welcome to America," someone called.

Rosie Prescott blushed bright red right to the roots of her hair.

. . .

WHEN RALPH WAS ALONE AGAIN he got up from behind the desk that had been delivered that morning and again looked out of the window onto the docks. People were moving around doing their business in the snow. No one seemed to care about the weather. The guffaw of laughter had given Ralph a warm feeling of welcome. He was going to enjoy America even more than he had thought.

Somewhere out there he knew Rebecca was going about her day. Ralph knew they could either meet in secret as if they were doing something wrong or he could first go and ask Sir Jacob if he may court his daughter.

Ralph began to pace his small office, deep in thought. Rosie had closed the door to his office to hide her embarrassment.

"Poor Rosie. She'll learn," he said to himself. "Poor Rosie." Not only did he know why she had been sent to America by his Uncle Wallace, he knew why Rosie had accepted. To tell her he was fond of her but not in that way would make everything worse. To say nothing would be unfair to Rosie Prescott. To add to his woes a stab of fear hit the pit of his stomach at the thought of meeting Rebecca again so soon. Was it just all letters? The build-up in their imaginations creating for each of them what they wanted from the other only in their minds. Would they meet again as lovers or strangers that the months had torn apart? He didn't really know the girl, he told himself. Just that instant attraction they hoped had changed their lives. How much was going to be real? How much was just a figment of their imaginations?

Before Ralph could make up his mind as to what he was going to do next, a young man in a smart uniform was shown into his office by Rosie. A Rosie who had regained her composure. The young man was grinning all over his face as he would at an old friend.

"Can I help you?" asked Ralph retreating behind his British reserve. So far as he knew he had never seen the man before in his life.

"Where do you want it?"

"Where do I want what, my man?"

"Your telephone. Am I too late? Did the other company get here first?"

"You have more than one telephone company in New York?"

"We sure do." Even Ralph found himself learning. In England, the telephone company was the government.

"Just on my desk. On the right. And an extension for Miss Prescott."

"Rosie's nice. Says I can have a cup of tea when I'm finished. Now that's nice... You British?"

"English."

"What's the difference?"

Stopping himself from a long conversation that would take neither of them anywhere, Ralph kept his mouth shut. He had had an idea. He was first going to pay a courtesy call on Sir Jacob Rosenzweig. After all, he was the local representative of one of Rosenzweig's larger clients... A plan was beginning to form in his mind.

THE LAST PERSON in the world Sir Jacob Rosenzweig expected to see walking into his office the next morning was Ralph Madgwick. By bad luck, he was standing at reception wishing a valued depositor goodbye by seeing the man to the lift. Sir Jacob's first thought was to ask Ralph Madgwick what he was doing in America, which would have been stupid. After the letter delivered to Rebecca in Central Park it was obvious they had been writing to each other. Sir Jacob had the bizarre idea the man had come to ask for his daughter's hand in marriage. After all, he had run out of England with Rebecca and destroyed Ralph Madgwick's letters to his daughter.

"Good morning, Sir Jacob. Well, this is nice. Came in just on the offchance. Took me a week to put the office together and quite rightly you are my first call. Rather pleasant to see a friendly face if you know what I mean... Both of us so far from home."

On the outside, Ralph looked as cheerful as the man who a day before had put in his office telephone. Inside Ralph was terrified. The palms of his hands were sweating just as they had before going over the top in a dawn attack during the war. His heart was pounding as Sir Jacob Rosenzweig gaped at him without saying a word.

"I'm Ralph Madgwick, sir."

"I know that."

"Of Madgwick and Madgwick, New York. The company is not yet incorporated but the corporate lawyer said it would be by the end of next month. The only thing that has taken any time, as a matter of fact. Which was why I came to see you before the shares are registered with the American authorities. I want to offer you twenty per cent of Madgwick and Madgwick Inc."

"What are you talking about?"

"You didn't know we were opening an American office?"

"No, I didn't."

"My Uncle Wallace said he had written to you, sir." Ralph felt the blush coming to his face at the lie but luckily Sir Jacob had turned his back and was walking away. It was all going worse than the worst scenario he had imagined.

"You'd better follow me to my office, young man."

Like the small boy at school following his housemaster into the housemaster's study for a caning, Ralph followed the tall, thin man with the face that reminded Ralph of a predatory hawk. At that point, Rebecca was clean out of his mind. All he wanted to do was save his skin. People were staring at him.

Inside the big office, Sir Jacob gently shut the door in a way more menacing than if the door had been slammed in Ralph's face.

"Have you seen Rebecca?" snapped Sir Jacob Rosenzweig.

"No, sir."

"Good. Sit down before you fall down... Now. What is this all about? From the very beginning. And don't lie to me. And yes, before you start, I did burn your letters, something I have yet to tell Rebecca."

Instead of the conversation he had planned in his mind, Ralph gabbled. All the statements of them both having the same God to being Englishmen fled out of his mind at the man's stare. All Ralph could talk about was his plans for his company. Even his request to be introduced to bank clients who might like his services was met with a cold, silent stare. At the end of the ordeal, Ralph stood up to go and put out his hand to shake hands with Sir Jacob. The man with the hawk-like face kept staring into his eyes without a word and without getting up from his seat.

"Goodbye, sir. It's been very nice seeing you again, sir. We did have a little chat at your company's anniversary in London, sir. A brief chat. Goodbye, sir. I hope you're liking America. Don't bother getting up, I'll see myself out. Goodbye, sir."

Like a man with lead feet, Ralph made it to the door, opened it, got himself out and shut the door to Sir Jacob's office without turning around. Then he walked to the lift. Everyone in the outside office was gaping at him.

It was the longest one-sided conversation Ralph had ever had in his life. Only when he reached the street did he begin to feel comfortable again. The snow was still falling on the wide streets of New York as Ralph walked the pavement, his mind seething from impatience.

"The old codger can't say I didn't try doing the right thing. Now, Sir Jacob Rosenzweig, it is war. War is something I know."

Not unsurprisingly, nobody on the busy street took the slightest notice of a man talking to himself. It took Ralph half the morning to calm down before he walked back to his office.

"So the ogre bit your head off?" said Rosie Prescott with a smile.

"Something like that. He didn't seem to want the shares."

"Or you. Good. Your Uncle Wallace phoned."

"How does he know our number so soon?"

"I told him. My first call. Alberto was right. The phone company are making money out of us the second day in our new office."

"At least someone is winning."

"What are you going to do, Ralph?"

"What did Uncle Wallace want?"

"We have our first client. You're to go and see them. Give you something to think about."

"I've plenty to think about, Rosie Prescott. It's just that right now none of it is very pleasant."

AFTER A YEAR IN AMERICA, Robert St Clair had forgotten Ralph Madgwick and his unrequited love for Rebecca Rosenzweig. Only when he reached New York with the finished manuscript of *Holy Knight* was the sequence of events brought back to him by Freya Taylor; the same week Ralph Madgwick opened his New York office.

Robert and Freya had been in New York a week and were walking slowly past Central Park, the pavement icy from the earlier snow, Freya holding Robert's arm in case his prosthetic foot caused him to slip. Robert had insisted on the walk to give him some fresh air. He was the only person Freya had ever met who left open the bedroom window in the depth of winter. Freya had long concluded the English were different despite their common ancestry and language.

A policeman in white gloves had stopped the traffic and was signalling to pedestrians they could now cross the wide road and go into the park.

"I gave her the letter right there," said Freya.

"What letter?" said Robert, having no idea what she was talking about.

"The one you sent Glen which I gave to Rebecca."

He walked on for a full minute without making any reply. She thought Robert had not heard what she said which was quite common. When the plot of the book was running through his mind, it was as if nothing around him existed. During those times, Freya completely lost him. She had learnt not to interrupt his thoughts or the scene in his head would go away.

They walked on arm in arm, which was nice. Freya was glowing with happiness. Not only was she now a fully-fledged journalist with her own syndicated column, but she was also the first person to have been allowed to read the handwritten manuscript of *Holy Knight*. Despite all the crossings and corrections, the story of Robert's ancestor who had gone on the Third Crusade had kept her engrossed right through to the end of the long story and the Crusaders' attempt to reconquer the Holy Land for the Pope.

"Strange how what at the time seems such a small thing can completely change a man's life. Will you marry me, Freya? I'm missing a foot and have spent more than half my life, which may make you think I'm not worth much."

"What are you talking about?"

"You and Ralph Madgwick's letter and Glen sending me your love in the cable. Doing one good turn gave us another. Or do you really think me too old and my book no good?"

"Cleaned up, typed and printed in a book, *Holy Knight* will sell better than *Keeper of the Legend*."

"I didn't ask how many copies it will sell, Freya... So it was back there at the crossing it all started. I wonder if anything became of the two of them?"

"Oh, yes. I was going to tell you weeks ago when I put the story in 'Juliet' under false names. Ralph should be here right now in New York. You were still absorbed at the end of your book and I didn't think you'd need the distraction."

"Did you hear what I said earlier on?"

"Lovers never marry, Robert. It's bad form. The moment they marry, they quarrel and split up. I don't want to lose you. In a better age, we'd just live together instead of running two homes."

"I will never understand women."

"They should have met by now."

"Who?"

"Rebecca and Ralph. Now that sequence of events should lead to a nice clean marriage."

"So seducing me wasn't clean?"

"You seduced me, Robert St Clair."

"Let's just say we seduced each other."

"I'll settle for that."

"So you won't marry me?"

"No."

"Then I'll just have to get you pregnant. That was how Tina Pringle married Harry Brigandshaw. I was up at Oxford with Harry... The St Clairs and the Pringles have lived in the same patch of England for centuries. There's a story about my brother Barnaby and Tina I won't tell you. Those two have loved each other since they were small children... Can you explain the world to me, Freya Taylor?"

"Yes, I can. Enjoy the moments while you have them. Like this one... I won't forget you proposed."

"I should jolly well think not... Freya, why are you crying?"

Their appointment with Max Pearl was at three o'clock that afternoon. He said he was going to tell them both what he thought of the book.

"Are you getting nervous about this afternoon, Robert?" asked Freya, sniffling into her handkerchief.

"Just don't let go of my arm."

ROBERT HAD ARRIVED from England on the RMS *Olympic* in January of the previous year. Having liked the change of London after so many years in the country, he had taken seriously Glen's suggestion of a small book tour to America. The idea of seeing Freya Taylor after so many years was part of his motivation. A woman who sent her love after so much time must be carrying a candle, he convinced himself before booking the passage on the boat. Sometimes Robert was not sure if the ideas he made for himself were not out of his book. His own life and the teeming lives of his characters often crossed and Robert was not sure what was fact and what was fiction. In his books, a woman who remembers a man after ten years has to be carrying a torch. Definitely, if they ask a third party to send their love.

They had found Robert a small cottage near a ski slope outside Denver where he could still write, as the book tour Glen put together with Max Pearl was limited to Colorado. The gestating book on the Crusades had exploded in his mind the day Freya Taylor showed Robert the snowbound cottage among the pine trees an hour's drive from Denver. By then it was the weekend and the book tour was over, three half-hour radio interviews that went out across America. Miraculously, the first sight of each other after nearly ten years had sparked the same excitement in both of them... Robert believed in sparks.

With the log fire going well in the grate of the small cabin, as Freya called the cottage, they had made love on the rug in front of the fire. They were older, both aware of the shortness of life. She was soft, warm, intelligent and just as interested in writing as Robert. Over the first weekend, alone in the snow-covered wooden cabin, Freya had written her 'Juliet' column and Robert's new book had begun to burst from his mind onto paper.

As it turned out, never before in his life had he finished a book in a year.

The whole setup was perfect. During the week, he was alone with no one to interrupt his writing. On the weekends, Freya drove out to the cabin where they talked, skied and made love. She brought with her the week's food. Robert liked cooking. Mrs Mason, the old cook at Purbeck Manor, had taught Robert how to cook his favourite dishes.

"If you know how to cook them, Mr Robert, they can never take them away."

"They are a legacy I will always treasure, Mrs Mason. A gift from you to me that will last a lifetime."

"You and your words, Mr Robert! Go away with you."

"The way to a person's heart is always through their stomach, Mrs Mason. Just you go and ask Old Warren. Why, he'd spend his entire life in your kitchen if you'd let him."

Mrs Mason had been in the house when Robert was born, a pillar of strength throughout his life. He had told Freya all about Mrs Mason when Freya asked him in awe where he had learnt how to cook.

During that first winter, the locals had taught Robert how to ski despite his wooden foot. It was all in the balance. For the first time since the war, Robert was mobile like anyone else, dashing down the white slopes, in and out of the pine trees, yelling like a maniac, feeling whole and real, in love and writing a better story than anything he had done before in his life. In the spring, they had a canoe to go out on the river, Robert's arms from the skiing strong as steel on the paddle. "I'll propose to her when I finish the book," he had told himself back then in the midst of his happiness.

Even her refusal did not matter. They were in love. If Max Pearl liked *Holy Knight*, his cup of life would be full. Always so much of Robert's life came back to whether people liked his books. Especially the one he had just finished.

"He'll have loved it, Robert."

"You can read my mind."

"Of course I can. We'll have a nice lunch at 21 and then go on to Max Pearl's office... Did I tell you I met Hemingway at 21?"

"Yes, Freya, but tell me again. He's the best writer in the world. Did I ever tell you that, Freya Taylor?"

Freya smiled up at him as she gripped his arm, a hollow pit of fear in her stomach caused by the worry that Max did not like the book... If he thought it wonderful as she did, why hadn't he phoned? He had had the book a week. Publishers and newspapers. Editors were all the same. Torturers the lot of them.

. . .

THE BACKGROUND for *Holy Knight* had come out of a hole in the inner wall of the banquet hall at Purbeck Manor. A St Clair ancestor had put the documents there after saving them from the family's seat Corfe Castle before Oliver Cromwell knocked it down during the years of the Commonwealth. Where the records had been during Cromwell's thirteen years as Lord Protector of England, the family had no record. As soon as Purbeck Manor was built with a safe compartment built into the stone wall of the hall, the records were placed inside and the wall sealed up to make the hiding place look like the rest of the building.

Robert's great-grandfather had stumbled on the inside cavity when he was drunk. His wife had thrown a silver goblet full of wine at him while he was licking spilt soup from the dress of the lady sitting next to him. The goblet had hit the wall with the sound of a strange interior echo. Or so the family story went. Robert's great-grandfather had denied he was licking soup from the girl's lap. When he came up for air he said he was picking up from the floor the girl's dropped napkin and putting it back in her lap, his denial meeting with a gale of laughter from the rest of the guests at the dinner. Family lore said his great-grandfather's parties were famous across the realm. By the time he died in his wife's arms at the age of ninety-two, he had gone through the family fortune and been forced to sell most of the land around the Manor to pay off his debts.

Robert had told Max Pearl the story when Robert handed him the manuscript of *Holy Knight* the previous week.

"It was the greatest love affair in our family history," he told Max.

"Is the story true? The cavity inside the wall?"

"I have the old parchments he took out of the hole in the wall. We were only knights in those days. Sir Henri Saint Claire Debussy went with Richard the First to the Holy Land. Where he built our first castle and made a fortune charging merchants from the East passage through his land. His grandson came back to England and built Corfe Castle that now lies in ruins. The documents in the wall are about our family in Palestine before the Mohammedans chased the Christians out again."

"Can they possibly be true? Could parchment survive so many centuries?"

"Why ever not? Read the book, Max. Make up your mind. A few hundred years in English history is nothing. Most families, rich and poor, know who their ancestors were and what they did."

"Can I see those documents? Can the public?"

"Oh, no. They belong to my family. There are bits I wouldn't want anyone outside the family to see. What's in the book are the nice bits. War, holy or not, is still war and never romantic. Always ugly. You have my personal word on that, Max. You read the book and tell me how I could possibly have imagined everything you read... I wasn't even there but you'll think I was... Or I hope you will!"

"Leave it with me for a week. Three p.m. next Tuesday back here in my office, Robert, and I'll tell you what I think."

"You don't look happy, Max."

"I don't like tall stories."

"You'll see."

"I hope so."

At that point, Freya had been pressing her nails so hard into the palm of Robert's hand, he thought she was going to break the skin. She was as passionate about *Holy Knight* as he was.

BY THE TIME they took a cab to 21, they were glad to be out of the cold. Robert thought if he looked in a mirror, he would find his nose had turned blue. Freya was relying on a table from her last time in 21 with Max Pearl. She felt part of the family. A member of the in-crowd who had talked to Ernest Hemingway and drunk wine with Jack Kreindler. When they got inside the speakeasy, clouds of smoke filled with heat and noise enfolded them. Someone at the table just inside the door had told a good joke. A fat man was trying to split his sides laughing. More than three tables through the cigarette and cigar smoke were impossible to see. They stood with their backs to the closed door knowing it was hopeless. The place was full. Robert had rarely seen a room so packed. Not even Clara's. Certainly not at this time of day. To add to Robert's surprise a big band started playing and it was lunchtime.

"Is this the only place in New York you can get a drink and food?" Robert asked Freya, annoyed with himself for letting the cab go before he had secured a table.

A florid man who ate well was beaming at Freya. Freya was beaming at the man with the florid face. The man had a cigar stuck in his mouth. All, it now appeared to Robert, was not lost. Robert, unlike in the clubs of London, felt quite out of place. He was again a country bumpkin up from Dorset for the day, or, as he said to himself, from wherever the bumpkins came from outside of New York.

The florid man now fixed Robert with his whole attention, ignoring Freya a moment after the first big beam. The man to Robert was obviously used to changing his allegiances at short notice. Robert looked behind to see if anyone was between himself and the door even though he could feel the doorknob in his back. After a year in their country, Robert still found American behaviour quite strange. Only brothers, fellow officers or old friends would greet each other with such familiarity. So far as Robert was aware he had never seen the man in his life.

"Hello there, Bob. Freya, you clever girl. Right where Max thought you'd bring the famous author for lunch. Welcome to 21, Bob. Max is waiting for you at the table. Follow me. You just stay as long as you like, Bob... You see. There he is... Here they are, Max! Captured at the door. Right as you said. Leave you now. Have a nice day, Bob. You can give me a drink later when the drunks have gone home."

Robert's American publisher had got up to move out a chair for Freya. Max Pearl was at the table alone. He was grinning at Robert like a Cheshire cat that had just done a good trick. His right hand was held out to Robert, preceding the grin. Robert thought Max was tight, which was true.

"Been here a while myself. Have a drink! Thought you'd bring him here to lunch, Freya."

"Who was that man?" asked Robert.

"Jack. Owns the joint. Or part of it. I've ordered the champagne."

"We can't talk drunk, Max."

"We don't have to. That book's the best book I've ever read. This is a celebration. Couldn't wait."

"Why didn't you phone me, Max?"

"And spoil the fun? Spoil the surprise. Sit down, Robert. Just don't take down your trousers and take off your leg or Misty over there will be killed in the rush the way she's looking at you. It's brilliant. We're going to print a hundred thousand for the first run."

The band stopped playing and someone tapped the microphone. The florid man's voice called for everyone's attention.

"Ladies and gentlemen. All the way from England, the famous author of *Keeper of the Legend*. The Max Pearl we all love whispered me there's a new book going to the press. Give the author a big hand. Bob St Clair. Right over there in the spotlight with the lovely Freya. Come on now. A big hand."

When the spotlight went away from his face and Robert could see again, it wasn't Misty's eyes popping at him that caught his eye. At the table next to Misty was a young girl looking at him with surprise written on her face. With her was a not so young man.

"Did you have to do that, Max?" asked Robert.

"Publicity, Bob."

"Don't call me Bob. My name is Robert. You're drunk."

"So will you be by the end of the day when I'm finished with you."

"Who's that girl staring at me? I think she's coming over."

"The price of fame, Robert. Have a drink."

The girl and the not so young man had both got up. The man was now following the girl. Robert was blushing from embarrassment. It was one thing for him to talk to the public on radio, another to be singled out for attention in public.

The rest of the throng had given him a gawp and gone back to what they were doing before Jack Kreindler took to the microphone.

Both Max and Robert stood up as the girl reached their table, the man hovering just behind the girl's elbow. Robert saw she was very pretty. A girl in her early twenties. She had the look of a woman who expected men to do what she wanted of them.

"I'm afraid I don't think I know..." Robert began. The band was now so loud Robert doubted the girl could hear what he said.

The girl smiled and said something Robert was unable to catch except for the word Barnaby. The only Barnaby Robert knew was his brother safely on the other side of the pond.

"Sit down, folks," shouted Max. "Have a drink. We're celebrating. My name is Max Pearl. I'm Bob's publisher. This is Freya. You want a book signed I don't have right now. But that just doesn't matter. You must know my friend Jack Kreindler?"

"My name is Stella Fitzgerald. I'm a friend of your brother Barnaby. Before I met John Lacey, my fiancé. John is the Marquess of Ravenhurst. I'm surprised you two haven't met."

"Have a drink," shouted Max just as the band stopped playing for some other reason as it was not the end of the song. "Have a drink. We're having a celebration."

"So are we," said Stella full of her own confidence. "This is John's first day in America. We are going to Boston for John to meet my father."

"Are you Patrick Fitzgerald's daughter?" asked Max, impressed. "Bob, move out a chair for Stella. How you going, marquess? Marquess? Isn't that French?"

"No, we're English. The French pronounce theirs like a large tent when you hold parties in the garden."

"Well, that's just fine. Just fine. Welcome to America. Have a drink? You two been engaged for long?"

"Just a week," said John Lacey. "It was in the *Times*."

"The *New York Times*?"

"The *Times of London*. Just below the Court Circular."

"I don't think Max knows the importance of our *Times*," said Robert, trying to help.

When the happy couple left to go back to their table, Robert was none the wiser.

"What was all that about?" he asked.

"Quite a lot," said Freya, wishing she could tell a real story in her 'Juliet' column. With real names.

BY THE TIME the three of them left 21 to walk down the cold street arm in arm with Freya holding them up in the middle, Max had made Robert drunk as he had promised. With some difficulty, Freya poured her escorts into a taxi. After being dropped at their hotel, Freya hoped the taxi would take Max straight home and not to an illegal bar.

Half an hour later was the first time since her childhood Freya had gone to bed at six o'clock in the afternoon. Robert was already fast asleep in their double bed. Brazenly they had booked into the hotel as husband and wife.

The last thing Freya thought of before she fell asleep was one hundred thousand copies of *Holy Knight* coming off the press.

CUDDLES MORTON-SAYNER HAD FOUND John Lacey after researching every titled family in the British Isles. Her eye was first caught by three lines in *Debrett's Peerage*. All it gave was John Lacey's full name and his titles. No regiment. No club. No address. The date of birth was 1888. No marriage. No children. When Cuddles made enquiries no one knew anything about the man, though she did find out he was the third of four brothers. His two older brothers had been killed in the war within a week of each other in 1915. In 1916, the 15th Marquess of Ravenhurst went down with his ship while serving in the Royal Navy off the coast of South America. Three months before the war ended the younger brother died of the flu. The mother had been dead for many years. All that was left was John who so far as Cuddles could find out had never done anything with his life that anyone knew about. The man who was the source of Cuddles's information had been in the army with the youngest Lacey before the boy died of the flu. It was clear to Cuddles if she could find the man, he was just what she was looking for. Not a duke, but a rank only one further down the peerage. Patrick Fitzgerald would surely be satisfied with his daughter becoming a marchioness.

Two months after the May Ball at Nuneham Park, Cuddles tracked him down in an old crumbling house in Lincolnshire. Cuddles had been too busy hunting down her quarry to go back to Riverglade to collect her clothes. CE Porter said the evening suit he had left in a small suitcase in Douglas Hayter's hall cupboard was too small around the waist for him anyway. Stella never mentioned the ball gown she had left behind.

Looking at the crumbling house surrounded by an unkempt garden from the lane, it was clear to Cuddles the Lacey family were not flourishing. She parked her small car and walked up what was once a driveway towards the brooding house. There was no sign of life. Cuddles tried to look in the windows, at least through the ones that were unhidden by unkempt shrubs. The windowpanes, all small, looked as if no one had cleaned them for years. Inside she could see the shapes of pieces of furniture.

Working her way round to the back, Cuddles found a well-kept kitchen garden that stretched into an apple orchard. The apple trees had been pruned the previous autumn; there was fruit on the trees.

From the field behind the orchard came the sharp crack of a shotgun followed by a small animal squealing. The squeals stopped abruptly. Someone began to whistle. Cuddles knew she was too far into the wilderness to run back to her car.

A man with a twelve-bore shotgun under one arm came into view. When he walked nearer, Cuddles could see he was carrying a dead rabbit. The rabbit's neck had been broken and was flopping head down by the man's side. The whistling stopped abruptly when the man saw Cuddles. He smiled and swung the gun up over his shoulder so the barrel was pointing behind him and not at Cuddles. He looked in his forties, dressed in old clothes that twenty years ago might have been in fashion.

"I'm John Lacey. Got a rabbit. Don't see anyone around here anymore. Have you been up to the old house? The roof leaks. Frightful bore. I heard your car. Sound travels in the country. We can have a cup of tea. Don't keep anything stronger I'm afraid. Probably just as well. What can I do for you, missus?"

Cuddles thought the man was nervous, speaking in short sentences.

"Miss Prudence Morton-Sayner. Due to a carry-over from my childhood, people call me Cuddles. Do you live here all alone, Lord Ravenhurst?"

"I haven't used the title for years. The tradesmen are less generous to the gentry. Quite alone. Ever since that dreadful war came to an end. The tradesmen don't come into the Lincoln marshes anymore. Well, not here. Feed myself." John Lacey held up the dead rabbit for inspection. "We had pretty much run out of money as a family before the war. A commander's pay in the navy isn't much... Do you know we were one of the most powerful earls in the sixteenth century? How the mighty have fallen."

They were walking in single file up the only trodden path. By the tone of his voice, the Marquess of Ravenhurst clearly thought the fallen mighty were better off as they were. The rabbit was losing blood out of its mouth, the blood dripping carelessly down the man's front and left leg.

"I grow my own fruit and vegetables and along with rabbits eat the odd unfortunate game bird that crosses my gunsight. I go into Grimsby once a month to buy dry provisions and post my month's work. Once a year the chaps at Oxford post me a small cheque... I hope I'm not boring you. We go in through the kitchen. The fact is, I can't open the front door anymore. Warped. Doesn't matter. Bell doesn't work and nobody knocks... Did you come all the way out here to see me? Well, you would, wouldn't you? There's no one else to see."

John Lacey, as he liked to be called, gave Cuddles a pleasant laugh and for the first time properly looked at her.

"Do you want to tell me now what this is all about?" he asked.

They were inside the kitchen, which was spotless. On the hob of the stove under a still glowing wood fire was a large pot of stew. John Lacey took off the lid and stirred his stew with a long-handled wooden spoon. Bending down, he picked up small logs of dry wood from the floor and fed them into the fire. The fire took up the left side of the old stove next to the baking oven. The stove was set inside an alcove with a chimney leading up through the ceiling. There were no lights in the room hanging from the almost black ceiling.

"This was the gatekeeper's house back in the old days when my family lived in the castle. You can see the ruins if you know where to look. I had a chap here last year who was studying old castles. Spent a couple of days. You'll forgive me if I talk rather a lot but I'm told people do who live on their own. Of course, I talk to myself. Take a seat, please. I'll make the tea when that old kettle on the hob boils again. The new wood will catch fire any moment... There it goes. Gives a nice taste to the tea, the wood fire. Or so I think. So used to it now. We don't have milk. I don't like having anything on the property bigger than myself and I can't milk a cow. Tried once. The cow didn't like my hands and kicked over the bucket... That was the trouble. We were taught things of no practical use. Certainly, nothing that could make us any money. One of the chaps up at Oxford gave up studying the humanities he had studied for three years and went into the City. Frightfully rich now. They say the stock market is going on up forever. They send me the *Telegraph* to the post office in Grimsby, which I read in date order when I come home. Every word. All I do for work is translating ancient Greek texts.

For pleasure, I read the *Telegraph* and my library, the only thing of value left of the family which I won't sell."

"And tend the kitchen garden, prune the fruit trees and shoot the odd rabbit."

"You saw! You can keep apples for six months if you stack them on trays so they don't touch. By spring, they are small and shrivelled but still nice to eat. I bottle the plums. Would you like some of last year's plums? How far have you come from today?"

"I drove up from London. I'm a social consultant."

"I say, what's that?"

"People who wish to move in good society but don't know how pay me for my services. I show them how to behave. Introduce them to the people they wish to meet... Have you been to America, Mr Lacey?"

"That's better, Cuddles. What a lovely name. There's so much in a name. No, of course not. The furthest I went was to Berlin before the war. Spent three happy years roaming the capitals of Europe after I came down from Oxford in 1909. Met a couple of chaps from America who were up at Oxford. There was even a chap from Southern Rhodesia who was reading geology. I tutored students in English that paid for my food and a small room. Sometimes there was enough for a good pint of German beer in Berlin or a bottle of wine in Paris. They were the happiest years of my life. Apart from Greek, I speak rather good German and French even if I have to say so myself. An educated man they used to call us, when it mattered more than the ability to make money... Now, there we are. By leaving the kettle on the hob, it boils quickly once the fire gets going. That wood was nice and dry."

During the one-sided conversation, John Lacey had hung the rabbit up by its back legs placing a small silver cup under its head to catch the blood.

"Hang them for two days in the summer. The hares I hang for a week. We had an old cook before the war when my mother was still alive who liked to see maggots in the hare's eyes before she would butcher and jug the hare in its own blood. Said it was the only way to judge if the hare was high enough before cooking the meat. Best jugged hare in the world... I let the tea leaves draw for five minutes. We will have to wait for a little for our tea."

"Have you read about America in the *Telegraph*?"

"They don't report much about America. More about the colonies. India. Africa. That sort of thing."

"There is a rich man in America who wishes for his daughter to be married to a peer. Are you married, Mr Lacey?"

"Don't be silly. The only love of my life was German but we couldn't marry as I did not have any money. The rich marry the rich. The educated poor stay single."

"He is Irish. His money probably dubious but real. Stella is twenty-two and very pretty."

"Stella is a nice name."

"I want you to marry her."

"Whatever for? Why would a pretty young girl want to do that in the first place? I'm old at forty in her eyes. And very poor. I doubt I have ten pounds in the bank."

"To become a marchioness. The father wants one of his sons to become president of the United States of America. He likes status. He really wants his daughter married to a duke."

"My word, he does have ambition... Did he steal his dubious money?"

"Not quite. He sells favours and bootleg whisky. Controls the pension fund of a large trade union. You have heard of prohibition and trade unions?"

"Even the *Telegraph* has heard of American prohibition and the trade union movement. How rich is this man?"

"And he's Irish."

"Oh, my goodness. What a pity they don't have trade unions for educated men with no money. But then they wouldn't get any fees would they, let alone take enough money to build up a jolly pension fund."

"Twenty million dollars, according to a friend's estimate. CE Porter is a business partner so to speak. And getting richer with every truckload of whisky into the States from Canada, according to CE."

"And he wants his daughter to marry an Englishman? Do I have to meet this Irishman?"

"Only if you sign a marriage contract. In the contract, you will receive one million dollars as a wedding present."

"Do I have to live in America?" Cuddles thought she heard a little sarcasm in his tone of voice.

"You can live where you like. May I pour the tea?"

"I'll find the sugar... Bless my soul... Are you serious?"

"Deadly. I get nine thousand pounds as a finder's fee. It would have been ten thousand if you had been a duke!"

To Cuddles's relief and amusement, the 16th Marquess of Ravenhurst burst into peals of happy laughter. Now, it was all up to Stella. Or so she hoped.

. . .

SIR JACOB ROSENZWEIG had sat alone in his office after Ralph Madgwick left, weighing the future against the past experiences of his life. They were going to see each other. That much was clear. Rebecca was twenty-one years old and free to do as she wished. With his elbows on his desk and steepling his fingers up to his mouth, Sir Jacob began to smile. He had probably been a fool turning the fickle emotion of young love into forbidden fruit. Had he let them be, they would have been sick of each other a long time ago. Unless there was a financial or family reason to stay together, lovers mostly moved apart, looking to rejuvenate the same feeling somewhere else. Instead of silently fighting his daughter making the image of love seem a condition that would last forever, which it never did in practice, Sir Jacob decided to be the bringer of glad tidings. He got up from his desk, put on his overcoat and hat, picked up his cane with the engraved silver handle and told his secretary he was going out.

"You have an appointment at twelve o'clock."

"Cancel it for me, Miss Cohen."

Outside in the cold street, it was snowing. Inside the taxi it was warm. Sir Jacob still thought of the New York cab as a taxi. He told the driver to go to Abercrombie Place. He hoped Ralph Madgwick had not yet made contact with his daughter.

Sir Jacob and Rebecca still lived alone in the sprawling apartment. Hannah had stayed in Golders Green. Probably with her old lover. They had all gone through the years living a lie. Why they had come together in the year before Rebecca was born he had never been sure. Probably Hannah had had a fight with her lover. At the time, he had been too surprised and too busy to find out. It had been like having an affair with his own wife, pleasant at the time and soon forgotten. His other children, all older than Rebecca, would most likely stay in England. The three boys worked well at the family bank. All three had married nice Jewish girls with rich Jewish fathers. He never asked as he never cared to talk about anything outside the business but if they had any sense they would have other girls on the side where brief love still mattered more than the family money.

"You are an old cynic, Jacob. An old cynic," he told himself as the cab drove through the wide streets of New York City, mostly in a straight line, which rarely was possible in the old streets of London. "Or a realist."

Sir Jacob was fully composed when the cab drew up at his apartment block. Striding into the building and travelling up in the lift with a forced smile on his face, he found Rebecca alone in the flat. The servant had gone out for some reason, which did not matter.

"What on earth are you doing home in the morning? Father, why do you look in such a good mood?"

"I have good tidings, Rebecca. Good tidings for you. Ralph Madgwick is in New York. He paid me a visit at the office. Madgwick and Madgwick are forming a company in New York and have offered Rosenzweigs twenty per cent of the equity that I have decided to take. Our contacts will bring them valuable clients so we will be adding value to the company as a shareholder... You didn't know Ralph was here? I was wrong about young Ralph. A nice young man. He did the right thing by calling on your father first. A young gentleman. I have decided to ask him to dinner."

"Here?"

"Wherever else, Rebecca?"

"You came to tell me that?"

"Of course. Isn't it important? No more little misunderstandings between you and me. You are a grown woman. This is America."

"But he is not Jewish!"

"I thought you knew that right from the start... Maybe back then you were too young to be serious, which is why I acted by going to see Wallace Madgwick. Fathers have to guide their daughters. Always remember your father has your best interests at heart."

"Oh, Daddy!" said Rebecca, running into his arms. She was crying.

When Sir Jacob left an hour later to go back to his office, he felt, in the words so often used at his old boarding school in the countryside, a right cad.

"Mr Madgwick gave me his card earlier this morning, Miss Cohen. On it was written his telephone number as you see. Please make a phone call and ask Mr Madgwick for dinner at my apartment tonight. Seven o'clock. Informal dress. You know the directions if he drives his own car. Tell him my daughter is very much looking forward to seeing him this evening."

"Very good, sir... I was unable to put off your twelve o'clock, Sir Jacob."

"Good. When the man arrives show him in to my office."

When he picked up the paper and read the financial page, Sir Jacob felt uneasy at what he read. The stock market had risen yet another point. It was all too easy.

Sir Jacob Rosenzweig was no longer smiling and read through the rest of the financial pages.

When Ralph Madgwick put down the phone ten minutes later, he was mentally scratching his head.

"The old bastard's invited me to dinner."

"Who?" said Rosie Prescott.

"Sir Jacob Rosenzweig. At his fancy apartment. With Rebecca."

Rosie Prescott had to turn away from Ralph to stop him seeing the smile that had sprung to her face. Once Rebecca and Ralph properly got to know each other, she would stand a much better chance.

"When?" she asked innocently.

"Tonight. Seven o'clock."

Somehow Ralph felt cheated. He had planned to visit Maryanne at the florist shop. To arrange a clandestine meeting with Rebecca. To meet in secret behind her father's back until Rebecca was prepared to run away with him and he won the war. Suddenly it was all going to be easy. The chase was over. It was as if her father had stolen some of the fun.

PATRICK FITZGERALD, Stella's father, had read three books in his life, all with difficulty. One had been a biography of Cecil John Rhodes the British imperialist who had made one of the nineteenth century's great fortunes by understanding the foibles of men. It was a phrase that had caught Patrick's eye: Every man has his price.

The price, when Patrick read the book, was not always counted in money. One man, a Jew, had sold Rhodes his mining company to get himself membership of the Kimberley Club, the first Jewish member in its history. Patrick had become a great admirer of the arch-imperialist who had died in his late forties with two countries in Africa called after him: Northern and Southern Rhodesia. Patrick was unable to aspire to a country even though the idea had appeal.

When Patrick met John Lacey, the day after Sir Jacob Rosenzweig supped with the devil, he had little concern about the man himself. The Marquess of Ravenhurst was a commodity he was going to buy for a million dollars. The Marchioness of Ravenhurst would dispel in the press the image they portrayed of Patrick Fitzgerald as a semi-literate from the bogs of Ireland. The rich Americans were as gullible to a title as a starving man to food, despite the republican foundation of the American constitution.

His daughter's engagement had been four small lines in the best English newspaper. In America, Patrick had leaked the story to every newspaper and magazine in the country who would listen. The woman in England who had bought him the peer for a nine thousand pound fee had researched the Lacey family back to their illustrious roots, giving the papers something to write about.

. . .

AMERICAN GIRL TO MARRY OLD TITLE. AMERICAN GIRL TO BE
BRITISH ARISTOCRAT. AMERICAN GIRL A MARCHIONESS.

THE HEADLINES WERE LEGION, the story the same. Patrick Fitzgerald's
daughter was marrying English aristocracy. Never once did the articles
mention the bogs of Ireland or how Patrick had come by his money.

So far as Patrick was concerned, John Lacey, the man, could turn out to
be an idiot for all he cared. The story had given the Fitzgerald family more
good press than money could buy. Unpaid for advertising was priceless
when it came as good story in the news columns of the press: especially the
kind of slush the public liked to read about the rich and famous. Seamus,
his eldest son, would be a shoo-in at the next Congressional elections. His
name, plastered across the press with the story of his sister's coming
marriage, was now familiar to millions, his Democratic nomination a virtual
certainty.

Patrick, when he put his hand out for the first time to his future son-in-
law, was well satisfied with his prize.

"Welcome to Boston, duke."

"I am a marquess, Mr Fitzgerald."

"What's the difference, duke?"

"A matter of rank."

The contempt in the American's eye and tone of voice was as obvious to
John Lacey as it must have been to everyone else at the railway station that
included a brass band and a full pack of newspapermen. John turned to
Stella to find the same look in her eyes, the look not even mingled with a
tinge of pity.

John, backing away for a moment into his own small world,
contemplated the rest of his life. However, he was able to look at it through
the eyes of his future wife and her family. He had been bought, lock, stock
and barrel, for a million of their bucks. The solitude of his old home in the
Lincoln marshes was more attractive than it had ever been before. Around
him on the platform was bedlam. The band's brass cymbals were crashing
sound into his head. Men with pens and notebooks were shoving forward,
all asking questions at the same time. Just a cacophony of sound. His
nightmare had finally begun. He was committed. The papers were signed.
The engagement to this Stella written in stone. Even with the help of an
army, there was no way out. Greed, his own stupid greed, mingled with a

little lust for the girl, had ruined the rest of his life. He who had read so many mistakes of the past had made himself the main player in what he now had little doubt would turn out a Greek tragedy. From England, and his brief visits to London at Cuddles's invitation to meet Stella in the midst of her social swirl, everything had looked different. In London, he was still the 16th Marquess of Ravenhurst with the right to take his seat in the House of Lords. In America, he was a freak. To add to his misery the brass band began to play 'Land of Hope and Glory', the trombonist messing up the tune.

"Father, it's wonderful," said Stella. "Isn't that the mayor of Boston?"

The whole family were having the time of their lives at his expense. The mother who brushed his cheek, the brothers who shook his hand, never looking him in the eye. Cousins of many stripes. Hangers-on. Everyone making the most amount of noise as possible greeting him, the man of the moment, not one of them seeing him as a man. In the war in France, the noise of bombardment had had a meaning. The meaning of death. Here with the train still waiting at the platform, the noise had no meaning for him at all. In the midst of so much noise and people, he had never been lonelier in his life.

"Stella," he said taking her arm in his grip, "I can't do this."

"Of course you can. You're in America. Please stop hurting my arm or you'll leave a bruise. My dress for tonight has short sleeves."

"Do you too despise me, Stella?"

"Of course not, John. What on earth are you talking about?"

"The circus. This is a circus."

"Well, it's some circus. The mayor is coming through. He wants to shake your hand for the cameras. John, please smile when they point at you with a camera... And let go of my damn arm."

To STELLA, it was all intoxicating. Everyone she had ever known in Boston had come to greet her return. Even Wesley, her younger brother, had been less condescending than usual. Seamus, the older brother slated for Congress, had actually kissed her on the cheek, something he had never done before in her life. Her tall, thin mother known throughout the Irish section as Big Annie, had given her a hug instead of telling her what she was doing wrong. Could eight months away in England have made them miss her in the family? For a fleeting moment, she thought it was herself they wanted. Then she saw her father milking the crowd for all he was worth... Seamus shaking hand after hand... Smiling at the press... Making brief one-liners.

The band had slipped into Irish tunes they knew better than the brief imperial indulgence of Elgar's music. The train that had brought them from New York pulled away from the platform. Her father took her by the elbow and together they moved out away from the grand reception.

When they reached the car her family were ready to leave. They all got in, Wesley at the wheel of a new car Stella had not seen before. They were driving to the family house on the bank of the Charles River, ten miles from the railway station. No one seemed to care John was still part of the crowd outside the car. Stella looked for him out the window, saw him and signalled. She was visibly annoyed he had not followed her closely. Whatever he thought, it was too late to change his mind... Make her a laughing stock. Father, she knew, would stop any of that nonsense. John Lacey was now in America.

They were going to live in New York where she would start her brilliant career as an interior designer. Everyone in New York would want the famous Marchioness of Ravenhurst to decorate his or her apartment. Her talent to paint would come to be an asset by showing her clients a picture of the room before it was redecorated and expensively furnished. She would be constantly in demand turning down clients who did not take her fancy. Important people. They would be her clients. She would mix socially with all the important people.

"Where's Lacey?" snapped her father.

"Outside still caught in the crowd."

"Keep a better eye on him, Stella. I don't spend that kind of money to be kept waiting."

"He's coming."

"About time, Lacey," Patrick Fitzgerald snapped as his future son-in-law got into the car. They drove off in silence away from all the hullabaloo.

"People in crowds make me sick," said her father.

No one else spoke all the way to the family's estate on the bank of the river.

In the back, John Lacey felt like a small boy on his first day at boarding school and just as miserable. Only with great self-control did he stop himself from being violently sick, something he regretted five minutes later. If he'd been sick over the back of the burly Irishman they might have mercifully thrown him out of the car. Silently he cursed Cuddles Morton-Sayner with all the power of his mind. He was trapped like a rat in a sewer with his wedding two days down the line. Cuddles had demanded and received the money before he left England... Her nine thousand pounds... His million dollars. John was even more convinced that anyone who said money made people happy should be shot.

Just before the car reached the modern-looking mansion perched next to the river up the bank, John Lacey began to smile to himself. Under his breath, he spoke words he had first heard from his mother, 'what's good for the goose is good for the gander'. Two could play tricks with money. After today, as he looked at Stella sitting next to him, he did not think he would be able to make love to her even had he wished. Whatever happened in the future, the seventeenth marquess would have no Fitzgerald blood in his veins.

"I'm glad to see you smiling, John," said Stella complacently.

11

AUGUST TO OCTOBER 1928 – WHEN THE CURTAIN GOES DOWN

*T*he one commodity Barnaby St Clair never wished to run out of was money. With money, the rest of his life did what it was told. Women came and went. Friends were used to mutual benefit. When there was no longer mutual benefit the friendship stopped. Life to Barnaby was one long trade culminating in money. Money, Barnaby had convinced himself, never let him down. Mostly everything else always did.

On the 13 August 1928, Barnaby calculated his net worth exceeded one million pounds sterling. Smiling to himself maliciously, he telephoned the seven independent stockbrokers who handled his affairs and told them to sell.

For three days Barnaby waited for the sales to be complete and only then relaxed.

Having secured his fortune, the next period in his life was to begin. The CE Porters, Douglas Hayters, the hundreds he had buttered up to get the financial information that made his money were now irrelevant. When his bank manager asked him to lunch, he declined. When CE Porter telephoned to find out what was going on, he was abrupt. When Cuddles Morton-Sayner asked him to do a client of hers a favour, he told her to go to hell. For the first time in his life, he no longer needed to use his charm on other people to get his own way.

For a week, Barnaby brooded, not leaving his Piccadilly townhouse except to walk across into Green Park. August had become September. The summer was good. His mind was at rest, the money in the bank earning a modest interest.

Since being sucker-punched by Harry Brigandshaw while watching Tina's legs as she picked up her skirts, he had deliberately kept his distance from the girl. What had once been fun had nearly cost him dearly if London had found out about his unceremonious dunking in the Thames: the idea of being laughed at was appalling. As Barnaby hoped and expected, Harry Brigandshaw had kept his mouth shut to protect his wife and children.

Like so many other dramatic moments in his life his running back to London soaked to the skin would have drifted into memory, even become a joke. Then as fate would have it, they bumped into each other when they were both sentimentally drunk.

Tina, he found out, had taken the children down to Dorset to introduce the new member of the family to her parents. Barnaby had seen the birth of Dorian in the birth column of the *Telegraph*, this time knowing with certainty the child had nothing to do with him. Barnaby had even smiled to himself when he first worked out the dates two months before he met Harry in the bar at Clara's.

They were both alone at one o'clock in the morning still not drunk enough to go home on a Saturday night. Taking his medicine and landing in the river had obviously brought Tina and Harry back together. Why else had they produced another son? Barnaby was feeling mellow in himself, forgetting the mental pain he had most likely caused Harry with the birth of Frank, a boy conceived when Harry was away on an extended trip to his farm in Africa.

Barnaby had lurched around on the bar stool he had been sitting on for five hours, coming face-to-face with his brother-in-law. Taking the bull by the proverbial horns, Barnaby began to turn on the charm.

"It's twenty years, Harry. I was a kid. You had just met Lucinda who was only fifteen years old back then. You had just come down from Oxford with Robert. That was the time they told you at Purbeck Manor your father had been killed by the Great Elephant. You went home to find the elephant and take your revenge. Can't we forget my mistakes and be friends again?"

Even having drunk too much whisky, Barnaby knew he was taking a God-sent opportunity to get back into Harry's good books.

"Did I break your jaw?" Harry's surprise, Barnaby saw, had now turned to mild amusement. The luck was still with him. Harry was well on the way.

"Only my pride, Harry. I was being an ass... She was five years old when I met Tina. You see I always thought she was mine but she wasn't. Didn't have the guts like you to marry the girl. She will make you very happy. I was just a fool... I read about Dorian in the *Telegraph*. Of course, it should be me married to Tina and you still married to my sister. Just how life goes wrong. That damn Braithwaite destroyed more than Lucinda's young life. And your child's. I did know about that. Lucinda was pregnant when she was killed. Then he killed Barend Oosthuizen and ruined your sister's life to add insult to terrible injury. Don't let us let him ruin our friendship. Harry, please let me buy you a drink and let bygones be bygones. Remember the good bits I say. There's good and bad in all of us, don't you think? I'm sorry. I'm not as good as you. Never could control myself when there was something I wanted. You have my word as a gentleman it will never happen again."

Harry stared at him for a long moment without saying a word... Barnaby continued, "Aren't you out alone late? Like me? I just felt like sitting here all night listening to the music and getting drunk. Sentimentally drunk. You know what, Christopher Marlowe, or whatever he calls himself, still can't play the piano. Did you know we first met in France during the war when he called himself Barrie Madgwick? Has a new show coming up, but you will know all about that as you finance his musicals... Please, have a drink, Harry? On me. They're playing a medley from *Happy Times*. Don't you think that is appropriate? We can't go on like this all our lives. You were once married to my sister, for God's sake."

"How are your parents, Barnaby?"

"They are fine... You drink brandy, I remember?"

"Thank you. I'll have a South African brandy. You're right. My father told me never to bear malice however appalling the reason."

"It was appalling. Utterly appalling."

"Yes it was, you were..."

Before Harry could say anything else, Barnaby asked, "Do you think this can be the last of it?"

"I think it can, Barnaby. For old times' sake. For all the people we have both known together in our lives that make up who we are. Apart from my own, you have the most wonderful parents in the world."

For the rest of the evening, Barnaby deliberately talked trivia until it was time to take taxis to their separate homes. The one thing Barnaby had learnt as he manipulated people throughout his life was when to shut up.

In the taxi back to his Piccadilly townhouse he hugged himself. Frank would go through life as Frank Brigandshaw and neither he nor Harry would say a word. He wondered what Tina would think of him had she been a fly on the wall.

· · ·

BARNABY AND HARRY had met on more than one occasion during the spring and summer. Outwardly, their old relationship had returned to normal. He just hoped his son looked like Tina when he grew up and not like himself.

AT THE END of his week of contemplation, Barnaby took his Bentley 3 Litre from the garage and drove out of London. He had told Edward his valet to expect him when he saw him and to tell no one what he was about.

He was rich and free as air. For once in England, the sun was shining, the road to Scotland clear. He wanted to get away from where he was to get a better look at where he wanted to go with the rest of his life. He was happy, he realised, something he had not been for a very long time.

DOUGLAS HAYTER WAS NOT SO happy and it had nothing to do with Barnaby St Clair closing down their lucrative two-way business. He had never liked the man, seeing him for what he was... A man who always took, giving back as little as possible. A man who only gave the appearance of being a friend. Everything about Barnaby was top surface, hiding the truth.

The first three months had been the worst, waiting for Stella Fitzgerald to come back to Riverglade for the clothes she had left the night of the Nuneham House May Ball. There had not been a May Ball in 1928. The one that had changed his life had been the last. None of them had come back to visit him. CE Porter had spoken business with him on the telephone. So had Barnaby St Clair until he sold out of the market, a fact Douglas kept to himself, as it was none of his business. Cuddles had vanished from the scene with her protégée.

At first, Douglas wondered if it had all been in his mind. The calling owls. The white light of the moon. The naked woman. The explosion in his groin. The brief surge of pure happiness. The feeling of fulfilment. The peace. The hope. The love... Had it all been a figment of his imagination? Had his body been there on its back that night straddled by the girl to whom he had talked all of the previous day?

He wondered more as the days of silence went from weeks to months, and not another word after so many down by the river after she had run pell-mell into his chest as he held the wheelchair from rushing back into the water.

Only after six months when he knew she was never coming back did Douglas act like a thief and look in her suitcase. The ball gown was there in all its blue and white, the smell of her as powerful as the night of the dance when she had shown him her finery. The smell of perfume, not the smell of raw sex, that stayed in his mind from her visit to his room in the middle of the night. Everything was there of her in the case, her memory lying before him, the only part of Stella he still possessed. Instinctively that first empty morning when he woke to find them all gone, he knew they had mutually taken each other's virginity. It was this that kept him certain the night had been real.

There was a room near the lounge his mother had always kept locked from the servants where he took the contents of her suitcase, turning the room into a shrine. Day by day, he wrote down every word they had spoken so none would be forgotten with the passage of endless time. The dress was placed on a stand he made himself. In all its splendour. The small shoes she had worn to the dance at the bottom resting on the old wooden floor. The rest of the bits and pieces he left in the case. The dress stood alone in the middle of the room he had cleaned of his mother's sewing and personal memories she had never wanted the servants to see. Who the man in the photograph was, he would never know. He had never seen the man before. Next to the dress, he placed a small mahogany table where he presented the writing of their conversations as they were done until each word was complete and would live with him forever. Each time he locked the door.

From then on, he only visited the room when the moon was full and the owls in the trees outside were calling. As a libation to her memory, he never again called back to the owls, his way of pouring wine for the gods.

Tina seemed quite happy after Dorian, and life went on. Harry Brigandshaw went to the office and performed well the job he hated, running a business like any big business, trying to give the public what they wanted with the help of Percy Grainger, the managing director of Colonial Shipping. Harry was chairman of the board. The bringer of new ideas or so he hoped, though mostly everything in the shipping line stayed the way it was. Ships were ships. Passengers to Africa came and went, as did the cargo. In Belfast, even the Short Brothers continued with their design of building a flying boat that would bring Harry's Africa so much closer to England. Harry knew in his frustration it was all still talk and research, nothing ready to fly a passenger route and make a profit.

Surprisingly to Harry, Tina had lost her figure after Dorian. She seemed to have little wish to get it back. She was thirty, smiling, good with the four children and, as he thought, seemingly happy. They had even met Barnaby socially without a mishap. It was as if all three of them had changed since the fight by the river.

He and Tina were even comfortable talking to each other except for one subject: Africa, where he had to go whether he liked leaving his wife alone or not. Whether he trusted her or not. Whether he loved her or not, he loved all four of the children.

Harry had not been home to Elephant Walk for three and a half years. Now his mother was sick and he was going. In a hurry. Flying again down Africa in a new hybrid flying boat with Ignatius Bowes-Lyon. A test flight for the future.

"I'm so sorry. Is she very sick, Harry?" asked Ignatius.

"Not very. It's me who is sick, Iggy. I need to go home to repair my soul."

"It will be a pleasure to go with you on the journey."

"This time we are taking a couple of engineers instead of passengers. Lots of spares. Onboard fuel. I need to get out of London. To breathe untainted air. To feel free again and walk in the bush. This new seaplane is a hybrid. It can land on water and an airfield. The small wheels are embedded in the floats."

"When do we go?"

"Thursday."

"SOD ME," said Barnaby St Clair, putting down the newspaper on the breakfast table. He was sitting in his townhouse two days after his return from his journey to Scotland to clear his mind of clutter. The clutter of his old business and the people who made it possible.

The morning newspaper had been brought to him at the table by Edward, delivered to the door. Instead of turning to the business section, he had read the day's news before turning to the social columns to see if there was anyone he knew. The name Brett Kentrich leapt from the page. The poor girl was engaged. Ever since Harry had dunked him in the river, according to rumour, Harry had kept away from his old mistress. The article announcing her coming marriage to the man who had written *Happy Times* also reported Christopher Marlowe's new musical was not to be staged for lack of a financial backer. Mr Harry Brigandshaw, chairman of Colonial Shipping, had withdrawn his patronage from the arts and was returning to his farm in Rhodesia to look after his sick mother.

"Bollocks, Harry. You're just cutting your ties with Brett."

Barnaby picked up the paper and reread the article properly. There was no mention of Harry's family going out to Rhodesia despite the rest of the detail. There was mention of Marlowe looking for a backer. Oscar Fleming had also pulled away from Brett Kentrich.

"Dirty old bastard isn't getting his oats," said Barnaby, the thought of which gave him an idea that might solve his boredom. When a man was too busy, Barnaby had found out for himself, he dreamt of a life of leisure... Breakfast at ten in the morning reading the paper. Pacing the day to fill it out and prevent long gaps with nothing to do... He had known the then Barrie Madgwick in France. He had even had a brief affair with Brett to spite Harry Brigandshaw, which he had no wish to repeat... It might just work. The idea of all the showgirls was appealing. Seducing young women was the one amusement left in his life.

A small part of his money would finance a West End musical. Hadn't Christopher's friend once confided in him he wished to put on a show from start to end?... Gert van Heerden, who lived in a room close to Christopher, had said he was tired of painting the sets, managing the stage. He wanted to produce a show in all its glory. He wanted the job being done by Oscar Fleming... They had both been drunk in Clara's, telling each other their life's ambitions. Barnaby knew he was lucky to always remember what he was told, even drunk, as he never knew when it would come in useful. He called it the dregs of his mind.

Barnaby put down the paper to think. If nothing else, he would have some fun losing some of his money. If the new Marlowe show was as good as the last one he might even double his money.

Barnaby began to smile as his hormones responded to temptation. A captive audience of pretty young things all wishing to please the man who put up the money.

"Best of all it will poke a finger in Harry's eye. Teach him to throw a punch when I wasn't looking. With a bit of luck, it will make him mad when he comes back to London... Marrying old Marlowe. Now there's a turn-up for the books."

With the idea fermenting in his mind, Barnaby picked up the paper and turned the page.

"Bugger me!"

Right in front of his eyes was a photograph of his brother next to a lengthy review of *Holy Knight*.

Barnaby sipped his tea as he read the review, which centred more on the lost and found parchments hidden in the wall of Purbeck Manor, purportedly found by an ancestor having a silver goblet thrown at him by his wife. Barnaby read on chortling to himself, impressed with his brother's acumen. The book, said the newspaper, had been a howling success in

America. Brother Robert was going to make a fortune. The newspaper even told Barnaby that Robert was back in London for the book launch the following week.

The review gave Barnaby another idea to relieve his boredom.

During the time his brother had lived in America, Barnaby had seen Portia Ramsbottom a dozen times. Each time she had asked about Robert while ignoring his flirtatious advances. Never being one who liked a girl's refusal, Barnaby had bided his time, aware each time they met of Portia becoming a beautiful young woman with exactly the type of sexuality he liked. He even knew the telephone number of the family home in London, Barnaby having made it his business to find out soon after Robert left on his extended visit to America... You never knew unless you tried, he told himself with a satisfied smirk.

When Barnaby finished his breakfast, he got up and walked to the telephone in his study. He gave the Pimlico number to the operator and waited for someone to answer. Within a minute, the operator had put him through... Luck favoured the forward. It was the girl herself.

"Portia, it's Barnaby St Clair."

"How did you know it was me?"

"I recognised your voice. Just read Robert's review. Thought I'd tell you to look it up in today's *Telegraph*. He's over for the book launch... Are you still there?"

"He hasn't phoned me. Hasn't written for months and months."

"Would you like a drink so we can talk about his book? Why don't you come over here? There are some friends coming for drinks at six. Cocktails the Americans call it. Very civilised. I'm only five minutes away in a taxi. I'll keep the paper so you can read the review. It's very good."

"What's the name of the book?"

"*Holy Knight*. Spelt with a K. About one of our ancestors in Palestine during the Crusades."

"Thank you, Barnaby. That's very sweet of you."

"Five o'clock. Just ring the bell. My man Edward will let you in if we are all talking too much."

When Barnaby put down the phone, he was smiling to himself with delicious anticipation. Best of all it would teach his brother a lesson in good manners. Both his brothers had been ignoring him for years. The seduction of Portia Ramsbottom might have to be put off until later.

Barnaby picked up the phone and gave the operator another number from his memory. A girl with an American accent answered the phone.

"Sorry. My memory for numbers must be wrong. I was looking for Robert St Clair, the author. It's his brother here, Barnaby."

"He's right here."

"Who's that?" he heard his brother say down the line.

"Barnaby."

"What do you want?"

"Where on earth did you dream up the parchments in the wall? Really, Robert. Fiction is fiction. What would the newspapers say if they knew?"

"Oh God. I didn't think Max was going to make such a song and dance. Most of what I wrote is folklore handed down the family through the generations. It just made better sense telling my publisher the family had found the stories hidden in a wall. We both know the stories were true about Sir Henri Saint Claire Debussy."

"Who was the girl on your phone, Robert?"

"Freya Taylor."

"Who is Freya?"

"She is a friend of mine."

"Then bring her for cocktails at five. And ask Merlin to be kind enough to come. We can discuss the review in the *Telegraph*. And the silver goblet thrown by our great-grandmother. You are lucky our father only reads the *Farmers Weekly* unless they reviewed your book... Where is Freya from, Robert?"

"America. Denver. Colorado."

"Five o'clock. There will be other guests. Including Christopher Marlowe and Brett Kentrich. I'm going to back Christopher's new musical. I'm sure Miss Taylor would like to meet a star of our London stage. A big star."

"Harry backs Christopher."

"Not anymore. He's gone back to Elephant Walk."

"With his family?"

"No."

"Will Tina be there for drinks?"

"Robert! Really! Whatever are you thinking? She's a married woman, for Pete's sake."

"What are you up to, Barnaby?"

"Have you taken Miss Taylor to meet our mother and father?"

"Not yet."

"Five o'clock. With Merlin and whoever he is escorting at the moment."

"All right. Please don't tell anyone about the parchments."

"Why ever would I do that? We are family, Robert. Families stick together. Had you forgotten?"

"Fine, see you later."

The line went dead. Barnaby jiggled the telephone.

"Can I help you, sir?"

Barnaby gave the operator Brett Kentrich's number. The least he could do was convey his best wishes for her forthcoming marriage.

"It's just getting better and better. The cat and the mice." Barnaby was chortling to himself.

"Brett, darling. It's Barnaby."

"What do you want? I haven't woken up."

"When does *Happy Times* close?"

"At the end of the month."

"Blimey... Congratulations on your engagement. Please bring Christopher and Gert van Heerden to my home at five o'clock for drinks."

"Whatever for?"

"To have a drink with an old friend, darling. Don't tell anyone but I'm out of the market. Sold all my shares... You remember my stock market dealings? I once tried to explain to you the art of selling short."

"Please not again."

"You can all spend a couple of hours with me before you go to the theatre. I'm going to back Christopher's new show which Gert is going to stage in its entirety."

"Are you serious?"

"Never more in my life... Five o'clock."

"Now I'm awake. How much did you get for your shares?"

"Just over a million pounds after paying back the mortgage on this house and the bank manager his overdraft."

"Barnaby, be serious."

"I never joke about money. Never... Five o'clock."

"All right, fine. We'll all be there."

Brett Kentrich had suddenly sounded wary. Barnaby clicked off his phone.

"I wonder if the engagement came before or after Harry announced he was going back to Africa? That's the trouble with sleeping with the boss. Once the affair is over people get fired."

With a trilby hat perched on his head, Barnaby left his townhouse for a walk in Green Park. It was a beautiful September day. He hoped all his guests were looking forward to their evening.

"Money, old chap. It's always about the money."

Then he crossed Piccadilly, dodging the traffic on his way to the park. Just in case it rained, he had brought with him his rolled umbrella.

· · ·

THROUGH THE DAY, Edward prepared the canapés. Barnaby did not employ a cook. He ate lunch and supper in clubs and restaurants. Edward was well capable of cooking their breakfasts. Even with all that money in the bank, it was silly to waste it. So far as he could remember, the only thing his great-grandfather had done in his life was waste the family money entertaining anyone at Purbeck Manor who liked to drink and eat good food. There was a family story about a silver cup thrown but nothing about an echo in the dining room wall.

When Barnaby came back from his walk in the park and saw all the ingredients Edward had bought for the snacks he decided to skip lunch. A good gentleman's gentleman was a real joy in a young man's life.

THE LAST PERSON Robert St Clair expected to find in his brother's house was Portia Ramsbottom, the girl who had once told him it was possible to love a man's mind. Robert remembered writing her letters from America right at the start before his life had been swallowed up by Freya Taylor excluding all other romantic thought that wasn't written into his book. Portia looked even prettier than he remembered. She was now a sophisticated woman who just looked at Freya with her American accent and smiled.

Earlier in the afternoon, Merlin had had no sympathy for his plight. The whole idea had grown from his conversation with Max Pearl when he had given the finished manuscript of *Holy Knight* to him.

"YOUR FAMILY MUST HAVE some written record of the knight?" Max had quizzed him again shortly before the book was published. "The publicity people will want some facts to promote a book like that. You seemed to imply the story was handed down by word of mouth but there's so much detail. The American public will want to know they are reading a real story about real people. They won't swallow seven hundred years of father to son word of mouth. No, sir. They want facts. You go and find the facts on which you based the story... Real facts, Robert."

"Of course some of it was written down."

"Where?"

"I told you, on parchments."

"Didn't Oliver Cromwell destroy your family's castle in Dorset? Burned it to the ground?"

"Well, yes." At that point in the conversation, Robert remembered his writer's mind going berserk, blurring family fact with family fiction. The natural born storyteller in the part of his mind that was Celt took over, spilling the storyline in a gush all over Max Pearl.

Robert remembered the rapt expression on Max Pearl's face.

THERE WERE OFTEN PARTS in his books that echoed his own past. This had just been one of them. Now Barnaby was threatening to catch him out and make a fool of him in the press on both sides of the Atlantic.

To make matters worse, Robert had arranged to meet Max Pearl at Clara's after the shows in the West End came out. Max had an early meeting with Robert's British publisher to which Robert had not been invited. When people talked money about his books it was none of his business. They paid him a royalty, which is all he wanted to know.

Christopher Marlowe walking into the room brought his mind back to the present, to his present very real predicament that could badly affect the men who had put their good money into his book. It was all typical of Barnaby. He always got his own way. Even as a child growing up. With all of them. He always seemed to find out something about each of them and demand his pound of flesh. In those days it was the threat of telling their mother about their indiscretions. Earlier, Robert had gone across to Merlin's flat in Park Lane.

"Barnaby is paying us back, Robert."

"He's paying me back, Merlin."

"Well. Yes. Why I'm not going for drinks tonight. It's your problem. Really, Robert. How could you possibly tell such a lie?"

"I'm a fiction writer, dammit. The stories are not even meant to be true."

"He's quite ruthless. Can twist anything to his advantage. Good luck, Robert."

"Merlin, will you stop laughing."

CHRISTOPHER MARLOWE WAS PLEASED to see Robert. He watched the slight embarrassment with Portia, who had also just arrived, play itself out before moving towards Robert St Clair.

"Thank you for helping Ralph with Rebecca," he said as they formally shook hands.

"You can thank Freya here," said Robert. "She delivered the letter. Hello,

Brett... All of you meet Freya Taylor from America with a big welcome. Portia, you look even more beautiful."

"Hello, Robert," he heard his old friend Gert van Heerden say. Christopher looked around the room. There was his lovely Brett. Gert, his old friend. Jane, Gert's girlfriend. Portia. Robert back from America with a girl called Freya. And Barnaby, as he had been told by Brett, who was going to finance *A Walk in the Woods*.

STANDING BACK, Barnaby watched the interplay between his guests. To make his brother feel even more guilty than he looked, Barnaby gave him a wink.

"Merlin did the duck I suppose," he said to Robert. "Left you on your own. He always did that when I was growing up. Do you know in those days the only birds and animals that did not run from Merlin were those of the night? The fox. The owl. The weasel."

He could read Robert like one of his own books, he knew his brother so well. He had also checked with Clara's whether his brother had a booking for a table any time that week soon after his visit to Merlin's flat.

"TEN O'CLOCK TONIGHT, MR ST CLAIR," Miss Clara had told him on the phone.

"Is that Merlin or Robert St Clair?" Barnaby had asked.

"The writer, Mr St Clair."

"Thank you, Miss Clara. I'd like a table for four."

"Can I put you at your brother's table? He has one male guest as well as his fiancée. His American publisher, I believe."

"That will be much better. My party will take in a show first. Ten-thirty, shall we say? By then I'm sure my brother will have talked out all the business writers talk with their publishers. How are you, Miss Clara?"

"Very well, thank you."

PLEASED YET AGAIN WITH his own guile, Barnaby smiled to himself. He had also been right about Gert van Heerden bringing a girl. A tall girl he had seen somewhere before. Probably a showgirl. The perfect cover for himself to invite Portia to a show and to dinner. The cocktail party went into full swing.

·   ·   ·

AT SEVEN O'CLOCK, Brett called for a taxi to take her to the theatre. Christopher was being dropped off at Clara's on the way. Gert and Jane Tamplin did not have plans for the rest of the evening. That much Barnaby had found out soon after they had arrived. Smiling, he put his plan to seduce Portia into action.

"Portia, how about the four of us taking in a show? The others have to work. Mr van Heerden and his lady have agreed to join me for the evening. The night is young. You just never know. Maybe we will all be together again before the night passes." Barnaby was smiling wickedly at Robert. "You might tell Merlin I'll catch him later, Robert. Don't forget what I said. The family must always stay together. A house divided is never strong. Till all shall meet again... Edward, I must congratulate you on such beautiful canapés."

Robert, fully aware of his brother's devious mind, had gone white as a sheet.

"Where are you going for supper, Barnaby?" he asked.

"Clara's, of course. Where Christopher plays the piano. I asked Clara to put us all on the same table but only after you and your fiancée have had a good chat with your American publisher. Clara said you were engaged which explains that lovely ring on your finger, Freya. Why didn't you tell me? Oh, heavens, everyone but Barnaby is getting married. Please, Portia, join me tonight. We will have a family celebration at a lovely restaurant where so many of our lives have crossed. At Clara's. It's a beautiful evening. Portia, why don't I find you a taxi so you can change for the theatre out of that stunning cocktail dress? Then I'll pick you up at eight o'clock."

"An evening out with you and Portia will be splendid," said Gert. "Jane is not in Brett's show tonight and can join us at Clara's. Don't you want to hear the music before you back Christopher's new musical?"

"Whatever for? I know nothing about music or the theatre except as part of an audience. Is it as good as *Happy Times*?"

"Better."

"There you are. I'll make a fortune. Harry doesn't know what he's missed. When did he leave for Africa?"

"Today."

"They always say one door closes while another door opens. Now isn't that so true? So it is settled. I will finance *A Walk in the Woods*."

"We are not exactly engaged," said Freya. "The ring is on the wrong finger."

"Very soon I'm sure my brother will put it on the correct finger and you'll both live happily ever after. I'm so looking forward to the launch party for *Holy Knight* at the Dorchester. I am invited aren't I, Robert?"

"Of course. You all are."

"Splendid. I have another brilliant idea. You and Freya can take in the same show with us and then go on to Clara's. Why, you must have talked out everything there is to say with your publisher who will love to meet another member of Sir Henri Saint Claire Debussy's family don't you think?... Is there something wrong, Robert?"

"Nothing at all I hope, Barnaby."

"Trust me. It's going to go on being a lovely evening... Freya was telling me earlier you met Stella Fitzgerald in America. At some place called 21 after they put the spotlight on you, Robert. She's marrying John Lacey according to the papers. She and I had a lovely evening at Lady Harcourt's May Ball. Harry was there with our old friend from my childhood, his wife Tina... So Stella finally got what she wanted. A husband with a title. I'm sure they're going to be oh so happy... Now... What show are we going to see? Probably have to find a spiv to sell us tickets if the show is sold out. Those chaps are a menace until you need them but everyone has to make a living. But first, we need a taxi for Portia to go home and change. What a pity Merlin did not want to come out tonight. All the brothers together. So much fun."

Turning his back on his brother, Barnaby went off to look for a growler taxi down in the street. For one splendid moment, he thought Robert was going to take a swipe at him... Revenge, when it came, was always so sweet he chortled to himself as he walked out of his house into Piccadilly. Within a minute he had flagged down a taxi.

THE FOLLOWING Tuesday Robert gave a brief speech at the launch of *Holy Knight* and asked the guests if they had any questions. The ballroom of the Dorchester Hotel was dressed to look like a mediaeval banqueting hall. Banners hung from the ceilings splashed with the emblems of long-dead knights. Suits of armour the publishers had borrowed from the British Museum stood along the walls. Effigies of knights in chain armour, their mailed hands resting at chest level on the handles of their swords stood at the entrance to the long room. Waiters dressed in smocks bearing the red cross of St George and England, were ready with trays of food and drink. They were to mingle with the men and women: the literati of London, Robert's few friends and family, the staff of Robert's British publisher who had worked so hard on the text and cover of his book along with the hangers-on who came for the free drink and food with no other interest whatsoever.

Merlin was there looking up at his brother on the rostrum, unaware of any possible drama. Lord and Lady St Clair, along with Robert's sisters, had declined a long journey from home to attend a two-hour cocktail party much to Robert's relief. On tables all around the room, Robert could see pyramids of his book. Later he was to sign copies for any of the guests inclined to take a copy, something Robert hated doing. The idea of himself in their eyes as a famous author had never sat well on his shoulders. Some people had the habit of trying to ingratiate themselves, which to Robert was the wrong way round. So far as he was concerned, they were doing him a favour by reading his book, the only way his characters could come alive. Inside the pages of a closed book, everyone was dead.

One reporter asked him if he was going to continue living in America. Robert said he was not sure. Another asked what the title of his next book was, and what it was about. Robert said he had yet to begin another book and that it took time for a new idea to grow. That he was going down to his family home in Dorset to walk and think despite having one foot... The papers had more than once talked of his wound from the war.

"Are you going to write a book on your experiences in France during the war, Mr St Clair?" The man had an American accent.

"No."

"Why not?"

"War is terrible."

"The Crusades were a war."

"A holy war."

"Not just a way for your ancestor to cut himself a farm in Palestine, build himself a castle and tax the trade route that passed through his property."

"My ancestor was providing security of passage for the merchant caravans. Robbers would have taken far more and likely killed the men and their camels."

"But he came home with a fortune and built Corfe Castle in Dorset."

"Yes, he did."

"Do you have proof?"

"It was a very long time ago."

"There were parchments in the wall, were there not? Every publicity stunt in America talked about your great-grandfather and the silver chalice hitting a hollow in the wall of your Dorset home. Wouldn't parchments locked away for so long have disintegrated?"

"No."

"May we see the parchments, Mr St Clair?"

"They are locked away."

"Proof, Mr St Clair. Why not the proof that your tale is true?" The man was almost snarling at Robert.

"There were things my ancestors did I don't wish to broadcast."

"So it was really just the same old rape and pillage back then?"

"Nothing changes."

"Will your brothers who are here tonight confirm the authenticity of Sir Henri Claire Debussy's hidden documents?"

Robert began to sweat in the growing silence. Max Pearl, Robert could see, was annoyed. Merlin had the expression on his face of horror. Robert looked at Barnaby a few feet away down on the ballroom floor. Barnaby was enjoying himself.

"You'll have to take my word," said Robert into the silence. Everyone in the ballroom was watching him. "There was no proof of King Arthur and Camelot. At least you can see the ruins of my ancestors' castle. No one has ever found Camelot but we all believe the legend to be true." Many of the guests were now smiling. Everyone liked to see someone richer or more famous than them come down a peg or two.

"Why can't we see the parchments, Mr St Clair?"

"They belong to my family. What we wish to be known is in my book on the tables. That much you're welcome to read."

"Very condescending of you, Mr St Clair."

Robert could see Barnaby moving towards the rostrum on which he was standing. His whole stomach was churning with fright. Barnaby stepped up next to him squeezing onto the rostrum before leaning forward towards the microphone.

"My name is the Honourable Barnaby St Clair. I am Robert's youngest brother." Barnaby paused. "I have seen the parchments and read them many times. Some of the reading was not good. I spent the last war mostly in Palestine. We British were not all saints then in Palestine. Neither were we before. Maybe we won't be again someday... There was a war on. People do things in war that look appalling from the comfort and security of peacetime. My brother has given you as much of the truth as the family wish to give. Warts and horrors stay in our flesh. They only belong to our family. Most of my ancestor, Sir Henri Saint Claire Debussy, is a wonderful story. Just read the book. For now, let us eat and drink... Be merry... Thank God England is at peace. Let us hope the clouds building again over Germany will not require more young men to give up their lives. Or, in the words of someone I heard say: 'Let the songs begin, the minstrels play and love be the food of life'."

"Was that Shakespeare?" called a voice.

"I have absolutely no idea," said Barnaby. "Though it does sound rather good."

The audience burst out into relieved laughter. The brothers stepped down together from the rostrum. The crisis was over for the moment.

"Thank you, Barnaby," whispered Robert.

"That Yank was getting on my nerves... I have another of my brilliant ideas I will explain when this shindig is over... I think it all turned out well, Robert. Most of the reporters I looked at were scribbling in their little books. The publicity for the book will be generous I should say. Very generous... I'm going to have a stiff drink. Sadly, Robert, you have to sign books. Work indeed is the curse of the working classes. For that little vignette, I give you Oscar Wilde." Barnaby caught the eye of the American who had questioned his brother, smiled and winked. He had learnt never to make an enemy of the press. Then he walked across to the American for a chat.

AFTER THE LAUNCH, Merlin found himself walking down Park Lane from the direction of the Dorchester to his flat. Robert and Freya had been whisked away to a celebratory dinner by the British publisher. Merlin was miffed at not being asked to go with them. Brett and Christopher had left early, Brett to the theatre, Christopher to Clara's. There was no one else he really knew except Barnaby who had been grinning at him for over an hour. Merlin was not sure what had happened. He knew the great-grandfather story was bunk. He had found out too often that stories told as true were not so. And not just by his eccentric family.

"You and I can walk home," Barnaby had said when he took his arm in the foyer of the hotel as Merlin was walking out alone.

"Let go of my arm, Barnaby. Those parchments don't exist. You told everyone a blatant lie."

"Not here, Merlin. Outside. Walls have ears... Portia was meant to have come or I wouldn't be on my own." Barnaby was smiling at Merlin as if he was doing his brother a favour by not pursuing the girl.

"Who is Portia?"

"She's sweet on Robert."

"Is he going to marry that American?"

"They live together. People who live together have usually had enough of each other before they get married."

"I don't believe you. It's a mortal sin."

"This time you can, Merlin. I'm hungry."

"You can eat on your own."

"Tut-tut. That's quite rude. If you let me buy you supper, I will tell you my plan, which will save the family honour."

"All right." Merlin felt weary. The whole evening had been most unpleasant the way people were looking at him in the Dorchester knowing he was a St Clair. "There's a nice Indian restaurant in Soho... Taxi! Taxi! They never stop when I want them. It's too damn far to walk."

Barnaby smiled. He liked irritating Merlin.

THE RESTAURANT WAS SMALL, low-ceilinged in complete contrast to the Dorchester and smelled of rich spices from the East. There was a small bar where they ordered themselves a drink.

"You and I should do this more often, Merlin."

"Shut up. You know perfectly well why I have been avoiding you. Your behaviour with Tina was despicable."

Barnaby was about to tell him his behaviour with Esther and his illegitimate daughter wasn't any better but kept his mouth shut. Instead, he managed to look contrite. Merlin really could be a pompous ass.

Barnaby waited for his brother to speak while he drank his whisky and soda.

"All right. What is this plan of yours, Barnaby?"

"I'm going to have those parchments made up for us. Warts and all."

"You mean forgery!"

"No, literary licence. There will be no difference between the bloody parchments and the bloody book. We can keep the press on the hook for months before letting it out bit by bit. In the book trade, I'm told, they call it free publicity. Nothing more fun than teasing up the press... I told that Yank he could come down to Purbeck Manor and visit with Mother and Father. The chap went quite limp... We had better order a bottle of wine."

"That American reporter was very rude."

"People prefer being told what they want to hear."

"Yes, they do... They'll have to be good forgeries."

"Good old Merlin, now you are talking sense."

"It's a matter of family honour. Such a scandal would kill Father. Will you promise me one thing, Barnaby? Never again to be alone with Tina Brigandshaw."

"Have you seen her lately? She's put on weight and lost her oomph. She's thirty. It's all behind me with Tina."

"Has she really gone off?"

"They all do in the end. Why men of your age like to go out with young girls. Tina will be all right. She's now a matron. Four kids... Now, let me tell you about the new Marlowe musical I'm backing. You're still out of the share market, Merlin?"

"Never went back after the war."

"Good. I'm out. Completely. If you ask me, the stock markets are going to crash. There is going to be another war with Germany."

"Nonsense."

Merlin to his great surprise found he was now enjoying himself. His brother always cut to the chase.

"Are you going to follow through with that invitation to the American?" Merlin asked as they sat down at their table.

"Of course not. But he doesn't know that. By the time he works it out, he'll be back in America boasting about my invitation to visit a real-life lord and his lady in their castle."

"But we don't have a castle anymore."

"We will have by the time he gets back to America. I also promised to give him copies of the parchments if the family ever changed their minds and decided to go to the press. That man is going to be our authenticity for the forgeries."

"That is wicked, Barnaby."

"Rather nice don't you think, seeing he brought up the subject. I'm going to keep leaking him the parchments one after the other. I'll tell him they are copies of course. That the originals would never survive the long journey to America. He'll stick like a fly to flypaper."

"You'd better get Robert to write the parchments."

"Whoever else? Then he can write a brilliant 'tell-all' sequel to *Holy Knight*."

"You mean pull their legs all over again?"

"Exactly."

ON THE LAST Saturday of the month, the curtain fell for the last time on *Happy Times*. Christopher Marlowe's musical that he had written with the help of Danny Hill for Brett Kentrich had run for three and a half years at the Globe. Everyone was at the last night, except Harry Brigandshaw who had left written instructions for the aftershow party before flying off with

Ignatius Bowes-Lyon earlier in the month to fly down Africa in the hybrid seaplane that could also come down safely on land. Once the patrons had left the theatre, the cast, friends of the cast and theatre personnel down to the doorman were to come back to the empty theatre with the curtain up for the party catered at Harry's expense by the Savoy Hotel. Oscar Fleming, the impresario who had staged the musical with Harry's money, was to read a message from Harry in his absence thanking everyone for the success of what had become, the previous month, the longest running show on the West End stage. The musical, according to Oscar Fleming's calculations, had run without a break every night except Sundays for twelve hundred and seventy-seven performances including the Saturday afternoon matinee.

After the ninth curtain call, Oscar Fleming called it quits, saying to the cast there was nothing worse than milking it to find the last call facing the backs of the audience as they walked away up the aisles. It was like someone had thrown a bucket of cold water over the entire cast. Everyone looked miserable. As if a living being had just died right in front of them.

Christopher watched with Danny Hill from the wings, his feelings mixed. *Happy Times* was closing but *A Walk in the Woods* would open in the same theatre at the end of October. The butterflies in his stomach were not for the end but for what the public would think of his new beginning in a month's time... Along with the critics.

From Danny's vantage place in the wings, he could look through at a section of the theatre where the patrons were still not getting up to leave.

"They are not going, Christopher. Everyone I can see through here is still facing the stage even though the lights have come up." Danny stopped looking offstage to look at the cast. "Now look at that. Am I wrong or is Brett crying?"

"She's crying."

"Women... Do you hear that? Oh, my word. Listen to that. They are yelling for the writer... Fleming's coming over to us. Grinning like a Cheshire cat. That man never smiles. Or not when I'm around... Good evening, Mr Fleming."

"I want you to go out to them, Christopher," said Oscar Fleming. "We'll pull back a flap of the curtain to let you out. This is very special, you must understand. Very special. To call for the writer on the last night. I hope there's a critic or two in the audience to see this."

"Only with Brett and Danny," said Christopher.

"All right... You will have to say something."

"What do I say?"

"How do I know? Now be a good chap. They are stamping on the wooden floor and this old theatre is beginning to shake. Just listen to them. Come along old chap, I'll push you through. The chap with the spotlight is ready. This is your big moment."

"I don't want it."

"Nonsense. Mr Hill! Give me a hand. Just the two of you. Brett's blubbing and her eye make-up is all down her face... Out, Christopher! Go forth and face your world."

"I need a drink."

"Out, Christopher! Out!"

Someone had pulled back the bottom of one side of the heavy curtain, making enough space for Christopher to go through to the front of the stage to stand just above the orchestra pit. The house lights dimmed as he went through. The spotlight picked him up immediately. When Danny Hill came through, the gap in the curtain vanished. There was no turning around. Christopher was still wearing the black beret he always wore in Clara's when he played the piano. His hair was down on his shoulders. He brought up both his hands. From shouting and banging came silence. Christopher was not sure which was worse. The entire audience stood up in front of him. Then they applauded as one, the new noise pouring into his face making him smile. Then as one, they went silent. Christopher held up Danny Hill's left hand.

"Mr Danny Hill, everyone. We wrote *Happy Times* together."

"Not quite, Mr Marlowe. You wrote the music in your head. I wrote it down on sheet music. Ladies and gentlemen, my friend and co-musician, Mr Christopher Marlowe."

"Thank you all," Christopher shouted over the new noise of the shouts and the banging on the floor.

Oscar Fleming had been right. He could feel the floorboards vibrating. The flap in the curtain opened behind them. Christopher and Danny backed off the front of the stage. It was over.

Inside the safety of the curtain, Brett ran into his arms.

"That, darling, was the shortest speech I ever heard."

Brett was now sobbing on his shoulder. The cast was again smiling. Excitement was all around Christopher as he smiled back.

"Everyone go and change. My friend Harry Brigandshaw has arranged a party. Everyone back here in twenty minutes. First drinks are already in the dressing rooms. We are all going to have a party which I hope will go on all night."

.   .   .

"If he expects me to tart myself up in twenty minutes he is daft," said Millie Scott, the comedienne of the show. "Blimey. Give us a drink and make it a stiff one... What a night. What a marvellous bloody night."

Friends were waiting out in the corridors as the cast filtered down to the changing rooms. Most of the cast were still milling around. Some had started to dismantle their costumes even before they reached their dressing rooms. Brett, the only one with her own room, had disappeared and shut her door. Millie was looking around hopefully for Merlin St Clair. She had asked him to come. She saw his brother, Barnaby St Clair, looking pleased with himself. On his arm was Portia Ramsbottom. The brother seemed in favour again now he was financing the new show. With him were his author brother and his American girlfriend.

"Where's Merlin, Barnaby?"

"He didn't come."

"Damn him. Always when I want a man they never turn up."

"I think he said he's coming to the party."

"That's something. They say there's booze in the dressing rooms. Excuse me."

"There he is."

Millie Scott turned with a smile which instantly froze on her face. Merlin was making his way through the milling crowd with his monocle fixed over the one dark eye. The blue eye was the only one that seemed to be looking at her. On his arm was a beautiful young girl. A very beautiful young girl. Tall, slim, with a perfect skin and no make-up. Even Barnaby stopped his trivial conversation with his brother Robert to look at the new girl with his brother. With seething, jealous rage Millie looked at the girl.

Merlin was walking straight towards her. Closer, Millie saw the girl was very, very young.

"Damn you, Merlin. Not this tonight. Tonight is special."

"I know, Millie," said Merlin as he smiled at her and then at his brothers in turn.

"Barnaby said you weren't in the theatre."

"Oh, we were... Millie Scott, I would like you to meet my daughter Genevieve... Genevieve wants to go on the stage, don't you, darling? She has just turned fourteen. Genevieve, I want you to meet Miss Millie Scott. We are old friends. And those two men with their mouths wide open are your uncles. Uncle Robert and Uncle Barnaby. Say hello to them. I thought tonight was a good night to bring my daughter out into the world. To meet everyone."

"She's beautiful," breathed Millie more in relief.

"Thank you, Miss Scott. Father has said a lot about you."

"Where's your mother, child?" The girl was certainly precocious.

"At home. Mother never goes out. Daddy comes to visit. Am I too young to go onstage?"

"You are never too young to go on the stage. Especially a beautiful young girl like you... Maybe your Uncle Barnaby can find a part for you in the new show. It's his money... My word, they do grow up so quickly. What do you think, Barnaby? A part in the show for your niece?"

Millie Scott was enjoying herself. Back in control. It was the first time she had ever seen Barnaby stuck for words.

"It will be my pleasure if the others agree. Merlin, you old fox. Never thought you had it in you... Hello. I'm your Uncle Barnaby. What a pity Harry Brigandshaw didn't know about this. He would not have backed out of the show. He was married to your late aunt, Lucinda."

"Who is Aunt Lucinda?"

"I can see there's a lot you don't know about your family," said Barnaby, recovering his wits. "Come on. Let the players change. We'll all go onstage so I can get a better look at my niece. At one of my future leading ladies... I just can't wait for Brett to get an eyeful of this. She hates competition."

Barnaby was actually giggling.

AN HOUR later after the speeches, Barnaby cornered Oscar Fleming before they had drunk too much and only wanted to talk rubbish. Danny Hill was down with the orchestra in the pit playing the piano. The staff of the Savoy had laid out a sumptuous buffet amid the defunct set of *Happy Times* that had till now been the pride and joy of Gert van Heerden. Oscar Fleming, like so many people when it came to money, had changed his mind once the money was found and agreed to produce *A Walk in the Woods*. This time with Gert van Heerden as his co-producer. When it came to money Barnaby also liked to hedge his bets. He had the best of both worlds. The young and the old. The new zest and the old tried experience that had made so much money for Harry Brigandshaw. Despite attending all the auditions for the cast he still wished to make money out of the theatre, and not, as he put it to Portia, throw his cash down the drain.

"Can you get someone into the Central School of Speech and Drama?" he asked Oscar Fleming.

"Probably. Why?"

"That's the one with its home at the Royal Albert Hall, I believe."

"The principal, Elsie Fogerty, is a friend of mine."

"Perfect. I will call a favour, Mr Fleming. If she is no good after the first year they can kick her out. Just getting in can be a problem without influence. You see the girl over there with my elder brother Merlin? That's the chap with the monocle. His eyes are different colours. As kids growing up the dogs all ran away from Merlin. The night owls were his favourites."

"You want me to speak to Miss Fogerty about the girl?"

"She's my niece. I only found out tonight. She wants to be on the stage."

"A good drama school is preferable. Even Brett Kentrich attended drama school. You can have all the talent in the world but you still have to know what you are doing. And that means you have to be taught... Mr van Heerden is very good but he still needs my guidance, you understand."

"Of course." Barnaby smiled to himself. One favour called for another, Oscar Fleming was still firmly in charge. "She's fourteen. Her name is Genevieve."

"Genevieve St Clair. How nice."

"Just Genevieve. She also needs to be taught how to speak properly. My brother is not married. Never has been."

"And the mother?"

"The truth?"

"Always the truth, Mr St Clair. Always the truth when two men are in the same business together."

"Her mother was a barmaid. Merlin met her during the war. Things are different in wartime."

"Yes, well, the war is over and the progeny must learn to speak the King's English if we wish to take them anywhere. Where is the mother tonight?"

"She stays at home. Merlin provides a flat and what she needs. A girl of simple needs. She is quite content not having to work for the rest of her life."

"How fortunate. Some of us are so fortunate." Oscar Fleming coughed delicately into his hand. "I thought it good manners to phone Mrs Brigandshaw this morning and ask her to the last night. She declined, which for some of us might be construed as fortunate. Such a pretty woman. I knew her well before she married Mr Brigandshaw, you understand. She had soon returned from Africa. She is worried about her husband, Mr St Clair."

"I thought that is all in the past."

"Oh, that. Yes, I did hear a little something. No, not the past, Mr St Clair. The present. She has received a wire from Rhodesia. From Mr Brigandshaw's grandfather wanting to know when Mr Brigandshaw will arrive on Elephant Walk."

"He left with Ignatius Bowes-Lyon three weeks ago. Must have stopped off on the way. Harry can be very impulsive. He was married to my late sister. I'll phone his office on Monday. They will have kept in touch I'm sure."

"Mrs Brigandshaw telephoned a Mr Percy Grainger on Friday. Mr Grainger is the managing director of Colonial Shipping, the firm founded by Mr Brigandshaw's paternal grandfather. Not the chap in Rhodesia. They have heard not a word since Cairo. Two and a half weeks ago."

"The aeroplane does not have a wireless. Harry told me himself. He has an aircraft engineer on board and a civil engineer. The civil engineer is going to build a dam across the Mazoe River on Elephant Walk."

"It is so nice to hear you are friends again with Mr Brigandshaw."

For a moment, Barnaby thought he was going to lose his temper. The old voyeur was giving him a look of lascivious understanding... Robert was now waving at him from across the stage. Christopher Marlowe had his arm around Brett Kentrich's shoulder, which annoyed Barnaby for some reason he wished not to admit even to himself. His good mood had changed. No matter what he had done to Tina, Harry was one of the few people in his life he had thought of as a friend. Someone he could go to. Three weeks was too long for two experienced pilots and a good mechanic to disappear. The plane they had flown had two engines. Harry had told him the day before they took off on the epic flight down Africa.

"You can fly this chap on one engine, Barnaby. The idea of flying again is wonderful. Free as a bird. I feel so clean when I am up in the sky. You must come up one day, Barnaby."

"Not me, Harry. I like to keep my feet on the ground."

"You should have thought of that when you dived head first into the river."

"It was a sucker punch."

"Probably."

"Are you and Tina all right?"

"We are now. And yes, Barnaby, I do understand she was your lady first."

"All our lives. From the time we were five years old. I was a bloody fool looking back. I should have married her."

"I'm glad she didn't marry you. She and I are going to be fine. We only have the one sticking point now. I want to live in Africa. Tina wants to bring up the children in England. Time will tell. It always does. We all mellow and change with the years. Our needs and wants become different. The slow evolution of getting older."

· · ·

Bringing his mind back to the present, Barnaby waved back at Robert.

"Excuse me, Fleming. My brother wants something."

"When's he going to write us a play?"

"I'll ask him. Yes, I'll ask him... They don't call it darkest Africa for nothing. I've been there. He could have gone by boat to Cape Town and caught the train to Salisbury and arrived by now."

"I'm sure nothing serious is wrong. He went right through the war, you know."

"He came over after his brother George was killed in Flanders. Please excuse me. You won't forget Genevieve?"

"I never forget a pretty girl. In a few years' time, she will be devastating."

The man was positively leering. Barnaby hated to think what was going through the old sod's mind.

Robert had watched Barnaby's mood change suddenly. One minute he was the soul of the party talking to Oscar Fleming. The next minute he was sour. It was one of Robert's attributes to sense people's moods. It helped him understand the way the characters in his books behaved... He watched Barnaby break off with the impresario and come across the stage between the trestle tables laden with so much good food.

"When are you two going back to America?" asked Barnaby.

"We are not. Not for a while, anyway. Freya loves England. She has rented a small flat close by. We are going down to Dorset for a stay. Freya will be Mother's guest."

"You'll have to behave yourself with Mother around."

"Barnaby! How could you suggest such a thing in front of a lady? We are always the perfect example of good behaviour, aren't we, Freya?"

"Quite perfect."

"Your brilliant idea has a flaw, Barnaby. Our ancestors spoke French. I don't speak French, let alone write it. The original parchments, had there ever been any, would have been written in old French."

"Nonsense. Not the ones that left Corfe Castle for the secret hiding place in Purbeck Manor. By then our illustrious ancestors would have translated the Sir Henri Saint Claire Debussy's words into English. By the time Cromwell knocked down Corfe Castle your precious parchments were written in Chaucerian English. Dear oh dear. Where is your imagination, Robert? I thought you said you were a novelist."

They all laughed as Christopher and Brett joined them. They were standing next to the buffet table. The music from the orchestra pit had stopped. Danny Hill was climbing back onstage and coming across to join them.

"Harry's missing, Robert. He hasn't arrived on Elephant Walk. No one has heard a word since Cairo."

Brett, who had turned as white as a sheet, ran off the stage without saying another word.

"You'd better go after her, Christopher."

"When did you hear?" asked Robert as Christopher went to look for her.

"From Fleming. Just a few moments ago. He had phoned Tina to ask her to come tonight."

"I'm sure Harry's all right. Engine trouble. They are fixing it. Harry is the ultimate survivor... When are you going to see Tina?"

"I'm not. Certainly not now. You'd better go and see her, Robert. With Merlin... Fleming's getting our niece into the Central School of Speech and Drama."

"That's a good idea. Cheer up. Harry will be fine. It's a long way down Africa... How long has it been?"

"Three weeks."

"Have the press got hold of it?"

"Not yet. I'm going to get another drink. A stiff one... Oh, and Fleming wants you to write him a play."

"How nice of him. I'm a novelist. The two are as different as chalk and cheese. A novel has to come to life in the reader's mind. A play comes to life on the stage and is looked at with the eyes of the audience."

"I have no idea what you are talking about, Robert."

"Think about it. The pictures are different ways around... Freya is still going to write her column for Glen Hamilton. Maybe Freya can write Mr Fleming a play. What about that, Freya? Then there is no competition. And we can live in the country."

"Where is Max Pearl, Robert?" asked Barnaby.

"Back in New York. Luckily, he didn't act on the parchment drama. The English edition of *Holy Knight* is selling like hotcakes."

"However, even more reason for forging those parchments."

"Do you know how difficult it is to write Chaucerian English?"

"How about Freya?"

"What a brilliant idea," said Robert.

"Count me out," said Freya, "I'm not a crook. There's something about being an accessory to the crime."

"How can there be a crime? The parchments never existed. You can't forge what never existed. Sometimes you have to give people what they want. A white lie at worst, Freya."

"I'll think about it."

"That's a good girl," said Barnaby. "Lies are always fine until they are found out. Germany says they are not re-arming. Now that's a lie. Churchill says it's a lie and when we find out, there will be a war. Lost and found parchments just don't matter. Except to that Yank... Oh sorry, Freya. That American. Let's give him what he wants and have some fun. Can where Robert found the ideas for his book make the slightest difference to how good *Holy Knight* really is? It's fiction. Entertainment. Based on fact. That much my entire family can vouch for."

"That 'Yank' got under your skin, Barnaby," said Freya.

"Yes, he did."

"I'll see what I can come up with. *The Canterbury Tales* were a set work at school. I'll read them again."

"That's a good girl."

"You say the press hasn't heard about Harry Brigandshaw disappearing in Africa?" she asked.

"No, not yet."

"They will. It'll make one hell of a story. War hero lost in the jungle. The fact he is very rich will make it all the better. I know. I'm a reporter."

"Robert, you and Merlin must warn Tina... Anyone like a leg of chicken? This food looks marvellous."

By ten o'clock in the morning on the following Wednesday, Tina Brigandshaw had the four children and the two children's nurses packed in a taxi on the way to the railway station. To add to her woes, on the Monday it was confirmed she was pregnant with her fifth child.

When she came back to the Berkeley Square house from her gynaecologist in Paddington, a man from the *Daily Mail* had been waiting on her doorstep.

"Is it true Mr Harry Brigandshaw has not been heard from in three weeks?"

"Who are you?"

"Wakefield. From the *Mail*. Does he have a will? Who gets his money?"

"My husband is not dead."

"After his aircraft went down in the jungle and not a word for three weeks?"

"My husband grew up in Africa. If he was forced to land he will know what to do. He was a fighter pilot. On board is an aircraft mechanic and Harry knows more about aircraft than most men alive."

"Will you inherit Colonial Shipping?"

"You don't listen. I said he wasn't dead. Now excuse me."

"Then you have heard from him?"

Tina had pushed past the man and slammed the front door in his face. She was crying. Frank was wailing somewhere inside the house. She and Ivy had tried everything to soothe his pain. He was teething or just being his usual self. When Frank did not get exactly what he wanted, he yelled his lungs out. The other three children had never given trouble. After the first week, Dorian had slept through the night in the nursery where the two nurses slept with the children. The reporter was ringing the front doorbell as if by right. Gritting her teeth, Tina pulled herself together. There was no point in feeling sorry for herself. It would not help the situation.

Going up the stairs to see what was happening in the nursery, she had decided to take everyone down to Dorset where she could think, away from people asking questions to which she had no answers.

As she was about to get into the taxi behind the rest of them, she stopped for a moment, standing up straight to look around. For the first time in her life, she knew what it felt like to be in love. Barnaby had always been lust. Harry, now he was gone, she knew to be love. The irony was not lost on her thirty-year-old mind.

She told the taxi driver where to go. Then she climbed into the back of the taxi. The family luggage was in the open compartment of the vehicle next to the driver. Her mother would know what to do. Her mother would know how to help. Merlin had told her to get out of London and he was right. Phoning Percy Grainger every day was worse than waiting by the phone for news. She hated Africa even more than in the past. For Tina, Africa was always dark and evil. Menacing.

When they all arrived later in the day at Corfe Castle railway station, her mother and father were waiting on the platform. This time she had not tried to fool her mother she could look after four children on her own. Ivy had the baby in a bassinet. The rest of the children stepped down from the train, each, in turn, holding Molly's hand. Ivy was nineteen, Molly seventeen. Frank had stopped being a nuisance. The boy ran to his grandmother and jumped into her arms – something he never did with Tina. Anthony at five years old shook hands formally with his grandfather. Beth was sucking her thumb and stroking her small blanket at the same time with her fingers. Old Pringle was in uniform and still on duty.

Being the very end of summer there were other people getting off the London train. The sun was shining and the day warm. The winter weather was still on the way. Tina looked up at the distant hill with the ruins of Corfe Castle prominent on the hilltop. How strange, she thought, if the ghosts up there knew Frank was one of them. None of the children had been told Harry was missing somewhere in Africa. Merlin had said they would not understand. Tina was glad Barnaby had the sense to keep away. He was the last person on earth she wished to see in her life at that moment.

Only standing on the railway station so close to where she was born did the premonition sweep over her, taking away most of the pain. Harry was still alive. She felt it in her bones. Then she walked across and fell into her mother's arms. The arms where she had always been safe. Always.

The taxi was waiting to take them all to the cottage by the river where the Pringles lived.

THERE WAS no telephone in the cottage, only at the station where Tina had phoned the previous day. She had told her father Harry was missing before someone told him from reading the papers. The only good thing that had come from the interest shown by the press had been the concern of the Royal Air Force. A man from the Air Ministry had phoned to say the RAF was sending a search party by air down Africa. They knew which path Harry had flown. He would have to pick up fuel on the way.

"He's got extra fuel on board in petrol cans. There are small ports on some of the lakes with petrol for the more sophisticated fishing boats. Bowes-Lyon was one of our best navigators. They were going to land on the lakes at the ports after landing on the Nile at Khartoum. Lake Tanner. Lake Rudolf. Lake Victoria. Lake Tanganyika. Lake Nyasa. They have a range of nine hundred miles with the long-range fuel tanks Harry had fitted under the wings."

"If they went down in the jungle wouldn't it swallow them up?" Tina had asked, not understanding a word of what the man had said.

"We'll do our best, Mrs Brigandshaw. I knew your husband during the war. We are all praying for their safe return. Everything will be done. Everything. You have my word."

. . .

LUCKILY FOR TINA, she was not in London on the following Friday morning when the news from the Air Ministry broke in the press. By then Tina was walking in the woods around her family cottage, trying to imagine life without her husband. Trying to tell herself what she was going to do.

'Like looking for a needle in a haystack or worse,' one paper editorialised.

Most of the other daily papers across England were equally pessimistic. Only the *Telegraph* with its 'they found Doctor Livingstone didn't they?' gave any idea of hope. For most people in Britain Harry's disappearance with his crew was just another echo from the past. Interesting. Sad. But a long way away.

As TINA'S stay in Dorset went into a second week, the papers were milking the story for the last drop. They touted Harry's war record in detail; the death of Lucinda, shot dead by Harry's wartime CO; the man himself shot by Tembo, the black man, after Braithwaite had shot dead Barend Oosthuizen, the self-proclaimed man of God, the preacher who had been saved from the bowels of a gold mine in South Africa to preach the word of God.

By THE END OF OCTOBER, Tina was still holed up in the cottage on the small river. The weather was wintry. The three aircraft of the Royal Air Force had returned to England with nothing to report. The search had been called off. Even Tina with her premonition now knew there was little hope anyone would be found. Harry, her husband, was dead in the festering jungle somewhere in Africa... It was all over.

TINA AGAIN PACKED up the children and went back to London, to her house in Berkeley Square, to face the rest of her life alone.

The story by then had faded from the newspapers, forgotten in people's minds. There were other stories of other people's misfortunes to read about. Only the few who knew Harry Brigandshaw or any on board the ill-fated aircraft had felt any pain.

THE DAY TINA BRIGANDSHAW locked herself up in Berkeley Square with her memories, the curtain rose on *A Walk in the Woods*. The lights dimmed and Christopher Marlowe's new musical began. This time Barnaby St Clair was the man who worried if the show would make a profit. It would take four months of good houses to even get his money back. So much depended on the first night, the stalls packed with newspaper critics all waiting to pounce.

In the audience, unknown to Barnaby, was Horatio Wakefield of the *Daily Mail* doubling for the night as the theatre critic. He was the same Horatio Wakefield who had waited for Tina on the steps of her Berkeley Square house. He was fully aware of the Brigandshaw connection with the theatre and his financing of *Happy Times*. There had been little good copy after the air force stopped the search for the missing plane in Africa. All the new breaking stories were domestic and boring to Horatio Wakefield. He had asked the theatre editor of his paper to let him cover the first night, hoping to find more juice in the Brigandshaw saga that had briefly lifted the sales of the *Mail*. Horatio was ambitious. Wanted to get on in life and be a success like Harry Brigandshaw, with a big house in Berkeley Square and a wife who looked like Mrs Tina Brigandshaw.

The overture had finished, the curtain rose, the show began; then Horatio watched a man get up and leave from the row in front of him that he thought was rude. Halfway through if the play was bad, but not just after it had started. He turned around and watched the man as he sat down again in a vacant seat at the back of the theatre. Horatio had no idea what the man was doing.

Looking back at the floodlit stage Horatio saw Brett Kentrich in all her glory and settled himself back in his seat. So far as he was concerned, the show could turn out lousy so long as this girl stayed onstage just in front of him. To Horatio, about to be married or not, Brett Kentrich was the most beautiful woman in the world. The likelihood of him ever getting to know her personally and shatter his dream was part of the attraction. Every time he saw her she was exactly the same: just perfect.

When the first act came to an end there was polite clapping. Horatio was still seeing Brett in his mind.

"She's just so beautiful."

The chap from the *Guardian* turned to look at Horatio. They had known each other as cub reporters on the *Daily Mail* before William Smythe moved up in the world and joined the *Manchester Guardian*. Horatio had known William was frightfully left-wing. They had met that night in the foyer before the show and juggled their seats with the other reporters to sit next to each other. The reason Horatio voted Tory was because his father voted Tory. Horatio and William never talked politics as it could affect their respective papers. They were good friends.

"She had a long affair with the chap you have been writing about."

Horatio smiled. They both thought of other men as chaps. Sort of a silly bond between them over the years.

"What are you talking about?"

"Brigandshaw financed *Happy Times*. Did you know he had put up the leading lady in a mews flat off Regent Street?"

"Does his wife know?"

"Before he married her. Your beautiful lady tried to break the marriage when Brigandshaw brought his wife back from Africa. The baby they brought with them was either premature or conceived out of wedlock. Take your pick. The other scandal in the family has to do with the chap who got up in front of us after the curtain went up. I saw you turn round and watch him sit at the back. There was a row with Brigandshaw who pulled out of financing the show. The Honourable Barnaby St Clair stepped in to spite Brigandshaw. They say the third of Brigandshaw's kids is St Clair's. To add insult to injury Brigandshaw was married to St Clair's late sister who was shot by that madman Braithwaite. Don't you know all this? You were writing about Braithwaite just the other day."

"I do know... So Brett was his mistress?"

"Something like that... When you put up big money for a show like this you get nervous. Why, I expect, St Clair went to sit at the back. Let's go and have a drink at the bar. It's a lousy show despite your beautiful lady who is about to marry the writer. Now did you know that, old chap?"

"You should work for a scandal magazine."

"I've thought of it. Trouble is, scandal is petty. Politics is vicious."

"Aren't you writing up this show?"

"Of course not. I'm a political correspondent. Picked up a free ticket from the night editor. Like you, Horatio, I like the look of Miss Brett Kentrich, the soon-to-be Mrs Christopher Marlowe."

"Is she pregnant too?"

"Why should I know?"

"You know all about Mrs Tina Brigandshaw."

"Now there was one really sexy lady. You should have seen her when she came over from Africa. Her brother is rich. A rand baron in gold and explosives. Put herself up at the Savoy. Wow, she was something."

"What else do you know about her background?"

"Born dirt-poor in a railway company cottage somewhere in Dorset. Just shows how far they can go in life with that amount of sex appeal."

"Whatever happened in her past, she's taken Brigandshaw's death very badly."

"Is he dead?"

"Must be. How could he have survived?"

"They say he grew up in the bush. His father was a famous big-game hunter... Come on. I need that drink before the curtain goes up again."

"You said the show was lousy."

"Not that lousy. Marlowe builds up in the second and third acts. There isn't much to the story but I like his music... Do you know my shares went up two thousand quid this month?"

"Why don't you sell them and take your profit?"

"Better to borrow from my bank manager and watch the shares go on up. Easiest money I ever made. Chap lends me up to eighty per cent of the current value of my share portfolio. The interest I pay the bank is piddling compared to the rise in the share price. Are you in the market?"

"I don't have any money. The *Daily Mail* doesn't pay as well as the *Guardian*. Why I do the stints as a theatre critic to get a free ticket."

"I'd better buy you that drink."

"The Brigandshaw connection was also my motive tonight. The cast is having a first-night party to wait for the crits in the morning paper. Why they opened on a Wednesday night. There are far more daily papers than Sunday papers."

"You really are a nit. I work for a paper. You don't think I know these things?"

"Anyway, after writing my piece for the *Mail* I'm coming back to the party. To see if there's anything more I can write about Brigandshaw."

"And ogle Miss Kentrich... Can I come to the party?"

"If you help me write a good piece. Shouldn't take ten minutes. The same taxi can wait outside the office and bring us back to the theatre where they are going to have the party. Not only do I get a free ticket for ten minutes' work, but I also get to drink the free booze. They like the critics to come to the parties. Fleming thinks it gets him better reviews... How much have you borrowed from the bank?"

"Twelve thousand pounds."

"That's a fortune, William! You don't earn that money in twenty years."

"I was lucky. A friend put me into the market early. Jock Shepherd. He heads up our financial section on the paper."

"Aren't you nervous?"

"Why should I be? My shares are worth more than my overdraft by over three thousand pounds. How can a newspaper reporter save that kind of money from his salary?"

"What if the market goes down?"

"I work for the *Manchester Guardian*. We have some of the best financial analysts in the world. They all say the market will go on rising as industry gets more efficient as all these new inventions come on stream. It's scientific inventions that make a man rich. The machines do the work. All you need is capital to buy the machines. It's working capital that makes the real money. Not working stiffs like you and me. Money makes money, Horatio. You should get on the bandwagon before you get left behind."

"I don't like owing anyone anything. Particularly money."

"What are you having?"

"A whisky and soda."

They were both by then standing at the bar in the foyer of the theatre. Next to them, with his back turned, Barnaby St Clair was ordering himself a large brandy.

"Looks nervous," whispered Horatio, who had recognised Barnaby as the man who had left the second row of the stalls at the start of the show.

"So would you be, putting that kind of money on a musical no one has seen. I never understand gambling like that with good money."

"At least he loses his own money."

"He's in the market up to the hilt. So Jock says. Borrowed right up to the hilt. The stock markets are a moneymaking machine, not like the theatre... You must know how many shows fail."

BARNABY LISTENED to every word without turning around. He was smiling to himself. When the riff-raff were in the market it was always the time to get out. Taking his drink in his hand, Barnaby moved anonymously among the first-night crowd. By the time he went to his seat at the back of the theatre, he was feeling better. The audience was just getting interested. If the second and third acts went as Oscar Fleming planned, there would be more than polite clapping when the final curtain dropped on the first night.

OSCAR FLEMING HAD BEEN QUITE specific.

"Never give 'em it all in the beginning. The end is what they remember. What they talk about when they get home. You got to build a show, Mr St Clair. Marlowe knows that as well as I do. Why his first musical made money. You do know his father was a leading man of business in the City? However much he likes to act the bohemian, Marlowe knows the end product that counts in life is money."

. . .

BY THE TIME Barnaby went for a drink after the second act, he thought his money was safe. When the curtain went down on the last act he was sitting in the seat where he had started. In the second row of the stalls. A little smugly, with his arms folded defensively over his chest, Barnaby watched Brett and the cast take five curtain calls. The old fox Oscar Fleming could have milked two more by the sound of the clapping from the audience. Only when people were certain the curtain had gone down for the last time did they get up to leave.

The theatre crowd gave off an air of excitement. They had enjoyed themselves, so far as Barnaby could see and overhear. He too was enjoying himself. Not only did the theatre give him something to do, but it was also going to make him money. All the girls were just one of the pleasant extras that came with life. Like so many women in his life, Portia had come and gone. When the chase came to its climax he mostly grew bored and looked for someone else to build his excitement. Barnaby knew he loved women. But in the plural. The more the merrier, he said to himself with a self-satisfied chuckle.

Barnaby followed the crowd out of the Globe Theatre. First, he was going to get himself a bite to eat at Clara's. Then he was coming back for the first-night party to see what he could find among all the young girls. Then they would all see what the morning newspapers had to say about *A Walk in the Woods*.

TINA BRIGANDSHAW READ the *Daily Mail* review sitting at her lonely breakfast table in her house on Berkeley Square. The children were still in the nursery on the top floor of the house where Ivy and Molly were feeding them their breakfast before taking them for a walk in the square. She was surprised reading the H Wakefield name as the reviewer of *A Walk in the Woods*. The same H Wakefield who had given her so much pain writing about Harry. She was numb, barely registering the new baby growing inside her, a child who would never know a father. Despite her premonition, Tina had now accepted Harry was dead. That she would never see him again. Never hear his voice except inside her head where she had conversations with him throughout the day and most of the night.

She was still in her dressing gown, picking at the food a servant had put in front of her. Tina knew she looked a mess. Were it not for having to visit Colonial Shipping at the request of Percy Grainger, she would not have contemplated getting dressed. Outside the breakfast room where she took all her meals, she could see the rain drizzling on the bare trees that had mostly lost their autumn leaves. Tina had no idea what Percy Grainger wanted. He had said it was important, and would she come to the office.

It had to do with Harry's business, which she knew nothing about. Why else would he want her to meet the other directors of the company? Percy Grainger had asked her to lunch in the executive dining room after the meeting but she had declined. Harry had once said something about entertaining clients for lunch at the office, which she now understood: Percy Grainger had settled with her for an eleven o'clock meeting that morning.

Leaving most of her food on the plate and her teacup half full, Tina got up to go and dress. She had read the review to try to stop feeling so sorry for herself. The visit to her mother and father had somehow made it all worse. The children had enjoyed themselves making a noise in the garden. They had run around screaming in the surrounding woods. Frank had got in the river up to his neck, frightening the wits out of Molly who had jumped in the water to pull him out. The children had known their father go away before. They were all too young to sense something dreadfully wrong.

Changing in their bedroom, Tina tried to put the pain of Harry out of her mind. The review was good. Ironically, Barnaby was going to make even more money by the looks of it. He had only made one call: the week the Royal Air Force called off the search, Harry's disappearance spread across a dozen newspapers. He had not come round, for which she was grateful. She had no wish for Barnaby to see her constant crying.

"You know where I am if you need any help. For what it's worth and despite everything we did, Harry was about the only friend I ever had."

"Don't talk of him in the past. He's alive. Somewhere. He roamed half of southern Africa after his father was killed by that elephant. If they didn't die in the crash, they can all survive. Harry knows the bush like you know women... No, that's a cheap shot. Thank you for calling, Barnaby."

"You'll have to come to terms with it one day, Tina. How long can you hope?"

"He'll walk out of the bush. You'll see."

"Tina, please be reasonable. It's been weeks since he must have gone down."

"I don't want to see you, Barnaby."

"That I understand. Just remember where I am if you need me."

"You didn't say when I need you."

"I know. Goodbye."

.   .   .

THE TAXI DROPPED Tina off outside the head office of Colonial Shipping in Billiter Street. It was five minutes to eleven o'clock.

The managing director's office was unpretentious when the receptionist showed her the way in. Percy Grainger got up from behind his desk. The room was full of men who all stood up. Percy Grainger introduced each one of them by name.

"We are sorry to bring you here, Mrs Brigandshaw. The board of directors have a problem. As you know, we are a public listed company with our ordinary shares quoted on the London Stock Exchange. The directors run the company. The directors have to be appointed by the controlling shareholder each year at our annual general meeting which is tomorrow. The controlling shareholder was your husband, Mrs Brigandshaw. I had asked your husband to sign a blank proxy form if he was ever away and unable to attend our AGM. He refused. There was something that happened in the war about tempting fate. He did not explain, only to say he was superstitious. Harry himself told me he did not have a will. In the event of him dying intestate, you will become, as his wife and next of kin, the major shareholder in Colonial Shipping."

"But Harry is not dead."

"Exactly, Mrs Brigandshaw. There is no proof of his death. Only his disappearance somewhere over the African jungle between Khartoum and the farm Elephant Walk. Our solicitors have informed us you may apply to the court in two years to have your husband declared legally dead. Please forgive me. This is just as difficult for me. In the meantime, we are asking them to give you power of attorney over your husband's shares in the company so tomorrow you can approve my recommendation for the continuance in office of the current board of directors without which the company may not legally function. I am now formally asking you to become your husband's proxy on the board until the end of the two years when you'll be able to dispose of your shares as you wish. I understand you know Mr CE Porter, who arranged with Harry for the company to go public some years ago. When Harry still lived in Africa, CE Porter voted his shares. He also had a seat on our board. I am sure Mr Porter will give you good advice in these terrible circumstances we all presently face."

"You want me to be a director of your company?"

"Yes, Mrs Brigandshaw, we do."

"I know nothing whatsoever about business or the company."

"It is more a formality."

"Can't we wait?"

"No, Mrs Brigandshaw. We want you tomorrow at our AGM with power of attorney to vote your husband's shares."

"The nightmare is getting worse. Frankly, I have no idea what you are all talking about."

"But you will do as we wish? For the company? For the staff?"

"Of course, Mr Grainger. My husband held you in high esteem."

"We have these papers for you to sign for our solicitor's appearance in court this afternoon. The company car will be at your door to pick you up at two-thirty tomorrow afternoon. The AGM begins at three p.m. In a moment our driver will take you home, Mrs Brigandshaw. With all our condolences. Harry Brigandshaw, like his grandfather, our founder, was a very special man to all of us. It is not wrong to say we loved him."

"He's not dead, you know. He's coming back."

"We all hope so. Now if you'll sign here and here, our receptionist will witness your signature and I will attend the court on your behalf this afternoon."

12

JULY 1929 – DOCTOR LIVINGSTONE, I PRESUME

*J*ohn Lacey, Marquess of Ravenhurst, was full of excitement. Not even the stifling heat in Madison Avenue where he was walking on the pavement between the towering skyscrapers of New York could dull his mood. His marriage to Stella Fitzgerald may have been a convenience for both of them but his money was real and growing every day. Every cent of the million dollars paid to him by Patrick Fitzgerald for marrying his daughter had been invested in the New York Stock Exchange. His new friends told him nothing could stop the Dow Jones going higher and higher. America was on an unstoppable roll. Stella's friends, and by association his, were stockbrokers, investment bankers, men of new money, richer than Croesus living fabulous lives in fabulous apartments newly decorated by his wife. Magnificent homes high above the city with views over Manhattan that took his breath away. The old crumbling house he had lived in like a hermit until Cuddles Morton-Sayner came knocking on his back door, was far from his mind. America had changed him.

The business of war and genteel poverty were gone with the bustle, the excitement, the brand newness of the New World he had not so much as imagined until they had set up home in their Manhattan apartment overlooking Central Park. Even the man in the flat below them was a titled Englishman, one of the breed of bankers who were making John Lacey enormously rich. His decision never to impregnate his wife with the old seed of the Ravenhursts had long been tossed out of the proverbial window. John now wanted an heir. An American heir. Not so much to inherit his title, as American citizens were unable to do so. He wanted the boy to inherit the fabulous wealth and lifestyle that went with being rich. Really rich and getting richer every day.

Finding the entrance to his wife's building where Stella kept a small, exclusive design studio only frequented by the rich, he went through the revolving door into the cool of an air-conditioned building where man lived at the temperature he chose for himself away from the fickle dictates of nature. The cool air that brushed over his face was utter bliss, the personification of everything he liked about living in America. John Lacey was quite happy to admit to himself that the real seducer had not been Stella Fitzgerald but America, a mistress he was looking forward to enjoying in luxury for the rest of his life. Suddenly England was a long, long way away, forgotten in his past, the weeds stalking through his ancestral home for all he cared. For a few dollars more he would have taken on an American accent were it not for his new American friends. They just loved the English marquess with his strange pompous accent that they said made him so much fun at their dinner parties. They wanted him to stand out. They wanted him to be different. John even suspected that was the reason he was so often invited into the sumptuous apartments across the island of Manhattan. 1929 was proving to be the best year of his life.

That night they were hosting a dinner party for ten of Stella's rich advertising friends who worked in the office building where he was now going up smoothly in the air-conditioned lift that did not require an operator: John had merely pressed the tenth-floor button to take him where he wanted to go, the doors closing automatically. Image, selling, advertising were all the rage in America. Everyone pushed. No one waited for the buyer to walk through the door, for the customer to ask politely if it was possible to do business. The polite old boy network of the old world had long ago drowned in the mass frenzy of getting the wealth every American strove for and wanted. Everyone had a chance, John understood. You just had to push.

On the door of the studio, John Lacey read his own family name:

STELLA, MARCHIONESS OF RAVENHURST – INTERIOR DESIGN

THEN HE WENT INSIDE to sit with the receptionist until his wife was free to see him. He wanted to take his wife to lunch. The only quibble John Lacey had with his life in America was not having enough to do. He couldn't very well wander around the fields with a shotgun over his shoulder in Manhattan. Or translate ancient Greek for a pittance.

The debacle of the brass band at the railway station in Boston no longer seemed what it was at the time. He even tolerated the brashness of his father-in-law, the 'I know we bought you' of his brothers-in-law. He had doubled their money on the stock exchange so to hell with them. They could patronise him any which way they wished.

When a young man about Stella's age eventually came out of his wife's inner office and blushed deep red when he saw him sitting at reception, he thought nothing of the man. Stella always did like doing business with men. John even gave the man a friendly smile. He had seen him somewhere before. At one of the many parties. Probably in his own house. When he got up and thanked the receptionist for the cup of coffee she had brought to him while he had been waiting, she did not look him in the eye for some reason. By the time John opened the door to Stella's office the man behind him had gone and the girl at reception was busy on her typewriter, hitting the heavy keys for all she was worth.

"What are you doing here, John?"

"I came to take you to lunch."

"Not today, John. I'm up to my eyeballs in work. Don't forget the party tonight. The caterers are coming at six so make sure to be there to let them in."

His wife was very often up to her eyeballs, an expression unknown to John. Stella had picked it up from Cuddles Morton-Sayner when Cuddles was searching the aristocracy for a husband to give a nice ring to her married name and to satisfy the ego of her brothers and father.

WHEN HER HUSBAND left the office five minutes later, Stella let out a small sigh. Even if she wanted him to, she doubted he was capable of making her pregnant. After six months she had given up seducing him and taken herself a young lover. Never once had John made the first approach. She had his name. He had her family money. Her friends liked him as a host at her parties, flattered by being flattered by an Englishman with a title. In some ways, she had grown quite fond of him. Like the faithful family dog she thought he had become. He dressed well at her insistence, not in old English tweeds, and his manners had always been impeccable. Best of all, John and his name were good for business. People liked to drop names. It made them feel more important: 'my apartment was decorated by the Marchioness of

Ravenhurst' had a nice ring to it. Her brothers dropped her new name all the time.

Just before she went back to the picture she was painting on a board for the chairman of Westgate Oil to show to his wife, so the stupid bitch could see what she was getting before she paid for the outrageously expensive decoration, Stella shuddered in the cold draught of the air conditioning. For a brief flash, she saw not the drawing board in front of her but a river through the trees in the light of a colourless moon. In her head, she could hear owls hooting across the moon-splashed night. It took another full minute to find her concentration and go back to her work. She wondered how he was. What he had done with her clothes. The man who had taken her virginity in his house on the banks of the River Thames. The man she seemed quite unable to get out of her head. In all the sex that had come to her after that first time, none other had been so satisfying. None other had satiated her lust. None had made her feel so good. Strangely, she found she could remember most of their day-long conversation, she sitting on the grass by his wheelchair. She could still feel the power in his arms when he had stopped her running head first into the river. More and more as the months went by, Stella regretted not going back for her clothes. Only when the painting for the bitch was finished did she realise what she had to do to lay the ghost. She would take a month's holiday away from her husband. She would tell him it was boring business. That it was best for her to go alone. Her husband was quite besotted with his new lifestyle anyway and never even talked of England, let alone the old house rotting away in the marshes he had so lovingly described when they first met in London. She would go to England and collect her long-lost clothes and find out what it was a legless man had done to her. Sitting at her desk, the one thing she wanted most in life was to see Douglas Hayter again. To talk to him all day. To make love all night while the owls called to her through the open French windows from the woods.

KEPPEL HOWLAND HAD GONE ALL the way to New York to make his old friend Ralph Madgwick a proposition. This despite their lack of correspondence during his years up at Oxford on a Madgwick scholarship reading English literature. He wanted Ralph to go back with him to Africa and look for Harry Brigandshaw. Keppel even had the title of the articles he was going to write to make himself a name in journalism: 'In the footsteps of Doctor Livingstone'. What he had read in the newspapers of the RAF flying over the jungle trying to look for a crashed aircraft under the trees, he knew was a waste of time. A publicity stunt to make it look as if the air force cared about its war heroes, the RAF high command prompted by the build-up in the press at two of their airmen's disappearance. What was needed were feet on the ground. An expedition like Stanley had put together in order to find and resupply Livingstone, Stanley a Welsh journalist who had concentrated the world on Africa, and the search for the famous explorer. With interpreters, Keppel could ask the locals questions. Probe any rumours of a devil crashing in from the sky. Even if Harry and the others were long dead, the finding of the crash site would make world headlines. Make him famous. If he found Harry Brigandshaw, it would repay Harry for the hospitality he had shown them when they left the leopard cave at Harry's invitation dropped to them from out of the sky. Harry in so many ways had been the start of his career as a writer. His first published article in the *Daily Mail* had been titled *The Leopard Cave*.

"It'll be a grand adventure, Ralph. Look, this office of yours is all very nice. I'm impressed. Ten staff in just over a year. But we owe it to Harry. I think I have a newspaper interested in sponsoring the expedition."

"Why don't you try Glen Hamilton in Denver? He knew Harry during the war. Helped to bring me to Rebecca thanks to Harry and his brother-in-law, Robert St Clair. But you don't understand about me, old friend. I'm flattered you came all this way with your proposition but I'm in love. I'm converting to Judaism which is a wonderful religion full of so much tradition. Then we will marry, I and my Rebecca. Look, why don't I ask Rebecca to lay another place at the table tonight where I'm going to dinner? The old man's a bit frightening the first time you meet him. But I like him despite everything. He'll remind you of one of those African eagles we saw on our safari. He has a nose like a predator's beak. He's a bit nostalgic on England despite his time in America. You'll have dinner with us and meet Rebecca. Then you'll understand. Wonderful seeing you, old boy. You'll stay in the flat of course. Where's your luggage? There's a pull-out couch in the lounge. My flat is pretty basic but you won't have to pay for a hotel. Just down from Oxford, you'll be skint. Do you remember how skint we were when we came back from Africa? Why don't I phone Glen Hamilton and put the story to him? He's chief editor of the *Denver Telegraph*. His assistant is going to marry Robert St Clair and we've promised to fly to Denver when they get married. The least Rebecca and I can do to repay Freya and Robert if Rebecca's father will let her go on our own. Freya, that's Robert's wife to be, gave Rebecca my letter when the old man was burning my mail. People travel long distances in America and think nothing of it. You really think Harry Brigandshaw could still be alive after all this time?"

"Stanley found Livingstone in the middle of nowhere. Livingstone had been gone longer when Stanley pronounced some of the most famous few words in history: 'Doctor Livingstone, I presume.'"

"You always were a man who got what he wanted. I wish you the best of luck. Just count me out this time. Your old schoolmate and fellow soldier is going to be a happily married man. Domesticated, with lots of children, all the girls looking just like Rebecca. You'll love her. She's absolutely gorgeous. You'll see... I hope you haven't told his wife you are going to look for Harry. She must be going through enough as it is without getting up false hopes. Yes, it'll make a good story for the press. Wouldn't surprise me if Hamilton didn't sponsor the whole expedition lock, stock and barrel. Do you remember that dinner party we both attended in Berkeley Square? I rather think you were bowled over by his wife that night the way you were looking at her like a lovesick calf. Good-looking girl is Mrs Brigandshaw. She must be going through hell. Just had Harry's posthumous baby in July according to the newspapers who won't leave her alone. Oh well. The price of being married to a famous man, I suppose. Tina won't mind your expedition if you find him. You can be sure of that, Keppel."

"No, I haven't approached the family or the company. I wanted to talk to you first, Ralph. We go back a long way. Couldn't think of anyone better by my side in unfriendly country. They say the bush in the Belgian Congo is thicker than anything we saw in Rhodesia. Why a plane going down in the trees could never be seen from the air. The canopy would literally swallow it up... You think this Glen Hamilton will pay my expenses in total, do you? That would be nice. After coming out here I don't have a penny. Put all I had into the boat trip over. Third class, of course."

"We can only ask him... Here's my address and the spare key. I keep the spare in the drawer of my office desk. In case I lock myself out of my flat... Get a cab. Nothing is formal on the nights I eat with the Rosenzweigs. I'll be home at six. We'll take a cab to Abercrombie Place. Rebecca will love to meet you. Spoken to her of our times together many times. And you're right, Keppel. We go back a long way. You can't make new old friends I read once in a magazine article on friendship. Now, be off. I have to work. Rosie Prescott outside keeps me on my toes. Did you see my Uncle Wallace before you came across the pond?"

"He wants to know when he can retire into the country."

"That's another story. Poor old Uncle Wallace. I think Rebecca and I are going to stay in America. We like the place. Her father thinks there is going to be another war in Europe. I've had quite enough of war in my life. I often think of our old school chum Malcolm Scott. Especially when I realise how happy I am with Rebecca. A splinter from the shell that killed Malcolm took the little finger off my left hand. You remember that. You were there. We are both lucky to be alive. No more wars for me... I'm soon going to become a married man."

Grinning at each other, they shook hands vigorously for the second time. Keppel picked up the key and left. He was already looking forward to the supper. He was hungry.

WHEN RALPH MADGWICK got home after work, he found the wedding invitation from Denver in the mailbox. The wedding of Robert St Clair and Freya Taylor was in a week's time. The invitation was the usual Mr and Mrs Taylor request. Ralph doubted any of the friends and family had time to come over from England. Certainly not Lord and Lady St Clair who never left Dorset, let alone the country. Not wishing to think badly of his friends who had made his beautiful life possible, he put the speed of the wedding down to compulsion, with the strange ways of artists who never seemed to do things like the rest of them.

Pushing the open invitation back in his pocket with the envelope, Ralph walked up the three flights of stairs to his flat and let himself in. Keppel Howland was fast asleep on the pulled-out couch. The man was incredible. During the war, Ralph remembered Keppel could sleep through a full bombardment whichever way the shells were flying.

Ralph prodded his friend awake.

"Where the hell am I?"

"New York, old boy. Glen Hamilton likes your idea. He's sending you a ticket. Or rather the name of the New York travel agent where you can pick up the ticket. Typical of Americans. They don't mess around here. They like an idea, they do it. None of all that British thinking in circles and finding someone else has pinched the idea. We can all go together. The wedding's next week in Denver, courtesy of an invitation I found downstairs in my mailbox. Have a quick bath and we'll go. Are you hungry?"

"Starving."

"The food is always good. Rebecca's a marvellous cook."

"Is there anything wrong with this girl?"

"Not a thing."

· · ·

WHEN THEY GOT into the lift an hour later at Abercrombie Place, it was necessary to push their way around two trolleys. On the trolleys were silver domes over silver salvers. The smell of the food was overpowering, making Keppel Howland feel quite weak from hunger. The last time he had eaten was on the ship early that morning before disembarkation. Keppel was always hungry and never put on weight, however much he fed himself.

"Someone having a party?" he said to the two men dressed as waiters who were attending the trolleys, standing aloof with their backs against the long mirror on the wall of the lift.

"That'll be the Marchioness of Ravenhurst," said Ralph. "They entertain every week in the flat above Rebecca's."

"Who's the Marquess of Ravenhurst? Never heard of him... Does Rebecca serve snacks before the meal?"

"Of course she does, Keppel. Why do you imagine I want to marry her?"

The waiters kept their noses in the air and said not a word. In a moment of mischief, Keppel thought of looking under the domes to see what His Lordship's guests were going to eat. Then the lift door opened and the moment was lost. The door to Sir Jacob Rosenzweig's apartment was opening and a girl prettier than a painting was smiling at his friend Ralph Madgwick.

"May I present my old school chum, Mr Keppel Howland?... Miss Rebecca Rosenzweig."

"You don't have to be so formal, darling," said the girl.

"Things must be done right."

The girl had dark hair that curled around her ears. Smouldering, brown eyes that only fleetingly looked at Keppel before slaking her thirst on his friend. She had a husky voice that caught in the lower cadence that shouted out her sexuality. No wonder, he thought, his friend Ralph was so besotted.

The father, a tall, thin man ten years older than Keppel had expected, was waiting for them in the lounge with an expression that spoke out of love and fear. The old man only had eyes for his daughter. Ralph Madgwick only had eyes for Rebecca. It made Keppel jealous of the girl, having so much love coming her way. The old man's eyes looked once briefly at Ralph. Keppel knew the religious story from before he had left England... Jews not marrying Gentiles... The look Keppel saw had nothing to do with religion. The old bastard was jealous. Jealous of his own daughter being in love.

Keppel shook the old man's clawed hand in a firm grip and the atmosphere in the room went back to normal. The two men of differing age looked at each other. Both understood.

"So you went through the war with Ralph?"

"The other schoolfriend was killed. There were three of us."

Keppel had no idea why he brought up Malcolm Scott. The old man made him nervous.

"I'm sorry. Let us all pray in whichever church we choose to prevent another war. My people in Berlin send me bad news. There is fear among our people."

"The doomsayers, sir. There won't be a war. The stock market will go on up. Modern science will enable everyone. Material want will be dispatched from the world. Educated men will again have the time to listen to music. To read all the books. Go to the plays. Be civilised. The ancient Greek Empire. Plato and Socrates. The Philosopher King. Rome before the fall. Before the barbarians."

Keppel knew he was gabbling. The old man looked at him and smiled, the smile changing the countenance of his face. He definitely understood. Keppel smiled. His friend Ralph Madgwick was going to be lucky to have this man for a father-in-law.

LATER ON, standing out on the balcony in the stifling heat of July looking back over the lights of New York between the buildings, they could hear the party going on in the apartment above. Keppel made out the well-bred English accent of the Marquess of Ravenhurst, or so he thought. Everyone else on the balcony above was speaking American.

Standing slightly apart from the invisible triangle that glued the girl to Ralph and her father, Keppel hoped Ralph was right. That this Glen Hamilton would pay for him to go back to Africa... Like so many other things in his past, his fate was in the lap of the gods. With a drink in one hand, Keppel went on munching the snacks. At that moment he felt much older than his twenty-eight years. If there was going to be another war he was still young enough to fight. Be the first to go. A trained soldier experienced in battle. Despite the heat, Keppel shuddered, unseen by the others in the triangle. Maybe this time, like Harry Brigandshaw, he was not going to be so lucky.

THEN THEY ALL trooped into the dining room for supper... Keppel's mind far away in Africa hoped Alfred was still to be found. The black man who had made the morning fire in front of their eyrie above the Zambezi valley, two thousand feet up on top of the Zambezi escarpment. Tembo would know where he was. Maybe Tembo, the black foreman on Elephant Walk, would come with them as well. Tembo even spoke English. Down below in the valley in the memory of his mind Keppel could hear the fish eagles calling to each other.

The food now in his mouth was delicious. The girl, indeed, was a good cook. Their children would be lucky. Love and good food. Perfect... Again Keppel Howland felt momentarily jealous of his old friend.

WHILE KEPPEL HOWLAND was listening to the voice of John Lacey and trying to imagine what he looked like, Glen Hamilton was sitting down to dinner in the Cattlemen's Steak House with Robert St Clair and Freya Taylor. His wife was joining them from the suburbs leaving the two children with their babysitter, who was eighteen and usually capable of keeping order.

For Glen Hamilton, the hardest part of running a daily newspaper was keeping up circulation and with it the price of advertising. The best-written newspaper was no good if it failed to make a profit. Which was why Glen had started Freya writing her 'Juliet' column, which she had carried on writing from England.

When Ralph Madgwick had phoned him from New York, the idea of mounting a Henry Morton Stanley expedition to find a modern-day David Livingstone had sparked his journalistic and business imagination. It was more than fifty years since the *New York Herald* had sent Stanley into the African jungle after Livingstone, reaping a fortune from the scoop in the process. Not to mention a place in history. With all the newspaper publicity given to Harry Brigandshaw's disappearance, Glen's old wartime friend was as well known to the public as Doctor Livingstone had been fifty years and more before. Ralph Madgwick had said on the phone that the young man who wished to mount an expedition to find Harry had a first in English literature. Now Robert St Clair had offered to put up money to look for his brother-in-law.

"The last place we know Harry to be alive is Khartoum," said Glen. "They can start at Khartoum and work their way down Africa. There must be places on the way they can send reports back to Denver."

"Go the other way," said Robert. "If I had two feet I'd go with them and write a book on the way. They must start from Elephant Walk and work up Africa. Harry went down somewhere in between. He could have been nearly home for all we know. Keppel Howland will need black men he can trust. Keppel needs Tembo. He'll know how to get through the bush better than anyone with a motive other than money. They can mount the expedition in

Rhodesia. The biggest cost will be sending Keppel Howland there. Horses. They'll need good, salted horses."

"What on earth is a salted horse?" asked Freya.

"One that has been bitten by the tsetse fly and survived... Here comes Samantha. Now we can order the food. Freya needs feeding in her condition."

"You don't have to broadcast to the whole world, dear Robert. This is the first time I'm glad you only have one foot... Do we really think this man can keep himself alive in the jungle with all those wild animals? Lions and tigers. The thought frightens me to death."

"Lions and leopards in Africa. The tigers live in Asia."

"When one of them eats you it doesn't make much difference which one."

GLEN HAMILTON REMEMBERED the first link in the chain that had now brought them together at the Cattlemen. Merlin St Clair. Twelve years ago in 1917, Merlin and Glen had met in France when Glen was a war correspondent with the honorary rank of captain in the American army. Both had leave due to them over Christmas. Glen had been invited to Purbeck Manor to spend Christmas. Merlin's ulterior motive had been to introduce him to Robert who had written a historical novel. The Christmas party, Glen also remembered, had included Harry Brigandshaw on leave from the Royal Flying Corps. Harry had been up at Oxford with Robert some years before the war. Even to an outsider, it was clear to Glen that Lucinda St Clair was in love with Harry Brigandshaw. Later, Glen had taken *Keeper of the Legend* back to America and shown the manuscript to Max Pearl who had published Robert's first book. Robert had visited with Glen in Denver when the book was launched in America where he met Freya Taylor for the first time. When Harry and Lucinda had been married in 1919, with a second wedding planned for Rhodesia, Harry had invited Glen to Elephant Walk. All of them had sailed on the SS *King Emperor*. The intention had been to go on safari. When Lucinda was shot dead by Mervyn Braithwaite at Salisbury railway station, Glen had gone back to America after a brief stay on Elephant Walk where he had met the black man they called Tembo. Glen remembered him as a man who hated the patronage of the English, which clashed strangely with his strong bond with Harry Brigandshaw. The two men were friends, not master and servant. They had grown up together.

. . .

"YOU ARE RIGHT, ROBERT," said Glen as his wife joined them at the table. He and Robert had both stood up to greet Samantha. "Tembo will be perfect if he is prepared to go and look for Harry... How are the kids?"

"All good. I came in a bit earlier to try on my dress for the wedding. Now, what's all this about, Glen?"

"We are mounting an expedition on horseback to find Harry Brigandshaw."

"Are you going, Glen?"

"Sit down, darling. Sit down. We have a young friend of Harry's out from England who wants to go and find him."

"Where is he?"

"He'll be at the wedding. With Ralph Madgwick and hopefully Rebecca."

THERE HAD BEEN a time when Freya Taylor thought she was going to marry Glen Hamilton. Men often married their secretaries and assistants. The girl in the office saw more of the man than a wife. Glen and his personal assistant had grown to know and like each other. Then Samantha had found Glen. She was right for him. A home-girl to bring up a family without another ambition in life to upset the tranquillity. The joy of cooking for a family and watching them grow up happy. Small fingers in the empty bowl after the batter was dropped in the frying pan. Small mouths licking small fingers with sweet, uncooked batter. Neither had ever been jealous of the other's part in Glen's life. They liked each other. Had become friends.

Freya listened to Samantha talking enthusiastically about her children and wondered if she herself would be a good mother. The doctor had told Freya she was nine weeks pregnant. Which had prompted the wedding. In a hurry. Only then did having children take on a life of its own. They had been happy, variously living with each other, keeping their own homes. Neither was the kind of person who plunged deeply into love. They were content with each other. With their lives. Once, when they had discussed getting married, both had said there was no point without children. Freya had been careless before and doubted she was able to fall pregnant. They had that night agreed to leave it in the lap of the gods. Let nature take its course. If she fell pregnant they would get married immediately. Were it not for the stigma of being pregnant at her own wedding, she would have asked Samantha what it was like to have children.

. . .

SOON AFTER ROBERT had stared dumbstruck at the piece of steak that covered his plate an inch thick, Samantha had steered the subject away from Harry Brigandshaw, a man she had heard so much about from Glen even before they were married. The man who had farmed in southern Africa was special to her husband. Someone unique. His brief visit to Elephant Walk, even amidst tragedy, a highlight of Glen's life. She had never met this Harry Brigandshaw and knew she never would. Glen was making a gesture, probably with publicity in mind. The poor man was dead as mutton somewhere in the jungle of Africa. Only the legend of the man would live after him. The legend and the legend's children. It was the thought of the poor children growing up without their father that made her change the subject. And the hope Freya would admit she was pregnant, as everyone around her knew. The girl was positively glowing. The idea of sharing with Freya the things that had to be done before the baby was born was going to give Samantha a lot of pleasure. She loved her family. They were everything in her life. Without them, there never could have been any reason for her life. The very thought of Glen going to look for Harry in the jungles of Africa had made her sick to the stomach.

"Where are you both going to live?" she asked.

"We are not sure," said Robert. "Probably have a permanent home in Denver as well as my flat in London."

"How can you do that with children?" asked Samantha.

"How do you mean?" said Freya, on the defensive.

"Oh, come on. You're among friends. Any woman who has had children can tell when another woman is pregnant."

"No, they can't."

"Then why the wedding all of a sudden? Where are you going to have the baby? Is he going to be American or English?"

"He'll be born in England," said Robert, seeing no point in lying. "I owe that much to my ancestors. Unless Merlin has children, our son will one day inherit the title."

"Goodness me. I never thought of that," said Freya. "Isn't Merlin looking for a wife?"

"He's so set in his ways he can't even change the menu for breakfast. After twenty years, Smithers is the housewife in that establishment."

"So Freya is pregnant?" said Samantha.

"We agreed some time ago to only marry if we had children. The whole point of a marriage is a family. Now are you satisfied, Samantha?"

"Not until I've had a good chinwag with Freya on her own. Real good women talk." She was smiling all over her face.

To change the subject again, Glen thought it time to speak. There was still a stigma in America for a child being conceived out of wedlock.

"Max Pearl was in Denver just before you came back from England, Robert."

"What did he want in Denver? Rather far from his New York haunts. Now there's a man who should find a nice wife and settle down."

"Again?" said Samantha. She knew from Glen, Max Pearl had been divorced three times.

"He questioned me about *Holy Knight*, seeing I introduced the two of you. He said a critic from the *Boston Globe* gave you a grilling at the London launch of your book. The critic suggested the parchments you based the book on don't exist. The hole in the dining room wall was part of your vivid imagination, Robert. Now you've come clean about the baby, tell me the truth."

"Why?"

"So I can shut up Max Pearl when he brings up the subject again. To tell a good lie you have to know the truth."

"Of course parchments nearly seven hundred years old don't exist. I got the story from Father. Passed down the centuries. Same thing without proof. Max wanted to know for certain before we published in America so I invented Great-Grandfather's dinner party. Yes, Great-Grandfather did go through the family money so the story to me had the ring of truth. The wine in the face and ducking the goblet. That bit did happen and the goblet hit the wall behind Great-Grandfather. Only there wasn't a hollow ring. Or there may have been but that wasn't told when the story was retold time and again. Our family have numerous stories from the past."

"You told Hank Curley of the *Boston Globe* you were going to send him the parchments, or rather Barnaby said he was going to send them. How did Barnaby get into the act?"

"We were going to forge them. Chaucerian English from the original French would have been my explanation. Until Freya went to the British Museum in London and realised just how hard it was going to be to make our parchments sound authentic. Harder than writing the actual book in today's English. Barnaby had invited Hank Curley to Purbeck Manor to meet my father and mother during a conversation they had at the launch party. Before we did all the work on our forgeries we told Barnaby to send the man a written invitation this time. The man never replied. Probably chasing some other poor novelist to expose, as if writing a good book is easy. *Holy Knight* is history to the *Boston Globe* thank goodness. Just don't tell Max. He is rather meticulous about the truth when he has vouched for it himself. The parchments in the wall were part of his publicity splurge. Anyway, that's over and I'm into another book now. That chalet on the ski slopes is just as beautiful in summer. And for me and Freya is just as creative. She's writing a play for Oscar Fleming. I told him I don't write plays. He produces Christopher Marlowe's with other people's money. First, it was poor Harry. Now it is Barnaby's money. Marlowe's good. Harry made a fortune out of *Happy Times*. Barnaby has got back his money already from *A Walk in the Woods* and the show is still running. He'll likely double his money."

"What's it about, Freya? The play?"

"She won't tell me so she won't tell you. What's this about Americans being so damn honest? I wish I'd never come out with the parchments in the first place. Max is so damn gullible, my tongue ran away with me while I wound him up. Lapped it up like a puppy dog."

KEPPEL HOWLAND ARRIVED in Denver the day before the wedding with Ralph Madgwick and Rebecca Rosenzweig. Rebecca was to stay with a family of a banking associate of Sir Jacob. The family were Orthodox Jews. Sir Jacob knew his daughter would be watched better than he could watch her himself. Especially when he looked back on the hours in his office during which Rebecca had found a way of contacting Ralph Madgwick. With Ralph becoming a Jew he would have to behave himself, Sir Jacob had rationalised. He had had the impression his daughter would have travelled to Denver anyway. The compromise with the Orthodox family was the way for father and daughter to keep faith with each other.

THE MEETING TOOK place that afternoon in Glen Hamilton's office. Within two hours the basic details were agreed upon. Glen was a little taken aback when Keppel asked for some of the money in advance. The expedition to Africa had not even got underway. As they were leaving for the church, Robert told him the story of the Madgwick and Madgwick bursary that had sent Keppel up to Oxford. That Keppel's father was not rich from running sheep on a farm in the Isle of Man.

"Chap's broke. Happens to all of us. Just scraped up the boat fare to New York. Staying with Ralph. I mean, you can't make money right away out of a Bachelor of Arts in English. How much did you give him?"

"One hundred dollars."

"You're a skinflint."

"I have to account for my money! I don't own the paper."

"Right. Take the money from me now. When your board of directors agrees on this expedition it can all be part of the accounting or whatever they do. I don't know. I'm a novelist. When I need money I just ask my publishers. Anyway, it's vulgar to talk about money."

Glen gave Robert a look which suggested the English were beyond his comprehension. Then they all packed into the one car to go to the wedding. Glen Hamilton was Robert's best man, Samantha the matron of honour. Closer to the church they were going to split up and make it look as if they had come in separate cars, the groom to wait at the altar for his bride like all good grooms.

"I can lie to you," Freya had said. "I can lie to myself. I cannot lie to God. God knows I am pregnant. Knows I have lived in sin. I asked him forgiveness for the white dress that signifies a virgin. Even my mother has not been told I'm going to have a baby. My father will count the days after the baby is born and not explain to my mother. My father is very pleased to have me out of the house, so to speak. He considers me at thirty an old maid. Now, Robert, please start the car so you and I can go and get married. This baby will wait for no one."

THERE WERE FAR MORE people in the church than had received invitations, the invitations going out at such short notice. Robert, one of the first in the church with Glen Hamilton, had kept turning around from where he stood all dressed up in front of the altar to find out what was going on.

"Who are they all?" he asked.

"Mostly the press by the faces I recognise," said Glen. "Didn't you know, Robert? You are famous. You make good copy. For all those people who have read your books. Take it as a compliment. Now turn round and face the priest. Here comes the bride."

FREYA, coming down the aisle on the arm of her father, was also surprised to see so many people she had never seen in her life before. She looked from side to side for friendly faces to smile at. One of them was the girl she had last seen at the pedestrian crossing into Central Park. They smiled at each other. The girl was radiant. A man next to her gave Freya a broad smile. The man was likely Ralph Madgwick. So many people weaving their lives in and out of each other. Touching each other with devastating consequences. How the generations came and went. Mostly by chance. Freya's whole mind was whirling around like a kaleidoscope, nothing making sense.

Robert was turning around with Glen Hamilton to have a look at her. The look of gentle pleasure on Robert's face turned in an instant to horror. For a moment Freya thought he was going to make a run for it. Then they were standing side by side being married to each other and the bells in the tower above in the belfry were ringing out. They were walking back. The car was waiting to take them to her parents' house where the guests would celebrate the wedding.

"What was that all about back in the church? You saw me and panicked."

"Hank Curley. He's at our wedding."

"My mother did say the press had been phoning ever since we announced the date of our wedding. She just told them to come along. She always has too much food."

"What are we going to say to him?"

"Nothing. Just hope he has forgotten all about your great-grandfather."

ONE OF THE first people to shake Robert's hand in the marquee was Hank Curley. People were swarming over the food and drink. Hank Curley had made a straight line for Robert.

"So Barnaby couldn't get here in time? He said he was going to catch the *Mauretania* but the time would be short. I really appreciated your father's invitation to visit with him in Dorset. Meet your mother. See the wall where the chalice hit the spot."

Robert tried his best to look natural. He even smiled at Hank Curley. Like an old friend.

"When are you going over?"

"Soon. Six days on the RMS *Olympic*. I like your British boats. Do me good, a sea voyage however short... Never met a real-life lord before."

"When does she sail? The RMS *Olympic*?"

"On the fifteenth of next month."

"Jolly good. Have a lovely trip. We shall see each other most likely. My wife and I are going to England for our honeymoon."

Glen had been standing behind Robert listening to the conversation. He left them to go and talk to Freya. To warn her she was now going to England for her honeymoon.

THEY LEFT for England the next morning. Mr and Mrs Taylor drove them to the airfield. Mrs Taylor was in one of her celebrated states at the thought of her daughter getting on an aeroplane.

Ralph Madgwick had phoned Rosie Prescott from Mr Taylor's study while the orchestra was still playing in the marquee that had been set up on the lawn between Mr Taylor's rose beds. Ralph was in the business of shipping. One good deed deserved another. Rosie had been instructed to use the influence of Madgwick and Madgwick to get the honeymooners a cabin on the *Mauretania*. The four-funnelled ship that held the Blue Riband for crossing the Atlantic in the fastest time had docked in New York the night before the wedding. The big liner was due to sail for England on the following evening two days after the wedding. With three stops including one overnight, the aircraft would get them to New York in time to board the *Mauretania* for Liverpool. The ship sprinted across the Atlantic in four days. It would get them to England well ahead of the RMS *Olympic* and Hank Curley of the *Boston Globe*. Robert would have almost three weeks at home to convince his parents to tell a lie. Three weeks would not have been enough time to forge the parchments. Robert's father would play the high and mighty. Tell Hank Curley, if he asked them, that the parchments were not for public scrutiny. That the skeletons in the St Clair cupboard were to be left by the family exactly as they were.

Barnaby was going to have to help. Their father would have to be coached properly or he would get it all wrong.

Robert hoped the threat of Max Pearl suing him for breach of contract would concentrate his father's mind. Robert was quite certain Max would turn any publicity away from himself. His reputation as a publisher was at stake. There were many other writers in his stable. Robert would be thrown to the wolves. Sued for the financial loss of all the returns of his books that would flood back from the retailers, let alone the lost sales in the future. Max would ruin Robert before losing his own hard-won reputation and who could blame him?

The only answer was for the St Clair family to unite. Hank Curley had to leave Purbeck Manor knowing the parchments were safe, but their contents were never to be divulged to the public. Barnaby's crackpot idea of forgery was now far too dangerous. This time Robert knew he was in a real crisis with no time for games. It was not the kind of wedding present he had expected giving to his new wife. But first, he told his feverish mind they had to reach New York in time to board the *Mauretania*. The next boat to sail with passengers for England was the RMS *Olympic*, making it likely he and Hank would arrive at Purbeck Manor with no time for him to properly warn the family. Convincing his father to lie was one thing. Convincing his mother quite another. Using a phrase in his mind he had first used in the first of his books, the one Max Pearl had been given in manuscript by Glen

Hamilton just after the war, Robert told himself he was tense as a turkey on Christmas Eve. Which barely made him smile. All they needed was for the car to break down. For the aircraft to break down before it climbed into the air. Robert now knew just how the poor turkey felt.

The airfield was a well-cut strip of grass in the centre of which was a long line of tarmac. At the end of the tarmac was the aeroplane. It looked small, with four round windows down the side facing them. A car was standing next to the aircraft. Mr Taylor drove onto the field. The pilot was waiting for them, his only passengers. Freya and Robert had overnight suitcases. They were going to buy more clothes in New York.

Mrs Taylor was holding onto her daughter as if she did not wish to let her go.

"Be careful, darling. For both of you."

Robert and Freya climbed up the rickety steps onto the plane. The small door was closed by the pilot from the inside. They sat down looking through one of the round windows. They could see Mr and Mrs Taylor on the tarmac. They all waved at each other as the propellers of the twin engines began to turn noisily. The aircraft began to move forward, to turn and face into the wind. Mrs Taylor was holding her stomach in a strange way, mouthing something the noise of the engines drowned out. The parents moved out of their line of sight as the plane's engines revved up in preparation for flight.

"Your mother knows," shouted Robert. "She knows you are pregnant. The 'both of you' had nothing to do with me."

"Relax. We're all going to make it. I'm sure your mother will understand everything."

"You don't know my mother. She's never told a lie in her life."

The one person Robert was not going to visit in New York was Max Pearl, even if they did have the six hours to spare as they expected.

As usual, Rosie Prescott had done a good job. She was going to meet them in the company car at the airport and take them shopping for clothes they would need on the boat where dressing up for meals was obligatory.

Freya was holding his hand. They were married. If he could think clearly for a moment he knew that nothing else much mattered.

WHEN RALPH MADGWICK returned to his office in New York and Rebecca Rosenzweig to her father's apartment in Abercrombie Place, there was a long message waiting for him from his Uncle Wallace in Rosie Prescott's handwriting. Rosie handed over the message with a look that spoke of sympathy and inevitability. She then quietly left his office that overlooked the docks and closed his door. Wearily, Ralph put the sheet of paper on his desk unread. Rosie's look had told him all he needed to know. The beautiful holiday in Denver was over in more ways than one.

Freya Taylor, now Freya St Clair, had given them the key to her car; Robert St Clair had given them the key to his cottage in the country where he was going to write his new book until he had to leave with Ralph and Rosie Prescott's help in such a hurry. Rebecca had told Mrs Levy they were taking a drive into the country and would be back in time for tea, a statement the American woman, who was Rebecca's chaperone while she was in Denver, barely understood. If the Americans had a time for tea, it was any time during the day. Mrs Levy and her family drank coffee. Good coffee from Brazil. Ralph, seeing her look of bemusement, had added the actual time of four o'clock in the afternoon which every Englishman and every Englishwoman knew was the time for tea.

They were truly alone. For the first time. In love, with eyes only for each other. Afraid to break the magical feeling that flowed between them by even holding hands. Mrs Levy and Sir Jacob Rosenzweig had no reason to fear the slightest impropriety.

Opening the cottage door into a room flooded with sunlight, they went to the big window on the other side of the room and looked out at the fir trees and hills, the slopes of green grass flowing in and out of the forest where Robert had once skied so easily despite his missing foot. The view of sun-drenched hills and dales, marched across by tall fir trees, was to both of them the perfection of nature's beauty. When Ralph opened one of the windows, they could hear a pigeon calling. There were other, beautiful bird songs neither had heard before. Birds only found in America. Birds not found in their native England or through the noise of New York.

In the small kitchen, Rebecca had lit the wood fire, putting on the kettle. This, they smiled, was definitely the retreat of an Englishman. On the counter, next to the kettle, Rebecca found a small wooden chest marked 'tea'. Inside was fine dry Indian tea, the blend made and shipped to Robert by Fortnum & Mason in London. The aroma from the chest was delicious.

"God bless the English," Ralph had said. "It's just so civilised. Here is one problem solved living in America. We don't have to drink their dreadful tea... And just look, Rebecca. A proper brown teapot made from clay. No tin teapot for Robert. Just look at this place. No wonder he thinks of staying in America. Just imagine the winter with the fire roaring, the trees out there hung with snow, the slopes covered from hill to hill in white. I think I too could write a book in this chalet... Even a tin of English biscuits. He'll be back looking at all this."

"Do you think the parchments exist?"

"Only Robert knows. When we've had some tea and biscuits we are going for a walk in the woods. It really is a lovely title for a musical. *A Walk in the Woods*. Full of romance. Of happiness. My brother is very clever don't you think?"

"So are you, Ralph."

"You are biased, Rebecca."

WHEN HE HAD READ the message, Ralph sat down hard on his office chair. He was recalled to England. Immediately. Under threat of dismissal. Rosie had already booked him a passage on a cheap cargo boat that was carrying some of their clients' cargo over to England. She had spoken to the English captain of the ship. Ralph was to leave the next morning from the dock just outside his window. Summoned home and not in style... Someone had told his Uncle Wallace that he was taking instruction from a rabbi. This was not going to be jovial Uncle Wallace at the other end. This time he had gone too far. He was going to be stripped of everything. His job. His new home in America. His livelihood. But worst of all they were going to strip him of Rebecca. He had challenged the British establishment. That old fox, Sir Jacob Rosenzweig, had known what he was doing all along.

When Ralph phoned the Abercrombie apartment there was no reply. There was no reply all afternoon and evening or in the morning, right up to the time of leaving his office and walking up the gangplank onto the small steamship.

When Ralph sat down to dinner with the captain and the three other officers in the small cabin that felt more like the wardroom of a warship, he knew the game was over. The captain had been ordered to give Ralph passage: by his company chairman on the phone from England. They knew. For all intents and purposes, he was their prisoner. A man condemned. It was going to be a long, silent voyage for Ralph. He had broken the rules. Without rules, they had taught Ralph at his public school, the empire would collapse: the unwritten rules were what held the empire together. British business. The establishment. The rule of law. If one of their own broke the rules, their world would collapse. The whole tiered system of class from the bottom to the top. Fifty million people and the rules had created the biggest empire the world had ever seen. A quarter of the world population subjects of the English King - Emperor right across the globe. Every public schoolboy had had this drilled into his brain. Never ever break the rules or you will be thrown out of the pack.

Suddenly Keppel Howland's expedition to find Harry Brigandshaw did not seem so distant. Ralph did not have to wait to hear his Uncle Wallace's words, the one glass eye boring into his soul. He knew. There was no way any of them were going to let him change his religion. He was born into the Church of England. He was going to die in the Church of England. Sooner or later. Depending on God's will, the same God of Abraham who Ralph knew was God of all of them.

When Ralph reached his minuscule cabin after the silent first meal he began to laugh. Soon he was laughing hysterically.

The whole ship listened as it continued to steam across the North Atlantic on its way to his personal cross where they were all going to stick him. He had tried and lost. They were too big for him. He was going to have to conform, like it or not. Like so many other times in his life, he was going to have to do what he was told. That or be ostracised to live alone somewhere far away in exile where no one would care whether he lived or died. A stranger. Just one poor lost stranger.

Standing alone on the deck of the ship the next morning, Ralph knew the day in the cottage would have to last them the rest of their lives. They would never stop loving each other for as long as they lived. The love they had would never have to die... In that one thought, was all Ralph had for comfort.

13

AUGUST 1929 – TO THE MANOR BORN

*I*t was Genevieve's fifteenth birthday, almost exactly a year after the last night of *Happy Times* that had changed her life so dramatically. This time she had extracted a promise from her father to take her down to Dorset to meet her grandparents which Genevieve thought was going to be fun: she did not even have a proper surname let alone grandparents she could claim as her own. He was so sweet and so easy to twist around her little finger.

"They don't even know you exist," said Merlin St Clair.

"Then they should. And you promised. I'm going to be a famous actress. Now that I speak properly why would they be ashamed of me?"

"Not of you, darling. Of me. For not marrying your mother."

"You married to Mother! What a giggle."

"Your mother is a very nice person."

"Never said she wasn't. She was a barmaid for God's sake. You're a toff and I love you."

"Don't take the Lord's name in vain, Genevieve. It's not nice."

"I'm sure they'll love an unexpected granddaughter."

"Father won't be too much trouble. His mind drifts off most of the time. Finding he has more progeny won't surprise him at all. Mother will be horrified. With me."

"Then I'll have to charm the old duck."

"Don't call your grandmother an old duck!"

"Then what do I call her?"

"I have absolutely no idea."

"Uncle Barnaby thinks I'm gorgeous."

"Of that, I have little doubt."

"What about your sisters? You do have sisters. My aunts, Uncle Barnaby told me. One is widowed and lives with her in-laws."

"That's quite enough for one promise."

"Oh goody goody gumdrops. We are going. Next weekend. The school is closed for the summer holiday. I'm free as a bird. You can take Aunty Millie if you want."

"My mother knows nothing about Miss Scott either. She's an actress."

"So will I be. I like Aunty Millie. She makes me giggle. I have free tickets tonight for the Albert Hall. It's Beethoven's fifth piano concerto. I love being at the Central School. We are at the centre of things in more ways than one. We can tell Gran we went to a classical concert. I took you. Should be very impressed... How old am I for Gran?"

"Grandmother. She's your grandmother and a lady. You are seventeen. Remember, I had to tell the Central School of Speech and Drama you are two years older than you are. They didn't take fourteen-year-olds."

"I look seventeen... Uncle Barnaby said I look eighteen and asked which one was my boyfriend in the class. He visited me at the Royal Albert Hall."

"Barnaby is a cross I have had to bear all my life."

"When are you going to buy a new car? That old Bentley is ancient. And it's black. One of the boys' fathers has a car painted silver. Very smart I must say... All right, Father. I'll do a deal with you. Your old Bentley 3 Litre with the hood down if we go to Dorset this weekend... I just can't wait to see their faces."

WHEN GENEVIEVE REACHED the small flat in Chelsea where her father paid for everything, she told her mother where she was going for the weekend. She was full of herself and forgot to talk in her normal East End of London accent. Instead, she imagined herself still with her father and his family and spoke to her mother in the new plummy accent she had learnt in school. Her mother looked horrified and slapped her across the face as if she was still a child.

"What's that for, Mum?" said Genevieve, the plummy accent knocked out of her head.

"For talkin' posh and being a bloody fool," said Esther. "I know you can make your dad do what you want. So what? Where're your brains? Everything we have here works and don't cost a penny. You goin' to that fancy drama school don't cost a penny. Your fancy new clothes cost nothin', not to mention your new plummy accent. Well, I don't know about you but I don't want to lose what I got. I don't want to go back to being a barmaid and listening to rubbish spoken by drunks all night. I don't want ever to work again, see? You make a fool of your father in front of his mother and father and he'll hate himself: I know Merlin. You and I tucked away nicely where he can come when he wants and put on his slippers, they'll all turn a blind eye to. They don't talk about them, let alone run their bastards down to the family seat in the bloody country. That's right, Genevieve. You're a bastard. Don't you forget and do that high and mighty on me. When something works leave it alone."

"His brothers know."

"Them's different. That's men among men. Barnaby was screwing that Tina Pringle long before she got rich. Did you know young Frank is your cousin? No, didn't think you did. See, everyone knows but no one flaunts it in polite society. Leave your grandma out of this. She's better off none the wiser. What Merlin was thinkin', I don't know. He can be a bloody fool too despite all his learnin' at fancy schools. Use your common sense, child. Don't rock the boat. We are all right, aren't we? Better than you being Ray Owen's kid and us living off sixpence from the government. See, I was married to Owen when you was born so they'd done give me an army pension but so small it wouldn't buy nothing as it turned out. And yes I was pregnant with you by your dad, Merlin, when I married Owen. Thought it would give you some protection, not thinkin' your dad would give us all this. Merlin in the trenches just like Ray and he too could have got killed and then where was I? You make a fool of Merlin, he'll want to forget us."

"I want to be part of his family. They are my family too."

"One day when you're famous. Maybe."

"You think I'll be famous?" With the resilience of fifteen, she was smiling again.

"Only if you keep your trap shut. Now go and ring your father and tell 'im you can't go. Quick. Before the silly sod does something and messes up my life. See, I'm selfish. We all are."

WHILE GENEVIEVE WAS on the telephone, trying to speak to her father and tell him her mother had bought theatre tickets for Saturday as a birthday present and being told by the operator the line was engaged, the *Mauretania* was docking at the port of Liverpool after a smooth crossing from New York.

Were it not for the sword of Damocles hanging over Robert St Clair's head, it would have been a perfect four-day honeymoon.

Living in the country in England and the cottage in Denver, Robert had had no idea how famous he had become. Even living in the flat in Stanhope Gate he had mixed with his own class who considered talking about another man's money or fame bad manners. Robert himself never even mentioned he wrote books. People would have thought he was bragging, which was not as bad to Robert as breaking any of the Ten Commandments.

THEY HAD REACHED New York by air with plenty of time to spare. The pilot and his navigator were trying to beat their own best time from Denver to New York. Rosie Prescott was waiting with the boat tickets. Robert wrote out a cheque to Madgwick and Madgwick for the fares. They all went to Fifth Avenue where the new Mrs St Clair enjoyed herself buying clothes, insisting she paid for them with her own money. Americans, Robert thought, were indeed strange. Robert went for an American-style dinner jacket with black tie and black shoes. The white shirt was soft, not starched to the texture of cardboard down the front. He had brought his own front studs and cufflinks in the small suitcase he had taken on the plane. In the end, they had two hours to window-shop and forget their problem before Rosie drove them to the boat in the company car.

"Don't wait and see us off," said Robert. "We'll be fine now. You've been wonderful to us, Miss Prescott. Did Ralph Madgwick explain my problem on the phone?"

"Call me Rosie. In America, everything is less formal. You are three weeks ahead of the RMS *Olympic*. I do hope you sort out the problem."

"It seemed so trivial when it started. Poetic licence. Not anymore... My word, she is a big liner. I always have a feeling of fear looking up from the ground just below such a monster. Man shouldn't build things this large."

"Don't be morbid, Robert. Come along. That's the first-class gangway over there. Not this one. Can't you tell looking at the people?"

"What's all this snobbery? I thought you were American... We'll be back, Rosie."

"Not until the baby is born," said Freya.

"Rosie doesn't know about the baby."

"Oh yes she does," said Rosie.

"Do you know, if Merlin doesn't marry, this baby inside me now could one day be an English lord?"

"Best of luck."

"Thank you again."

"Go on. This is the right gangway. Up you go. The weather forecast is perfect, for what that is worth. Have a lovely trip. Give England my love. How was Ralph with Rebecca?"

"We gave them the car and the key to Robert's cottage on the ski slopes."

Rosie Prescott went white, shook their hands formally and left.

"What was that last bit about?" said Robert.

"She's in love with Ralph, you idiot."

"How do you know?"

"The way she nearly dropped dead at the thought of her love alone in a cottage with another woman."

"But the whole reason for coming here was about Ralph and Rebecca."

"Doesn't make any difference. When are they due back in New York?"

"The day after tomorrow. We'll be halfway across the Atlantic."

THAT NIGHT they had been invited to sit at the captain's table which was when Robert first saw fame staring him in the face. Within the first five minutes, the people at the table were asking him about the parchments, everyone fascinated by how his family had stumbled on the story of Sir Henri Saint Claire Debussy. All the Americans at the table, the women dripping with jewels, wanted to know the truth behind *Holy Knight*. Somehow every night for four long days the subject came up again and again, drawing Robert further and further into the mess, the imagined nightmare now become real. The readers of his book had had their imaginations sparked more by the story of Robert's great-grandfather having a silver chalice thrown at his head than the book itself. Should the public ever find out he had told them a blatant lie, they would tear him and his reputation to pieces.

AS A WRITER he would be finished, he told himself as he finally hurried down the gangway onto English soil.

The first thing Robert did was find a telephone in the offices of the shipping company. The luggage was still being carried off the ship. From two small suitcases going on the plane in Denver they had grown to a cabin trunk the size of a baby elephant.

The first call he made was to Barnaby. It took the operator half an hour to put him through.

"It's far worse than we ever imagined," Robert said to Barnaby down the telephone. "You and I have to go down to Dorset and make our mother tell a lie. Curley is on a boat right behind us. He said he had accepted your written invitation to visit Purbeck Manor."

"A bit belated but I did receive his acceptance. So what? Show him some of the forged parchments instead of sending them in the post."

"We didn't have time. It's a monstrous task. Can't be done. Bloody terrible idea of yours. This is all your fault, Barnaby."

"Nonsense. You told Max Pearl the family story. Not me. You invented the thrown wine cup. So don't blame me for trying to help."

"I'm going to telephone Mother now. To tell her Freya and I are coming home for a while."

"Is she pregnant?"

"Of course. Why do you think we married in such a damn hurry?"

"Does Mother know?"

"Certainly not and don't you tell her. If the child's a boy he could one day inherit the title. Why he must be born in the Manor: an Englishman."

"Mother can count."

"Our mother never thinks badly of any of her children."

"We can drive down together."

"Thank you, Barnaby."

"Give Freya my congratulations."

When Robert put down the phone he could hear his brother still laughing. Then he had put a second call through to his mother in Dorset. By the time he had finished organising his own crucifixion, the large trunk was in the customs warehouse ready for collection.

Two hours later, while Genevieve unbeknown to Robert was still trying to call her father to cancel her own journey down to Dorset, he and Freya boarded the train for London.

"LADY ST CLAIR," said Mrs Mason to Old Warren as they were drinking tea together in the kitchen of the Manor house, "is in a right royal fluster."

THE FIRST CALL to Lady St Clair had come from Merlin saying he was driving down to Dorset for the weekend and bringing with him a surprise. Lady St Clair's first thought was to pay a visit to her hairdresser in Swanage. Merlin, she was sure, had at last found himself a bride.

Half an hour later the second call came from Robert in Liverpool. No sooner had Lady St Clair digested the fact of her new daughter-in-law being in England, Barnaby telephoned. They were all coming down for a visit. All three boys at the same time.

To add to her sense of panic, Barnaby said an American was coming down at the end of the month: a friend of Robert's who wished to spend a few days with British aristocracy, whatever that meant. The American, Barnaby had called Hank Curley, would be better off in a good hotel with servants of an age that did not require walking sticks to help them around.

As always, the thought of seeing Barnaby made her smile. He was her youngest. Only to herself did she ever admit he was her favourite.

The corridor was dank and dark and smelling of must... Children! What would she have done without her children? If only all the girls could be with them. All except Lucinda, the thought of which set Lady St Clair off worrying about Harry Brigandshaw.

"Are you all right, Lady St Clair?" called Mrs Mason. The footsteps in the corridor leading to the kitchen had stopped.

"I was just thinking, Mrs Mason."

"Come and have a nice cup of tea."

"What a lovely idea..."

"It's going to be so nice with the boys in the house."

"It is, isn't it?... So silly. You have so many children you can't get them out from under your feet. Noise. Arguments. Laughter... Then they go. All of them... What was the point?"

"A weekend like the one we are going to have. Old Warren's going to slaughter one of the pigs."

"I think Merlin has found himself a wife. He's bringing down a surprise. I was thinking I should go to Swanage to have my hair done but it is all so far."

"Your hair looks very nice."

"Do you think so? The girls these days are all so well groomed... I live in the past, Mrs Mason."

"We all do at our age. It's one of the pleasures of growing old. Memories. Nothing wrong with memories."

LITTLE MAVIS, at sixty the youngest of the servants, had gone off to throw open the windows in the old house. To let the smell of summer waft into the rooms. Old Warren, with the help of Lord St Clair, made the Atco motor mower start, the engine sending a cloud of blue smoke across the garden in front of the house. The lawn had last been mowed three weeks before. By the time the one piece of front lawn had been cut in straight lines, the summer air smelled of newly cut grass mixed with a slight whiff of petrol fumes.

Mrs Mason took herself off to the station at Corfe Castle driven by Lord St Clair in the Rover 14 which Barnaby had given to his father earlier in the year. Going as far as the station with Lord St Clair at the wheel was quite enough for Mrs Mason. After that, she took the train to Swanage for her day of shopping. She and Lady St Clair had prepared a list in the kitchen over the cup of tea. The boys had their favourite food. On the shopping list was a small barrel of herrings which Mrs Mason was going to souse in vinegar with fresh herbs cut from the garden outside her kitchen: fresh bay leaves from the big tree, sorrel, thyme, mint and wild oregano. The herrings she would lay out in dishes, deep enough for the split-open fish to be covered. The fish would be soused in time for Sunday lunch in the garden under the walnut tree. Honey she needed for the cakes. Dried fruit. Spices. The list went on for a page and a half. After the long shop she would have a cup of tea with Mrs Pringle, the young Mrs Pringle married to young Edward, Mrs P's son who had worked on the fishing boats. Then the train back and the taxi to the Manor. It was going to be a lovely day. A nice change away from the old house that would look so nice when she came home... Mrs Mason's heart was all of a flutter with happiness at the thought of her house being full of people once again... They were such dry old sticks on their own, she told herself. Old people needed the young to liven them up. To remind them what it was all about. Why they had had such long and happy lives... Mrs Mason couldn't wait to see Barnaby again. Despite all his nonsense, he was still her favourite.

BARNABY AND ROBERT were the first of the boys to arrive at the Manor on the Thursday afternoon. Lord St Clair had heard Barnaby's car from far away, as it drove the high road through the Purbeck Hills. Most times the family used the small door cut into the side of the big Gothic front door of the Manor house. The doors stayed closed. Imperious. In one of Lord St Clair's grand gestures, they had all helped open them, the creaking sound going out far into the hills. Through the grand doors gaped the hallway into the old house.

They all waited on the high terrace above the newly cut lawn. Everyone who lived in the house. A tradition that had come to them down the centuries when the knights of old came home from the wars.

When Barnaby's Rolls-Royce came into sight at the end of the driveway through the trees, everyone took a deep breath. Like Merlin's Bentley, the car was black, shining black with newness, Barnaby having only driven his new car out of the showroom in Regent Street the previous day.

Lady St Clair smiled down on them as they got out of the car. The bride looked radiant, confirming Lady St Clair's suspicions aroused by the sudden invitation to the wedding in Denver. Even if their invitation had come months in advance of the day, neither of them would have travelled to America. They were too old. Robert was married and going to be a father which was all that mattered. All mothers could tell when a girl was pregnant. There was so much happiness in their eyes.

Walking forward as the trio came up the steps onto the terrace, Lady St Clair went first to her daughter-in-law and gave her a hug. They were old friends from the time Freya had spent at the Manor while Robert was writing one of his books. Then they looked at each other at arm's length.

"Welcome home, Freya. Welcome home. I just know how happy you two are going to be... Robert... Barnaby... What a lovely surprise."

"Why are the big doors open?" said Robert.

"My sons have come home," said Lord St Clair awkwardly. He never liked to show his emotions.

"Merlin is on his way," said Lady St Clair, kissing her sons on the cheek in turn.

"What's Merlin coming for?" asked Robert.

"He's bringing a surprise."

"Did he tell you anything?" asked Barnaby.

"Of course not. He's bringing down a girl who is going to be his bride."

They all trooped into the house.

BARNABY WOULD GO BACK for the luggage after he had had some tea. He was nervous. All three of them were nervous. The big house was silent with disapproval. Only when the dogs burst out from somewhere inside did the old house seem normal to Barnaby. His mother was looking at Freya, directly at her stomach. After shaking hands, the servants had gone. Barnaby had given Mrs Mason a hug. Everything to Barnaby had seemed to be in slow motion. He and Robert had yet to agree on a way of broaching the subject of the parchments. They had agreed to say nothing the first day. Neither of them was sure who to speak to first. Now he was at home, the idea of asking his parents to tell a lie was impossible. All the bravado of being thirty years old and rich had evaporated. The disaster of Tina and Harry was nothing in comparison as to how he felt now.

By the time they had drunk tea at the table laid out under the walnut tree in the garden, neither of his parents had mentioned the wedding. Or Harry Brigandshaw. His mother kept smiling at Freya. There was no doubt in Barnaby's mind his mother knew Freya was going to have a child. He was not sure whether the smiling complicity was a good omen or bad. Barnaby just wished Robert would stop fidgeting. Maybe Merlin's big surprise was telling their parents the family home was about to be dragged through the mud. Typical of Merlin. Doing it the right way. In person... As the idea of Merlin broaching the subject first made it seem worse, he got up from the tea table to take the dogs for a walk. Robert gave him a look of panic. The dogs began barking, dashing around the table with excitement.

"What's going on here?" said Lady St Clair. "What's the matter with you two? If you're worried about me finding out Freya is going to have a baby, I think it is wonderful. Truly wonderful for both of you. Children are the glue that holds together a good marriage."

"Oh, it's not the baby," said Robert with a faraway look of doom on his face.

"Then what is it, Robert?"

"I want you to both lie for me, Mother. Or my reputation, and with it this family's, is in tatters."

"Sit down, Barnaby!" said Lady St Clair. "Now. Freya, you are now part of my family so you will stay. I presume you also know what is going on?"

"We wanted to be sure we could have children."

"Very sensible. What we preach and what we do in this life are usually two very different things. Very sensible. Have you seen a gynaecologist?"

"Only a doctor."

"You need a specialist. Especially for a first child at your age. This is your first child?"

Freya nodded. Robert gave his mother a weak smile.

"Right, Robert. You are the man of words. While your father is still sitting down, what do you want me to lie about? There are no secrets in this family, I hope... Out with it and don't beat about the bush."

For ten minutes Robert tried to make out what he had done was all part of the business of writing books. Of how he wrote his books. Neither of his parents said a word until he had quite finished.

"It wasn't your great-grandfather who spent all the money," said Lord St Clair, "it was your grandmother who threw the chalice at your grandfather. My father. Jolly good shot by all reports... You have a tremendous memory, Robert. I haven't told that story for more than thirty years. You must have been a small boy. Everything you told your publisher and this Hank Curley is quite true. Only jumbled. All the family bits you heard as a boy have come together in a jumble. Only when you wrote it down in *Holy Knight* did it all make sense. I've read your book twice. You have my full approval. There are certain parts in all our lives we don't shout about. Certainly not to strangers. We must just hope we learn from those mistakes."

"But we don't have any parchments to show Hank Curley," said Robert miserably. "However true my story may be based on fact, I told Max Pearl I had proof. Not legend passed down through the generations."

"But we do have proof."

"Where?"

"I think we all deserve a glass of sherry. The proof can wait. It's been in the house long enough. Suckling pig in the dining hall tonight. Done especially by Mrs Mason on the spit. Stop looking so worried, Robert. Do you think all those years ago I would tell you family stories that were not true? That would have been telling you a lie. Something your mother would never have permitted."

"Where are the parchments?" asked Barnaby.

"Whoever said parchments? You said you wanted to show Mr Curley the proof. Then we shall. The parchments you thought of as paper are tablets in stone."

"You mean the family history is written in stone?"

"Exactly. I rather think we had something to do with the saying, written in stone. But I'm not sure, so I would be lying if I claimed it for the family."

"Where are the stones?"

"At Corfe Castle. Naturally. Where the story of our family began."

"But it's a ruin. Clumps of pulled-down building blocks covered in grass and moss. Apart from the old keep there's nothing left taller than a small tree."

"That's what the ruins look like now. It's what is underneath that I will show you. The castle in its heyday went down as far as it went up. Deep into the hill."

"Why didn't you tell us children, Father?"

"The one who inherits the title is told. Can you imagine all the archaeologists digging away if it became common knowledge? We St Clairs were not saints, you know."

"What about Curley? If he finds out what is under the ruins he will tell the world."

"Leave Mr Curley to me. Now, let us men go into my study for a glass of good Spanish sherry and let Freya talk to my wife in private. Can't you see they are both bursting with things to say they would never let us men hear for a moment?... Does Merlin know all about this?... Good. I'll show you all after he arrives with his big surprise, whatever that is going to be."

ROBERT THOUGHT he was walking on air to his father's study where they found the windows flung open by little Mavis who was still letting in the summer air to compete with the smell of old books. Being told to go to his father's study as a child was never good. Robert still expected the worst. How could something so valuable go unknown for centuries he asked himself, as his trembling hand took the first glass of brown sherry. Unlike most people who drank sherry in England, his father liked the sherry to taste sweet.

"Maybe you had better sit down, Robert. I'm your father, don't forget... She's a very lovely lady and better still, she has brains. You are a lucky man... Now, let me see if I can find what I'm looking for."

The two brothers sat and looked at each other not saying a word. Both quickly finished the sherry. Barnaby sniffed as usual at his father's bad taste in sherry. The paler, the drier was how his friends drank it in London.

"Here they are," said Lord St Clair a few moments later. "Some of them anyway." He was carrying under his arm what looked like tubes made from rolled up paper which he put on his desk in front of his sons... "Now. What have we got here? This one is in French. So is this one."

Lord St Clair had unrolled what was in his hand.

"What is it, Father?" asked Barnaby.

"Here we are. One of the ones I was looking for. They're all jumbled up I'm afraid. This one is in English, Robert. Come and read over my shoulder while I hold the damn thing open. They spring back into a roll if you let them go. I used brass weights at either end when I read them after inheriting the title. You were about six, Robert. I must've told you everything I read, not imagining you were taking it all in. Do you remember those winter nights around the big fire in the cosy room where I went to relax after a day's difficult work? I must've been bursting to tell someone but couldn't, according to the will."

"But these are the parchments I'm looking for," said Robert, reading over his father's shoulder.

"Not really, Robert. Anyone with knowledge would know at a quick glance the paper is nineteenth century. This was the work of your great-grandfather. He was a scholar. My father was the reprobate who spent all the money and had the wine thrown at him by his wife. The fifty-year great love you talked about, Robert, was true but it was one generation back. From your child's memory, you put the two stories together to come up with the thrown chalice across the great dining room table, the table that has been in the family for all the centuries. I must've talked about parchments. *These* parchments, but they were not in the wall of the great hall. Yes, there was a hollow ring when the silver cup hit the wall behind my father. Yes, there was a secret cavity but there was nothing inside when my father had a look. He was looking for something valuable to sell. To pay his debts... What we are looking at is one part of a book written by our ancestor's grandson. Sir Henri Saint Claire Debussy's grandson. In French, naturally. We came over with William the Conqueror from France... You are not the only writer in the family, Robert. Like so many things, what we are is passed down to us from our ancestors."

"But this is in English," said Barnaby.

"First my grandfather copied the tablets down in French. Then he translated the old French into modern English which is what you are reading now."

"Do the original tablets really exist?" asked Robert. "Or was my great-grandfather just a writer like me? Making stories up around the family legends?"

"Oh yes, they exist all right. I'll show you. When Merlin arrives. But of course, they are written in French so you won't be able to read them... Now, who would like another glass of brown sherry? I heard a rumour that Mrs Mason is making her famous soused herrings you like so much, Barnaby."

"And suckling pig, tonight," said Robert. "But you never slaughter piglets."

"Well, this time we had to – the poor old thing. Sally-Sue the sow had nineteen piglets. To paraphrase Old Warren, there weren't enough tits, though I think he meant teats. They are the two smallest we are eating tonight. The rest of the piglets wouldn't let them drink their mother's milk. Nature has some terrible ways of making life survive. Every one of us is in a fight for survival and it never stops... Don't you worry about this American, Robert. Leave him to me. The St Clairs have been around a long time... Now I have another good idea. Why don't the three of us take those dogs for a walk in the fields? If you think about it, the mess you were in, Robert, was all my fault for talking out loud all those years ago and having no idea a small boy was taking it all in. Let alone going to write it down in a book thirty years later. It must be a great blessing in your work to have an almost total recall from that far back."

.   .   .

THEY WALKED for two hours in the summer evening, father and sons. Taking the same path on the same land the family had owned for centuries. Looking at hills and oak trees with the eyes given them, like the land, by their ancestors. They talked little and only about the nature that flourished all around them. Three men content with life, enjoying each other's company and not having to talk.

At the top of one hill, they looked back towards the village of Corfe Castle seven miles away. Behind the village that had nestled at the bottom of the hill for all the same centuries, they could see the ruins of Corfe Castle where it had all begun. Where the English St Clairs had morphed from the French Saint Claire... No one spoke as they looked.

Then they walked back to Purbeck Manor in the soft gloaming, even the dogs silent, their tongues hanging loose to let them perspire from the evening's exertion of fruitlessly chasing rabbits that always bolted back into their warrens.

When they reached the manor house all the windows were still open. Only the big Gothic door had been closed. There was another legend in the family that said that if the great doors stayed open after the sun had set, the sun would also set on the St Clair dynasty. The sun, as Lord St Clair said, as they walked through the small side door cut into the old oak, that would set that night behind on Purbeck Manor but never set on the British Empire, God save the King.

When Barnaby heard his father go off on that one, he was not sure if the old man was being serious or pulling their legs. Like when he appeared to lose his memory when it suited him: when Father liked to become the vague old man living in the clouds and giving exotic names to his pigs.

LATER IN THE vaulted dining room that was only now used on special occasions, Freya was happy to see the piglets for the first time, cooking over the fire on the spit looking more like pork than pig. Only the one big, walk-in fireplace had a fire burning and just enough to roast the sides of the suckling pigs. Freya was told Mrs Mason had sat on the comfortable bench inside the fireplace for two hours with a long silver basting ladle and one of His Lordship's bottles of brown sherry that Lady St Clair had brought to her earlier in the kitchen where the rest of the night's feast was being prepared... Roast potatoes in the wood-fired oven cooked in lard... Roast chestnuts mixed with almonds and walnuts, all from the estate, chopped together into a paste and baked the size of dumplings in the same oven... Five vegetables from the garden... Rhubarb batter encrusted with brown sugar for dessert,

which Mrs Mason knew was Barnaby's favourite when he was still a child...
Apple sauce with cloves and brown sugar... A rich sage and onion sauce
made with herbs from the garden... Gravy placed in pewter gravy boats and
left standing near the fire to keep warm, collected from Mrs Mason's long
basting, the juices flowing from the suckling pigs into catch-trays, the fire in
the middle of the two suckling pigs that Mrs Mason had turned and basted
as she drank down the bottle of sherry, throwing the last of the sherry over
the pork, the crackling hard, thin and richly brown, just the way Barnaby
liked his crackling, Freya was told by Lady St Clair as she sat down to dinner.

On the long black oak table, pitted with age, were their platters, the
trenchers waiting for the food, while next to the trenchers had been placed a
single knife and fork. At each place setting stood a wine glass emblazoned
with the family crest. Bottles of rich red French wine waited open along the
table where the family now sat away from the heat of the fire, their corks
having been drawn to let the wine breathe before the men went off to walk
the ancestral fields.

Freya had never seen anything quite so feudal. So old. So traditional. So
beautiful. Quietly, as she sat at the table whose top was six inches thick all
the way down to the distant end of the room where she was told in times
gone by the servants sat below the salt, Freya pinched herself to make sure it
was all real, that she, Freya Taylor from Denver, Colorado was now part of
all this. That the child inside of her was a product of so much history.

Looking across at Mrs Mason on her bench inside the biggest fireplace
she had ever seen in her life, Freya was sure the old cook was as tight as a
tick. Robert had gone over to carve the pigs. Barnaby had poured wine into
the crested wine glasses and taken one, brimming, over to Mrs Mason who
looked as if she was about to go to sleep, her work done. As Freya watched,
little Mavis brought in all the trimmings of the meal from the kitchen on a
trolley that looked as if it had come out of the ark, the smell wafting into the
great hall where the high windows were wide open to the last of the day's
twilight, the birds outside singing an evensong.

As Freya tried to take it all in, her silent wish was for her mother and
father to be with her at the table.

Lord St Clair stood up, wine glass in hand.

"I give you the King, ladies and gentlemen. The King, God bless him."

Everyone stood up. Freya was not sure what to do until she remembered
the St Clair child in her belly. Awkwardly she got up with the rest, raising
her own glass to the King with the others, drinking the toast to the King of
England.

Then she sat down, slightly bemused as Robert and Barnaby waited on the rest of them, making her evening in the great dining hall just that bit more bizarre.

By the time the pork and the array of side dishes had been eaten into, and the rhubarb batter came out from the kitchen, Freya looked across and saw that Mrs Mason was fast asleep, stretched out on the bench.

"Why didn't she eat?" Freya asked Barnaby.

"She nibbles when she cooks. Just look at the size of her for goodness sake. The worst sin for a cook is to be thin... Are you enjoying yourself?"

"More than you can imagine. And we don't have to worry again about Max Pearl and those damn parchments."

"More wine, Freya?" said Lord St Clair.

"I'll be tiddly."

"So will we all. That's the whole idea. We St Clairs have been some of the best trenchermen in history. We love good food and good wine."

"And good women," said Robert, looking at his wife.

"Robert, you are tight."

"Of course I am... That food really was good. The wine perfect."

ARM IN ARM they made their way out of the dining room as everyone said good night. Mrs Mason was still asleep on her bench. Someone had placed a blanket over her despite the summer night. The windows in the house were still all wide open.

When they reached Robert's second-floor bedroom where they were sleeping together as man and wife in the single bed that had been Robert's for most of his life, the owls were calling from the woods. There were three owls Freya could hear calling intermittently. A dog-fox barked from somewhere behind the cowshed. There was not a breath of wind.

After they climbed onto the bed and hugged each other they fell asleep.

The moon came into the room later but neither woke up.

THE SUN WOKE FREYA. It was morning. The birds were singing. Pulling her one arm out from under Robert gently so he would not be woken, Freya got up to look out of the open window. Her arm was fast asleep, full of pins and needles. The view out to the hills over oak and elm trees was just as beautiful as the view from the cottage outside Denver.

"I'm happy," she said aloud. "I'm truly happy."

"Now that is nice to hear, Mrs St Clair... Come back to bed."

When she was safely back in the small bed, they made love.

Only afterwards did they both go back to sleep in each other's arms.

LATE IN THE AFTERNOON, they all heard the engine of the Bentley coming to them from up on the high road of the Purbeck Hills. The car was going fast, the sound echoing across the silent valley. There was not a breath of wind.

"Must be Merlin," said Barnaby. "Why's he driving so fast?"

"To impress someone," said Robert. "Come on. If we walk fast, we'll meet them in the driveway. We can all take the Rolls to Corfe Castle. I want to get this over with once and for all."

Freya was clutching a bunch of wild flowers she had picked on her walk as they hurried along despite Robert's prosthetic foot.

WHEN THEY REACHED THE TERRACE, the Gothic doors were wide open again. Lady St Clair had one hand on the waist-high balustrade. The black Bentley 3 Litre was coming up the long drive between the trees. Lord St Clair was standing next to his wife, waiting to greet his eldest surviving son. Only Mrs Mason was absent from the terrace to meet the current heir to the title and the estate. The hood was down. The woman in the passenger seat was half out of her seat trying to get a good look at Purbeck Manor for the first time.

"She's very pretty," said Lord St Clair, smiling.

"She's very young," said Lady St Clair.

"No point in marrying a woman your own age when you want to start a family at the age of forty-four."

The car was coming to a halt in front of the steps that led up to the terrace and the gaping doors of the Manor house. The young woman was on the side of the car nearest to the terrace. She was looking straight at Lady St Clair.

"She looks familiar," said Lady St Clair.

"Never been down here before," said Lord St Clair. "I'd have remembered by Jove."

"What's the matter, Freya?" said Lady St Clair. Robert and Freya had moved nearer to the balustrade to get a better look at the passenger.

Freya had her right hand over her mouth. Robert had his eyes wide open. From behind Lady St Clair, who was racking her brains to remember where she had seen that face before, Barnaby gave out a giggle. The car engine was turned off. Merlin took off his goggles and waved before getting out of the car. The woman waited for Merlin to come round to open her door before she prepared to step out. Lady St Clair saw she was very tall and slim. Like a calf. Her skin was unblemished. Smooth and soft white with a tint of fresh rose blushed on both cheeks.

"She's very young," Lady St Clair repeated as the woman looked up at her and smiled. The eyes that looked at Lady St Clair were of different colours, the one darker than the other.

Small feet crunched on the gravel as Merlin took the woman's hand. Lady St Clair had never seen her son look at a woman in such a way. Usually, Merlin was aloof. Untouched by anything around him. Himself all the time. The couple was coming up the steps towards her, past the earthen flower urns with the red petunias. Lady St Clair was now staring at the girl.

'She's only a child,' thought Lady St Clair. 'What on earth is Merlin thinking, marrying a child?' From a broad smile of welcome, Lady St Clair looked with hostility at the girl and her son.

"Mother," said Merlin still smiling broadly, enjoying himself. "This is the surprise I promised you. Genevieve, say hello to your grandmother. Mother and Father, I want to introduce my daughter, Genevieve. Genevieve already knows Uncles Robert and Barnaby and Aunty Freya." Merlin with the monocle over his dark eye was grinning maliciously, enjoying everyone else's discomfort. Proudly, he watched his daughter step forward.

"Hello, Grandmother. How are you?"

Just in front of Lady St Clair, Genevieve curtsied as she had been taught at the Central School.

"Now I know why you look so familiar. I have old photographs of my mother inside, just like you... Come here, child... How old are you?"

"Well, Father tells the school I'm seventeen. But I'm fifteen."

"Which school, child?"

"The Central School of Speech and Drama at the Royal Albert Hall. I'm going to be an actress."

"The different coloured eyes would have given it away," said Lord St Clair, who was chuckling with good humour now he knew what was going on. "Let's pretend you are seventeen and go inside for a glass of brown sherry. Welcome to my home. Where is your mother?"

"My mother never travels."

"No, I suppose not. Why we have never seen you or her before at Purbeck Manor. Well, Merlin, this is a surprise."

"My mother is not married to my father. She told me not to come here. That you would be annoyed with my dad. Ashamed of me. But I still wanted to come. You see, however it all happened you are still my grandparents." Genevieve gave the old pair her most delicious smile, the one that always got her her own way from the age of five.

Freya was looking at the girl with genuine admiration. She thought with a few more words, Genevieve would have them all in tears.

"You promise, Grandmother, not to be mad at my father or I'd never forgive myself for insisting he bring me to meet you both."

"Of course we won't. Of course we won't. I was looking forward to a good surprise. Maybe sherry is not such a good idea. You must be hungry, Genevieve, after such a long journey. Mrs Mason isn't feeling so well today. You and I will go into the kitchen together and see what we can find. Do you like cold pork with apple sauce? Barnaby always liked cold roast potatoes. Now come on into the house. All of you. Later, Merlin, you and I are going to have a long talk. In private. I want everything out in the open. Genevieve must have been born during the war when you were in France. Terrible times have stranger consequences. What may seem wrong now was right then when so many of our men were dying."

"Isn't she just lovely?" said Merlin.

"Yes, she is. Very lovely... Come here, child."

Formally, and on both cheeks, Lady St Clair welcomed her grandchild to Purbeck Manor. Then they all trooped inside through the open Gothic doors.

With Grandfather and Grandmother leading the way in front of them, Genevieve gave her father a quick wink.

Then Genevieve swept into the house as if to the manor born.

WHILE GENEVIEVE WAS GETTING around her grandparents, four miles away, on the banks of the stream that ran along the path from Corfe Castle to Purbeck Manor, Tina Brigandshaw was reading her second book on maritime law. She had brought her five children down to the railway cottage to stay with her parents, to make some sense out of her new life as a director of Colonial Shipping, the holding company of the Castle shipping line which owned the SS *Corfe Castle* that plied to and from Africa. Harry Brigandshaw named it for Lucinda St Clair's family before Lucinda was shot dead by Fishy Braithwaite at Salisbury station in Rhodesia, making Harry a widower. Tina's life had more than one connection to the barons of Purbeck.

For weeks, Percy Grainger had been coming of an evening to the house in Berkeley Square to explain the ramifications of Tina's inheritance of Colonial Shipping. The chances of Harry being found, after disappearing with his aircraft over the African bush a year ago, were small. After another year, the courts would rule him dead with Tina the new owner and all the consequences of death duties, something Tina had never heard of in her life before.

"YOU'LL HAVE to sell thirty per cent of your holding to pay death duty," Percy Grainger had warned her on his first visit to the townhouse on Berkeley Square. "The best way will be to sell the Castle shipping line to someone like Nicholas Kayser, of Kayser and Irvine, and retain the customs clearing and confirming side of the business."

"What is the confirming side?"

"You don't have to know, Mrs Brigandshaw."

"Oh, but I do. I have four of Harry's children to think about. Soon to be five. I am now, thanks to you, a director of the holding company, I think you called it."

"But you know nothing about boats and shipping cargo."

"Then educate me."

"Why, Mrs Brigandshaw? You and your children will still be rich."

"By the time the children are grown up there won't be a company for them to go into if I don't do something now."

"You don't even have a formal education."

"You should have met my tutor in Johannesburg, Miss Pinforth. She knocked more sense into me than any school. I can read, write and do arithmetic. The last is rusty. Fact is, it was never very good. Mostly we women leave adding up and making money to our men while we bring up the children and nurture their small brains that one day will be big... Or so we hope."

"What do you want me to do, Mrs Brigandshaw?"

"Educate me. Answer my stupid questions until I make some sense. I want books to read. Books on ships. Books on trade. A book, definitely, on British death duty tax. On income tax and any other damn tax that takes my husband's money away from our children. If I want to give away our money to charity, I'll give it away myself. Not some inefficient government."

"I have a company to run, Mrs Brigandshaw. A big company. My job and your late husband's."

"You have to eat at night. Come to dinner twice a week. Bring your wife. Tell her to bring her knitting. I will not let him down."

"So you think Mr Brigandshaw's dead?"

"Of course he's dead, dammit. Don't you start getting my hopes up. He's dead, get it, Harry's dead. Dead as mutton."

Tina remembered the conversation almost a year ago word for word.

Now Keppel Howland was stirring up her hopes with another expedition to find Harry.

That damn reporter from the *Daily Mail* had heard something in America of all places and wanted her confirmation. Horatio Wakefield had phoned her three times. Why people could not leave her alone with her misery she had no idea.

The company driver had brought her down to Dorset in the company Rolls-Royce that had previously been allocated to Harry and was now at her disposal. It was the only part of the trip with the children and the nurses that had made her smile. At her father's expression as she stepped out of the car at Corfe Castle station where he still worked as stationmaster, clerk, ticket seller and porter, all rolled into one. For the one train a day on its way to Swanage from London and back again. Even Ivy and Molly had let out a giggle.

Tina put down the book on the bench under the tree overlooking the stream and went across to the pram where Harry's new son was sleeping. Kim, named after a Rudyard Kipling character, was four months old. The boy had blue eyes the colour of cornflower and a smile that always looked up at his mother whenever she looked down into the pram.

"What are you so damn cheerful about?" she said, picking him up. Ivy and Molly were off somewhere into the woods with the other children. Now she had stopped concentrating on the book she could hear their treble voices far away behind the trees. If she were not so lonely for Harry her day might have been perfect, the sun shining, birds and insects humming in the summer day, the lovely sound of water running over rocks, the smell of newly cut hay from the fields that still belonged to the St Clairs after so many centuries. Idly, Tina wondered what Barnaby was now doing with his life after selling out all his shares. For a while, there had been Brett Kentrich and Christopher Marlowe's new show. Once the show was up and running there was nothing for Barnaby to do, Tina remembered. Remembered Harry when he had put his money into *Happy Times*. And watched it run on, night after night, with nothing more for Harry to do.

Gently putting Kim back in the pram, Tina walked to the bench and picked up her book and began reading where she had left off, barely a word penetrating her brain.

"Concentrate, you idiot," she scolded herself, starting the same paragraph again.

Before she had to take over the company in less than a year's time she was going to know what she was talking about... Unless Keppel Howland found them.

When the children started to drift back with Ivy and Molly, Tina was still dreaming of hope. She could hear them coming from half a mile away. Happy children with not a care in the world. Still too young to understand what had happened to their father. The terrible hollow that would never be filled in their lives once they realised he was never coming home.

She recognised Frank's voice over the others. The only one to have a father still alive. A father he would never even know about if she had her way.

High up on the top road going along the spine of the Purbeck Hills, Tina heard the engine of a car and frowned. The car was her own Rolls-Royce that was meant to be outside the Greyhound railway hotel in Corfe Castle where the driver was staying. There was a pub in the hotel but the man must have grown bored and gone for a drive. Except the car was going towards Corfe Castle and she had not heard the car leave, the sound of a car or motorcycle engine so distinct in the silence surrounding the hills. She must have been concentrating reading the book on maritime law after all.

The fact her car was going the wrong way brought back her feeling of disquiet. The last conversation with Percy Grainger started playing through her mind again.

"I HAVE some good news from our solicitors, Mrs Brigandshaw. They have come to an agreement in writing with the Department of Inland Revenue concerning the amount of death duty that will be payable from your husband's estate at the end of the two-year waiting period when Harry is pronounced legally dead. And sorry, Mrs Brigandshaw, but we have to face facts. Over three hundred thousand pounds in a deceased estate and the government take eighty per cent in death duty. The good news is we have agreed on the share price of your husband's Colonial Shipping shares that'll be used when the solicitors file probate in a year's time. The nice point of the law says the shares will be valued on the date of death to establish the value of a deceased estate. Harry and his aircraft disappeared without a trace in September last year. The share price for the purpose of death duty will be that which prevailed on the 13 September 1928, two weeks after the aircraft was last heard of in Khartoum."

"Please, Mr Grainger. You are sounding more and more like a lawyer. What does this all mean?"

"The price of Colonial Shipping shares have risen on the London Stock Exchange by thirty-two per cent since the 13 September last year, negating a large amount of what you will owe the government. A large part of the death duty will be paid from the increase in the value of the shares."

"And if the shares go down?"

"Don't be silly. There is nothing wrong with Colonial Shipping. We are steaming ahead, if you will excuse the pun. Why, our ships are ninety per cent full of passengers and eighty per cent full of cargo. We are very profitable."

"I'm not questioning your company, Mr Grainger. I may know nothing about business. But who determines the value every day of the shares?"

"Why, the buying public. There are no sellers. Only buyers waiting to snap up our shares. In a year's time, they will have gone up even more. This agreement means you are making money on the shares that if Harry had been found dead right away would have been sold to pay death duties... Don't you understand?"

"I rather think I do... Where is the rest of my husband's money invested other than Elephant Walk and my house on Berkeley Square? The balance of the money he received when CE Porter took the company public some years ago."

"My word. You have been reading. Well, of course, the money was invested in shares. You and your husband live most comfortably off the dividends."

"And the price of the other shares?"

"The average price on the 13 September 1928 as quoted on the London Stock Exchange at the time. They have also gone up considerably. You are very lucky, Mrs Brigandshaw."

THE NAGGING at the back of Tina's mind would not go away. The value of a share was determined by a willing buyer from a willing seller, she had read in one of the books. Not by the price listed the previous morning in the *Financial Times*. Yesterday's price, to her layman's mind, was still yesterday's price. And Barnaby had sold every one of his shares and put his money in the bank. And Barnaby was greedy. He had always been greedy. Barnaby knew something... What if her shares fell below the share price on the 13 September 1928? She would have to pay the government eighty per cent of a much higher price than she could sell them for. The Department of Inland Revenue would take all her money. She'd be back to the railway cottage. With five children. Broke. And not knowing how to make a penny for the rest of her life. No one would marry a penniless widow with five children however much she flashed her eyes. Certainly not Barnaby. Why should he? Why should he indeed?

With cold fear suffocating all her other feelings, she finally understood the implication of the solicitors' agreement with the Department of Inland Revenue. Percy Grainger might think her an uneducated fool but she was not.

Hurrying with her book back to Kim's pram she put the heavy volume at the baby's tiny feet, gave him a kiss on the forehead and yelled for her children. At least the Rolls-Royce was on its way back to Corfe Castle. They were going back to London. To find out exactly how much she would owe the taxman. So she could sell enough shares to have cash in the bank ready to pay him when the time came.

"Men can be so bloody stupid," she said as Ivy and Molly came through the woods with the other four children. Were it not for having to push the pram she would have run all the way back to Corfe Castle to get in the car and drive back to London. Instead, they all walked back to the railway cottage. Ivy was sent on foot to Corfe Castle with a note from Tina asking the driver to pick them up at her parents' house as soon as possible. Then she began to pack. The void of doom in her stomach was making her sick.

WHILE TINA and Molly were packing the children's clothes, Barnaby stopped his brand-new Rolls-Royce at the foot of the hill below the ruins of Corfe Castle. Looking up at the centuries of decay since Cromwell tore down his family castle stone by stone, he found it hard to believe there was anything up there other than overgrown rubble where some of the bigger blocks of stone still pushed out of the overgrown grass and moss. As a child he had played cowboys and Indians with his friends through the ruins. The other game they had played was hide-and-seek. Never once had any of them found an entrance that led down into the rubble.

Silently, they all got out of the car, each armed with a big torch. Often the lights went out in the Manor house and battery-powered torches were part of their lives, a change from the earlier candles Barnaby had once carried up to bed. Merlin looked subdued. The interview alone with their mother had been less friendly than the display on the terrace. Genevieve had been taken off by Freya to get her out of the way while his father showed them the tablets. Barnaby was still sceptical. Such historical treasure would surely have been found a long time ago and vandalised. Even the pyramids had finally been penetrated and looted even if some of the content had ended up in Cairo's Egyptian Museum. Tablets depicting the Crusade would be known throughout Christendom. They were all on a wild-goose chase armed with their torches. His father was senile after all, his mind playing him tricks. At least the nineteenth-century parchments would go some way in keeping Hank Curley from the truth. That the real parchments, or whatever the story was first meant to have been written on, were a figment of Robert's imagination. A good, vivid imagination, which was why people liked his books and bought so many copies in England and America. The sudden thought of Curley arriving at Purbeck Manor at the end of the month made Barnaby start thinking of new ways to handle the situation. Relying on his native wit had got him out of enough holes in the past, he told himself, why should this one prove any different? "I'll just have to keep my wits about me," he said to himself, smiling as he followed his father and two brothers up the steep path that led to the top of the hill and what was left of Corfe Castle.

THEY WERE all puffing from exertion when they reached the top of the path and went through the gap in the overgrown piles of rubble that had once been the keep of the castle, their father still leading the way looking like a man who knew exactly where he was going. In the centre of the square that had once been the inner fortress stood an oak tree so ancient there was only one limb sprouting leaves, the great bowl of the tree surrounded by yew trees and undergrowth that had finally sapped the life out of the old oak. Why his ancestors had let a tree grow in the centre of the castle was a question that had never entered Barnaby's head. It was there. Had always been there, and a place he could get to as a child when he wanted to relieve himself away from the eyes of his friends. He remembered, as they all followed Father across to the foot of the old tree, there was always a faint smell of urine behind the thick bushes at the base of the tree, Barnaby not being the only small boy to use the place as a toilet.

Now, late in the summer evening with the sun going down on a beautiful day, there was not even a sign of an inquisitive tourist or anyone else.

"If there is anyone around we'll have to come back tomorrow," his father had said when they stepped out of the car at the bottom of the footpath. "We can't let anyone see where we are going."

Barnaby watched his father now stride to the part of the yew tree behind which was his favourite spot to use as a toilet.

"It'll be smelly, Father," Barnaby said, wrinkling his nose from the memory.

"I want you all behind the bushes. Now. Quickly."

At the foot of the old oak, behind the yew, was another pile of old rubble and signs of old, used toilet paper. The place now stank, Barnaby thought, let alone smelled.

Their father was pulling away clumps of grass and picking up pieces of old stone, carefully putting the stones down so the moss that had grown on top of the old Purbeck stone would not be torn off.

"Now careful. When we return, all this has to be put back where it was, including the bits of toilet paper."

"Where are we going, for goodness sake?" asked Merlin. To Barnaby, their mother's dressing down had made Merlin visibly irritable.

"Under the bole of the tree," said Lord St Clair. "There's a passage cut between the tree's roots when we get rid of the stones. The trapdoor was once of oak. I made an iron door when I inherited the title. The old wooden one was rotten, the big stones about to fall in the hole. That first time I had to move all the stones myself. The second time when I fitted the iron door, Old Warren gave me a hand. Took us all day in the depth of winter when there wasn't any likelihood of people being around. Old Warren and I have never mentioned that day since so don't ask him."

"What happens if someone comes when we are inside?" said Barnaby to humour his father. He still thought the expedition was going to end in one big laugh.

"It'll be dark and the trapdoor will be back in place. The door will be covered in rocks we stuck to the iron. In the old days, someone covered the trapdoor when anyone was inside... We were Catholics before the time of Henry VIII. Like many Frenchmen. After Henry founded the Church of England with himself as defender of the faith, we said we followed our King but we didn't. We stayed faithful to the Pope in Rome until the 18th century, when the eleventh baron decided all the deception wasn't worth the risk. That God was God, Pope or no Pope. Before that this was the priest's bolthole. Before that the chamber where our first family history was written... Here we are, you see. My beautifully camouflaged trapdoor... Barnaby... Come and help me lift it out. I was a lot younger when I picked this damn thing up all those years ago. Robert, go check outside if all is clear. Be quick about it."

"Are you going to take Curley down there?" said Robert, looking down into the hole when he came back from his brief reconnaissance.

"Of course not. Only family. Come on."

Barnaby was now not sure if he wanted to go down the hole. He followed in last and pulled the trapdoor shut over his head. Once down inside, Barnaby shone his torch on a flight of ancient, well-worn stone steps that curled down into what seemed like the bowels of the earth. The others had climbed down the wet steps while Barnaby had let the trapdoor down into place over his head, cutting out the last of the evening light and the smell of stale urine.

For ten long minutes with their torches showing them the way, they climbed down the gently circling flight of ancient stone steps. Once past the top few, the stones and the walls were bone dry. There was an echo from the sound of their movement coming back up to them from far down below. Strangely, Barnaby told himself, he felt quite at home. As if the darkness below was friendly. As if somehow, long ago in history, he had climbed down the same steps before.

"These iron brackets were for lighted torches," his father said, pointing out the old brackets beside them. Then they were down in a chamber.

"This is where the Catholic priest stayed when the King's men visited the castle. Queen Elizabeth would have chopped off all our ancestors' heads and then where would the four of us have been? Not even born. Can you see the tablets through the dirt, Robert?"

"What tablets? It's just a wall."

"Give me your handkerchief... Now can you see? This is the one I wanted to show you. The words are in French but the picture carved on the stone underneath speaks for itself."

"What is it?" said Merlin.

"The corpses of massacred Mussulmen, their wives and children. The knight standing on top of the pile with his sword on high is our illustrious ancestor, Sir Henri Saint Claire Debussy... Look carefully at what people, our own people, do in the name of religion. In the name of God. The same God of those dead Mussulmen. That's why Mr Curley will never be shown this chamber. This is the ugly side of our family. The skeletons in our closet. Robert wrote about the brave side of our founder. This is the ugly side. As you can imagine, this tablet was not copied onto those parchments in my study. Without realising it, I told Robert the truth when I had no idea he understood or would ever remember. This is why every Baron St Clair when he inherits the title is made by his father's will to visit this room. So we will never do that again. I always hope it has made us a better family, knowing the ugliness in our own being. The ugliness in all of us, now and in the future. Whichever one of you becomes the eighteenth baron, you don't have to come here again. Just remember what you have seen... Now we can go and have a pint in the Greyhound before it closes. After, of course, we have covered the trapdoor and made the old rocks good and smelly so no one will want to pick them up and find what is underneath. We may think of ourselves as aristocrats but we still have to piss like everyone else. If at any time you get too big for your boots, remember that. And remember the content of this chamber. What is written and the picture that is carved into the face of the rock that is the thirty-second tablet. The last tablet. The one someone must've thought was Sir Henri's greatest triumph but in fact was a terrible sin before God."

AT THE END of the month, Hank Curley arrived from Boston, Massachusetts, having sailed to England on the RMS *Olympic*. Robert met the train with the Rover 14 at Corfe Castle station. Barnaby had stayed in London to watch the rehearsals of Christopher Marlowe's new musical that was to run concurrently at Drury Lane with *A Walk in the Woods* at the Globe. For the first time, Brett Kentrich was not the leading lady of a Christopher Marlowe musical. In July, ten months after Harry Brigandshaw's aircraft disappeared, she had married Christopher Marlowe in a lavish wedding at St Giles church in Ashtead, Surrey. She was to continue in the female lead of *A Walk in the Woods* at the Globe.

Barnaby had spent a day in London showing Hank Curley the sights and starting the process by warning the American to watch out for the family ghosts at Purbeck Manor, telling him the place was haunted. Only then had he put him on the train for Corfe Castle with his luggage.

While waiting for the train, Robert talked to Pringle the stationmaster.

"How's Mrs P, Pringle?"

"Doesn't complain, Mr Robert. Don't do no good complaining. Our Tina was down start of month. Five children, poor Tina. Poor Harry. Trying another expedition to find him on horseback they are, much use that'll be. Went back in a hurry did our Tina. In a Rolls-Royce. Tax problems. Death duties."

"Hadn't thought of that."

"Blokes up town won't let Tina sell nothing till Harry lost two years and officially declared dead. Say she don't inherit till next September. Didn't understand trouble. You know anything about taxes, Mr Robert?"

"Not a thing. Let my publishers handle that. Excuse me. There's my man. Remember me to Mrs P. Always remember sandwiches and pickled onions Mrs P made for us kids on our way back to boarding school. Five kids you say? Didn't know about the last one."

Half an hour later at Purbeck Manor, Lord St Clair was surprised to meet a small man with a large head. The man had bat ears and round glasses that only just covered the eyes. Lord St Clair had been expecting a large man in a cowboy hat drawling English he was unable to understand. Instead, the man giving them all the trouble spoke like the well-educated Irishman Lord St Clair had met up at Oxford in his undergraduate days. On his way through the small door in the larger Gothic door, the man looked nervous as was intended.

"We've put you in a room on the ground floor, Mr Curley. Welcome to Purbeck Manor. You call the ground floor the first floor I believe in America. Well, our bedrooms are usually on the three floors above but for centuries, only the family had been able to sleep properly above the ground floor... Your room where we're going now hasn't had any trouble for years."

"What kind of trouble, baron?"

"Just call me St Clair... Why ghosts, Mr Curley. The whole Purbeck peninsula is haunted by the ghosts of some of my more unfortunate ancestors. The priest is another problem. The priest is usually the big problem actually."

"What priest, baron? I'm a religious man myself. If you introduce us I'm sure there won't be a problem."

"The priest was strangled on the orders of Queen Elizabeth herself, so that won't be possible I'm afraid. He was a papist you see, we all were in those days. The priest was trying to get down into the bolthole when the Queen's men caught and strangled him. Poor chap has haunted the Isle of Purbeck as we call the peninsula ever since. Trying to escape. Trying to get back down the bolthole and shut the trapdoor over his head to stop the Queen's men finding him. I've seen him a few times, poor chap, with his eyes bulging. You can hear him at night chanting in Latin. Not every night I'm pleased to say. When he wasn't down the bolthole he lived in the attic at the top of the house. Why we bed down our honoured guests as far away as possible from the attic on the ground floor. I wonder what he will think of an American? We haven't had one of those at Purbeck Manor before. No, not ever... Now, how does your room look? I'll leave you to unpack. If you run into trouble ring that silver handbell that belonged to the seventh baron."

"When was the seventh baron, St Clair?"

"Good chap. Now you've got my name right. He was Lord of the Manor during the latter part of Queen Elizabeth's reign, when the family were up at the castle. Did Robert point out the old ruins at the top of the hill? Oliver Cromwell knocked our castle down after they made him Lord Protector of England. After he cut off the King's head. Another of my relatives was beheaded by Cromwell right up there on the hill. We usually see him three days before Christmas on the anniversary of the day Cromwell cut off his head for following the King."

"How many ghosts are there?" asked Hank Curley in a small voice.

"Hundreds, I think. How many, Robert? You do the family research."

"Currently haunting the Manor or known from the past?"

"All of them."

"Three hundred and twenty-two reported sightings of different ghosts. Only twenty-four have been seen in the last five years, mark you. The older they got the less we see them... Look, Hank, when you finish unpacking, trace your way back to the hallway and look for the passage to the right. We'll be down in my father's study to welcome you with a glass of sherry."

"You mean, on my own?"

"Oh don't be silly old chap. Ghosts don't go about during the day. Only at night. Usually just before dawn for some reason. Mostly you can only hear them. Bangs and groans, that sort of thing. They all died violent deaths... Quite usual in very old English houses, ghosts. Something you don't get much in America, which is why Freya and I are going back to live there after our son is born... Or would you like me to wait while you pack?"

"Please."

Robert, hearing the squeak in the man's voice, just managed to control the laughter building up inside of him... He had left Freya up in their new suite of rooms they were painting, quite certain his wife would never have been able to keep a straight face.

AFTER HIS THIRD glass of brown sherry in Lord St Clair's study, Hank Curley began to regain his composure. He had come to expose the English, he told himself, not be frightened by them. He had never seen a ghost in his life and never would. In America or here in some old house in England. A house was a house, however old. Dead people were dead people. This Lord St Clair, Baron of Purbeck, in front of him was just a bumbling old fool and his son was a fraud. Making up stories to fool the American public who had the right to know the truth. Sir Henri was a figment of the son's imagination. The parchments, that obviously did not exist, a way of catching the public's eye so they would buy more copies of *Holy Knight*, thinking the story was based on truth. The American reading public was being made fools of, buying something with good dollars that was not what they thought it was. Not what this Robert St Clair and his publisher Max Pearl had said it was on the radio and in numerous newspapers across America... His own book on the American War of Independence was based on fact. All of it was true. It was well written. A good story. If Max Pearl published historical novels based on truth he had no right to reject *All Men are Born Equal*, a book that had taken him ten years to write. That should have made him rich. Famous, just like Robert St Clair.

"I think these are what you are after," Lord St Clair was saying to him, interrupting his train of thought. "The original as you can see is written in French. This is the English translation so you can read the facts upon which my son based his book. I, personally, can vouch for the truth as can these translations."

Hank took the scrolls and pulled them open. The English version and the French.

"I'm sorry, baron. Pull the other leg. These are not fourteenth century."

"No, but the original tablets are. From which my grandfather copied down what you have in your hand."

"Then I want to see them, don't I?"

"Maybe."

"Why I came all the way from America... Where are these original parchments that have lasted so many centuries and not turned to dust? Where are they?"

"The originals of my son's parchments that he talked about with his publisher are tablets. Carved into granite, or Purbeck stone as we call it in these parts."

"And no one else knows about it? Come on. How many? Tablets! Sounds more like Moses."

"Thirty-two. If you see them you will be the only person to see them who was not a direct descendant of Sir Henri Saint Claire Debussy."

"Of course I'll see them if they exist. Why else did I come all this way? I'm a newspaperman. Either put up or admit your son is a cheat."

"My son is not a cheat, Mr Curley."

"Then where are these tablets you now spring on me after I tell you this here means nothing? Might as well throw them on the fire. Your son made these parchments, baron."

"Please don't throw them anywhere," said Lord St Clair icily.

"Then take me to see the tablets and stop the horseshit."

"Tomorrow night... My family have guarded these secrets for centuries."

"Then why these translations?"

"Not all the tablets were translated. Which is why they have never been shown to anyone outside our family."

"Why?"

"Because there are some things in our history we are ashamed of. The parts that did not go into *Holy Knight*."

"Where are they, baron? I'm getting bored with all the bullshit."

"Down the priest's bolthole. Deep in the granite under Corfe Castle. Under the ruins that you looked up at on the hill when you stepped off the train from London."

"Which priest?"

"The one who haunts us to this day, Mr Curley. Why you are roomed on our ground floor. The papist priest who was strangled and still walks the lands of the St Clairs looking for his sanctuary dressed in a brown robe, his head half covered by a cowl, his eyes bulging from the strangulation that killed him back then in the reign of Queen Elizabeth. Long before we English had thought of colonising America. Tomorrow night, Mr Curley, I will take you blindfolded and let you climb down through the trapdoor, down the hundreds of ancient stone steps until you find our family secret at the bottom and read our shame."

"You will show me yourself?"

"No, sir, just the bolthole. You go down alone. Only if you don't come up alive will I go down and fetch you even as old as I am."

"What about Robert?"

"He only has one foot; the other was blown off in the recent war. He walks with a prosthetic foot strapped to the stump. He is unable to make it down those steps into the bowels of the earth. Tomorrow then. Enough of quarrelling. Next, we go to the dining hall, to eat supper, the old vaulted chamber of the house where my family and retainers ate together at the same table in years long past where tonight you will dine as my guest."

AFTER A GOOD SUPPER and red wine, Robert showed Hank Curley back to his room.

IN THE MORNING, there was no sign of the American. Only his luggage remained which Robert packed up nicely, ready to take to the railway station and put on the one o'clock train to London for Barnaby to collect at Waterloo station and give to Hank Curley in his hotel room if he was in England and had not gone straight back to America.

IN THE LAST dark of the night, the whole family had been woken to a blood-curdling yell that came from the ground floor followed by the frantic ringing of the silver bell. No one took any notice.

When Mrs Mason went down to make the tea, she saw the small man with the big head sneaking out of the small side door into the first light of dawn and heard his feet on the gravel, crunching away towards the path by the river that led to the village of Corfe Castle.

OVER BREAKFAST, Robert thought his father looked particularly smug.

"What happened?" asked Robert.

"Old Warren dressed up as the priest, tapped on the window. Why I put Curley on the ground floor. Old Warren had put just enough fluorescent paint on his teeth and round his eyes to make his face glow in the dark. His eyes have always bulged, as you know. You had better go and thank him after breakfast, Robert."

"Would you have taken Curley up the path to the oak tree?"

"Of course. And put him down the hole with a torch. And put back the trapdoor for a couple of hours. After less than five minutes the battery would have given out. I don't think our friend would have wanted to go down again with a new torch however much I told him the word of an English gentleman was at stake."

"It might have killed him."

"He was young. No one has really ever died of fright. Or at least I don't think so... Can you pass me the marmalade?"

"He paid one taxi man in Corfe Castle to drive him all the way to London. I phoned Pringle at the station to find out if he had gone."

"Good. I hope it was expensive. Teach him to doubt the word of an Englishman... There is no doubt, Robert, Mrs Mason makes the best marmalade in England."

"I'll go see Old Warren."

"Finish your breakfast. I don't think Old Warren's stopped laughing. By the way, what was he all about? The American?"

"Max turned down his book on the American Revolution."

"Hell hath no fury like a woman scorned or another rejected."

"Amen."

Freya, looking from father to son and back again, had a broad grin on her face. She couldn't wait to tell Glen Hamilton the story of the man from the *Boston Globe*, but only after her baby was born. A boy she hoped. A boy who one day might have to climb down to the priest's bolthole and look at a picture of his ancestor gloating over the bodies of Mohammedans. She hoped he too would learn his lesson. That God meant what he said, thou shalt not kill.

14

SEPTEMBER TO NOVEMBER 1929 –
THE GREAT LAKES OF AFRICA

*K*eppel Howland and Ralph Madgwick sailed for Africa from London on the 4 September 1929 on board the SS *Corfe Castle*, their boat trip paid for by Colonial Shipping as their contribution to the expedition sponsored by the *Denver Telegraph* and partly paid for by Robert St Clair. No one saw them off, not even Rosie Prescott who had crossed the pond on the RMS *Olympic* all too late.

The row with Uncle Wallace had ended with Ralph's resignation from Madgwick and Madgwick. Sir Jacob Rosenzweig as the local partner had appointed an American to manage Madgwick and Madgwick, New York. Having lost his temper, Ralph had returned to Uncle Wallace the furniture and the lease on the flat in South Kensington that had been a bribe to make Ralph train to take over the family business. Uncle Wallace had been anything but the friendly uncle. A staunch member of the British establishment and the Church of England, he had also lost his temper. When Ralph walked out of the senior partner's office, that was up till then going to be his if he had stayed the course, as his uncle put it, he was virtually penniless. Keppel was staying with him in the flat while his friend licked his proverbial wounds. Keppel also had been on the RMS *Olympic* along with Hank Curley who was then on his way to England to expose Robert St Clair. Keppel had been travelling third class with Rosie Prescott while the *Boston Globe* reporter had been travelling first on his expense account so neither of them met. Ralph was still in the flat that he was due to vacate at the end of September when Keppel arrived in London to start his expedition to Africa to find the crash site of Harry Brigandshaw's aircraft.

"Come with me, Ralph, I asked you before. Things have changed. Get away from it all and find a perspective. Everything looks different from a distance. Even love. As your Uncle Wallace said, all love affairs end sooner or later in disappointment."

"Shut up."

"Let's go out on the town. The best way to forget a girl is to find another one."

"You want me to throttle you? Then shut up. You've never been in love. Rebecca is the only woman I want in my life. And don't throw back at me what my uncle said. I told you the whole sordid drama in confidence."

"You'll still inherit your share of the family company one day. Your mother and uncle won't be able to stop the inheritance of you and Christopher once they are dead. Everyone dies."

"Now you are macabre. How dare you talk about my uncle or my mother dying?"

"Calm down, Ralph. I'm your friend. Come on the expedition and together we'll find Harry. Planes can't just disappear. Even in Africa. The event would have been so big it would have filtered into African folklore by now. The drums. The drums would have sent the message of the plane crashing out of the sky far and wide. We'll pick up something and trace it back. If Harry and Ignatius Bowes-Lyon are still alive the black people may not have wanted them to go."

"What are you talking about?"

"African superstition. Just imagine you're a black man and four men in a flying machine they could not even imagine, dropped out of the sky into your backyard or whatever they have outside mud huts. Moreover, the men are different. Look nothing like you. Your skin is black and their skin is pinky-white. You'd probably think Harry, Ignatius, Fred Dwyer, the civil engineer, and De Wet Cronjé, the flight engineer, were something sent from heaven. By the ancestors. What if they had dropped into Spain during the Spanish Inquisition? The Pope would have said it was a true act of God's miracles and made all four of them saints. Saint Harry, Saint Ignatius, Saint Fred and Saint De Wet. Why do the Afrikaners give their children their ancestors' surnames as first names?... But I'm digressing... That's better. Smile. We've known each other a long time. Come with me, Ralph. It'll be like old times. The two of us again on safari. Let the mess you've got yourself into sort itself out on its own. Let's go out for a drink: let's go to Clara's. Is your brother still playing the piano now he's married to the famous Brett Kentrich? I must say I envy Christopher Marlowe. She's gorgeous."

"He's still playing the piano."

"Still wearing the black beret? Good. Let's get drunk. If we stay long enough, Miss Kentrich, the new Mrs Christopher Marlowe, may appear. Or does she call herself Mrs Barrie Madgwick, which must surely be her legal name? Poor old Uncle Wallace. He'll never get to retire into the country and ride his horses. The one plays the piano in a nightclub and the other has just thrown his toys out of the cot."

"All right. Just a couple of drinks."

"I'm paying. Or rather Robert's paying. Says he won't come up from Dorset with Freya to see me off. Into another book. Wish I could write a bestseller one day like *Holy Knight*. It's still in every bookshop in the country. What's Rosie Prescott going to do? She was on the boat with me. You do know the girl's in love with you? All she talked about was you, Ralph. All the way across the Atlantic. Very boring."

"Uncle Wallace has given her back her old job. She's his private secretary again. He never did find a good enough replacement. And she's not in love with me, you idiot. We're friends. Business colleagues... Have you any idea how much I miss Rebecca?"

"So you will come with me to Elephant Walk? We are going to find Harry."

"Have you seen his wife?"

"Yes. She told me to mind my own business and burst into tears. I saw Percy Grainger the Managing Director of Colonial Shipping to get some funds for the expedition now I have Glen Hamilton and Robert St Clair behind me. I think he'll spring for another ticket at least. He's having a row with Mrs Brigandshaw. She wants to sell a large number of Colonial Shipping shares to cover death duty due next September. I think she's right. The markets are jumpy for some reason. Or they were in New York. Grainger won't let the solicitors authorise the sale. Says it will look bad if the Brigandshaws start selling the shares of their own company. Says people in the market will think there is something wrong with the shipping company. I didn't listen properly. More interested in extracting a big fat donation to help look for Harry."

"How much did you get?"

"My passage and hopefully yours. We can share the same cabin. The only extra cost will be food. I'll stand for the drinks. Drinks are cheap on board. No duty on booze outside territorial water so the cost isn't a problem. She's lost a lot of weight."

"Who?"

"Mrs Tina Brigandshaw. Now there's one good-looking broad, to use a rather vulgar American expression. You remember when we first saw her on Elephant Walk in '23 after Harry dropped us that message wrapped around a spanner from the cockpit of his Handley Page? Always did rather fancy her."

"She's going to be one very rich woman if we don't find her husband."

"But we will. Kind of ironic don't you think?"

"Why? Do you think she fancies you? You're an ugly-looking bastard."

"I have no idea. The idea of taking on five kids would probably put me off. And I'm not a bastard. I have it on good authority of both Mother and Father, who I should go and see in the Isle of Man before we leave for Africa but I don't have time. My poor mother. She puts up with so much and gets very little in return. I'm selfish. I admit it. Why are we all so selfish, Ralph?"

CHRISTOPHER MARLOWE HAD NOT GONE to Tilbury Docks to see his brother off. He thought Tina Brigandshaw had gone through enough pain without Keppel Howland and Ralph adding to her woes. The expedition was a publicity stunt. To give Keppel Howland a boost at the start of his career as a journalist. The comparison even in the English papers to Stanley finding Doctor Livingstone was in Christopher's opinion a lot of rubbish. In Livingstone's day, there were no phones or aeroplanes. Africa was not even colonised. The colonial powers had brought a semblance of civilisation to Africa. Africa was no longer the dark continent of Joseph Conrad's *Heart of Darkness*. If Harry and his crew were still alive after a year, the world would have heard about it. Glen Hamilton and Robert St Clair were in bad taste but it was none of his business.

Ralph had appeared in Clara's with Keppel Howland a month ago when Christopher first heard of his resignation. If he was really honest with himself, his feeling of guilt was part of the reason for his animosity. As the older brother, he should have been the one to take up the family responsibility at Madgwick and Madgwick, instead of indulging himself playing the bohemian piano player and writing musicals for the West End stage however successful they might have become. A man born into wealth had his duty to do and Christopher knew plainly he had avoided his family responsibilities. Now Ralph had done the same thing and poor old Uncle Wallace, with one eye missing from the war, was still in a job he hated in the

City instead of retiring, as he well deserved to do, in the country where he had wanted to be all his life, instead of answering the call of duty. Even if Mr Postlethwaite largely ran the company.

Ralph was now a disgrace. He himself was a disgrace. And since he had married Brett Kentrich his life had been stood on its head. He was no longer the happy-go-lucky piano player in a black beret playing mediocre piano every night to people getting drunk. He was married to a star of the West End stage and now did what he was told to do.

No longer did he live in the attic. No longer did he shop for food in the Portobello Road. He was now living in Brett's flat in Regent Mews, the one she had been given by Harry Brigandshaw back when she lived with Harry as his mistress... Before she was famous. He even had had to cut his hair and buy clothes that Brett considered more in keeping with his new position as her husband... When Christopher looked in the mirror he knew his long chase of Brett Kentrich had come to a ghastly end. Only when they were married did she tell him she never wanted children. That having children would make her look fat. Interrupt her career... When he confronted her, she said he could take it or leave it. She had married him hadn't she?... The beautiful moonlit night on the banks of the River Thames was forgotten. Never mentioned.

All they had together was the show and the eternal social round with people Christopher would have rather never met, let alone hobnobbed with. They were all rich, artificial and vain, not interested in who they were but what people thought of them, their false image enhanced by being seen out with a famous actress and a man whose name they rarely remembered but who wrote musicals. Christopher's last sanctuary had been Clara's and even that had been taken away. Were it not for the new musical in rehearsal away from his wife he would have been even more miserable. Which, when he finally admitted to himself, was the real reason why he had not gone to the docks to see Ralph off at the start of the search for his wife's ex-lover.

To add to his loneliness, Gert van Heerden was going back to Africa, the itch of the theatre finally scratched out of Gert's life. Gert was going to be a farmer. He was going to make wine. He was going home where he said he really belonged. For Christopher, the new musical at Drury Lane was just a money machine. The fun had gone. There was no difference in making money out of a musical than sitting in an office. The only thing in the end that people wanted to know was how much money he was making. Brett was the star. He just wrote the musical, an anonymous name on the programme. Not even his picture. When he went down to Ashtead to see his mother for the first time since the wedding in Ashtead church, she laughed at him.

"Well, Barrie, finally you have grown up. Up until now, you were living in a dream world. She's nasty like all the rest of us. All we want is our own way. You followed her around like a puppy dog and look what you got."

As usual, his mother was right. He would just have to make the best of a bad job… It was just so strange how people changed once you married them.

WHILE CHRISTOPHER MARLOWE was commiserating with himself on the reality of marriage, CE Porter was reassuring Tina Brigandshaw. The stock markets of the industrialised world were safe as the Bank of England, where a pound sterling was backed up by gold in the vaults of the bank to the exact amount promised by the bank on the note.

"I had the honour to take Colonial Shipping public. While your late husband was away in Africa, I sat on the board of directors. The company is sound, rich in assets with little liability and a spread of income from many spheres of business. Stop worrying. The agreement the company solicitors have come to with the Department of Inland Revenue is a stroke of brilliance. Why, the shares went up again today, minimising your exposure to otherwise exorbitant death duties, which in my mind are quite immoral. They will be why every great British company is destroyed, the ancestral management cast to the four winds. Then who is going to run the companies? The government! Goodness gracious me. This is not democracy. This is legalised theft by the masses from the few who know how to run a company. Bring the whole empire down, that sort of thing and then where will the poor people be? Turning on each other I should think. Scratching each other's eyes out for the few scraps left. My oh my, what greed can do. You can have all the workers you like and nothing happens. People have to be put to work by people who know what they are doing. Leave your shares where they are, Mrs Brigandshaw. You may have lost your husband in a terrible accident but you still have your children and a beautiful home. Go home and enjoy them."

Not sure whether to be rude at so much pomposity, most of which she did not understand, Tina resigned herself to having done her best. It was, as they say, a man's world, she told herself. She just hoped the men knew what they were doing. In Tina's life, enough money was enough. She would far rather cover her debt now and know there was enough left over for the children, like any good housewife. As she got older, and the more she saw of great wealth, the less she understood people's reasons for wanting more and more when they would never be able to spend what they had in three lifetimes.

Leaving CE Porter's office in the City, she still felt sick in her stomach. All the new book learning was only adding to her fear. In her own mind, Tina compared the stock market to one large gambling casino controlled by the rich. And the rich, from her perspective, were not always as clever as they thought they were... Except for Barnaby, which set Tina thinking of Barnaby comfortably sitting on the fence with his money safely stored in the bank... For one brief moment, she even thought of going to see him. To ask his advice. But she knew how all that would end. With her in tears, feeling even lonelier than she now was in the taxi on her way back to Berkeley Square.

By the time Tina reached the house, she was thinking of Harry and the new expedition to find his remains, which was surely all they would be able to find if anything at all.

On her doorstep was Horatio Wakefield from the *Daily Mail*. They just never left her alone.

Brushing past the newspaper reporter, who had hounded her before, she refused to give him an interview.

"Have they at least left for Africa?"

"Yes," she said going into the house and slamming the door rudely in the man's face.

Outside the closed front door, Horatio Wakefield gave her a smile and a wave... For him, it was all in a day's business.

ON THE MORNING at the end of September when Tina was back with her parents in the small railway cottage having done what she thought was her best, the family doctor was visiting Freya St Clair further down the path that led along the stream to Purbeck Manor. He had come to check on her pregnancy, which took him less than five minutes. Everything, he said, was exactly as it should be for someone five months pregnant.

Walking the doctor back to his car, Robert told him the story of Old Warren appearing at Hank Curley's window, Robert's conscience still nagging at the back of his mind as to whether a man can indeed drop dead from a fright. To make his family seem in the best light in the circumstances, Robert told the doctor a large part of the story, only leaving out the priest's bolthole and the tablets in the form of panels carved onto the walls of the sanctuary deep down under Corfe Castle.

"You see, can a man be frightened to death?" asked Robert hopefully.

"Oh, indeed. Probably grounds for a police investigation. Not Old Warren, of course. He was just told what to do. Following orders like they have to do in the army. You are lucky the man ran away on his own two feet and was not removed in a coffin. Couldn't have signed a death certificate for death from natural causes under those circumstances, Mr St Clair. Not even for Lord St Clair, but please don't tell him that... Very dangerous. Have you heard from this man since?"

"Not a word."

"My goodness. Sometimes they die a few days later. We call that aftershock."

"But no one would know what had happened."

"Probably not... You say he took the Corfe Castle taxi to London? Very expensive, poor chap. Better, I suppose, than dropping dead. Did the right thing, he did, getting away from the Manor house. Another big fright would have killed him. The first one would have weakened his heart. The second dropped him on the spot like a stone... Have you spoken to the taxi driver?"

"The American got to London but never went back to his hotel where we sent his luggage. I packed his suitcase myself."

"Jolly good of you. Well, I'll be off. Same time, same day, next month. Isn't your wife an American? What did she say?"

"Laughed her head off. You see, my publisher turned down Mr Curley's book on the American War of Independence... Now I feel absolutely terrible."

Unbeknown to Robert, the doctor waited until he was down the driveway safely inside his car before he began to laugh, which he did in bursts most of the way back to Swanage. The doctor had felt quite sorry for the American even if it did serve him right.

By the time Robert had carefully drafted a letter to Max Pearl asking him as a favour to Robert to think again about publishing Hank Curley's book on the American Revolution, the doctor was back in his surgery telling his nurse the story. By dinner time, it was halfway around Swanage.

THE NEXT DAY Robert took the Rover 14 to Corfe Castle and posted his penance letter to Max Pearl. Only then did he feel a little less guilty.

Walking across to the Greyhound to have a pint of beer, he felt the weight lift off his shoulders.

"Frighten your guests to death," said Barty Shead, the landlord who had pulled Robert's first pint the day Robert had turned eighteen.

"Oh my God. It's all over the county. Old Doctor Dorkin was pulling my leg."

"Laughed himself all the way to his surgery. Nurse Shead told me the story on the phone. She's my cousin."

"But couldn't he have died of fright?"

"Not without a dicky heart in the first place. Probably not even then. Now, right from the beginning, Mr St Clair. Good stories like this don't come often. This will keep the locals amused for a week and drinking my beer, bless 'em. American, you say he was? Fancy Old Warren pulling that kind of stunt. Served the bugger right for pushing his nose into other people's business. My old mother always told me to mind my own business. Now that's good advice."

WHILE ROBERT WAS DRINKING his second beer in the Greyhound, in southern Africa the horses were moving through the mopane forest. Last year's leaves crackled under the hooves of the horses it was so dry underfoot. The rains were still a long month away for the riders in the sweltering heat of the Zambezi valley as the expedition moved away from the river deeper into Mozambique on their way to Nyasaland. They had crossed the Zambezi River one week after leaving Elephant Walk.

The only one of the three white men who was not bothered by the heat was twelve-year-old Tinus Oosthuizen, born into a family with three hundred years of ancestors in Africa. Tinus was having the time of his life. He was going to find his Uncle Harry and show the two men from England what Africa was all about. The day before, while the black men under Tembo had built the raft to ferry the horses around the islands that dotted that part of the Zambezi River, Tinus had shot the eye out of an impala from two hundred yards and carried the carcase back into camp to feed themselves and the porters. Even Tembo had given him a faint smile of approval, having taught Tinus to shoot after his Uncle Harry stayed in England with his new wife.

The argument with his mother on Elephant Walk had lasted two days. Tinus had had to whine and plead with the two men leading the expedition to find Uncle Harry when they arrived on the farm to recruit Tembo to take them up Africa on horseback. The men had wanted Alfred to go with them but Alfred had long gone back into the bush. Tinus thought Alfred had gone off to find himself a wife, which was only sensible. Tembo had three wives and kept them on the farm. One day Tinus expected Alfred to come back with three wives, build each of them a round hut by the river, make a vegetable patch and brew maize beer so he and his friends could get drunk on Saturday nights, like Tembo.

According to Tembo, they were going to find Uncle Harry as Tembo, in a dream, had spoken to his ancestors who had seen Uncle Harry beside a big,

big river that was so big they could not see the other side, despite the ancestors being up in heaven. Uncle Harry was well and living with the tribe beside the river. Tembo said the ancestors had only seen Uncle Harry. Uncle Harry was now a god and living in the same hut with the holy man who threw the bones and made everyone in the tribe do what they were told.

Tembo said he had had the same dream many times for a whole year so Uncle Harry was still alive, and Tinus was going to find him and bring him back to Elephant Walk to teach him how to fly the Handley Page, which was still in the shed with the tyres flat. Many times Tinus and Tembo had started the engine but neither of them knew how to fly the aeroplane. To stop it going off on its own they had tied the wings to the ground and left the tyres flat.

The row with his mother had only ended when his great-grandfather, who was as old as the hills, had said he should go and look for his Uncle Harry as Great-Grandfather loved Uncle Harry like the son he had never had, whatever that meant. Afterwards, Tinus thought, it was a good thing Great-Grandfather had never had a son as his grandmother then joined in the row, two against one, and the next day he was on his horse with the rest of them, which was just as well. Even though the two new uncles had lived in the bush before, they knew nothing about what was going on. Only then had the dogs gone wild with the rest of them while his mother sat down and cried. Tinus thought, maybe his mother did not love Uncle Harry as much as the rest of them, which to him made sense. Uncle Harry was his mother's brother and there were times when Tinus hated his elder sister Paula but not all the time. When Tinus had looked back from the saddle on his way out of the family compound with the rest of the expedition, Paula was holding one of his mother's hands and his younger sister, Doris, the other. Just then, he had liked both his sisters and given them a wave.

Even as Tinus looked back at the river for the last time, he knew it was going to be a very long journey. If the ancestors could not see across the big, big river from up in heaven, how much bush did they have to cross to find Uncle Harry?

KEPPEL HOWLAND WAS WORRIED about Ralph Madgwick. Even on the ship, Ralph had said little. Now in the saddle, he stared far ahead, only seeing what Keppel suspected were the replays of pictures in his head. Many times Keppel had asked Ralph what he was thinking of and the answer was always the same: "Rebecca." It was like travelling with a man whose spirit was still in America.

On board the SS *Corfe Castle*, without being noticed, two pretty girls had tried to penetrate Ralph's shield. The man who once raced his way through the bars and clubs of London never even looked at the girls. To Keppel, the friend he had been to school with and fought through a year of war in the trenches beside, was emotionally dead, just waiting for the physical death to take him out of his misery. Trying to talk to him was a waste of time. The man refused to listen or make any sign he had heard. Even the kid was better company and a lot more enthusiastic about the outcome based on Tembo's dreams.

So far there had been nothing. In Salisbury, they had picked up a Nyasa who spoke Chinyanga as his home language and a little Shona. Both were Inguni languages but as different as French and English with their common influence of Latin. Tembo and the man who called himself Parsons could communicate enough for Parsons to pass on the fact that no one he met on the road had heard of four white men lost in the bush. In the year since Harry disappeared, there had been no word on the bush telegraph as they reached the southern tip of Lake Nyasa at the end of September, the day after they crossed the Zambezi. They had passed through the small capital, Blantyre, of the British Protectorate of Nyasaland on their way to the great lake where Harry had been due to make a landing in his hybrid according to the flight plan he had filed in England. Keppel had found the man in the capital whom Harry had written to to supply the plane with petrol. The weather-beaten Englishman who looked to have been in the tropics too long for his health had cashed Harry's cheque and waited with the petrol drums at the lake for a week.

When the expedition had reached the lake later in the day to make camp, they even found the petrol drums still full of fuel a year after they had been dumped but no one had heard of the plane or a crash further north.

Instead of riding up the shore, Keppel booked them on the passenger boat that sailed up the lake. The boat had space at the back for the horses and the expedition's equipment. It was hotter than hell. The mosquitoes on the shore were worse than the Zambezi valley. The captain of what he called a ferry said out in the lake it was free of mosquitoes.

The first report posted to Glen Hamilton in Denver from Blantyre was dated the 30 September 1929. Keppel wondered how many weeks it would take for the Royal Mail to reach America.

"It's got a long way to go, ducks," the postmistress from the East End of London had promised. The big, blowsy woman was a surprise to Keppel in the middle of Africa. "Don't rightly know how long. First, it has to go to Salisbury in Rhodesia by horse and then to Beira in Mozambique by train.

After that, your guess is as good as mine. Mind you, it'll get there. It's the Royal Mail. The Royal Mail always gets through."

With nothing about Harry to say in his report, Keppel had sent a brief cable saying the report was on its way. Luckily the expedition was proving cheaper than planned for in America. Even if Keppel only arrived back in America with his diary, Glen Hamilton would have recouped his money. Just the idea of a Stanley–Livingstone type rescue mission had generated enough interest for the story to be syndicated.

As Keppel looked across the water with only mountains visible on the other side, Tembo's dream began to take on a life of its own.

THE WATER in the lake was crystal clear with small, colourful fish darting in and out of the swaying weed that grew near the shore. For the first time since leaving England, Ralph Madgwick began to feel alive. The warm water was smooth on his suntanned skin, the site of the shoals of fish a happy surprise as he swam above them peering down through the surface of the water.

Back on shore at the camp, the sky was blood red in the west where the sun was sinking behind the mountains. Near the big fire, the mosquitoes left him more or less alone. The tsetse had stopped attacking them at sunset and sunrise once they had climbed out of the Zambezi valley. The shores of the lake were free of tsetse.

Tembo and the porters had caught Nile perch in the lake and were cooking the fish over the open fire. Behind them in the mopane forest, Ralph could hear hyena.

Very slowly, without Ralph realising what was happening to him, his depression began to lift. The depression that had gripped him ever since he walked out of Uncle Wallace's office had thrown his whole life to the wind.

A lion roared just behind them bringing Ralph right back to the present, his .375 at the ready. The ferry captain who had joined them for their company gave a short laugh.

"That's old Simba. Smelled the fish. Couldn't kill a bloody fly he's so old. One day I'll have to shoot the poor bastard. Now, Mr Madgwick, won't you have a little of my whisky? Looks like Simba woke you up. Best thing in life is to get drunk with a stranger and tell him all your woes. You're a young man. What's the matter? Is it love?... Ah, yes... Love... Whisky, young man. Have a whisky, the only love of my life I can still remember... You planning to stay in Africa for the rest of your life?"

"I rather think so. Thank you. I'll have a drop of your whisky."

"Splendid. Now we can all get started. Properly started. Drinking with a sober man is a terrible thing for an Irishman. Indeed it is."

"How long does it take to sail up the lake?"

"As long as you like."

THE NEXT MORNING they embarked on the *Mary Magdalen* and headed up the long lake of Nyasaland. They were the only passengers on the boat. For Captain O'Leary, it mattered little if the boat sailed or not. The old boat was paid for, the cabin just as comfortable on the lake as tied to the old jetty. He was going nowhere for the rest of his life.

O'Leary had paid ten pounds for the boat he liked to call a ferry. He had bought it from a drunk. There were no papers, no record of how the wooden boat came to be on a lake in central Africa. Looking at the hull, O'Leary could see the boat had been made in four pieces each the length of an ox wagon. The heavy diesel engine had been dropped into the boat later. The old masts were still in place, no one having bothered to take them out. The sails had long ago rotted away in the tropical heat.

There was good fish in the lake, game on the shore and no one asked him for taxes. Singleton, the governor's ADC, brought the whisky when he visited for a weekend every month. There was nothing else to pay, Singleton was O'Leary's only friend. A good drinking friend. Sometimes they talked of Ireland. When drunk, Singleton talked of his wife who lived in England with the children. O'Leary had never had a wife or children so far as anyone had told him. He and Singleton had both been too old for the war. Singleton had reached the rank of acting major at the end of the Boer War which was how he came to Africa. Singleton liked the isolation and the freedom from his nagging wife who had married him when she thought he had prospects just out of Sandhurst. The governor had been at a minor public school with Singleton and did not like his wife who lived on the family estate in England with their children. All the governor's children were girls who had never married. None of them liked Africa or their father. The governor and Singleton had much in common. O'Leary, looking at the governor and his ADC, was glad he never married. Getting drunk once a month with Singleton convinced O'Leary he had not wasted his life. In a perfect world, O'Leary would have liked more whisky. Only when a safari wanted to go up the lake to shoot lion and elephant did O'Leary have any money. Then he drank solidly for days in Blantyre until his money was finished, at which point he went back to the boat.

Sometimes the black people wanted to go up the lake. He took them when there were enough to cover the cost of the diesel. O'Leary was paid in long-legged chickens that he sold in Blantyre.

If the *Mary Magdalen* could run on petrol, the dumped drums by the lake would long have been finished. Twice O'Leary had tried to move the drums up onto a wagon on his own but the forty-four-gallon drums were too heavy for one man. He had thought of asking the black men to help him steal the drums, but that would have been crossing the line. Whites, however poor and in need of a bottle of whisky, had responsibilities to keep up appearances of doing right. All the blacks knew the drums belonged to another white who had never come. The abandoned drums were a small legend and would have been stolen, except only white men bought petrol.

Strangely, O'Leary knew he was happy on the boat in the sun. That his years by the lake were the happiest years of his life. Mostly he never had to think, which was good. Only on the boat the first day out did he discover what the men he was ferrying had come to do on the lake. They had come to look for Englishmen who had flown out from England and never arrived. O'Leary suspected they were the same Englishmen who owned the drums of petrol he had tried to steal. Then he got to thinking as he steered the old boat up the lake.

IT WAS MORE like something in the ether. Spoken of so obtusely by the blacks that O'Leary knew it did not exist. Slowly, months ago, the wind blew it in. The story. Vague. Ethereal. Not real. A feeling more than a fact. And like so many things about God no one was sure whether it was true. Only those with faith were sure there was a god. Only the believers. O'Leary had little faith by this late stage of his life.

It was the Celt in O'Leary that made the hair on the back of his neck seem to stand on end every time he heard the blacks whispering the story. It was one of the quirks in O'Leary that had made him learn Chinyanga... The gods had come down from heaven, sent by the ancestors, he overheard. The gods from heaven were among the people. Far to the north. So far away no one knew where they were. Only that the gods had come down from the heaven to be among men. Strange gods who looked like men but were not. Gods with great power. Gods who could fly in the sky.

At the thought of telling Keppel Howland what was floating in the ether, O'Leary had to cross himself and say not a word. O'Leary was more superstitious than religious. The expedition did not carry whisky in their baggage, which was lucky. The little people who were part of O'Leary's existence from the past would have been angry with him for telling such a lie. God was up in his heaven not floating in the sky. Without whisky, O'Leary hoped he would be able to keep his mouth shut.

AS THE SUN went down red into the lake, the hairs rose on the nape of his neck warning him again. The blacks were heathens. What did they know about God?... Steering away from the sunset into the night, O'Leary knew he had been an old African hand for too long. Even the superstitions of the black people were getting to him. In many ways, he was becoming like them.

WHEN HE STOPPED the boat and dropped anchors for the night, a sickle moon had come up. The symbol of doom. Looking up at the night sky, at the moon and three layers of stars studding the black heavens, O'Leary was certain something bad was going to happen. Shuddering in the heat, he went down to his cabin. There was nothing more for him to do. On the *Mary Magdalen*, people cooked their own food. It was the way it was done.

All night O'Leary tossed and turned in his bunk, waiting for the dawn and the swim in the lake that would cleanse his soul of the bad spirits floating in the ether.

When he slept, he dreamt of the moon so thin it wanted to cut off his head.

RALPH MADGWICK WOKE to the sound of the hobbled horses shuffling on the lower deck. The first moment brought panic, not knowing where he was. The silence was like the prelude to going over the top of the trench in a predawn attack when the artillery barrage had just stopped. The smell of horse manure was sweet on the air and comforting. There were no live horses in the front line. Ralph relaxed.

Lying on his back on the upper deck where it was cool, Ralph marvelled at the depth of the heavens above and knew where he was. The moon heralded the change at the equinox, giving little light to the sky and making the stars brilliant. Only the planets did not twinkle. Ralph found and traced the Southern Cross to find the north and the south: a sailor could steer by the stars in the sky from the time of the ancients. Ralph looked but there were no shooting stars in the heavens. The last time he and Keppel had seen a shooting star it was up on their eyrie, the cave that looked out from the top of the escarpment over the Zambezi valley. The next day from a clear blue sky had come Harry Brigandshaw in the Handley Page. In the forward cockpit, standing up holding the side, was a small boy. The same small boy still sleeping soundly on the deck next to Ralph, the boy who was now twelve years old.

The lap of lake water on the old wooden hull mingled softly with the sound of the horses. Ralph hoped there was enough fodder for the horses in the morning. To be strong the horses needed to eat a great deal of hay. The hay was in bales tied with wire. If they ran out of hay they would go into shore to graze the salted horses they hoped would be immune to the infectious bite of the tsetse fly.

For the first time since being told by Uncle Wallace to leave America, when Ralph thought of Rebecca, he could see her smiling face with the soft brown eyes and not sink into depression. Instead, the memory made him smile. From such a great distance, they could still smile at each other in the night. He knew he would never hold her again. Knew he would never go back to England. If he were lucky, he would find an old boat like Captain O'Leary and spend the rest of his life on his own. Being alone with his memories was better than having other people around and have to look at their happiness.

The night beyond the rails of the boat was quiet, without either bird call or the bark of an animal. There were no mosquitoes so far out on the lake. For as long as he could keep himself awake, Ralph lay on his back, looking up at the stars, smiling at Rebecca.

IN THE FIRST light of dawn, Ralph threw the rope ladder over the side and dived into the water. He had been told there were no crocodiles in the middle of the lake. That the water was too deep... He was naked. Had been all night in the tropical heat. As he came up to the surface, water cascaded down from his long hair that hung over his face. Water had never felt so good. Life still had a chance. They could take away Rebecca but they would never be able to take away the memory locked in his mind.

Striking out away from the stationary boat, Ralph revelled in the soft touch of clean water.

Later, floating on his back and moving his arms and legs to keep afloat in the fresh water, he looked back at the *Mary Magdalen*. The old captain was leaning on the rail watching him from a hundred yards away. Ralph waved. The old man turned his back. Ralph could smell the old man's first pipe of the day. Ralph felt the man's sadness from right across the water. The rest of them were still asleep or lying on the deck. The porters were down with the horses. He could hear them sluicing the deck. On the opposite lower deck, someone must have been hauling up buckets of lake water. Ralph continued to swim around for a while.

When he reached the side of the boat, he climbed up the rope ladder. It was already getting hot. Captain O'Leary went and fetched him a mug of coffee as Ralph pulled on his trousers over his underpants. Only when the sun began to scorch his skin would he put on a long-sleeved shirt. They had been back in Africa long enough for his tan to come back. His skin was no longer red and raw as it had been the first months with Keppel and Alfred soon after the war.

Ralph smiled at the captain as he took the mug of coffee. Their eyes met. The old bastard knew what he was thinking without saying a word. There had once been a woman in the old Irishman's life. A long time ago. Living alone wasn't so bad after all. The captain seemed about to say something and changed his mind, turned and walked back to the engine room in the centre of the boat. The engine drove the propeller down a long shaft. The quiet was broken by the sound of it. They were underway as the captain pulled in the small anchors that were not necessary for the tide-less centre of the lake. Or so it seemed to Ralph.

Ralph found he was hungry and went to look for the cold fish they had cooked the previous night before coming onboard. Afterwards, he went to check the horses. They all had dark soft eyes as big as chicken eggs that spoke of love. Ralph's own horse whickered when she saw him. The fodder was almost finished: they must have been eating through the night by the light of the stars.

BY TEN O'CLOCK, the reflection of the sun off the surface of the water was so strong none of them could look at the lake near the boat as it chugged slowly forward. Again, Ralph thought the captain was going to say something important. Above there were white puffs of cloud in the powder blue sky. A pair of ducks were flying fast just above the water. Ralph could hear them but knew better than to look and sear his eyeballs. Young Tinus was hopefully trawling a line for tiger fish. Keppel was sitting in the shade of the small cabin. The porters had put up the canvas to shade the horses and themselves. Tembo was scratching his crotch, which reminded Ralph of his own heat rash that had cooled earlier in the water when he swam. There was something very satisfying to Ralph about a man scratching his crotch when there were no women about.

Ralph began to wonder what Rebecca was doing in America. Then he wondered what everyone else was doing including Rosie Prescott and his

Uncle Wallace. They had all probably forgotten him by now, which was just as well. Then Ralph too began to scratch his crotch, which was the worst thing to do for heat rash.

Ralph was hungry again. The cold fish had gone. There was cold venison somewhere. He stopped scratching himself and went to look.

MANY DAYS LATER, on the day they reached the end of Lake Nyasa now in British Tanganyika, unbeknown to any of them on board the *Mary Magdalen*, the stock market crashed in New York changing the face of the world.

A WEEK LATER, when the expedition was deep into Tanganyika after a four-day rest to shoot game and dry the meat, a man who had been rich jumped from the window of his office in Wall Street killing himself when he hit the pavement down below. Oblivious of anything but themselves, Keppel and his party reached the shore of Lake Tanganyika and found another boat to take them up the new lake. By then, Captain O'Leary was back next to the drums of petrol at the south end of Lake Nyasa and Singleton had come aboard with the monthly whisky. With nothing else really to tell each other, O'Leary told Singleton as much as he knew about Ralph Madgwick.

"Women. How strange when we can't have them," said Singleton, when O'Leary finished the story. By then Singleton was drunk. "And when we have them we behave like me and the governor... What was the poor girl's name?"

"I don't know."

Singleton cracked open the second bottle of whisky and began to pour.

THE NEW BOAT was a steamboat owned by an Arab from the island of Zanzibar in the Indian Ocean off the shore of Tanganyika. And Zanzibar was British, the new captain told Tinus in English. The man spoke Arabic, Swahili and not very good English. On the lower deck with the horses and the porters were stacks of cut wood that fired the boiler.

Tinus, who was always interested in a good story, had made friends with the new captain soon after the steamer left the shore going north, trailing smoke and a small, wide, U-shaped wall of water made by the front of the wooden boat. Tinus watched the thin line on the water spread back over the smooth surface of the lake. They had not swum in the lake while they were looking for a boat camped on the shore. They could all see the Nile crocodiles on the sandbanks watching them during the daytime. When the captain told Tinus his boat had once been a Nile steamer at the time the Mahdi killed General Gordon, the Lord preserve his soul, Tinus thought all things on the lake came from the River Nile: the steamboat, the perch and the crocodiles. Tinus had no idea who the Mahdi had killed or whoever the Mahdi was, but thought better than to ask questions. The captain had a dark, leathery face with a big hooked nose and eyes like a fish eagle. Except the captain's eyes were black. Tinus liked the captain very much. He told stories of ancient times whenever Tinus joined him at the wheel of the steamboat. There was one other crew member, a black man whose job was to feed the boiler all day with the chopped wood stacked on the lower deck. The black man only spoke Swahili. Tinus tried twice speaking to the black man in Shona but without any effect.

Slowly, day after day, with the rain clouds building in the east presaging the rains, they steamed up the lake going further and further from Rhodesia and his home. Once or twice Tinus thought of his mother. It was better not to think of his mother. Mostly Tinus tried to think of Uncle Harry and Uncle Harry teaching him to fly the Handley Page. Tinus thought it would be quite simple to blow up the tyres again and fly up into the sky.

The new uncles had asked the captain to ask the black man if he knew of any aircraft that might have fallen out of the sky somewhere. The man had rolled his eyes, showing the whites of his eyes. Always the black man kept far away from Tinus and his uncles. Tinus thought and hoped the man had something to say rather than roll his eyes and be frightened. For the first time in his life, a man was frightened to look at him. If they could only just talk, Tinus told himself, as the days went by.

Every night the new captain took his boat inshore to cut more wood. The horses liked the stops. Right through the nights, the horses grazed the grass that grew on the banks of the lake. The grass had roots in the water and was green.

At night, they made two fires and listened to the wild animals while they slept around the fires under the nets they hung up under the trees. The black men liked a fire to themselves even though they all came from Elephant Walk. The captain liked to sleep close to Tinus. Tinus slept next to his gun in case he had to protect the horses on their long tethers in the middle of the night. Tinus was the only one who knew all the animal noises in the night and knew when to get up with his gun. He would walk around the horses in the light of the fires, with flickering firelight going up to the top of the trees and far into the bush, which had been brown all the way down to the lake due to the dry season. It had been better for the men on the *Mary*

Magdalen away from the mosquitoes but not for the horses. The mosquito nets they slept under made Tinus hot. Only when the lions roared did the horses not like being on the shore. With the sound of the lions, Tinus would stand with the horses close to the fire as the animals whickered with fear. The look of fear in their eyes was the same look of the black man who put wood in the fire of the boiler, and mostly when he saw Tinus or the uncles coming his way. Never before had a black man been frightened of Tinus. Something was wrong.

On the fifth night up the lake, a group of black men on the shore were standing watching the boat as it came into shore. They had likely seen the Arab captain many times before. At their feet were wild fruit and vegetables they were going to trade, or so it seemed to Tinus as he watched them getting bigger.

The black men ran away leaving the fruit and green vegetables where they were when the uncles jumped into the shallow water to wade ashore. Tinus had stayed on the boat with his gun pointed at the water looking for crocodiles. When everyone was on shore, only then did he jump in himself.

Once on shore, the blacks who had brought the fruit were nowhere to be seen... Something was not right... Probably the black men on shore had never seen whites before. That was what he thought.

WHEN THE NEXT day they sailed into the lake port of Ujiji, where Stanley had found Doctor Livingstone many years before, they learnt of a party of whites from America hunting the area where they had camped the night before. The British had built a railway line from Dar es Salaam to Ujiji. They were almost back in civilisation. The British Resident informed Keppel Howland he was wasting his time looking for the plane crash. If there had been an aeroplane crash anywhere between Ujiji and Khartoum he would have heard. Something so awesome for the blacks would be talked about and he would have heard: reporting to the British governor in Dar es Salaam was part of his job as the British Resident.

Sending a second report to Glen Hamilton on the train to Dar es Salaam, Keppel and Ralph discussed what they should do. So far, no one had been ill with fever. The mosquito nets they hung up under the trees when they slept near shallow water had been successful. The rains were about to break. They could take the train to the coast, sail down to Beira on the next liner and take the train up to Salisbury. There seemed no point in going any further. Like Stanley at Ujiji, they had come to the end of their search.

· · ·

TINUS, listening to the uncles, hoped he could go home. Now he knew of Americans hunting big game near the black people who had left their fruit and vegetables on the shore, his last hope of finding Uncle Harry was dashed. The fear in the black man's eyes held no deep secret for Tinus. Tembo's dream had been wrong. Uncle Harry was never coming back to teach him how to fly an aeroplane.

ONLY ON THE boat that had sailed down Africa through the Suez Canal on its east coast way to the Cape did they hear of the panic in the world stock markets. Ralph thought how it might affect Uncle Wallace and Sir Jacob Rosenzweig. Rumour had it on the boat, companies that had been trading for centuries were going insolvent and closing down. That walking down Wall Street in New York was hazardous to a man's health. That nothing financially would ever be quite the same again. Some of the passengers who had started their journey rich were saying the world would plunge into recession. That Hitler's Nazis would now win the election in Germany and take Europe back into war. That America stripped of its economic might would worry about its own problems and have no wish to sort out other people's arguments this time around. That America would mind its own business if it came to another war in Europe. Tinus had no idea what they were talking about. He was happy to be going back home to Elephant Walk. Looking forward to seeing his mother. Even looking forward to seeing his sisters. The uncles had said nothing happening in Europe and America would ever affect Elephant Walk and that was all that mattered to Tinus. He would tell his mother they had tried very hard to find Uncle Harry.

WHILE KEPPEL HOWLAND in the writing room of the liner was writing up the journal he was going to sell to American and British publishers, the Arab captain was finally sailing out of Ujiji with a full cargo of trade goods that had come up the new British railway line from Dar es Salaam. On board were the horses he had bought for a good price from Keppel Howland. Instead of waiting for customers up on the north shore of the lake, he was going ashore with the horses packed with the products from English factories. The blacks wanted pots and pans. Drums to carry water. Blankets for the winter nights. He wanted elephant tusks and the horns of rhinoceros that were so valued in Arabia for making the intricate handles of daggers which every rich Arab carried at his belt. This time he was going to barter enough to go back to Zanzibar and become a trader in ivory and horn. The young boy on the expedition always asking him to tell a story had made him want a wife and his own family before it was too late. Before he died not leaving behind his own self on earth. He wanted to be rich. Dressed in fine silk. His wives dressed in fine silk. His children educated. Able to read and calculate. Able to trade and make money. With the horses and the porters who were now working for him under the instruction of Tembo who spoke English like himself, he, a descendant of the great Saladin who had conquered the infidels in the land of his forefathers and run them out of Palestine, was finally going to be rich and live in a palace. Only money and God brought happiness. He was going to be happy like Tembo said the porters were going to be when they finally went back to their home in Rhodesia.

Buying the horses had been the difficult part of his plan. He was frightened the Englishmen would ask too much money which he did not have. That the Englishmen would put the prized salted horses on the train down to Dar es Salaam where they would fetch a much better price. The one called Ralph was happy to give him his horse. The horse and the man had come together in the months they had travelled. The horse had looked at the man and whickered when the man left. The horse had known the man was not coming back. The man called Ralph had said it was good to give the horse to a man who loved horses, which the captain understood. A man and his horse in the bush or the desert had to rely on each other to survive. The horses and the porter all came from a place called Elephant Walk to which they were returning after helping to make him rich. The porters believed the Englishmen who said they would be paid for going on the expedition to find an aircraft that had fallen out of the sky. The captain had heard them jabbering in a language he did not understand while the Englishmen were deciding whether to go home or go further north. The Englishmen had camped near the wooden jetty alongside the tied steamboat. The captain had asked Tembo in English what the porters were talking about.

"Their wages which they will receive on Elephant Walk. When they reach home, they will buy cattle to exchange for wives and build huts by the river. They are paid by the week. They can either go home on the train and a big boat on the sea or help you trade for ivory. They know you are going to buy the horses. The young boy Tinus told them. If the expedition goes on, they will have enough money for three wives who will work their fields and make beer so they can get drunk with their friends like me. This is my plan. I will help you take these goods you are buying deep into the bush where the elephant are thick. We will shoot the elephant ourselves while we look for more ivory to trade from the tribesmen. You will pay the porters their same weekly wage in gold when we all reach Dar es Salaam. Plus a big bonus for me."

"You don't make sense, my friend. You are the black chief on Elephant Walk. Why don't you want to go home now?"

"That is my business. We all have our own business."

"Then we will all go up to the north of the lake. Together helping each other we can all become rich."

The Arab captain was puzzled by Tembo being rude. Telling him to mind his own business.

"The rains are about to break. It will not be easy," he said to Tembo, not wanting to ask him any more questions.

"Nothing is ever easy getting rich." Tembo was now smiling, the look of an ulterior motive gone from his eyes.

"There is one life on earth, God be thanked," said the Arab captain.

THE DAYS WAITING for the Englishmen to make up their minds had seen his one worker who stoked the fire and cut the cords of wood, refuse to get off the boat and go into Ujiji to help bring the trade goods to the jetty. Something was not right with the man. Whenever something is wrong there was money to be made. His man was frightened of the Englishmen. Like the blacks who had left their fruit and vegetables and run away into the bush. Something was wrong and the captain was going to find out what.

He would like to know what he had seen in Tembo's eyes when the black man told him to mind his own business.

TEMBO HAD TOLD Tinus he was staying to look after the porters and the horses. Keppel Howland had listened to the advice of the British Resident in Ujiji. Tembo had been more interested in the strange behaviour of the stoker when he found himself anywhere near one of the white men. And on shore the people had run away when they could make out the skin colour of the Englishmen on the boat as they steamed into the shore. No one worked to bring fruit and vegetables to the boat and then run away. It was not the way of any man, whatever the tribe. Tembo would have liked the captain to question the stoker. To ask him what was wrong with the white men that he would not even look in their faces. There was something around he could not catch hold of. Something that became more real the further north they travelled. Even the Irish captain had known something he was not telling them. Twice Tembo had watched the old man about to say something to young Tinus and change his mind.

If the two men from England wanted to go home taking young Tinus there was no reason for him to give up the search. He may have to wait through the worst of the rains with the rivers swollen and impossible to pass. They would all live on the steamboat under the nets so as not to get sick. Now it was every night he was having the same dream. His ancestors were talking to him and only a fool ignored the ancestors when they spoke directly to a man in a dream.

Tembo had asked in Ujiji. The next lake north they called Victoria was so wide in the part that was Uganda, a man could not see the other shore. It was to Uganda Tembo wanted to go. However long it took. The Arab had been sent to him by the ancestors. It was why every night now they kept showing Tembo the great sea in his dreams.

As THE STEAMBOAT moved away from the small village by the lake that was Ujiji, Tembo smiled to himself. His wives had been bickering for the last year. It would do them good to live without him for a while longer. So when he went home they would appreciate him more and stop nagging... Then he smiled a bigger smile at the thought of all his children. He was a rich man. All those girls would bring him many cows when they married, when he was too old to drive the car and make everyone behave themselves on Elephant Walk. An old man needed many children to support his old age... Which brought him back to thinking about his wives. If they were still as nasty when he got home, he would find a fourth, very young wife. That would really make them bicker. But only after he had made them all pregnant again would he look for the very young wife.

THE STOKER LOOKING up from tending the fire in the boiler saw Tembo's face and smiled. Intentionally not looking back at Ujiji, in case the three gods had come down the jetty to see off the boat, he felt better.

When the village eventually sank into the lake behind them in a flash of crimson and red, the colour reflected in the clouds floating high over the water, he felt even better, the spirit of the unknown lifting from his mind. To the north behind the mountains that came down to the lake, thunder was rolling, the gods clapping their hands in approval up in heaven where they lived. Not down on the boat where he worked, frightened every day out of his wits every time one of them tried to catch his eye.

On the lower deck with the horses under the shade of the canvas, the porters were singing a song the stoker had never heard before. It was a lonely song though he did not know the words... But he understood... The porters were a long way from home and singing a lonely song that all together made them feel better.

That evening, the boat anchored out in the lake, not going into shore. They had brought tight bales of hay in Ujiji that would feed the horses all the way up the last third of the lake where they were going to leave him to look after the boat while they crossed on horseback to the bigger lake in the north. The stoker was looking forward to having the peace of the steamboat all to himself without having to work and feed the boiler all day long in the heat. If he was lucky, he would find a young girl to keep him company while he waited for his captain to return with the men from the south who never understood a word of what he said. Even when he was telling them about the gods who had come down from the sky and his captain was trying to listen to what he was saying. Oh, yes, he told himself, he was going to have a good time on his own. He hoped the rains would go on for months keeping the others away and leaving him in peace to live on the comfortable boat far enough out in the lake at night so the mosquitoes did not bite. A peaceful night free of the flies was worth firing the boiler. Better still he would stay out on the lake fishing. Once he had found himself a woman and got her on the boat.

The men who said, through the captain, that they were Shona, had stopped singing. He could smell their cooking so he went down to the lower deck to see if they would give him some of their food. It was a lovely evening out on the lake and his heart was singing. Life sometimes was very good. She was going to have a very big bottom, which he liked.

Putting on his best smile, he was glad to be greeted with a tin plate covered in hot food. The food when he ate it with his fingers, pinching the maize meal and dipping it in the meat, was good... For some reason, everyone on board was in a good mood. Even the captain who was standing on the upper deck looking at them, with the canvas roof down, and the sun sinking into the lake. The Shona were all chatting with each other in their own language, which was a pity. He would very much like to have joined in their conversation. The conversation between old friends eating, talking and smiling with each other. Such evenings on a boat were the best a man could have in his life. In his mind, he wished them all a safe journey to the north and a safe journey home.

· · ·

TEN DAYS LATER, the remnant of the expedition to find Harry Brigandshaw, struck out northeast from the northern shore of Lake Tanganyika, headed for the southern shore of Lake Victoria. They were still in nominally British territory. The Arab captain was with them mounted on Ralph Madgwick's horse. Most of the paraphernalia that had left Elephant Walk at the start of the expedition had gone on the train at Ujiji. The packhorses now carried trade goods, the animals following the riders on long leads. The sky had thundered every day for two hours before dusk. Quick, violent showers soaked them to the skin but the main rains that flooded the rivers had yet to break. So far, none of the tribesmen had appeared with tusks and horns. A few had come with skins, most of which were domestic cattle that would cost more to get to Dar es Salaam than they would fetch.

Sebastian Brigandshaw, Harry's father, had first taught Tembo how to shoot, just like he had done with Harry's boyhood friend, Tatenda. There were four great white hunters in southern Africa at the time: Selous, Hartley, Brigandshaw and Martinus Oosthuizen, the grandfather of young Tinus who would soon be back at school in Salisbury learning how to be a white man. Tembo had heard the story many times, of how Sebastian had found Tatenda when the Matabele of King Lobengula had raided his village. The men had been killed with the stabbing swords of the Matabele impi, the cattle stolen, the young women and girls taken as slaves and the huts burned to the ground. Tatenda had been minding the cattle in the bush some distance away from the village. It had been some years before Cecil Rhodes conquered the Matabele when Sebastian found Tatenda and took him under his wing. That was before Sebastian had gone back to England to claim Emily and bring back his son to the sanctuary of Africa.

Moreover, as he had done with Tatenda, Sebastian the young man with white hair who spoke Shona like everyone in the village, taught Tembo how to shoot. To get the range. Judge the wind. Judge the height of the target, to lift or drop the bullet into the heart or head for a clean kill. To thank the ancestors for the kill. To never kill an animal without a reason.

For most of Tembo's life, he had shot game for the pot. Now he was going after elephant for their tusks and rhinoceros for the big and small horn, like Sebastian Brigandshaw so many years ago when he was young.

FOR DAYS they rode on through the open bush cutting the tusks from the elephant he shot with his .375 Winchester rifle. Always killing with the first shot.

Somewhere weeks after they left Ujiji, the rains broke and the rivers came down in a flood. They were caught between the two great lakes, if Tembo had properly read the stars. They were alone in the wilderness. Not the first time in Tembo's life. Cut off from the world. Comfortable in their isolation.

"We build huts and wait," Tembo told the captain of the steamboat. "Be sure we all sleep under the nets. When the river in front of us goes down we will go on and find the great lake. There will still be elephant to shoot even if they don't come down to the river to drink. By now there will be new waterholes all over the bush. The animals have dispersed far and wide. Be patient. In Africa, we always have to be patient."

While Tembo was sitting out the main rains, Sir Henry Manderville, Harry Brigandshaw's maternal grandfather and the father of Emily, was reading a month-old newspaper that he subscribed to in England. When he put down the paper to look at the rain pelting down outside his window, he was glad not to own any shares in the world's stock markets. The price of Colonial Shipping shares were half what they had been at the peak of the market and the markets were still going down all around the world. Companies were laying off workers as people stopped buying their goods. Banks were calling in overdrafts. Bread lines were spreading across America where the financial situation was the worst in the world.

So far as Sir Henry could see in his mind's eye that no longer focused on the lashing rain, the entire system of capitalism had collapsed making Karl Marx, the father of communist economics, a hero. Only in Russia were people still in work, even if many of them stood on the assembly lines doing nothing. In Russia, the money was spread thin but it was spread over everyone provided they did not argue with Stalin and the Russian state. Greed, Sir Henry told himself, the worst instinct of man had finally made the system of private capital bankrupt.

In America, it was only a matter of time before the banks collapsed under the weight of bad loans. Even the man who had been prudent and put his money safely in the bank was going to lose everything. People were going to start fighting over food. The civilised world was going to tear itself apart and there was nothing the government appeared able to do except tell their people not to panic, which made it worse according to the paper Sir Henry had just read. It was not even any good trying to sell shares. There were no buyers. Only sellers.

Houses were going on the market at ever-reduced prices. Like shares used as collateral for loans from the bank that were now being sold by the banks for any price, they were also selling the houses ordinary folk had bought with a bank mortgage they could no longer keep paying. In his many years of life, Sir Henry had never read anything like it. Even during the terrible war in France, a man's money had not disappeared through no fault of his own. Everyone was going to pay for the greed of the few. Luckily the farm was solvent, the new crops in the ground, the rains good. Elephant Walk owed nothing to anyone, he told himself, until he suddenly went cold all over. Harry! Harry was dead. When the courts finally declared him dead the government would come calling for a slice of the estate. Death duty.

Ignoring the rain, Sir Henry went out of his small house in the family compound to talk to his daughter. If the British government added Elephant Walk to the rest of Harry's estate, there would be a huge bill to pay. Somewhere he had read the top rate of death duty tax was 80 per cent, a punitive tax introduced by socialism to stop the wealth of England staying in a few hands. Even though they were nearly eight thousand miles away and self-governing, Southern Rhodesia was still a British Crown Colony. The British and Rhodesian estates of his grandson Harry would be lumped together for the purposes of British death duty.

EMILY BRIGANDSHAW SAW her father come out in the rain and wondered what was going on. The old man never went out in the rain. Now Keppel Howland and Ralph Madgwick had gone from the farm having safely brought back her grandson Tinus, there was no one else living in her house. Madge and the girls had their own house in the compound. The children were all in school in Salisbury, only coming home at weekends. Ralph Madgwick was only due back on Elephant Walk if he made up his mind to take the job.

When she opened the door for her soaking wet father to come in, he looked as if he had seen a ghost.

"Did Harry register the farm in his name?"

"Father, you are soaking wet. What's the matter?"

"Death duties. They can take the farm. In whose name is the farm registered in Salisbury at the deeds office?"

"Probably no one... I'll get a towel and make you some coffee... Seb took the farm before they had such things as deeds," she said over her shoulder. "The land was empty of people. He had built a house in the wilderness. Only much later did we put up the fences to stop the cattle going off into the bush. The fence became our boundary I suppose."

"So we don't own the farm?"

"Probably not. Legally. It never seemed to matter as we never borrowed money from the bank using the farm as security. Seb never liked owing anyone anything. Never liked being obliged."

"So we are squatters in the legal sense?"

"I suppose so. What a terrible word."

"Did Sebastian leave a will?"

"Don't be silly. He never thought of things like that. Why he liked living in the bush away from civilisation. No one expected an elephant to kill him so young."

"So legally what he had, you inherited as his wife?"

"I didn't move out of the house if that's what you mean. You must remember? At one stage he and Tinus owned half the farm each. Sebastian bought his share when Tinus went to live in the Cape before the Boer war. In those days people didn't write things down. They trusted each other. They were big-game hunters and farmers. Not in business to cut each other's throats."

"When the rain stops you and I are going into the deeds office in Salisbury to straighten this out. You have to register Elephant Walk in your name, Emily. Quickly."

"I think Madge owns some of it. Through Barend. I'll have to ask her. What on earth does it matter? No one's going to do anything with Elephant Walk. It's ours. It belongs to the family like the huts by the river belong to the blacks. You don't have to write down things like that in Africa. It would be far too complicated. People have to trust each other. And Tembo has not come back. They said he and the others were going to help some Arab for a while and then come home overland. I worry about him."

"You worry about everyone. He's also caught by the rains. Don't worry about Tembo. If there's anyone who knows what he's doing it's Tembo."

"You're shivering. I'm going to run a hot bath. Was the fire lit under the boiler?"

"Just give me the towel. I'm old but not an invalid... So you are sure the farm is not registered in Harry's name?"

"Pretty positive. Now stop worrying. That's my job in the family."

RALPH MADGWICK SAW his old friend off at Salisbury station. In the parlance of his childhood, it was raining cats and dogs. Never before had Ralph seen so much rain fall out of the sky. Visibility was less than twenty yards. Ever since leaving Elephant Walk the heavens had opened.

Sir Henry Manderville had lent him the car which was falling to pieces from the bad road. That way he had to go back to the farm or have someone drive the car for him. The job of a learner assistant on Elephant Walk solved his problem of where to live but not what to do. Did he want to become a tobacco farmer in the middle of nowhere on his own? With Rebecca, it would have been perfect. On his own, at the age of twenty-nine, he was not so sure.

As the two old friends shook hands for the last time, they silently wondered when they would ever see each other again. Keppel was going back to be a famous journalist having finished writing up his journal of the journey while they stayed on Elephant Walk as a guest of Harry's mother. The rain was pouring down their faces much as it had done in the trenches eleven years before. Eerily the sight of all the rain on his friend's face brought back the feeling of danger.

"What's this for, Keppel? Two fivers." Keppel had put the money in Ralph's hand.

"You may be stuck in Salisbury in this rain. The rivers will have come up. I still have some of the money given me by Glen Hamilton and Robert St Clair. That's why I just went to the bank. That's for helping me, Ralph. For being my friend. I don't know. I'm just getting sentimental. Even though we did not find Harry it was a worthwhile trip being with an old friend again for three months. You look after yourself, Ralph. Take the job or come back now with me to England. You can't just lie down and die without her. I've never been in love like you, so I don't know what it feels like. You have to go through the same things to understand... Well, there goes the whistle. What's it to be, Ralph?"

"I need time to think."

"Sometimes too much thought is dangerous for a man's mental health."

"I'm not going crackers. I don't think I am. Goodbye, old friend. Hope the journal sells for a fortune. Hope Glen's happy even though there was nothing big to report."

"So long."

Keppel got into the carriage of the train that was going to take him back to Beira and a ship to England. The heavy metal door clanged shut. The train began to jerk forward and then picked up speed. Keppel was leaning out of the open window for a moment. The rain quickly took him from view.

Ralph never felt more lonely in his life. The five-pound notes of the colony of Southern Rhodesia were still in his hand. The car that belonged to the farm was waiting. He would have to stay in a hotel. Keppel was right. The rivers would be flooding over the low-level bridges that crossed the dirt road in so many places between Salisbury and Mazoe. He would never get through in the car. Tears of frustration and loneliness finally mingled with the rain as Ralph turned away from the station platform to face the rest of his life... What did a man do when there was nothing he wanted out of life? Or nothing he was allowed to have which he wanted.

Walking back to the old car, Ralph wondered if back in America Rebecca was feeling just as miserable... Probably not, he thought. Other people got on with their lives. The old bastard had most likely found her a nice Jewish boy she was happy to marry and move forward to live a good life with. If not now, then later, Rebecca would forget him.

Moving the car slowly through the rain, Ralph drove to Meikles Hotel. There was a space to park near the entrance. The old Zulu doorman was still there in his ceremonial skins, his big shield against the wall out of the rain. Ralph gave him a thin smile of recognition, glad his tears were hidden by the rain. With ten pounds, he could stay drunk for a very long time if he took the cheapest room at the back of the hotel. Somehow, he would get the car back. Somehow, he would make up his mind... The trick now was to stop himself from thinking.

With steam coming off his bush jacket, his bush hat in his left hand and his socks pulled up, Ralph sat in the hot humidity at the bar with the punkah going round and round over his head making not the slightest difference to the heat. Miraculously the beer was cold... Halfway down the pint, Ralph began to feel better. Six beers later he was drunk, his shirt dry, his mind back wallowing in the misery of losing Rebecca. After that, he couldn't remember a thing until he woke up in a strange bed somewhere in the hotel.

Sheepishly, Ralph went down to look for the car. The car was gone from outside the entrance.

"We moved it for you, Mr Madgwick," said the big Zulu. "You gave me the keys. Remember? Your car's in the garage out of the rain. You won't get back to the farm for quite a few days. Anything you want just ask... I'm sorry you didn't find Boss Harry. He was a good man."

Looking blank, Ralph turned around and went back into the bar he had been in the previous night. He was in good hands. Maybe he should take the job and come into town once a month for the rest of his life to get drunk like the rest of them and make some friends.

In the bar at ten o'clock in the morning, Ralph recognised two of the men from the previous night. All three of them drank beer silently until they felt better... Then they began to talk.

. . .

THE RAIN EASED off by late afternoon. Ralph could see across Cecil Square where earlier he had not been able to see across the road. Someone had told him in the bar that Cecil Square was named after the third Marquess of Salisbury whose family surname was Cecil. The marquess had been Prime Minister of England when the pioneer column hoisted the Union Jack over Fort Salisbury when Cecil John Rhodes proclaimed the territory British on the 13 September 1890. The man at the bar had been full of information for a newcomer who was thinking of settling in the colony. Ralph remembered most of what the man said except the man's name. The history lesson had been somewhere before the seventh beer the previous evening or before Ralph became drunk. Looking out over a square in a city named after a dead man, Ralph wondered if it could all really last. There were so few of them. The British Empire was everywhere. Right around the globe. An island barely the size of Southern Rhodesia trying to run the world in its own image.

"What the hell," he told the pigeon in the jacaranda tree outside his window. "I've lost everything. What else can I lose?" The pigeon flew off over Cecil Square.

On Elephant Walk, Ralph had seen Sir Henry Manderville was in a bind. He had told Ralph he was too old at seventy-seven to stand in the lands and supervise the growing of the tobacco crop. He could still get around enough to look at what was going on in the lands, the curing barns and the grading shed, but he needed someone else to be his eyes all day long, now Jim Bowman had gone off with his family to farm on his own.

Jim had been the tobacco manager. Jenny his wife had run the clinic on the farm. Ralph was told the two came from the same village in Lancashire. That the Crown land farm they had been allocated in virgin bush by the Southern Rhodesian government was the first land either of their families had owned in their history. Jim Bowman had proved to the Rhodesian government he knew how to grow tobacco after learning to farm on Elephant Walk. His bonuses from the tobacco crops he had managed were enough to grow a first small crop and put up six curing barns. Jim Bowman was now on his way to creating a dynasty. Ralph, if he took the job of learner assistant, would begin his own chance to found a dynasty on his own without having to rely on his family in England which, as Sir Henry said with a smile, was by the sound of it the only way to go... Ralph had told him earlier about his falling out with his Uncle Wallace but not the real reason. "Couldn't stand working in an office," had surfaced as Ralph's explanation... There was a roundhouse in the family compound Sir Henry called a rondavel that would be his. Peregrine the Ninth and Colonel Voss had previously lived in the house, whoever they were... Ralph was constantly being bombarded with the names of strange places and strange people.

For a long time, Ralph stared out of the bedroom window on the second floor of the hotel trying to make up his mind about nothing. There was nothing to make up his mind about. He had nothing. He had no alternative. He had to live somewhere... Best of all, Africa was far enough away not to remind him of Rebecca. He would let the future take care of itself. The chances for Rhodesia were the same as the rest of the world. Some even thought England would be back in a war. Ralph had had enough of war. He never wanted to be part of another one. If Europe started to blow itself to pieces again, a small round hut in the middle of Africa was the place to be. Far enough away for Ralph never to be involved... America would have been all right but that part of his life was over. By now Ralph had begun to hate his Uncle Wallace and Sir Jacob Rosenzweig.

Making up his mind, Ralph decided to let the spruits and rivers go down. Then he would drive the old car back to Elephant Walk... Beggars could not be choosers. He was lucky to have anything at all... Maybe later if he liked it he would get a farm of his own like Jim Bowman... Then Ralph laughed aloud at what it might've been. There was, he told himself, nothing worse than working in the City of London. Catching the eight-ten train from Ashtead station to Waterloo for forty years every day of his life. Living in the suburbs however much money he would have made out of Madgwick and Madgwick. However big his suburban house with the tennis court, the croquet lawn and neighbours all around. And life in New York would not have been any much different... Except for Rebecca, which set him off again thinking in circles.

DOWNSTAIRS IN THE HOTEL, Ralph found himself a small table in the dining room and ate himself a good dinner. Outside the rain had stopped. He was feeling brighter. There was nothing better for a man than to make up his mind, he told himself firmly. At least he spoke enough Shona, which he had learnt from Alfred and from the trip with Keppel up the lakes. He had even learnt a few words of Chinyanga from the black man they had picked up on the journey who had called himself Parsons. Even a few words of Swahili from the stoker on the steamboat. The blacks who worked the tobacco lands would be able to understand what he said. Tembo would soon be back after helping the Arab captain to trade for ivory. Tembo would show him what to do. Tinus had become a young friend who said Alfred would one day come back to Elephant Walk with three wives. Ralph had a new family. The loneliness he now felt on his own would go away. The porters on the trip were his friends and they would be back with money enough to buy themselves wives in the African tradition. He would never marry himself, of that he was certain, without Rebecca. Instead, he would watch other people's children grow up. Paula and Doris, Tinus's young sisters, home from school at weekends. They would make him laugh. He would get himself a cat. A dog: a Rhodesian ridgeback of his own to add to the pack on Elephant Walk... In the end he would be happy. Surely, in the end, he would be happy. Pain like the one he knew from the war which killed Malcolm Scott right in front of him slowly faded from the mind. His old schoolfriend was now young in his mind, not smashed by the shell that had cut off Ralph's small finger clean as a whistle.

Signing the bill against his room number, Ralph walked from the dining room into the bar to talk to his newly made friends. They were a lively lot. And friendly to a stranger all alone... After all, they were British. And far from home. They all needed each other to survive. Of one thing Ralph was certain: Harry Brigandshaw was dead. Lost in the great, empty vastness of Africa.

15

MAY TO AUGUST 1930 – TEMPTATIONS AND DESPAIR

*B*y the end of May, Tina Brigandshaw was at the end of her tether. In four months' time, they were going to sell her up when Harry was legally declared dead by the court. The shares in Colonial Shipping. The portfolio of shares. The house in Berkeley Square. Elephant Walk. Everything Harry had owned. To pay estate duty to the British government. The amount now owing was more than the current value of all the assets in Harry's estate. Percy Grainger was denying he stopped Tina selling shares before the crash. He had merely advised her of the soundness of Colonial Shipping with no mention of what it would do to the public's and institutions' confidence in the stock price if the controlling shareholder began selling large quantities of her shares. The managing director of Colonial Shipping now said it was her decision as Harry's sole heir to do as she wished. That there was no dispute as to her ownership of her late husband's assets even if he had not left a will. She was his next of kin. The law was clear on that matter. Percy Grainger said all he was doing was trying to help the widow. The continuing fall in share prices around the world was out of his control and nothing to do with him. Mrs Brigandshaw was not the only person who was unfortunate. Many pensioners who relied on their dividends would be destitute when companies that had been making money before the crash began to lose money and not pay dividends: the inference, Colonial Shipping was not going to make a profit... They were all in the same boat.

No one wanted to have anything to do with her. Except for Barnaby they all had enough financial problems of their own. The agreement between what turned out now to be her solicitors and the Department of Inland Revenue was a valid legal document. A small man in a small government office asked her: if the share price had gone up instead of down, would they have been able to claim the agreement invalid and demand from Mrs Brigandshaw a vastly increased amount of death duty? They were sorry. They had an agreement which she had signed when her adviser Mr Grainger pointed out their generosity at fixing the date on which her late husband's shares would be valued. Ignorance on behalf of the widow had no point in law, or everyone would change their minds after the event if it suited them. The price of the shares was that on the 13 September 1928. Nothing anyone could do would change that fact. The man had even had the cheek to wish her a very good morning as she left.

When the letter came from Sir Henry Manderville, Tina had to smile. The irony was so beautiful. Harry dead was going to get what Harry wanted alive. The only place for her and the children to go was Elephant Walk. It turned out the farm, for some reason Tina did not understand, was not Harry's property. It would not be sold. She was welcome to live with the family in Africa. The farm was largely self-sufficient and owed no one a penny. Up until the letter, she had thought her only place to live was with her mother and father in the Dorset railway cottage, but where the money was coming from to feed them all she had no idea. She had never worked in her life. The reading she had done so diligently was commercially worthless. Once she was forced to sell her shares in Colonial Shipping, the Rolls-Royce would go back where it belonged and Mrs Brigandshaw would be voted off the board.

So there it was, she said to herself looking at the letter. She was going back to Africa in four months' time whether she liked it or not... To add to the misery at the thought of living again in the African bush, all her children big enough to understand whooped with joy. To them, they were going home to be with their father if their father wasn't coming home to them. To Tina, they were all going to grow up as little savages far away from the civilised world.

As Tina tried to tell herself, it was not meant to have turned out this way. Whatever she had done in the woods with the Honourable Barnaby St Clair, damn his eyes. The sins of the mother were about to be visited on the children. Even Tina could see it. Young Frank at nearly five years old was the spitting image of Barnaby St Clair.

. . .

WHILE TINA WAS CONTEMPLATING the implications of burying herself in the African bush where theatres and restaurants had never been heard of, Barnaby was having the time of his life. There was nothing better than watching people who had only recently been stuck-up prigs come crawling. The ones who had been particularly high and mighty in their previous life Barnaby cut dead, pretending he had no idea who they were. CE Porter was high up on his list. Brett Kentrich was no longer the condescending star of the West End stage since *Happy Times* had finished its run and said she was currently resting. Christopher Marlowe's new show, *Sweet Moments of Life*, was now the rage and Brett was not in the cast. Looking back at better times appealed to the public. It took them out of their present misery. Barnaby even had a little gloat within himself at how the mighty were fallen. It was not in his nature to cut Brett. Once they were lovers. All he did was give her a look that said everything she did not want to know. The only surprise to Barnaby on the Brett Kentrich score was Christopher Marlowe. The poor man was still besotted with the woman. Barnaby even suspected the stupid fool was in love and marrying Brett had nothing to do with marrying a star.

Soon, when the stock markets started their inevitable small recoveries only to continue the downward slide, Barnaby was going to sell the market short. All the way down. The money he had made and put in twenty different banks to spread his risk was going to be nothing to how much he made on the way down. As the financial backer of *Sweet Moments of Life*, he was still making money from the theatre. They seemed to need him even more. Oscar Fleming now treated him as an equal, not quite so condescending. So far Barnaby had had brief affairs with four members of the cast. To Barnaby, being rich when everyone else around him was thinking of money going down the proverbial drain made it all better than it had been before. The game of life was on again. At full pelt. To be, as he put it to himself, rich, almost thirty-three years old, in the prime of life was positively spiffing... It really was a shame about poor old Tina. It could not have happened to a nicer gal. The fact he had kept his hands off the widow had something to do with his satisfaction. She might just have asked him for help.

To add to Barnaby's happiness as he sat at the breakfast table, Edward brought in the morning newspaper with the second cup of coffee. The markets had taken another shuddering fall. Another well-known financier in America had shot himself. Unemployment had reached a new height in the industrial world. Hitler's Nazis showed stunning gains in German elections. Everything pointed to a bear market for the stock exchange and Barnaby's war chest was safe. The only question on his mind was who to take out to dinner that night. Something a little different. Showgirls were fun for a while but rather stupid: they had nothing to say. Just looked good. To get Barnaby excited there had to be something more. Like a very young girl or someone else's wife. Especially if someone else was fool enough to love his wife. Or at least be jealous when she went off to bed with another man. Robert came into his mind which gave him the idea. Robert, the new father of a bouncing little boy which had made Barnaby jealous. Robert's Richard was legitimate. His Frank was not. One day Richard was going to inherit the family title... The idea of bedding Freya had never crossed his mind. She was too old. Like Tina, children made her fat despite Tina losing all the weight worrying about Harry, or so Barnaby was told by mutual friends who liked to keep him informed. Even he had his limits of bad taste when it came to women. His brother's wife and Harry's widow were off limits. But not Portia Ramsbottom, now in town from Yorkshire for the summer season someone had said. Perfect, he told himself going to the phone where Portia's London number was in his book. He would play the intellectual for the evening. The patron of the arts. She would love it... Only when Barnaby reached the telephone did he remember. The girl was now married having finally given up on Robert when Robert came back to England married to Freya.

"Anyway, you idiot," he said putting down the phone, "you had her once before."

It was after she came to the townhouse for drinks with Robert bringing Freya Taylor in his wake, he now remembered. He rather thought he was drunk at the time, which usually blocked his memory. No wonder the girl had been easy. She had done it to spite his brother, poor girl... The things people did to each other... Now, who on earth could he take to Clara's for supper?... There had to be someone he could think of he hadn't been to bed with before... And Clara needed the business or she would close Clara's and go off into the country to hibernate as she had promised so many times. The countryside. Why did they all want to live in the countryside?

Barnaby's right hand went out again to the phone. He picked up the receiver and put it down again. For a moment, almost, but only almost, he was going to phone Tina and ask her out to dinner. Taking his hand off the receiver he wondered how she was. What she was going to do. What she felt like in his bed... And then he began to sweat... She was still the only woman who could make him want her as much as before.

"And she's old, damnation."

"Did you want me, sir?" called Edward from the kitchen.

Ignoring Edward, Barnaby went out of the house, slamming the front door behind him. Crossed Piccadilly into Green Park. It was something he had done before. Walking off his frustration. Always with the same woman in his mind.

When Barnaby came back to the house for lunch he had still not thought of anyone he wanted to take out to dinner other than Harry Brigandshaw's widow, the only woman that had ever been in his life.

When he strode through the house to the telephone he had made up his mind. The girl had lost weight. The girl was vulnerable. Would fall all over herself with gratitude.

"Hello, Tina? This is Barnaby. How are you, old girl?"

"Go to hell, Barnaby. I have enough problems without you trying to come back into my life."

"How's Frank?"

"You really are a sod."

He could even see her face at the other end of the line as she slammed down the phone.

When Edward brought him a badly cooked lunch, Edward only being good at breakfasts, Barnaby was still smiling. Only then did he have a bright idea. Leaving the food to go cold on the table, Barnaby went to the phone and called Cuddles Morton-Sayner. Sometimes a man needed a pimp.

"How strange you should call, Barnaby. I was just thinking of you as I ate my lunch. The Marchioness of Ravenhurst is in town. On her own. I'm sure she would love to see you."

"What happened to John Lacey?"

"Poor chap went bust. Had his money in the wrong shares. The ones his so-called friends told him would double overnight. Lost over two million dollars in less than six months. The old saying. Easy come, easy go."

"What is Stella doing in England?"

"I have no idea."

"Stella doesn't really come into my mind. Poor old John Lacey. I've been out of touch. You do know I did not have a penny in the stock market?"

"It's my business to know, Barnaby. What can I do for you on this lovely day in May? Don't tell me you have run out of pretty girls?"

"I want a challenge, Cuddles. I think I'm starting to get bored."

"There's a cocktail party at the Dorchester starting at six. I'll put you on the guest list. I'm the party organiser. Your brother Merlin has been invited for some reason. All very arty-farty but you will fit in. The Royal Albert Hall is trying to raise money to fix the roof. You won't know a soul apart from your brother. A small donation, Barnaby. I know you don't like wasting money. Just tell me who you like the look of first and I will tell you who they are. If you think it will make a good challenge I will do the introduction. How does that sound?"

"Will Stella be there?"

"Of course not. She doesn't have any money. Defunct titles are two a penny these days."

"Isn't her father rich?"

"Not anymore. There's a scandal in the pension fund for his trade union. He'll be lucky not to go to jail."

"How do you know all these things?"

"Do I ask you your business? Stella Fitzgerald, as she was when we did business, is history. Like so many people these days. You can't believe how many people who once looked down their noses at me are suddenly so nice."

"I think I can, Cuddles."

"Six o'clock in the ballroom of the Dorchester. It's a big party. The roof is a mess... Got to go."

WHEN CUDDLES MORTON-SAYNER put the phone down she was having a good giggle. She knew all about Barnaby St Clair and Mrs Brigandshaw. Again she picked up the phone.

FROM THE OUTSIDE, Riverglade looked the same as Stella remembered. Except for the shutters. She had hired a motorboat in Oxford to make the last part of her journey, to come ashore at the same place she had fallen into his arms and been stopped from going head first into the River Thames. The grass down from the house to the river was cut, the flower beds she could see near the river free of weeds. Everything looked the same except the shutters on the windows making the house look blind.

Since the October stock market crash, Stella's life had never been the same. The sham of her marriage was over. The clients that begged the Marchioness of Ravenhurst to decorate their Manhattan apartment no longer had money. The easy money had stopped. The money no one had had to work for. The creation of vast wealth on paper had gone with the wind. People were lucky to hold on to their jobs and their apartments. The days of ostentatious spending had stopped. Like a big door slammed into their collective faces. The free lunch they had all taken for granted was over and with it Stella's design studio and her husband's money which, when given to him by her father for making his daughter a marchioness, had seemed unimportant, a fragment of Patrick Fitzgerald's wealth. The man himself, whose sons were going to run America, now stood mired in the filth of accusation. People who had once fed from the same trough were snapping and snarling at her father, happy to push him under to save themselves. The wonderful people who were making America so rich in September were now hated speculators, liars, fraudsters and cheats. For Stella, it did not seem fair but she knew it was. There was always retribution for ill-gotten wealth.

John Lacey, the 16th Marquess of Ravenhurst, was the first to go. Her husband. The man who had seemed to be having such a good time deluged with all the flattery. For a brief time the man of the moment. The curiosity who had something the others could never have: a title, whatever that was worth, except for those to whom it was forbidden by the Constitution of America. All these *nouveaux riches* who made the most noise proclaiming their new wealth but found it hollow, realising that just having money made no difference to their lives. They were still the same men who built houses, sold bonds, sold anything. They found out in the end, they were no different to what they were before. No different to everyone else, despite their apartments being full of strange expensive objects put there by the Marchioness of Ravenhurst... Stella could still feel the hollow ring echoing through the emptiness... It was all for the sake of appearances which only mattered to the other person, never to themselves. All the art and pictures would never change who they were, not even an ancient title for a million dollars.

Stella had come without a man to drive the boat, showing the hirer in Oxford she knew all about boats from her days out on Massachusetts Bay. Whatever happened she wanted to see the place again. Where she had been happy for her one perfect day. Herself alone. Not once trying to impress or play the bitch she knew herself to be. She had come back alone at last to the place of her dream.

Tying up the small motorboat to the wooden jetty, Stella went ashore. No one came out of the house, which was good.

Walking up the path slowly, the same path she had run down into his arms, the arms that had led her down into taking her virginity, she felt the silence of the morning, heard the call of the pigeon, thought of the night calls of the owls and was happy again, the weight of her depression lifting from her mind.

A man she had never seen before came round from the back of the house. He seemed to be waiting for her. As if he knew who she was.

"My name is Stella Fitzgerald. I've come to see Douglas Hayter."

"Yes, I thought so... What a pity. You are six months too late. Mr Hayter hanged himself. I am the butler. Well, I was the butler. Have you come for your clothes at last? What a pity... Please come with me into the house. Mr Hayter put it all in a special room where he hanged himself. He had put a pulley up over the beam. Another rope with a noose. He was very strong in the arms."

So that's how it ends, she told herself. He killed himself.

"Was it because of the stock market crash?"

"Oh, no. Mr Hayter was a trader. He never bought shares."

"Then why did he hang himself?"

"You will understand when I show you the room. He had hauled himself up in the wheelchair with the pulley, put the noose around his neck and fell forward out of the chair. It snapped his neck. Far less pain than when the Germans blew off his legs."

Numb in mind and body, Stella followed the man into the house through the corridors and into the room. Her blue and white ball gown from the last May Ball given by Lady Harcourt was draped over a frame that made it look as it had been on the night of the ball. Except she was not inside the dress. Her evening shoes were at the foot of the flared gown. In front was a mahogany writing desk. There was a photograph of a strange man who by his dress had lived fifty years before. The frame was covered in thick dust from years of neglect. In the middle of the desk was a wooden box.

Stella lifted the lid of the box and took out the sheaf of papers that were resting inside.

"Will you excuse me, please?" she said to the man.

"If you need anything."

"Thank you. I'll let myself out."

Then she read the pages of their conversation the day of the ball that she remembered so well. Every word was there.

Putting the sheets of handwriting paper back in the box, Stella closed the lid and walked out of Riverglade to take the same path down to the river. Taking the boat out back to Oxford, she would travel by train and then by boat to America to face the rest of her life alone.

Later, she hoped, she would be able to cry for both of them.

When she returned the motorboat in Oxford, she knew there was one last job she had to do in England. She had to go and apologise.

John Lacey, 16th Marquess of Ravenhurst, was making tea in the kitchen at the back of the house when he heard the car. The last unannounced car at the old house in the Lincoln marshes had been Cuddles Morton-Sayner. He just hoped the car outside had nothing to do with him. He was back translating ancient Greek for a small living. He was happy back in his own house far away from everyone. The man he had been in America had nothing to do with him. Later in the day he would go into the woods and shoot himself a rabbit for his supper. The game birds were still out of season. He never shot birds who had young. Only the rabbits were in season the whole year round as they bred too quickly. Since running away from his life in America, John Lacey had himself fixed the new leaks in the roof of the old house. He had dug and planted a new kitchen garden. Pruned his fruit trees in the depth of winter.

When he looked up from pouring the tea, Stella was standing in his doorway. He had never before seen her looking ill.

"I came to apologise for being a selfish bitch... Can I tell you a story that happened before we were introduced like slabs of meat on a butcher's hook? It's not a nice story. But then I'm not a nice person and deserve what I get."

An hour later, they were still sitting at the old kitchen table with its thick wooden legs. The room was warm with the afternoon spring sun coming through the window. They had fallen into silence, not knowing what to say.

"Can I stay the night, John? It's a long way to the nearest hotel."

"You can stay as long as you like. However it happened, you are still my wife. In America, once the business side of the affair had disintegrated, I thought there was no point in staying. I was superfluous. Anyway, I was penniless. Those people don't like the poor. So I came home to the last part of my family inheritance. I didn't think you had seen me go."

"I like the house."

"It's comfortable. Even in winter, if I have cut enough firewood during the summer."

"Do you think he killed himself?"

"The war killed him, Stella. He thought he wasn't a man without his legs... How is your father coping with the pension scandal? Your brothers?"

"They want to put him in prison."

"That wily Irishman! Never. He's got too much on too many people... Does he want his million dollars back now I've gone? He can't even have this house as it is in a trust entailed to the son I never had. Someone will claim the title and the house when I die. There must be some male descendant I don't know of. All he has to do is prove direct lineage back to one of the Ravenhursts. If no one comes forward, the property reverts to the state."

"Unless we have a son."

"Stella. Be sensible. After a month in this wilderness, you will be going round the bend."

"I'm nothing in America."

"Poor girl. You really are in a state. Don't say any more. Just see what happens... Rabbit stew for supper. How does that sound?"

"You will have to teach me to cook... Do you think there'll be another war in Europe?" Stella said, for something to say when her husband did not pick up on the idea of them having a son together.

"There are always wars in Europe. Humanity always fights among itself."

"What are you doing for money?"

"Translating ancient Greek texts. I'm an educated man, Stella, for what that is worth financially. That is all I am... Did I ever tell you I can also speak French and German? Good. That would have been boasting. I was taught a gentleman should never boast about himself. My goodness, Stella, you look terrible. When did you last have food?"

"Yesterday. I think it was yesterday... Thank you for being so kind to me."

Only then did the tears break.

TINA BRIGANDSHAW BOOKED them all on the SS *Corfe Castle*, the encounter with Barnaby St Clair finally making up her mind. She was still the major shareholder in Colonial Shipping and entitled to the owner's cabin when she wanted to take a trip. Everything was free until the Department of Inland Revenue sold her up in September. Share prices, despite her hopes, were still going down around the world.

The trip she planned was in August. There were other jobs she had to do, like the letter she had written to Brett Kentrich a week before she received the phone call from Cuddles Morton-Sayner saying how much the Royal Albert Hall needed a new roof. Flattered someone had phoned to include her in a social event, something that had not happened since Horatio Wakefield stopped writing about Harry in the *Daily Mail*, she had accepted without thinking why the woman would want her at the Dorchester. The devious Cuddles never did anything without a reason. A last-minute invitation should have warned Tina something was wrong. Maybe because the Dorchester was round the corner, she accepted on first impulse. Giving the Royal Albert Hall money that would be claimed by the government in September also had something to do with it, which set her to thinking of stashing cash away where no one would know where to look for it.

She was back wearing the size of clothes she had worn before her first child was born. All the worrying had given her little appetite for anything, which included food. The children had their food in the nursery given them by Ivy and Molly, who had both surprised Tina by wanting to go on the boat.

"We love the children," Ivy had said.

The thought of five children running riot around the first-class deck of the *Corfe Castle* had gone through her mind. In Africa, the family would give her nannies to look after the children. With so many things on her mind, Tina had said yes to the nurses and booked another cabin for Ivy and Molly. It would cost her nothing. Maybe the girls would find themselves rich husbands in Rhodesia where Tina knew the young men outnumbered the young girls four to one. She could see Ivy and Molly were pretty enough in their nurse's uniforms and caps. Ivy had a pert little nose.

As she confidently walked through the entrance to the Dorchester Hotel, Tina was hoping her life was going to fall into some kind of place. Waiting for her in the lobby was Barnaby St Clair with a grin on his face. Only then did it dawn on her what Cuddles Morton-Sayner was up to: looking after one of the few young men in London still stinking rich.

"This is not a coincidence, is it?" said Tina, caught between the door and the reception desk of the hotel.

"It was not my idea. I'm surprised you fell for one of Cuddles's old tricks. How are you, Tina?"

"Didn't I tell you to go to hell?"

"You look wonderful. Most important I hear you need my financial expertise. Not my money, Tina. My expertise. I thought I would be sadly wanting if I did not help such a very old friend. Anyway, you forget I have an interest in the whole debacle."

"What have you heard?"

"That you wrote to Mrs Marlowe, our esteemed Brett, to the effect the government would likely sell her leasehold flat. That Harry had given her the keys to the flat in Regent Mews and the keys to the red car. That he registered neither in Brett's name. Christopher phoned me. They've moved out already. He's back in his attic, can you believe the man? Now she's out of a part on the stage, she's singing at Clara's. With Christopher back on the piano. The strangest part is they look happy... I can never figure out people... You see, we need a chat. First, we go up to the ballroom and give the roof some money. Then you and I are going to Clara's. Did I mention you look smashing?"

"Barnaby, you are incorrigible."

"I know."

Tina's knees had gone weak as usual at the sight of him.

. . .

CLARA'S, when they got there after the cocktail party, was not as full as usual. What the papers were calling the start of a world depression was affecting everyone. Christopher Marlowe waved from where he was sitting on his piano stool. There was no sign of Brett.

They sat at the bar looking at each other, not having to say a word, just looking at each other. It was one of the nice things, Tina told herself, about knowing a man for the whole of one's life. Neither of them was forced to talk.

Danny Hill was playing the trumpet again. Harvey Lyttleton was crooning through an old number he had been singing for years. Clara was moving comfortably from table to table, talking to her guests. It all looked so normal except she was sitting with Barnaby and not Harry. What was she going to do, she tried to ask herself? Her mind told her to bolt out of the restaurant. Her body was craving for his company. Nothing over all the years had ever changed. Not even Frank. Not even having a son together. They were looking at each other. Knowing. Knowing what was to happen. That this time there was no one to hurt but themselves.

When Brett came on to sing with the band, they both sat up and took notice. Tina had not seen or heard from Brett after writing her the letter about the flat. The bar and the small bandstand were on the same level and not so far apart for Tina to know something had changed in Brett other than where she was living.

Brett had looked at Christopher as she stood in front of the microphone with a look of intense familiarity. Christopher back with his black beret on the top of his head and pulled to one side had gently smiled back, tinkling the first bars of the tune she was going to sing. The love song from *Happy Times*. The tune that had made both of them famous.

Right through the song, Brett sang to her husband. Barnaby said not a word. Both of them watched, transfixed by what they were seeing. The girl was in love. Despite the loss of her leading part on the stage and the loss of her flat, Brett was intolerably happy, making both Tina and Barnaby look sad and envious at the same time. The tune finished. Harvey Lyttleton joined Brett to sing the Cole Porter duet. Again, instead of singing the words to the crooner, Brett sang to the man in the beret sitting at the piano.

"Can you tell me what's going on there?" Barnaby asked, turning to Tina.

"She's pregnant. Brett's pregnant. And happy."

When Tina saw the expression on Barnaby's face, an expression of pained, faraway sadness, she understood. Barnaby had yet to see his son.

"We can go back to the Berkeley Square house. They'll all be asleep. That's as far as it goes. You understand?"

"Thank you, Tina."

For the first time Tina had ever heard, Barnaby sounded humble. Their unexpected evening had taken another turn.

"I'm going back to Africa in August. With all the children. Do you want to do this?"

"Of course. He's my son."

There was no hurry. They had the rest of their lives to work through the problem they had created. Barnaby ordered another drink for them both. Tina knew she was drinking too much. Had been drinking too much for some time. Even on her own in the Berkeley Square house. Africa, she knew, would be worse. Far worse. It was the national recreation, getting drunk when the sun went down.

A distinguished old man in evening clothes that had gone out of fashion in the era of the flappers sat himself down at the far end of the bar. He was alone in white tie and tails direct from the theatre or a concert. The old man, Tina noticed trying not to look at him, had a glass eye.

A few minutes later a much younger woman came out of the powder room and sat with the old man. The girl's looks had faded. The dress she wore was also old-fashioned. She was definitely not the old man's paramour. They were familiar and comfortable with each other. More like old friends who had used each other to go to the theatre, something they could not do on their own. The man to Tina had been in the military by the look of his bearing. His back was straight, his presence quiet while the one good eye was directed at the piano player. The woman was also looking at the band.

The one good eye was boring into the back of Christopher Marlowe's head, making Christopher look round and hit a false series of notes. Used to the mistakes, Harvey Lyttleton sang louder to let Christopher look for the right sounds. Even Clara stopped on her way between tables in alarm, looking quickly at the piano player... Tina smiled. Tina thought it nice to be a famous musician and still make a mistake. Only when Tina saw Clara look from Christopher to the old man at the bar did she realise something was wrong. That the false notes had come from the gimlet-eyed look of the old man.

To add to the strange moment in time, Brett appeared at Tina's elbow.

One minute she had been singing with the band, the next she was standing next to Tina looking sarcastically at Barnaby who was somehow looking sheepish under Brett Kentrich's glare.

"Well, this is nice. On my way to placate Uncle Wallace who do I find?"

"Did you get my letter, darling? Such a shame. Harry was always bad at things like that. He never expected to die or I am sure he would have put your name on the leasehold. Of course, I don't mind. You were his mistress after all. It's just the government."

"It's better than losing everything. So sorry. Anyway, Barnaby is still rich."

"Oh, I forgot. You also had a brief affair with Barnaby."

"Better than giving birth to his bastard son. Poor Harry."

"That's enough," said Barnaby. "Not in public."

The two women smiled thinly at each other. Despite Harry being dead, they were still competitors. To Tina, the bitch coming back in Brett was a relief. The one thing Tina would have hated was Brett Kentrich being happy.

"Christopher and I are going to have a baby. Tonight is my last night singing in public. You must stay and have the lovely food. Christopher I know would love to talk to Barnaby between sets. *Sweet Moments of Life* is doing so well. You should be pleased, Barnaby. But then you always did have the Midas touch."

"You mean you are not going back on the stage?"

"Not with a family."

"You can't all live in an attic?"

"Of course not, darling. Christopher is rich. We can do what we like. We were going to give up the flat anyway. The attic is pure nostalgia. Where it all started for Christopher. We are making a new start to our lives."

Tina watched her adversary walk down the bar to Uncle Wallace, who stood up from his stool at the bar. Tina understood. Harry was dead. They were both making new starts in their lives. The world was full of false starts and cross purposes. She had her five children. That would have to be enough.

"What does this Uncle Wallace want?" asked Tina.

"The usual. Christopher to take over the firm. Or rather Barrington Madgwick to take over the firm."

"I thought it was Barrie."

"That was Christopher again. Changing his name."

"And the woman with Uncle Wallace?"

"His secretary. She's been in love with Ralph Madgwick for years. Rosie Prescott. Followed Ralph to America and back again. Uncle Wallace likes the theatre and so does she. Convenience... Poor old bugger wants to retire to the country. Some people have all the bad luck... She's jealous of you."

"Rosie Prescott?"

"Brett Kentrich. Poor old Harry. I miss him."

"You mean that don't you?"

"I'm not a very nice person, Tina. You of all people should know that. Harry saw clean through me. He was a friend. Not had many of those in my life... But you can't have everything, now can you? You should know... Now may I go and see my son?... What's he like?"

"You."

"Poor chap. He'll need a skin as thick as a rhinoceros."

UNCLE WALLACE HAD WATCHED Brett join Tina Brigandshaw and Barnaby St Clair at the bar. He knew exactly who they were. Rosie Prescott had told him when she sat down at the bar. All the young people seemed to know each other. Madgwick and Madgwick was collapsing. Uncle Wallace had come to Clara's from seeing *Sweet Moments of Life*, which he had enjoyed for the third time. Secretly he was proud of the nephew who liked to call himself Christopher Marlowe.

Uncle Wallace liked to say his worst enemies did him the biggest favours. Like the Germans knocking out his left eye, sending him back to England before they killed him. The stock market crash, though not a person, had done the same thing. At last, he was free from family obligations. He could go live in the country the last years of his life. Hunt, shoot and fish to his heart's content.

"What are you going to do, Rosie? The American company will stay afloat under Sir Jacob Rosenzweig. We'll lose our shareholding and they will change the name of the New York company but there will still be a job. Not like the new owners in England who don't want our staff. Only our clients."

"Not without Ralph."

"You still love that stupid nephew of mine after all he has done?"

"Because of what he did. He loves her. She loves him. Why should religion get in their way?... Oh, I'm sorry. I don't see straight when it comes to Ralph."

"Ever thought of being a housekeeper in the country?... Can you ride a horse?"

"Even some of us who choose to live in London can ride a horse. But not to hounds. I find the idea of chasing a poor defenceless fox appalling."

"They are vermin. Kill the pheasants. Breed like rabbits if we don't hunt them down. Anyway, that's enough. Here comes his wife. She must think I'm here for a riot act on family responsibility... Ironical, really. All my years as senior partner after their father died was a waste of time... Why are so many things in life a waste of time, Rosie Prescott? Like the last war and the next one. And the next one... There's always another war... Brett! How lovely you look. You know Miss Prescott from your wedding reception. Fine wedding. Fine old Norman church, St Giles. Backbone of England. When that nephew of mine has finished tinkling the ivories tell him I have something to say to him. He doesn't have to be frightened. Fact is, Barrington will have a good laugh. Saw his show again tonight. Good, but not as good as it would have been with you in the lead, Miss Kentrich. No, indeed. Have a drink. Fact is, when you all hear what I have to say we'll have a good few drinks... Did I hear you say to those people you were going to give up the stage? Oh, congratulations. I may have one eye but I have two ears and both are very good. Have your children but stay on the stage. London would miss you. You would miss the stage. I'm sure Barrington is writing a new show just for you, Brett... He really is a lousy piano player... Did you hear all those false notes when he saw me sitting at the bar?... Poor Ralph. Gave him a hard time and now he's staying out in Africa. His mother tells me he's going to grow tobacco and build himself his own farm... She'll be all right. Not all her money was in the firm. Lately, she has lived quietly, my sister-in-law."

"What are you talking about, Uncle Wallace?" asked Brett expecting trouble.

"Madgwick and Madgwick are going out of business."

EVEN AS TINA and Barnaby opened the door to leave Clara's, they heard Brett's peal of laughter.

Then they found a taxi to take them to see their son.

CHRISTOPHER MARLOWE KNEW his days of playing the bohemian were over. When Uncle Wallace told him between sets that Madgwick and Madgwick were going out of business, the company's bad debts equalling the firm's assets causing the fire sale, the irony was not lost on him. Brett had told him that morning she was pregnant. The responsibility he owed to one family was being replaced by another. Being a father would change everything he did in his life. After Tina's letter saying the flat still belonged to her as Harry's widow, they moved back into the attic. Christopher had kept on paying the attic rent out of nostalgia for an easy life without complications when Gert van Heerden returned to Africa to face his own responsibilities. For some reason, Brett had been happy to live in the attic to please him. Now he knew why. His wife, who had said she never wanted children, was consumed by the knowledge she was going to have a child of her own. Her euphoria was tangible. As the father, some of Brett's new-found happiness flowed his way. As if he was terribly clever. Even Christopher knew most women changed at the thought of actually being pregnant. It was built into them or the species would never have survived. Like his own understanding that he now had to make a stable home and provide for his child. That too was in his human make-up. Nothing was really terribly clever in life. Everything they did was ordained by their own evolution from time immemorial. How they themselves had survived the fight for life to be born. Every child had to be nurtured before it could stand on its own two feet.

Smiling and listening to Uncle Wallace, he knew he had had a good run. It was now time to settle down. Thankfully without having to sit every day in an office to provide for his children... He was thirty-seven years old.

"I'll even have to change my name back to Barrington Madgwick. Can't have a son with a different surname to his father. Brett can keep her stage name but not me."

Uncle Wallace was smiling. He knew. Rosie Prescott was downcast. Christopher understood. In the end, sadly they all had to grow up with the facts of life.

THE BOYS' bedroom was quiet, the night candle resting on the small table between the two eldest brothers. Ivy, Molly and the three other children were asleep in the room next door. Tina quietly closed the connecting door that stayed open once the children were asleep.

"Won't we wake them?" whispered Barnaby, not sure whether he wanted this after all.

"Once they go to sleep a bomb going off won't wake them." Tina picked up the thick candle on its silver dish, relit it and held the light above Frank. The boy had his thumb in his mouth. Tina was smiling gently. "They are such angels asleep."

"Is that my son?"

"Yes, Barnaby, though I want you to swear you will never tell him."

"Not even if he is in terrible trouble?"

"You won't know. We will be far away in Africa."

"It's a strange feeling looking at your own flesh and blood... Are you sure?"

"Quite sure."

"How can we prove it?"

"The way he looks. The way he behaves. The total difference between him and the rest of them. Maybe one day they will be able to tell. Anyway, to you it does not matter. You are going to have nothing to do with Frank. You owe that to Harry's memory."

"That boy there removes any burden from my future. I don't have to marry and give up my freedom. I understand now I have a son. I will go on when I'm dead. The reason for my life is right there in the bed. The only way a man can reincarnate himself is through his children. I was very clever. I've got what I need without having the responsibility of having to be a father."

"You're a selfish bastard."

"Look after him, Tina. He's my son. He'll always be with me in my mind till the day I die."

"The taxi is waiting downstairs."

"You won't let me stay?"

"Not after what you just said... Why I cared about you so much, I don't know."

"We play the perfect tune together, Tina. Never forget it. Very few people in life ever get to play the perfect tune. When they do, they stay together one way or the other. You'll never be rid of me, Tina Pringle. Any more than I will be of you. Some call it fate. It's much simpler. Sexually, we are the only two people on earth who can satisfy each other. Now and forever. Don't forget about it. Even in Africa... He's not a bad-looking boy when you come to think of it."

They were smiling at each other. They both understood.

Tina stayed with her children as Barnaby left the house. In the still of the night she heard the front door click shut and the taxi drive away.

Blowing out the candle, Tina opened the connecting door so Ivy could hear if the boys wanted something. Or something went wrong. Ivy or Molly liked to look at the children during the night. They were both light sleepers.

Then she went to her own bedroom, undressed and got into bed. She was still awake when the dawn paled the sky over Berkeley Square. Only then did she fall into dreamless sleep.

WHEN TINA WENT ABOARD at the end of August it was not as bad as she imagined. The SS *Corfe Castle* was the same ship on which she had seduced Harry, half intentionally getting herself pregnant and leading to the chain of events that now led to herself and her five children sailing to Africa. Nothing had changed with the money. Colonial Shipping shares were still going down like everything else. America was in a depression with banks across the nation going broke. The percentage of workers unemployed had reached 20 per cent and Europe was not very much better according to Horatio

Wakefield in the *Daily Mail*. Tina had bought the paper for something to read, not knowing if she would ever again see an English newspaper. A brass band had played them off as the tugs pulled the ship into the Southampton Solent on its way to Cape Town. All the old choke in the throat Tina told herself while wiping the unwelcome tears from her eyes. For Tina, it always took a ship too long to sail. For the hawsers to be released from the bollards, the tugs to get a grip and painfully, slowly, drag the ship from the jetty. 'Land of Hope and Glory'. 'Greensleeves', for some reason. All the pomp and patriotism expected from the empire encapsulated in music. The longing for belonging. The longing for home as they turned their backs and headed out into the world from so small an island. The whole history of England slipping away with the notes of the music floating out on the water, reminding Tina what she was losing.

To Tina's surprise, the one thing she would not miss was all the obsequious fawning by the staff of Colonial Shipping, the captain, and the crew of the SS *Corfe Castle*. Once she had everything money could buy, including people's deference, it seemed unimportant. There was no excitement in all the attention anymore. Only for a brief time had Tina's ego been impressed. She had found through her life that once she had what she wanted, she didn't want it anymore. She was still the same self whatever she possessed. It made no difference to her being. The only difference was the perception of the captain who in another life, when she spoke a broad Dorset accent and lived in a railway cottage with love, he would have ignored. She would have been too insignificant for him to be rude to. Her difference was the power of great wealth she was leaving behind which was fine by her... As she said to herself, looking over the side at the receding shores of England, there were some things in life she would never understand... One of them was why people were so impressed with the rich and famous.

THE CHILDREN WERE ALREADY RUNNING riot despite the best efforts of Ivy and Molly. Poor girls. For them, it was going to be a long trip before they reached the space of Elephant Walk where Anthony and Frank could shout their lungs out without anyone caring about the noise. The dogs would join in. The wild geese, now tame, would honk their way to the river... Only Harry would be missing.

To Tina's surprise, Barnaby had seen them off at the railway station in London. He was looking smug and rich. Barnaby liked to look rich. He liked what people thought of him in a condescending sort of way. He had laconically waved as the train pulled out of the station, quickly turning his back and going off somewhere in a hurry. Barnaby liked to look in a hurry. Tina had smiled and pulled up the window of her carriage. It was cold even in August... From that moment the children started their mayhem.

By the time the ship sailed down the English Channel, Tina had found the first-class bar despite women not usually going to bars on their own. She needed a drink and she only had twelve more days of being the owner. Everyone knew who she was. Everyone left her alone. The children, bless them, were not allowed in the bar.

"Money, old girl, does have some advantages," she said, lifting her glass. She would make it up to Ivy and Molly when they reached Rhodesia by train from Cape Town... The children would have to make their own way through life. In September, the silver spoon was going to fall right out of their mouths.

WHILE TINA BRIGANDSHAW was ordering her third gin and tonic on the SS *Corfe Castle*, in the heart of Africa, Tembo was drinking from a bowl of white maize beer in the shade of a tree on the shore of Lake Victoria. They had arrived at Mwanza on the southern shore of the lake a week earlier. The rains had been intense, locking them between rivers until the end of April when they broke out from their camp to continue the journey north. During the rainy season, Tembo had shot nothing but small game to feed them. The big game was always too far away. Never in one place. To shoot and wound an elephant was a sin likely to be paid for with the life of the next human being that came across the wounded elephant. Tembo had known an elephant to attack a village, rampaging through the mud huts years after being shot and wounded by a white hunter. When Tembo killed the elephant, he found a festering cyst in the shoulder behind the big ear that was years old, by the look of it, and still giving excruciating pain to the elephant. Hunting down the wounded beast to protect the villagers had taken Tembo a week.

The two small carts bought in Ujiji by the Arab captain had caused most of the trouble in the wet. Loaded with the few tusks of elephant shot by Tembo before the rains came down, they had to be manhandled much of the way through the bush between the north shore of Lake Tanganyika and the south shore of Lake Victoria. Only a span of oxen would have done the job properly, something not for sale in Ujiji. The harnessed packhorses had tried their best. Anywhere wet in the low country, the carts sank into the mud. With all the men on the wheels, they could pull the carts from the suck of the mud. Their journey to Mwanza had been long, heavy work with little reward. Only once did the Arab trade his Western goods for rhino horn.

When the Arab reached Mwanza he had hired a boat to take him up the lake, leaving Tembo to guard the small pile of ivory. The Arab thought it would be easier to trade for ivory and horn from a boat than hump the tusks through the bush without an ox wagon inspanned to eight powerful oxen.

The British had built two spurs to their railway line out of Dar es Salaam to open up the heart and lungs of Africa to trade. The one spur had gone to Ujiji, the other to Mwanza where the Arab was going to entrain with his ivory and horn leaving Tembo and his Shona to go back to Rhodesia overland on horseback unencumbered by trade goods or tusks. They had blazed a trail. Going back would be easier. With gold for helping the Arab to accumulate his ivory and horn they would buy passages down Lake Tanganyika and Lake Nyasa, reaching Elephant Walk with money and the horses.

Tembo, drinking the smooth white beer out of the old wooden bowl, was well pleased with himself. He was going to be rich. The open bar under the tree was to his liking. The woman who served him the beer when he wanted was big in the bottom and big in the breast. Young. Just as he liked his women. The man who called himself Parsons and spoke Chinyanga with a smattering of Shona had stayed with Tembo. He was going to take the train from Mwanza to Dar es Salaam. He also thought himself rich, a man following his whims through life, going where life took him without a care in the world. Mostly, the locals spoke Swahili in Mwanza so Parsons was of little use to Tembo's quest for information other than as a companion with whom to drink beer and listen for any gossip they might understand. Many men came to the shade of the tree to drink beer.

IN THE MONTHS on the journey, Tembo had learnt his own smattering of Chinyanga and Swahili. Some of the black people who worked for the British even spoke English. The British, Tembo understood from Rhodesia, liked to teach the blacks English rather than have to learn so many African languages, hoping one day English would be the common language over the territories they had colonised stretching all of the way up East Africa to Egypt.

Drinking beer and listening, sitting comfortably in the shade of a great tree with a pretty young girl serving his beer, was all Tembo asked for from life, the nagging of his own wives far away in the back of his mind.

There was a small fire under an iron grille that was kept burning all day giving off the pleasant smell of woodsmoke and making coals always ready to cook. At the bar counter at the trunk of the old tree were trays of butchered meat and fillets of Nile perch. On the side of the fire stood two three-legged iron pots with domed lids. In one, slowly cooking in their own juices, were dried beans now turned soft by the slow cooking. In the other large pot, maize meal was cooking, occasionally stirred with a long spoon by the young girl who always leaned over the pot showing Tembo her large black bottom and white knickers. Tembo hoped she was doing it on purpose... There was plenty of time. The Arab and the porters first recruited by Keppel Howland were going to be away a long time... Or so he hoped. Even in the day, by the great lake that had no end in sight, the temperature was pleasant under the tree... Cool at night with a soft breeze off the lake.

When Tembo was hungry he went to the counter. In the mornings he ate fish. In the day and evening, a piece of meat: all were cooked as he liked them over the hot coals on the iron grid, sipping beer. Added to the beans and *sudza*, his food was just right. Tembo's days and nights were perfect. There was nothing a man could want more. Most nights he and Parsons slept under the tree next to the fire covered in blankets, listening to the wild animals before they fell into dreams satiated by good food and beer. Drinking beer all day was an art that required slow drinking and good stories. Tales to be told and tales to be heard. Sometimes Tembo told a long story in Shona which no one understood. Everyone smiled and drank their beer, listening to every word, savouring the day under the big tree by the great lake whose shores none of them could see across, the great stretch of clean blue water, the one great lung of Africa that helped them breathe the pure clean air. It was good to be alive by the side of the lake with his friends.

The days folded gently into each other. Tembo was so lazy he just looked at the young girl with appreciation, not bothering to take it any further... Sometimes he knew it was better not to eat what was in front of him. Fulfilment was always too short. Once a woman was taken she was rarely as exciting anymore... Something Tembo reflected on sadly as he thought back over his life in the shade of the big tree.

THE BEST PART of Tembo's day was the sleep after lunch. Half an hour under the tree settled the morning beer and made room for the rest of the day. It was part of the drinking ritual passed down through the generations. A hut near water, fat cattle, three wives to work the fields and bring the brewed beer and a sleep after lunch was in Tembo's mind the attainable pursuit of every man's life... A long, lazy life of luxury and pure contentment.

TEMBO WAS HALF-ASLEEP when the two black men came to the tree and bought themselves each a beer. They were well dressed and looked important. The young girl in her rush to serve the men spilt beer from the bowls of white brew, receiving a frown from the older of the men. It was none of Tembo's business so he went off to sleep where he dreamt of the great ocean that had no end. In the dream, people were speaking to the part of the dream that was himself making Tembo wake up with a start. Never before had he dreamt in the white man's language. Being awake too early annoyed him. The ray of sun through the boughs of the tree rested on the same spot in front of his foot. He had slept not a minute despite his dream being much longer, which was always the case... A dream was all in one picture, he was told. An instant event with all the sequences coming in one, which the brain formatted when the sleeper woke up. When Tembo first became a man he had asked the sangoma about dreams, the wise man who lived far from Elephant Walk. When Tembo wanted something, he always went to see the same wise old man. The sangoma could talk to the ancestors, which was why he knew so much... All the knowledge of all the ancestors in all their lives long. It was important to listen to such a man.

When Tembo was wide awake, still lying under the tree in the shade except for the one shaft of sunlight that had not moved, nothing happened. The dream did not take on a life of its own showing him everything. Instead, a different story was going on that had nothing to do with what was spoken in the dream. Tembo lifted his head from the ground to make sure he was awake. The man who called himself Parsons for a reason Tembo never understood, was sleeping soundly, fluting through his open mouth, making sounds like a whimpering dog, a sure sign he was having a good dream... Tembo sat up and looked around to see what was going on.

To Tembo's astonishment, the two well-dressed black men seated on high stools at the bar were speaking to each other in English. Not very good English, Tembo could hear, but still having a conversation that both appeared to understand. They looked very different from each other, which probably explained why they were speaking English. The one who was younger had a coal-black skin and a small neat-looking nose with small nostrils. The older, the more arrogant of the two, who was pretending not to look at the young girl who was stirring the pot of maize meal with the long spoon, leaning over and showing the old man her big bottom and the knickers she had probably bought in the Mwanza bazaar, had a nose squashed all over his ugly face with nostrils so big Tembo was sure the man could stick two of his fingers right up to the top. The coal-black man with a kind of face Tembo had never seen before was telling the story while the older man looked at the young girl's bottom, making Tembo jealous, as was his right, having spent days and a large sum of money looking at the girl while he made up his mind what to do. The man was talking about white gods who lived with a tribe in the jungle on the far side of the great lake. The gods had fallen out of the sky, little nose was telling big nose, which made Tembo sit up straight.

The older man, bored with a tall story, got up. He went over and patted the young girl's bottom, which she seemed to like. The girl must have seen by the old man's clothes, big nose was rich. Every old rich man took young wives when the others grew old and ugly. When she saw Tembo looking at what was going on, she tossed her head, telling Tembo without words to mind his own business.

Tembo stood up.

When Tembo reached the bar the younger man was still talking, telling his story.

"Where are these white men?" asked Tembo in English, which surprised the man and stopped the flow of his story.

"No one knows," he said. "The rumour of the gods has been circling around us for years."

"How many years?"

"About two."

"But nobody knows for certain if the gods really exist?"

"Or which tribe they live with. It is just the making of a legend."

While the older man went off with the young girl down to the lake, Tembo and small nose explained to each other how both of them spoke English. The coal-black man came from Uganda, another country run by the English with their mission stations and schools. The old man with the big nose came from Kenya, a British colony like Rhodesia where he too had been taught to speak English. Both Uganda and Kenya, like the Tanganyika territory they were now in, owned part of Lake Victoria. Along with territory owned by the King of the Belgians.

"Who is the King of the Belgians?" asked Tembo, enthralled by the man's knowledge.

"Another white man."

"That explains... Where did the story start? Of gods from the sky?"

"No one knows."

"Why are you here?"

"We are going to England. To see the King. In our countries, we are important men. We came down the lake. Tomorrow we take the train to Dar es Salaam... The old man likes the young girl."

"Yes, he does. She is my girl."

"I am sorry."

"It does not matter. There are many young girls."

When the old man came back from the lake, Tembo left them alone. The young girl came back five minutes later.

When the two men were leaving, Tembo was drinking from a bowl of beer.

"How many white gods?" he called.

"Fifty. Exactly fifty. Five times two hands. Why are you interested?"

"It's a long story."

"Are not they all?"

"Is there any truth to it?"

"Whoever knows?"

"Have a good trip."

The old man turned round and glared at Tembo.

In his frustration, Tembo went down to the water's edge where he threw small stones from the beach out into the water sparkling in the sun. It was all so big. Where should he go? Unless Harry Brigandshaw was alive and walked out of the bush on his own, Tembo would never, in all the lives of his ancestors put together, be able to find where he was... It was just another African rumour. When the others came back on the hired boat with the Arab captain he was going to take them home. With the money in his pocket, he could buy a very young wife and not have to stare at the young girl with the big bottom.

When Tembo fell asleep that night, he was drunk. All night long it was black in his sleep. Not one dream. Not even as he woke to the dawn. His head was throbbing. Even before he got up from the floor, Tembo was in a bad temper. If the Arab wasn't back soon, Tembo was going to put the tusks of ivory on the train himself... There was something going on that had to do with Harry Brigandshaw, the white man who treated him as more a friend than a servant. He owed it to the man... Otherwise, the rest of the white men could go back from whence they came. All these aeroplanes, trains and boats with steam engines were interfering with the tranquillity of his life. The way he and his ancestors had lived as far back as time.

16

SEPTEMBER 1930 – NEW BEGINNINGS

*W*ith the turmoil in the world's financial markets, Sir Jacob Rosenzweig had a lot on his mind. Not the least, Rebecca's wedding at the end of the month. The idea that buying out Madgwick and Madgwick in London would explode in his face had never entered his head. The chapter in his life that included Ralph Madgwick had been closed for him once and for all by Colonel Wallace Madgwick, who had vitriolically reacted to Ralph becoming a Jew. Benny Levy, a gold-digger in all probability, was a far better husband for his daughter. A man hungry for success with just the right amount of ruthlessness. Sentimental businessmen in Sir Jacob's experience almost always went bust. There could be no sentiment in business. Only in charity.

Madgwick and Madgwick were owed large sums of money by their clients who were unable to pay. To prevent Madgwick and Madgwick being put into liquidation, which would lose a lot of money for people other than Rosenzweig Bank, Sir Jacob, through a bank nominee organised by Westminster Bank, had made an offer gladly accepted by Wallace Madgwick who, along with Ralph Madgwick's mother, had personally guaranteed Madgwick and Madgwick's overdraft facility with Rosenzweig Bank. In reality, nothing but the staff of Madgwick's changed. The Madgwick clients still owed the same amount of money, but now directly to Rosenzweig Bank. When business returned to normal, as it always did in the end, Rosenzweig's would get their money back with interest and own Madgwick and Madgwick for nothing.

When he told Rebecca he had saved Ralph's mother and Uncle Wallace from having to sell their other assets to make good the guarantees to Rosenzweig's, he thought it would help to restore a relationship that had gone from bad to worse from the moment Wallace Madgwick pulled his nephew out of America... Rebecca exploded. Flew into a rage. Ran out of the front door of the Abercrombie apartment and slammed the front door in his face.

For hours Sir Jacob had waited for his daughter to come back. Despite the chaos reigning at the bank.

"You did it on purpose. Not enough to ruin Ralph and make him penniless. Now you've taken it out on his family... I hate you. Hate you."

All day long, his daughter's words kept ringing in his mind, the thought of his wife arriving in America for the wedding not helping one bit.

REBECCA HAD GONE STRAIGHT to the flower shop and her friend Maryanne. Maryanne was still not married to Shaul. Her life was in the same mess. Both girls agreed it was difficult enough to find the right man to marry without being prevented from doing so... Let alone ending up having to go through life with a spouse picked for them, something that was about to happen to poor Shaul, business and family overriding any kind of love. Other people's interests were important, the religious incantations an excuse for the family to get their own way.

When Rebecca had come down from the height of her indignation she was not sure if picking a fight over the forced sale of a company in England had not been an excuse. The very thought of Benny Levy even touching her made her flesh crawl. The man was physically repulsive. All he ever talked about was business and himself. The business of Rosenzweig Bank.

Exhausted from finding Ralph running off into the African bush on a wild-goose chase that was going to get him killed, she had had no fight left in her to do battle with her father. Sometimes, she had told Maryanne, taking the line of least resistance was the best alternative. Without really taking a proper look at Benny Levy, she had agreed with her father to marry him. If nothing else, it seemed to make her father happy, the other man in her life she loved.

Benny, ever the calculator, had obsequiously kept his distance until the marriage was arranged. Only then had he come out flying his true colours, something Maryanne was quick to point out to her best friend Becky.

"He's insinuating himself into the bank. Through you, he can become a partner, especially when you have his children. On his own, he'll stay an employee. The man's a creep, Becky. How can you bear the thought of kissing him, let alone anything else? Just imagine what your children are going to be like, rubbing their pudgy hands, insinuating their way through life. Were it me, Becky, I'd vomit."

Rebecca and Maryanne were both twenty-four years old. At the peak of their power as desirable women.

They both agreed when Rebecca came storming into the empty flower shop that if they did nothing now they were doomed to misery for the rest of their lives. That time was running short. That time was running out.

Moving in that night with Maryanne, Rebecca made up her mind to go to England. From the papers, she knew the expedition to find the English pilot had failed. Ralph would be back in England. There was nowhere else for him to go.

Having carefully saved up half her allowance, Rebecca took her life into her own hands and bought passage to England. To hell with religion. To hell with everyone. This time she was going to follow her heart and not listen to anyone.

WHAT REBECCA DID NOT KNOW WAS that by following her own desire she was breaking her father's heart. A condition that was not helped by the arrival of Sir Jacob's estranged wife for a wedding that was not going to happen.

In the peace and calm of the Abercrombie apartment with only Rebecca as his constant companion, Sir Jacob had forgotten why he was happy his wife had stayed in England. The woman was a foul-mouthed shrew whose only joy in life was finding fault in other people.

DAYS WENT into weeks and still no word from Rebecca. Not that Sir Jacob did not know where she had gone. Passages out of America were no secret if the shipping lines were given a good reason. One of which was runaway daughters without money.

After the third week, Sir Jacob telephoned Wallace Madgwick. Uncle Wallace was in the middle of moving out of his office with the help of Rosie Prescott.

"Where's Ralph, Wallace?"

"No idea, old boy. My word are we having fun. Can't wait to get into the country. Lovely month, September. Sold everything I own and bought a place in the Cotswolds. Going cheap. Everybody's selling. Chap was only too glad to get out. Bought the furniture as well... Have to go, old chap... Why did you phone?"

"Where's your nephew, Ralph? Rebecca's run away."

"Always did like that gal. Where's she run to?"

"England."

"Well, he isn't here... Rosie, where's Ralph?"

"In Rhodesia."

"Hear that, old chap? Still in Africa."

"Has Rebecca made contact with you?"

"I'm not very high on her list. About down the bottom with you, old chap. The girl's in love. Nearly a thousand acres. Don't shoot as well with one eye but a man can't have everything. Cheerio, old chap."

IN SIR JACOB'S office at the bank, the line went dead. He'd lost her. This time he had really lost his daughter... There was nothing he could do.

"Just be happy," he whispered.

If Wallace Madgwick knew where to find Ralph, his daughter would find out and go to Rhodesia. Picking up the phone he called his secretary.

"Find me a map of the world."

After searching British East Africa on the map, Sir Jacob looked further south. There were two of them. Northern and Southern Rhodesia. Even on the map, they looked like the farthest place on earth.

When he went home that night, his wife said she was going back to England to the rest of the children. He was going to be alone... For the rest of his life... Then he smiled. His wife was still talking and he still wasn't listening... That part of his loneliness would only be a pleasure... Maybe he would join a club... Maybe. Just maybe he would find himself a mistress... Somewhere he had read it was never too old to fall in love... Only then did he notice the chatter had stopped... His wife had left the apartment... In the midst of all his new thoughts, he had not even noticed she had gone.

THE LAST PERSON Christopher Marlowe expected to see in London was Rebecca Rosenzweig when she arrived at the door of Robert St Clair's flat in Stanhope Gate. With Brett's pregnancy making the attic room impractical with its distant bathroom, Robert had lent them his London flat. Freya had finished her play for Oscar Fleming soon after Richard was born. She hoped Christopher's influence would help Oscar Fleming take on the play.

"Rebecca! What a lovely surprise. How did you know I was here?"

"Where's Ralph?"

"In Rhodesia. He's learning to become a tobacco farmer, though for some reason they call it a tobacco grower. On Elephant Walk. Come in. Come in: with Harry dead and Jim Bowman off on his own, Harry's grandfather offered Ralph a job. In five years he's going to apply for his own Crown land farm, whatever that may be. Rhodesia is vast and thinly populated... Doesn't he write?"

"Not since he went to Africa with Keppel Howland. He said it hurt too much. That time and distance would leave us with wonderful memories. The only thing we had left... Oh my God. I don't have enough money to get to Rhodesia. I had an allowance but not very much. Father wasn't stupid... Your poor family. Forcing you to sell him your business."

"He did us a favour, Rebecca. Rather ironic. Now Ralph and I don't have to think about our family obligations. Poor Ralph paid the price. He hated working in the City."

"He was loving New York. Then Uncle Wallace pulled the rug from under him. We all believe in the same God. Everyone forgets that."

"Where are you staying?"

"I just arrived on the boat train."

"Who told you to come here?"

"Rosie Prescott."

"Poor Rosie Prescott. She's loved Ralph since he joined the firm."

"I never knew."

"Neither did Ralph... My brother is a lucky man... When do you wish to go to Rhodesia?"

"As soon as I can."

"I'll phone Colonial Shipping and book you a passage to Beira. It's only a day to Salisbury from Beira on the train. From Cape Town, it's three days on the train."

"Isn't Cape Town quicker? How am I going to pay?"

"I think I owe that much to my brother. As the elder brother, it was my job to join the family firm and run the business... Brett's taking a nap. She likes to sleep a lot with the baby on the way. Says it is good for him."

"She's pregnant?"

"Five months. You can stay here until you go. Robert's only coming up from Dorset next month. For the launch of a book. An American by the name of Hank Curley. Max Pearl launched *The American Patriot* in America. Robert's British publishers are doing the honours in London. You'll be long gone on the way out to Ralph. You should get to know Brett. You're going to be sisters-in-law if I know that look of determination."

Rebecca, looking at Christopher's kind face, burst into tears.

"Who's here?" called Brett from the main bedroom.

"Rebecca. She's come over from America to marry Ralph."

"Good for her."

WHILE CHRISTOPHER MARLOWE was arranging passage for Rebecca to Cape Town, Percy Grainger was sitting at his desk feeling pleased with himself. The sale of Mrs Brigandshaw's assets was over, including the Berkeley Square house. The figures were in front of him, the sum total enough to pay the British government what was their due with a few thousand pounds left over for the widow. A woman who at one time had thought she was going to be telling him what to do. The Brigandshaw family were finally out of Colonial Shipping, a company he had been running for so many years, without due respect.

With a carefully chosen syndicate of investors including top management he was now in control of Colonial Shipping. In a deal with the tax inspector, the syndicate had bought Harry Brigandshaw's shares. The Rolls-Royce and driver were at his command. The executive dining room his to entertain. Power, real power, was right there in his hands.

PERCY GRAINGER HAD NEVER FELT BETTER in his life... A whole new world was in front of him. New clubs who would now let him join. New friends who before would not deign to talk to him. New respect... For the first time, people who mattered were going to look at him as an equal. He was now a society man.

As was his duty, Percy Grainger cabled the figures to the widow in Rhodesia, signing his name with the deepest respect for the last time.

Only when the cable was sent did he catch a glimpse of a smiling face in the small picture frame on his desk. Instead of the photograph of his daughter, Percy Grainger saw the face of Harry Brigandshaw.

With shaking hands, the new chairman of Colonial Shipping went to his cocktail cabinet. The drink was partly to lay the ghost, partly to celebrate.

"To life," he said, holding the empty glass up to the ceiling. Only then did he shiver. As though someone had walked over his grave.

MERLIN ST CLAIR had finished the exact same breakfast he had eaten for ten years in the alcove of his flat overlooking Hyde Park. The weather outside had changed from a brief shower to warm sunshine. At the age of forty-six, life was good. He still smiled at keeping his money in three per cent government bonds while everyone was telling him to buy stock. For Merlin, the secret of life was not to have to think about money. The chequebook, an instrument that paid the merchants without worrying how much money was left in the bank.

Merlin had heard the front doorbell ring, something he ignored. The financial pages of the paper were full of bad news which had nothing to do with him. Flipping to the sport's page, Merlin read the cricket scores with more satisfaction. Middlesex had beaten Surrey by an innings and six runs.

Smithers's cough made Merlin turn round and look at the door.

"The Honourable Barnaby St Clair, sir," announced Smithers as if he did not know his own brother who was standing in the door to the lounge.

"Thank you, Smithers. What do you want, Barnaby?"

"A cup of coffee."

"Tea, I'm afraid. Bring my brother a cup, Smithers. There's enough in the pot... Do you want breakfast?"

"That would be nice."

"You'd better sit down... What's it about, Barnaby?"

"Is it always about something?"

"Always."

"Freya has written a play. Fleming showed it to me. Wants me to back a production. Funnily enough, there's a young girl in the play."

"She doesn't know enough yet!"

"It's said some learn faster on the job. Genevieve looks much older than she is. Loves the part."

"You showed her?"

"She wants to talk to Daddy... Did I tell you I saw Frank?"

"Don't even mention that sordid story."

"For brothers who both have illegitimate children, you are a prig, Merlin."

"Esther wasn't married."

"Tina was mine first."

"Harry was your friend."

"Don't worry. Tina and her children have gone to Rhodesia. I'll just keep a long-distance eye on the boy. It's nice to be a daddy... Are you going to pour the tea?... Thank you, Smithers. I'm hungry. Lots of toast."

"Two eggs underdone. One sausage. Tomato. Bacon."

"Perfect, Smithers... What a lovely day out there in the park now the rain has finished. London is such a civilised place. Poor Tina. She hates Africa. It must be terrible not to have money... Who won the cricket?"

"Middlesex. By an innings and six runs."

"Lord's in July. Gentlemen playing county cricket. What can be more perfect?... Can you pass me the sugar?"

∽

DEAR READER

~

Reviews are the most powerful tools in our kitty when it comes to getting attention for Peter's books. This is where you can come in, as by providing an honest review you will help bring them to the attention of other readers.

If you enjoyed reading *To the Manor Born,* and have five minutes to spare, we would really appreciate a review (it can be as short as you like). Your help in spreading the word and keeping Peter's work alive is gratefully received.

Please leave your review on the retailer site where you purchased this book.

Thank you so much.
Heather Stretch (Peter's daughter)

PS. We look forward to you joining Peter's growing band of avid readers.

PUBLISHER'S NOTE

~

Peter Rimmer completed writing his *To the Manor Born* on the 13 July 2004. We at Kamba Publishing began the process of typing up the manuscript and editing the novel in late 2017. We had anticipated releasing the book a lot soon than November 2018 but a number of other things prevented us from doing so, including the extremely sad loss of Peter who died in July 2018, very suddenly. This was a heartbreaking setback for us but determined to release this new book, we got back to working on it as soon as we could. Peter wouldn't have wanted it any other way.

We hope you enjoy *To the Manor Born*.

As Peter would often say, "I hope you enjoy reading my books as much as I enjoyed writing them."

Heather Stretch (Peter Rimmer's daughter)
Kamba Publishing

PRINCIPAL CHARACTERS

~

The Brigandshaws

Harry — Central character, Harry is the son of Sebastian and Emily

Tina — Harry's wife and Barnaby St Clair's one-time girlfriend

Anthony, Beth, Dorian and Kim — Harry and Tina's children

Frank — Tina and Barnaby's love child

Sir Henry Manderville — Emily's father and Harry's grandfather

Emily — Harry's mother

Sebastian — Central character of *Echoes from the Past* (deceased)

The St Clairs

Barnaby — The youngest brother of the St Clair children and Tina Pringle's love interest

Merlin — Brother to Barnaby and Robert, a confirmed bachelor

Robert — Harry's university friend and author

Genevieve — Merlin's bastard daughter

Ethelbert, 17th Baron St Clair — Robert, Merlin and Barnaby's father

Lady St Clair (Bess) — Robert, Merlin and Barnaby's mother

The Oosthuizens

Tinus — Harry's nephew

Paula and Doris — Tinus's sisters

Madge — Harry's sister, mother of Paula, Tinus and Doris

The Madgwicks
Clive — Barrington and Ralph's dictatorial father
Ralph — Youngest son of Clive
Barrington — A bohemian. Eldest son of Clive who also goes by the stage name of Christopher Marlowe
Uncle Wallace — Uncle to Barrington and Ralph

The Rosenzweigs
Sir Jacob — A Jewish bank owner providing services to Madgwick and Madgwick
Rebecca — Sir Jacob's youngest daughter and Ralph Madgwick's love interest
Hannah — Sir Jacob's estranged wife

The Fitzgeralds
Stella — A wealthy Irish heiress
Patrick — Stella's wealthy trade-union father from Boston, USA
Seamus — Minor US politician and Stella's brother
Wesley — Stella's younger brother

The Ramsbottoms
Portia — The youngest of three sisters whose mother is looking for a husband for each of her daughters
Mr & Mrs Ramsbottom — Coal mine owners from Yorkshire
Hermione and Clarissa — Portia's older sisters

Other Principal Characters
Alfred — Ralph and Keppel's African guide
Brett Kentrich — Harry's one-time girlfriend, an actress
CE Porter — A devious stockbroker in the City of London
Clara — Owner of Clara's supper club
Douglas Hayter — Business friend of Barnaby's who is wheelchair-bound
Esther — Merlin's ex-mistress from the Running Horses, Mickleham, and mother of Genevieve
Freya Taylor — Glenn's personal assistant and writer of the column 'Juliet'
Gert van Heerden — Barrington's South African friend
Glen Hamilton — Colorado Telegraph editor and friend of Harry and Robert
Harvey Lyttleton, Danny Hill, William Blake — Band members at Clara's

Ignatius (Iggy) Bowes-Lyon — Harry's chief pilot and cousin to the Duchess of York, Elizabeth

John Lacey —The impoverished 16th Marquess of Ravenhurst

Keppel Howland — Ralph's friend from the army

Max Pearl — Robert's American publisher

Millie Scott — A chorus girl and Merlin's current girlfriend

Oscar Fleming — Theatre Impresario

Percy Grainger — A senior manager at Colonial Shipping

Postlethwaite — Uncle Wallace's business assistant

Prudence (Cuddles) Morton-Sayner — A lady who sells social favours to make a living

Rosie Prescott — Wallace Madgwick's secretary who is in love with Ralph

Smithers — Merlin St Clair's manservant

Tembo — Harry's boyhood friend and servant on Elephant Walk

ACKNOWLEDGEMENTS

~

With grateful thanks to our *VIP First Readers* for reading *To the Manor Born* prior to it's official launch date. They have been fabulous in picking up errors and typos helping us to ensure that your own reading experience of *To the Manor Born* has been the best possible. Their time and commitment is particularly appreciated.

Alan McConnochie (South Africa)
Felicity Barker (South Africa)
Hilary Jenkins (South Africa)

Thank you
Kamba Publishing

ON THE BRINK OF TEARS (BOOK FIVE)

~

Unknowingly betrayed by one of his own, Harry Brigandshaw returns from the dead. But salvaging all that he's lost comes at a price...

The Tutsi tribe have kept him captured for more than two years. His disappearance extensively reported worldwide. Ingeniously escaping in 1931, Harry heads for Dar es Salaam. Dishevelled and unrecognisable he hides on the beaches waiting for a ship to dock. But little does he know all that has happened, with Colonial Shipping stolen...

Securing his berth, he convinces the captain of who he is, only to learn of the duplicity. Harry needs to weigh up the options open to him. But, on arrival in England Harry is rushed to hospital, critically ill. His whereabouts undisclosed...

Harry will need all his strength to recover and fight back but is it all too late?

Made in the USA
Las Vegas, NV
18 February 2024

85943222R00246